Comparative Doctrine

"Beloved, do not believe every spirit, but test the spirits to see whether they are from God, for many false prophets have gone out into the world."

1 John 4:1

- Learn How to Let the Scriptures Define Your Doctrinal Beliefs.
- Learn How to Quickly Find Scriptures to Teach Biblical Truth.
- Learn about Multiple Religions and What they Teach.
- Learn About Many Unscriptural Beliefs that Some Churches and Cults Teach.
- Be Able to Quickly Identify the Scriptures that Address Those Common False Beliefs.
- Learn how to Build Scriptural Chains that Support Various Biblical Doctrines.
- Learn How to Build Scriptural Chains that Will Help Address All False Teachings Identified in this Work!

F. Russell Crites, Jr. and Derek Russell Crites

Comparative Doctrine

Published by CPC Dallas, Texas.
Printed in the United States of America

Library of Congress Control Number: 2022917288

Comparative Doctrine: Letting Scriptures Define Your Religious Beliefs F. Russell Crites, Jr. & Derek Russell Crites

Religion

ISBN: 979-8-9869377-0-0

Revised and Updated Edition

The work was originally published in 1980 by Bible House in Abilene, Texas (now located in Searcy, Arkansas) and was titled, 'Sharpening the Sword on False Doctrine'. In this new revision, a study of several religious organizations has been added in order to help the reader develop a better understanding of what they teach in comparison to what the Bible says regarding specific doctrinal beliefs. In addition, a brief Historical study of the development of many different Churches or Beliefs, a Scriptural Study of Core Scriptural Beliefs, and a Scriptural Study of Common Theological Differences have also been added.

Acknowledgements

Special thanks to my son, Derek Crites. Without his help, this update
and major revision would have taken much longer to complete. He gave beneficial feedback,
generally edited this work and helped with some of the new content.

We would like to give special thanks to those who helped check cover and content: Pamela, Paul
and Tammy, Tim, and Phillip. Thanks again for taking a more detailed look at the contents and
for the suggestions you made. We also want to give our thanks to several others who gave us
helpful feedback regarding content. Again, thanks to you all. This would not be the work it is
without the feedback we have received.

Authors

This significantly updated work was revised with the help of Derek Russell Crites. His help as a co-author regarding this work has been immensely helpful. Derek also co-authored the Sharpening the Sword on Mormonism manual and has continued to help with other works that are being revised. He has also edited works for other authors.

Russ has written and co-authored many works; Journey Into Discipleship, Discipleship Groups, Discipleship Group Curriculum, Sharpening the Sword on False Doctrine, Advanced Sharpening the Sword materials on Mormonism, Spiritual Gifts and Ministry and more. He has been a youth minister, a singles minister, an involvement minister and a counseling minister in different churches over the years. Initially, this work was titled, Sharpening the Sword on False Doctrine and was written in 1980.

In addition to writing, teaching and doing programs for churches Russ has spent much of his life working in the field of psychology. He worked for the public schools for over twenty-five years where he did Psychological Testing for a variety of conditions. Russ has been a consultant for public and private schools, psychiatric hospitals, a variety of agencies, and has had a private practice for over thirty years. Russ currently holds a license as a marriage and family therapist (LMFT), a professional counselor (LPC), and is a licensed specialist in school psychology (LSSP). He is a Certified Clinical Hypnotherapist, is a Certified Professional Coach (CPC) and holds many other certifications. Over the years he has spoken at local, state, regional and national conferences. Topics for some of those conferences or programs were Family of Origin Issues, Codependency, Assessing Family of Origin and Codependency Issues, Marriage & Family, Couple Issues, Parenting, Bipolar Disorder, ADHD, Executive Function Disorders, Depression, Anxiety, Motivating Resistant Learners, Learning Issues, Self-Esteem, and much more. Russ has also provided staff development training for school districts, businesses and other agencies. He is the founder and director of Crites Psycho-Educational Consultants. Russ completed a B.S. in psychology with a minor in Bible and a M.S. in Clinical/Counseling Psychology from Abilene Christian University. He has completed post masters work in Marriage and Family, Counseling and Psychology in order to meet the requirements for additional licenses and certifications.

Comparative Doctrine

Table of Contents

Comparative Doctrine

The Purpose
of this Scriptural Study

Section One

In a world filled with numerous religions, theological differences and varied interpretations regarding Scripture, it becomes increasingly important to be able to identify what you believe and where in the Bible you can go to show what you believe. We all have a tendency to believe what we have been taught by our spiritual leaders.   Our goal is for you to let the Bible be your guide, not any man, e.g., the Pope, a Preacher, a Priest, an Elder, a Bishop, a favorite teacher, the founder of your church, writer, etc. In Philippians 2:12 it says, "Therefore, my beloved, as you have always obeyed, so now, not only as in my presence but much more in my absence, work out your own salvation with fear and trembling." It is your responsibility, by studying Scriptures, to identify what stance you should take in regard to specific doctrinal beliefs.   If you don't know what the Bible teaches about specific doctrine, it is very difficult to identify a body of Christ who closely follows Biblical teaching.   We also want you to keep in mind, that we believe that no Scripture should be taken out of context.   However, all Scriptures that Identify specific doctrine should be believed and accepted.   With all the above in mind, we have three important pieces of information that we want share with you. They are:

- The Basic Tenets of this Work
- Understanding the Comparative Doctrine Coding System
- The Purpose of this Work

Quotes or Summary Statements

All quotes within this work have quotation marks around them. If there are no quotation marks the statement is a summary of what is found in that particular document or comments by the authors.

Basic Tenets of this Work

Before you begin this study, there are some basic tenets regarding this work that we want you to keep in mind. Each of the tenets shown below are important. Our hope is that you will either agree with us or will grow to agree with us as you study this work.

- We believe that knowing what the Scriptures teach is at the very least essential for someone who claims Christianity. You must know what you believe. You must know what Doctrine the Bible teaches so that you can be sound in the faith. You must know what the Bible says about how we treat each other, how we help others and so much more. However, having knowledge about what the Scriptures say is only the first step. You must also learn to apply the Scriptures in your life. Without application the Scriptures are just a compilation of facts. However, God's plan does not stop with application. Once you know the Scriptures and you see how to apply them, you also need to constantly seek to internalize them, or make them part of you, so that you can grow and mature in Christ. However, if you don't know the facts shown in the Scriptures, and if you don't seek to apply them, you will probably never internalize God's Word in order to grow and mature. We are told in multiple Scriptures that God wants you to grow and mature. He wants you to possess the qualities that will help you mature or grow in holiness. He wants you to consistently increase your knowledge, application and internalization of these facts and qualities so that you can become more like Christ (Galatians 2;20; Hebrews 5:11-14; 2 Peter 1:3-11). You also must develop self-control. That simply means that you have to choose to make right choices (Proverbs 25:28; 2 Timothy 1:7; 2 Peter 1:5-7; Titus 2:11-12; 1 Corinthian 9:27).

- We believe that the Bible, specifically the New Testament, is the last will and testament of God the Father and Jesus His son. Any 'new' revelations, no matter where they come from, are not God inspired and should not be accepted as being God's will. Some men try to 'interpret' God's will, while in reality they simply distort it for their purposes.

- We believe that the Bible does not contradict itself, especially when it comes to New Testament doctrinal beliefs. In regard to the New Law, if a Bible verse communicates a doctrine, it cannot contradict itself somewhere else. When there appears to be contradiction it is up to us to see how the Scriptures work together to communicate the whole truth. So, if two Scriptures seem to contradict one another, it does not mean one is right and the other is wrong. It means that if you truly understand the concept, both will be right in some way. One Scripture does not, and never will, negate the other. Many churches have developed their own doctrine by choosing one Scripture over the other when there appears to be a conflict. Our belief is that all Scriptures are of God and all should be accepted.

- The New Testament reflects the teachings of the New Law (Law of the Spirit), and takes precedent over the Old Testament Law of Commandments. Keep in mind that the Old Law (Old Testament) and the New Law of the Spirit, that is found in the New Testament, do conflict at times. However, the New Law is a fulfillment or completion of God's Law for man, and He wants us to focus on the New Law for doctrine (the Law of the Spirit found in the New Testament). The New Testament is always the final answer. That does not mean that there isn't some valuable information found in the Old Testament.

As you work through this book you will find that there is very little opinion or comment. If there is, we will let you know in advance. Initially, this work was developed to help you prepare to share Biblical truth with others and to help you combat the forces of the evil one. This current work has five basic areas that are addressed. We hope to help you identify:

1. What the Bible says about False teachers or False Doctrine and what responsibility we have when faced with False teaching or doctrine.
2. Doctrinal areas where some churches or beliefs contradict Biblical teaching.
3. The core beliefs that most all Christ-Centered beliefs adhere to.
4. The common doctrinal issues where there is disagreement among various Christian Churches.
5. False doctrine that is often found in some Churches, Cults and non-Christian beliefs.

Understanding the Comparative Doctrine Coding System

You will notice when you look at sections four, five, six and seven in the table of contents that there are letters next to each identified doctrine. These are short codes that represent each specific doctrinal issue. You are given the option of chaining several Scriptures for each doctrinal issue in your Bible. To do that you need to have a code of sorts so that you can differentiate different doctrines as you go from one identified verse to the next. It simply makes it easier to identify the appropriate Scriptures for any specific doctrine. For instance:

- Jesus Is The Christ - Deity (JIC)
- Bible Inspiration (BI)
- Death (DE)
- Forgiveness of Sins (FOS)

At the back of this work there are further explanations regarding how you chain these doctrinal issues. There are also handouts that you can paste into your Bible that have the initial Scripture that will address that specific doctrine. Obviously, you can choose to utilize these chains or simply use this work as a resource.

Understanding the Purpose of this Work

Overall, there are two things we hope for you as you study this information. First, we want you to develop a strong belief in the Bible and the doctrine within it. Second, we want you to have the Biblical knowledge necessary to help those who, 1) have never really understood what the Bible teaches, or 2) have been pulled away from the truth by False Religious beliefs. After you have worked through this book, we hope that you will be able to:

Let the Bible Determine Your Doctrine or Biblical Beliefs

We want you to clearly see what the Bible says regarding Biblical teachings without us or others telling you what to believe. As stated above you should never allow another person to determine what you believe. It can't be your Preacher, a Priest, an Elder, a Bishop, a favorite teacher, a writer, a friend or anyone else. We want you to see what the Scriptures say, and let them speak for themselves regarding doctrine. Be open and listen to what the Bible says, not what others say it means. Listen to the Scriptures and decide for yourself what they are communicating.

However, what do you do when it doesn't appear that the Scriptures are clear on an issue? You may also ask, how do you decide what the Bible is trying to communicate when it is not extremely clear, or when others seem to share a different belief? I personally struggled with this issue when I was younger. Before we go on, I want to personally share a memory that impacted how I more clearly define my personal doctrine. When I was a teenager we had an older minister, his name was Brother Burns, who had a tremendous impact on what I believed and why. He believed in focusing on what the Scriptures said and constantly told me to search the Scriptures when I wasn't sure what to believe. One day we were talking about the Bible and how people were finding ways to change, alter or minimize Biblical doctrine. He told me a story that has lived with me to this day. Here is the story. I hope that it helps you as much as it helped me. It sounds a bit like a New Testament parable and could be if you used chariots instead of a car.

A rich man had taken very good care of his driver for years and they had grown close over their time together. However, one day the driver came to him and said, 'I love my job. I love working for you and I can't thank you enough for allowing me to be your driver all these years, but it's time for me to retire. My eyes aren't as sharp as they used to be, and my reaction time is much slower. I don't want to put you in danger. I will need to stop driving for you soon. So, I will stay on for a short period of time until you can find another driver.' The rich man was upset because his driver was exactly the kind of person he wanted for a driver. He trusted him, and the driver had always taken care of him....had always kept him safe. He had also become a close friend.

The rich man advertised that he needed the best driver that he could find to replace his friend and driver who was retiring.

He immediately received multiple resumes from drivers across the land. In time, he settled on three. There would be a test to determine which driver would be the best for him. He took them up to a mountain road that had multiple hair pin turns as well as a few stretches of road that were straight. He told each one in turn, 'The person who can show me that he is the best driver for me will get this job.' They had to drive up the side of the mountain making multiple turns and then come back down. The rich man also told them that he would be watching them with his binoculars and timing them.

The first driver sat down in the car and the rich man waved at him to start. He took off with tires spinning. He raced up the road, but was careful to stay away from the edges, but went as fast as he could on the straight sections of road so that he could get a good time. When he returned the rich man nodded his head as he wrote down his notes and the time it took.

When he looked up, he nodded to the second man who immediately got into the car. As he did, he said to the rich man, 'Watch me, I can do better than that.' As soon as the rich man nodded for him to begin the tires squealed again and the second driver was on his way. It was phenomenal. He far outpaced the previous driver with speed and was actually proving his ability showing that he could get close to the edge and handle it with ease. There was actually one place where he took a turn on two wheels showing how much he could control the car. When he returned the rich man nodded, jotted some notes and the time.

The third driver shook his head as he looked at the other two drivers. He tipped his hat to the rich man and stepped inside the car. He put on his seat belt. The rich man nodded, and he turned his head and quickly scanned the road behind him before he took off. When he did, he did not squeal the tires. He slowly increased speed. When he came to corners, he slowed down. When faced with dangerous hair pin turns, he moved over as far as he could to ensure safety. He was not in a hurry at all. Sometime later he was back at the starting point. The rich man jotted down some notes and noted his time.

The three men stood in front of the rich man waiting for his answer. He looked at the first man and said, 'You did well. However, the next man did the same as you, but was faster and proved he could handle a perilous situation best. So, thank you for coming, but I am not choosing you. The first man nodded his head, got into his car and left. He stepped up to the second man who was smiling and said, 'You proved that you are obviously skilled as a driver by showing your willingness to go fast and stay close to the edge while maintaining extraordinary control. You are without question a very good driver. However, you are not who I choose. The man's smile fell as he walked over to his car and left.

The rich man stepped over to the last driver who had been so slow and careful. "You were deliberate. You did what you could to stay safe as you drove up and down the mountain and made it a point to stay away from any situation that was dangerous or questionable. You broke no laws and proved to me that I would be safe in your hands. I don't need sparkle. I don't need excitement. I don't want a driver who gets close to the edge, and takes chances when it is not necessary. I need a man who carefully does his job. I would like you to be my new driver."

So, in regard to our personal beliefs, we don't want to find ways to prove a doctrinal point if Scriptures cannot clearly…**clearly** support it. We don't want to bend the Scriptures to prove our point. We don't want to add 'sparkle or excitement', if those things cannot be found in the 'New Law' (Law of the Spirt—New Testament). We don't want to accept something as theological truth if it conflicts with another part of the New Testament. We believe there is always an answer if you look closely. We would rather believe what the Bible says, and if there are questions about what something means, we would rather stick with what it is telling us instead of making suppositions. This work is based on this philosophy. We'd like to think that this story might help you also. With this in mind, let's go forward.

New Law vs Old Law

When Jesus came, He instituted a new Law; the Law of the Spirit. This new law replaced the law of commandments that had been established in the Old Testament. For Christians, this New Law takes the place of the Old Law. So, in determining doctrinal belief we will focus on what the Scriptures in the New Testament have to say. In other words, the New Law or Law of the Spirit take precedence over Old Law.

As you think about the story, there are a few other things we would like you to consider as you study the Bible. First, it's important that we all accept that the Bible is inspired and communicates God's will. The Holy Spirit working with Godly men penned words that communicated God's story. His story is truth. Second, any interpretation that comes short of communicating what the Bible truly teaches is not truth. Both Jesus and the Apostles struggled with men who wanted to alter or change the truth. Third, our role is not to make the truth comfortable for others or to make it compatible with their desires or beliefs. It is to simply share the TRUTH in love. However, to do so, we too must know what God's truth is, and where it is found in the Bible. Last, we must accept that God's truth transcends all cultures, personal desires, etc. Biblical truth does not and should not vary because of our culture, our preferences or our personal desires. It's the same today as it was in the Apostolic age.

One of the primary purposes of this work is to provide you with a tool that will help you investigate God's Scriptures objectively. In other words, we want you to look at what the Scripture says about a variety of beliefs **without the words of man being used to communicate what it means**. In most cases you will clearly see what God's truth is by simply reading the words found in the Bible.

Understand What the Bible says About False Teachers and What to do About Them

False teachers were evident when Jesus walked this earth. He warned us about false teachers saying, "See that you are not led astray. For many will come in my name, saying, 'I am he!' and, 'The time is at hand!' Do not go after them" (Luke 21:8). This has happened many times since Christ left this earth.

It didn't take long for churches to split because men wanted to take control in a variety of ways. From Jesus' time until today, men have attempted to alter God's intent for the church and what He intended to be taught in His Holy Word. The warnings are clear in the Bible that men would distort His will, and the consequences are evident. It is important that we all know the difference between false teaching and Godly truth. This work will also help you see how Christians have been warned about false teachers and what we as Godly men and women should do when we are faced with untruth or distortions of God's truth.

Learn what Various Beliefs or Cults Teach

If you are to help others who want to know more about Biblical truth, you need to know what the Bible says about multiple doctrinal issues. You also need to know what other religions teach that are contrary to what the Bible says. Many will surprise you. Some will shock you. You will learn about several churches or beliefs, what they teach and how they are in contradiction to the Bible.

Quickly and Easily Communicate your Theological Beliefs using Scriptures

We also want you to be able to quickly and easily share Scriptures in the Bible that support specific biblical doctrine. As part of this work, we will present many Bible passages that address doctrinal beliefs. A chaining system is included that will make it easy for you to share Scriptures specific to each doctrinal issue addressed in this book. Once you learn how to use this system you can add other topics, beliefs and Scriptures later if you like.

This current work is a practical and easy way to study the Bible so that you can learn what it teaches regarding God's desire for you and others. It will also help you be better prepared or equipped to have ready answers to many major questions and issues that you may be confronted with regarding the Bible and what it teaches. This knowledge will help you to obey God's charge to, "Preach the word; be prepared in season and out of season; correct, rebuke and encourage--- with great patience and careful instruction (2 Timothy 4:2)." To accomplish this we will be providing you with Scriptures that support, explain or refute, 1) core beliefs that most Christ-

centered churches adhere to, 2) common theological Issues where various Christian churches seem to disagree, and 3) false doctrine that is taught by a variety of churches. beliefs or cults.
Using specific Scriptures as a guide, we want you to be able to quickly and easily refute false doctrine that is taught by various religions, cults, etc. The Bible is very clear regarding false teaching. 2 Peter 2:1-3 says, "But false prophets also arose among the people, just as there will be false teachers among you, who will secretly bring in destructive heresies, even denying the Master who bought them, bringing upon themselves swift destruction. And many will follow their sensuality, and because of them the way of truth will be blasphemed. And in their greed, they will exploit you with false words. Their condemnation from long ago is not idle, and their destruction is not asleep." 1 John 4:1 says, "Beloved, do not believe every spirit, but test the spirits to see whether they are from God, for many false prophets have gone out into the world." Both Peter and John were concerned about false teachers and false doctrine. When you look at what some religions teach (shown in this work), it becomes evident that their warnings are just as important today as they were when their concerns were initially penned. We will present many false beliefs that are taught by at least one religion, and the Scriptures you can use to refute them in love as you have opportunity. It will be evident that some religious groups are in conflict with what the Bible teaches. The beliefs of some churches will surprise you, maybe shock you, once you look at them. In such cases the names of those religious affiliations will be identified so that you can maintain an awareness of some of their beliefs. This will be very eye opening when you look at Scriptures and compare them to what various churches, beliefs and cults teach. Just keep in mind that you need to believe what the Bible says, not what someone says the Bible means.

Quotes and Summaries: Most quotes are directly from works of various religious beliefs. However, sometimes there are multiple pages referenced or very long references. At times we have chosen to summarize what is found. However, you can go to the identified work and see the actual words for yourself if you choose.

Keeping everything above in mind, we do want to say that some doctrinal issues need a deeper study in order for us to have a better understanding. A second work is planned. It will be titled, Comparative Doctrine: Supplemental Study of Specific Topics. This work will look in greater detail at some specific doctrinal issues where multiple Christ centered churches have some disagreement, e.g., Original Sin, Once Saved Always Saved, Instrumental Music, Women's Role in the church, End Times (Eschatology) and more. Regardless, Scriptures or pieces of information are included in this work regarding some of these issues for you to consider.

Author's Note

It should be apparent that it would be nearly impossible to address all the contradictory or false teachings that can be found in this world today. With that in mind, we have picked some of the more basic or obvious issues that Christians may face when discussing God and the Bible with others. These teachings can be found in two places:

1) In Section Six, under each Church or Cult name there is a description of some of their unique core teachings. Some of their teachings are not in the body of this work. There are simply too many to address.
2) Section Seven Identifies Core Scriptural conflicts with other church or cult teachings. In most cases you will see direct quotes to show what they believe.

Warning About False Teaching

Section Two

Even as the Bible was being written, New Testament writers were concerned about false teaching that would subvert what Christ intended for all those who would follow him. Jesus was concerned about this problem. In Matthew 24:24 He stated, "For false messiahs and false prophets will appear and perform great signs and wonders to deceive, if possible, even the elect."   In 2 Timothy 4:3-4 Paul warns us about this same issue. "For the time will come when people will not put up with sound doctrine. Instead, to suit their own desires, they will gather around them a great number of teachers to say what their itching ears want to hear. They will turn their ears away from the truth and turn aside to myths."   As you will see in this section, warning after warning has been given regarding false teaching. Yet today there are many churches or cults that teach doctrine that is foreign to what was intended by Christ and the New Testament authors.

This section simply reviews the concerns and warnings communicated by New Testament writers.   Even in their time, there were people who were attempting to teach a 'strange gospel'. Today, we now have people who have subverted the Gospel and New Testament teachings by writing other works that 'explain' what the Bible means. Some have gone so far as to say that the Bible is not complete and as a result further 'revelation' is necessary in order to know what God's will is for our lives. Others have completely abandoned the Bible, using texts or writings of man saying that their writings are also from God. Yet, others say that God doesn't even exist. There are also those who believe in the Bible, but they distort the message and change what is actually taught. Regardless, for Christians it has become even more important to know what the Bible teaches.   The following warnings about false teachers are found in this section:

- The Problem with Current Day Prophecy and False Teachers
- Identifying False Teachers or False Doctrine
- Scriptural Review Regarding False Teaching in the Bible
- The Prophet Test
- New Revelation or Works from God and False Teaching.
- Eastern Religions and False Teaching

The Problem with Current Day Prophecy and False Teachers

Most Christians believe that the Bible is God's will and that there is no further need for revelation. However, that is not true with many religious beliefs. Why do so many religious groups claim to have current day revelation? The answer is simple. They want to change, add to, or delete from God's true Word. From the dawn of Christianity, the writers of the Bible have warned us about those who would teach any doctrine other than the one found in the Bible.

Old Testament Warnings

"And if you say in your heart, 'How may we know the word that the LORD has not spoken?'-- when a prophet speaks in the name of the LORD, if the word does not come to pass or come true, that is a word that the LORD has not spoken; the prophet has spoken it presumptuously. You need not be afraid of him" (Deut. 18:21-22).

"Let the prophet who has a dream tell the dream, but let him who has my word speak my word faithfully. What has straw in common with wheat?" declares the LORD (Jeremiah 23:28).

"Behold, I am against those who prophesy lying dreams, declares the LORD, and who tell them and lead my people astray by their lies and their recklessness, when I did not send them or charge them. So they do not profit this people at all, declares the LORD" (Jeremiah. 23:32).

New Testament Warnings

"His divine power has granted to us all things that pertain to life and godliness, through the knowledge of him who called us to his own glory and excellence," 2 Peter 1:3

"Now may the God of peace who brought again from the dead our Lord Jesus, the great shepherd of the sheep, by the blood of the eternal covenant, equip you with everything good that you may do his will, working in us that which is pleasing in his sight, through Jesus Christ, to whom be glory forever and ever. Amen." Hebrews 13:20-21

"Not that there is another one, but there are some who trouble you and want to distort the gospel of Christ. But even if we or an angel from heaven should preach to you a gospel contrary to the one we preached to you, let him be accursed. As we have said before, so now I say again: If anyone is preaching to you a gospel contrary to the one you received, let him be accursed." Galatians 1:7-9

"Beloved, although I was very eager to write to you about our common salvation, I found it necessary to write appealing to you to contend for the faith that was once for all delivered to the saints. For certain individuals whose condemnation was written about long ago have secretly slipped in among you. They are ungodly people, who pervert the grace of our God into a license for immorality and deny Jesus Christ our only Sovereign and Lord." Jude 3-4

Jesus Warns Us

And he said, "See that you are not led astray. For many will come in my name, saying, 'I am he!' and, 'The time is at hand!' Do not go after them" (Luke 21:8).

Identifying False Teachers or False Teaching

Before we begin we need to understand that false teaching come from the father; the father of Lies (John 8:44). Because of this God wants us to be aware of Satan's schemes (2 Corinthians 2:11). Why? Because he and the angels and demons that follow him are constantly seeking to find ways to, 1) keep us from finding God, and 2) attempts to take away our life that we have in God in a variety of ways. His desire is to deceive the whole world, each person so that he or she will not accept the Grace of God (Revelation 12:9; 20:3, 8).

One of Satan's Greatest Schemes

We believe that one of Satan's greatest schemes is to change how the Scriptures are understood in small ways that cause division. On Pentecost, when Peter preached about Jesus and the Kingdom of God one church was formed. It was the church that Jesus wanted all people to be part of across the whole world. The apostles often had to deal with those who wanted to alter the message. Over two thousand years later there are hundreds of churches that have specific doctrines they believe in, ways that worship must be conducted and much more. How did that happen? Satan has encouraged men to alter God's word. Sometimes this was done in small ways. Sometimes he encouraged dramatic changes. Regardless, as false teachers spoke of their beliefs the Word of God was altered, minimized, or taken out of context and new churches arose. Many share a close resemblance to the New Testament church we read about. Others look completely different. Who would do this? Who would promote these often small, but doctrinally important changes? They are called False Teachers, and that is one of the main purposes why this work was written.

So, it is obvious that false teachers and false teaching is problem for us today. It's easy to see. If you look around you will find many different religions that have distorted Biblical teaching or cults that have developed their own beliefs. It quickly becomes obvious that there is a significant problem with false teaching in our world today. Actually, Jesus dealt with this when he still walked on this earth. He knew that they would be a problem while He was here and after he had gone home to the father. In Matthew 7:13-14 He left us a warning. He stated,

> "Enter by the narrow gate. For **the gate is wide and the way is easy that leads to destruction,** and those who enter by it are many. For the gate is narrow and the way is hard that leads to life, and those who find it are few."

His words suggest that out of all the people who have lived in this new dispensation, only a few will make it to heaven. Why? It's certainly not because He or his Father doesn't want everyone there. It's simply because false teachers who communicate false doctrine will send people down the wrong path. That gate and the path to that afterlife is extremely wide and easy to get through. However, I sadly suspect it will be a bit crowded, simply because false teachers who teach false doctrine will sway many from the truth. Those false teachers are doing their father's will. Just to be clear their father is Satan. He wants to take as many people to hell with him as he can.

In another Scripture Jesus expressed his concern about this very issue. In Matthew 7:15-16. He stated,

> "Beware of **false prophets, who come to you in sheep's clothing** but inwardly are ravenous wolves. You will recognize them by their fruits. Are grapes gathered from thornbushes, or figs from thistles?

Paul was also concerned about this issue.

In 1 Timothy 1:3-6 Paul was concerned about false teachers who were teaching false doctrine that was causing some to wander away from Godly truth and focus on vain discussions or meaningless talk. Paul stated that those false teachers should be told that they should not "teach any different doctrine." In this case it appears that he was speaking about teachers who simply didn't understand the truth and ended up teaching doctrine that was not Godly truth. They were to be told not to teach false doctrine. We would like to hope that also meant that they could be taught the truth so that they could then teach Jesus' doctrine. They needed correction.

> "As I urged you when I was going to Macedonia, remain at Ephesus so that you **may charge certain persons not to teach any different doctrine, nor to devote themselves to myths and endless genealogies, which promote speculations** rather than the stewardship from God that is by faith. The aim of our charge is love that issues from a pure heart and a good conscience and a sincere faith. Certain persons, by swerving from these, have wandered away into **vain discussion, desiring to be teachers of the law, without understanding either what they are saying or the things about which they make confident assertions**.

In 1 Timothy 4:1-3, 7, Paul bluntly states that some Christians will leave or depart from the faith as a result of devoting themselves to deceitful spirits and teachings of demons. This is much worse than teaching incorrectly as a result of a lack of knowledge or understanding.

> "Now the Spirit expressly says that in later times **some will depart from the faith** by **devoting themselves to deceitful spirits and teachings of demons**, through the insincerity of **liars whose consciences are seared**, who **forbid marriage** and **require abstinence from foods** that God created to be received with thanksgiving by those who believe and know the truth. For everything created by God is good, and nothing is to be rejected if it is received with thanksgiving, for it is made holy by the word of God and prayer."

Paul also addresses false teachers in 1 Timothy 6:3-5. In this Scripture he was even more direct regarding those who would teach false doctrine. In this scripture he identifies qualities or characteristics of false teachers. Obviously this is helpful for us today as much as it was for those in Paul's day. What did he say about those who would teach false doctrine?

> "If anyone teaches a different doctrine and does not agree with the sound words of our Lord Jesus Christ and the teaching that accords with godliness, he is **puffed up** with **conceit** and **understands nothing**. He has an **unhealthy craving for controversy** and for **quarrels about words**, which produce envy, dissension, slander, evil suspicions, and constant friction among people who are depraved in mind and deprived of the truth, imagining that **godliness is a means of gain**."

Cause and Effect

Let's look at the cause and effect in this Scripture. It's an interesting way to look at Scriptures and often helps you understand the meaning a bit better. When something occurs (cause), it almost always produces an effect. Let's dissect 1 Timothy 6:3-5 and see the cause and effect.

Cause: Someone teaches a different doctrine that and does not agree with the Jesus Christ and His teachings.

Effect 1: The effect of such teaching is: envy, dissension, slander, evil suspicions, and constant friction among people
Effect 2: The effect is he uses his teaching as a means of personal gain.

Neither effect shown above is acceptable to God or Christ and can contribute to difficulties for those who are either seeking Christ or seeking to become a more mature Christian.

Unhealthy Qualities of False Teachers

When we look at the Scriptures there are several unhealthy qualities of False teachers that are identified (1 Timothy 6:3-5; 2 Timothy 2:22-23; James 3:15; 1 John 3:12). Let's look at several qualities that False Teachers may have within themselves.

1. Puffed up with conceit
2. Understands nothing
3. Has an unhealthy craving for controversy
4. Quarrels about words
5. Pride
6. Jealous
7. Selfish Ambition
8. Godliness is a means of Gain

None of the above are qualities that any Christian should have. To take it a step further, no teacher should ever exhibit any of the above qualities. Should a person be teaching others when he has these issues within himself? Any of the issues mentioned above could easily end up causing significant issues in a church. A person who has these qualities should be on the receiving end in his Christian relationships. He should have other Christians seeking to help him rid himself of those qualities and instead internalize the very nature of Christ.

Characteristics You Often See in a False Teacher

There are several undesirable characteristics that are seen when a false teacher is given opportunity to speak or teach. We have listed ten characteristics below that you may want to watch for so that you can determine if someone is speaking for God or himself. Let's look at each one.

- The individual seems to be the focal point of the church.
  - ➢ He defines or clarifies the unique doctrine of that 'church'.
  - ➢ The focus is on the work of the individual.
  - ➢ He often highly benefits from his work.

- The Fundamental truth about Jesus or his deity is minimized, denied or questioned (1 John 2:22-23)!
  - ➢ Jesus was just a great man of God.
  - ➢ Jesus was not born of a virgin.
  - ➢ Jesus did not complete his mission.

- Ungodly character is revealed (Galatians 5; James 3:13-18).
  - ➢ Pride may be evident.
  - ➢ Caught up in immoral activities.

- The Gospel is being distorted by requiring more than God requires (Galatians 1:6-9).
  - ➢ Circumcision being required.
  - ➢ Following tradition over Biblical teaching.
  - ➢ Addition of requirements for those becoming part of the Kingdom of God, a member their church or for those who are members.

- People are being exploited for personal gain (2 Peter 2:1-3).
  - Focus on self wants and needs; expensive tastes, cars, houses, jewelry, etc.
  - Prestige!

- God's grace is being perverted into permission to do what Scriptures say is immoral or wrong (Jude 3-4; 2 Peter 2:1-3).
  - Cheap Grace. Sin all the more so that Grace will abound.

- Scriptures are altered, minimized, added to, removed or taken out of context (Gal.1:7-9).
  - Use of only one Scripture that is contradicted in other Scriptures.
  - Literally altering the text in your own interpretation of the Bible to support an unscriptural doctrine.
  - Ignoring Bible doctrine that contradicts the Biblical stance you have taken.
  - Scripture is twisted out of context to prove a doctrinal point.

- Promotes current day revelation that reveals some of God's will that is not found in the Scriptures. This includes anything beyond what Jesus or his Apostles taught and wrote (Hebrews 13:20-21); 2 Peter 1:3.
  - Individuals within the 'church' have new revelations by which the 'church' must abide or follow.
  - New writings that are from God are shared as God's new covenant to man.

- False or unfulfilled prophecy has occurred.
  - The founder, priest, preacher, teacher, etc., makes a prophecy that is false or unfulfilled (Deuteronomy 18:20-22).

- Afterlife is also altered to benefit believers of that religion.
  - Offers salvation after death, e.g., could be taught by a pervious member of the church who is dead, can be prayed for so that they can be saved after death or some form of obligation can be met by family or others to get the person out of the hadean world (Hebrews 9:27; 2 Corinthians 9:10).
  - Must have one or more reincarnations, rebirth or reorganization, to finally get it right so that you can go to a better place (Hebrews 9:27).

> Loving Jesus and loving People
> means exposing lies that prevent
> people from seeing Jesus.

How to Identify False Doctrine

The entirety of this work is in part dedicated to, 1) identifying Scriptural doctrine that all Christians and Bible believing Churches should adhere to, and 2) specific false doctrines that cannot be identified in the Scriptures. Here are five core tests you can give any doctrine to see if it is from man or God.

1. **Test the Origin of the Doctrine:** Any doctrine that is identified and taught from any other book than the Bible, specifically the New Testament is False Doctrine (Galatians 1:7-9; 1 Thessalonians 2:13). See Revelation-Current Day Prophecy in this work.
2. **The Test of Addition:** Any doctrine that has been added through revelation that alters New Testament doctrine is false doctrine (Mark 7:6-8; 2 Peter 2:1: Jude 3-4). See Revelation-Current day Prophecy in this work.

3. **Test of Acceptance of God's Word:** Any doctrine that deletes, minimizes, changes or disregards Scriptures is False Doctrine (Hebrews 13:9; 1 Timothy 1:3).
4. **Test of Minimization or Denial:** Any doctrine that minimizes or denies the deity or work of Jesus Christ is false doctrine (John 14:6; 2 Peter 2:1; 1 John 4:3).
5. **Test of Scriptural Consistency:** Any doctrine that has been identified using specific Scriptures to prove a doctrinal point, that do not consider how other Scriptures may be in disagreement, is probably false doctrine.

Comparative Doctrine
Identifying False Doctrine Checklist

Doctrine To be Checked:	Yes	No
Did this doctrine come from any other work, personal beliefs or any other means other than the Bible?		
Was this doctrine identified as a result of any new revelation other than what is shared with us in the Bible and New Testament teachings?		
Does this doctrine delete, minimize, change or disregard the Bible or specifically the New Testament teachings?		
Does this doctrine minimize or deny the deity or work of Jesus Christ?		
Does this specific doctrinal point use a selected Scripture or Scriptures as proof, instead of considering how other Scriptures may be in disagreement?		

Note: If you answer "Yes" to any of the above questions, the doctrine you are considering is most likely a false doctrine. If you answer "Yes" to several of these questions it becomes more obvious that the doctrine you are checking is false. Keep in mind that the truth about any doctrine can be found in the Bible and no other book.

Scriptural Review Regarding False Teaching in the Bible

Jesus himself knew that there would be false teachers who would seek to lure people away from the truth. Luke 21:8 states, "And he [Jesus] said, "See that you are not led astray. For many will come in my name, saying, 'I am he!' and, 'The time is at hand!' Do not go after them." In addition, other writers of books of the Bible warn us against those who would pervert, add to or take from Scriptures. Let's look at the Scriptures and let them speak for themselves.

Instructions:

1. Read the verse and summarize what it says in the right-hand column.
2. If you choose, you can underline these Scriptures in red ink or pencil designating that those particular Scriptures address false teaching.
3. You can also make a chain out of these Scriptures if you like. See Section Seven: Scriptural Study for False Doctrine for an example for how to set up a chain.
4. Put the 'Warning of False Teaching' in the 'Personal Quick Reference' guide (shown in Section Nine), or in a preferred place in your Bible so you can easily find the initial Scripture.

Scripture on False Teaching or Doctrine	Your Understanding of this
Matthew 7:15-23	
Matthew 15:8-14	
Matthew 24:11	
Matthew 24:23-24	
Mark 7:6b-9	
Mark 7:11-13	
Luke 21:8	
Acts 20:27-31	
2 Corinthians 11:13-15	
Galatians 1:7-9	
Philippians 3:2	
Philippians 3:18	
Colossians 2:28	
1 Timothy 1:3c	

1 Timothy	1:6-7	
1 Timothy	4:1-2	
1 Timothy	6:3-5	
2 Timothy	4:3-4	
Titus	1:10-12	
Hebrews	3:9a	
2 Peter	2:1	
2 Peter	3:17b	
1 John	4:1b-3	
2 John	7-10a	
Revelation	2:20	

Sharpening the Sword (STS) Bible Study Method:
You may _underline_ these scriptures in **RED** for False Teaching.

Comparative Doctrine

The Prophet Test
Example Using Mormonism

In Deuteronomy 18:20-22, we are told how to determine if a proclaimed prophet is truly from God. If a prophet is 100% accurate in fulfillment of his prophecies, then he is from God. If he makes one false prophecy, then he should not be considered one of God's prophets. Rather, we should heed God's warning when He spoke through the Apostle Paul, "But though we, or an angel from heaven, preach any other gospel unto you than that which we have preached unto you let him be accursed" (Galatians 1:8). There are multiple individuals who have claimed to receive prophesy from God. You can use this Prophet Test with any religion that suggests that they are currently receiving revelation from God.

The Prophet Test

False Prophecies in Mormonism

Prophecy	Fulfillment	Prophecy True	False
In Doctrine and Covenants 84:1-5 Joseph prophesies that, "the New Jerusalem and its Temple are to be built in Missouri in this generation."	This was prophesied in 1832 and has not occurred.		X
In Doctrine and Covenants 124:56-60 Joseph Smith prophesied that, "Nauvoo House was to be built and that it would belong in the Smith family forever."	The house no longer belongs to the Smith family.		X
In History of the Church (vol. 2, p. 182), Joseph prophesied that, "The coming of the Lord which was nigh . . . even 56 years should wind up the scene."	It's been much more than 56 years and Jesus has not returned.		X

There are many other false prophecies that could be noted, but only one is necessary. Whenever you are dealing with a member of a church that has its own "prophet," give him God's Prophet Test. To do this you would need to understand what has been prophesied by someone in that particular church or cult.

New Revelations or Works from God and False Teaching

Our belief is that God gave us His will through the writings of the Bible. With this in mind, it is obvious that many 'new' revelations, writings or interpretations of the Bible or God's will has been suggested by multiple people throughout the ages. Let's look at some of them.

Primary Work or Works Defining Doctrine	Who it was 'revealed to' or who is the primary author.	Church Belief or Cult	Explanation
Bible Mystery of the Ages The Real Truth The Pillar Magazine:	Herbert Armstrong	Armstrongism Worldwide Church of God, Grace Communion International.	Believes the Bible has a hidden code that he discovered to reveal the truth about God's will.
Bible Book of Mormon Doctrine and Covenants Pearl of Great Price And many more!	Joseph Smith	Church of Christ of Latter-day Saints	Received knowledge of golden plates from the Angel Moroni. Additional Revelations.
Bible Catholic Catechism	1992 Pope John Paul II officially approved the definitive version of the Catechism of the Catholic Church.	Catholic Church	Doctrine interpreted and changed as Pope believes is correct. He is infallible in all things doctrinal. The Catechism defines Catholic Church beliefs.
Science and Health with Key to the Scriptures Miscellaneous Writing Retrospection and Introspection.	Mary Baker Eddy	Christian Science Church	God revealed the information found in Science and Health. There is no matter, no illness, no death.
Divine Principle Unification Church 120 Day Training Manual. Unification Theology Unification Theology and Christian Thought And more!	Sun Myung Moon	Unification Church	Moon is the second coming of Christ. He fulfills Christ's mission by getting married. The perfect family. The Divine Principle is God's new will for man.
Studies in the Scriptures (7 Volumes) Thy Kingdom Come Let God Be True. The Truth Shall Make You Free New World Translation of the Holy Scriptures And more!	Charles T. Russell	Jehovah's Witnesses	144,000 will reign in heaven. All good people will live on the New Earth. Evil people will be annihilated. New World Translation and Studies in Scriptures suggest core doctrine.

Qur'an or Koran	Muhammad	Islam	Muhammad received revelation from the Angel Garbrial and the Qur'an was written.
Dianetics: The Modern Science of Mental Health The Factors: Admiration & the Renaissance of Beingness. Scientology: The Fundamentals of Thought.	L. Ron Hubbard	Scientology Church	Scientology begins with the concept that man is 'basically good, and that his spiritual salvation depends upon himself, his fellows and his attainment of brotherhood with the universe.
Seventh-day Adventist Church Manual. Seventh-day Adventist Questions on Doctrine: An Explanation of Certain Major Aspects of Seventh-day Adventist Belief. Steps to Christ The Desire of Ages The Great Controversy. Believe His Prophets Writings And more!	Ellen G. White	Seventh-day Adventists	God reveals new beliefs in Questions on Doctrine and many other works.
Jesus Christ Heals. Metaphysical Bible Dictionary Christian Healing; The Science of Being The Revealed Word Teach Us to Pray	C. Fillmore	Unity Church	New works like the Metaphysical Bible Dictionary, Jesus Christ Heals and other works teach beliefs.
Eastern Religions			
All Eastern Religions Deny the Deity of Christ and some Believe the Bible is just one of many messages to man.			
Dhammapada	Gautama, Siddhartha 'Buddha'	Buddhism	A man who wanted the best for all mankind.
Gleanings from the Writings of Bahá'u'lláh,	Baha'u'llah	Baha'i	Based on Hinduism. Keep living life over and over until you merge with 'God'.
The Upanishads Bhagavad Gita The Visnu Purana: Sanskrit Text	Hinduism:	Hinduism	Believes it is the oldest form of religion in the world. Keep living life over and over until you merge with 'God'.

Compatibility of Eastern Religions with the Bible

Eastern religions often teach many concepts that are in conflict with Biblical teaching. For instance, they don't accept Jesus Christ as Lord and Savior. They have completely different perspectives from Christianity regarding salvation. Their 'salvation' is often through self-works that can be attempted over and over again in different reincarnations. Often their founding fathers were mortal men. Here are some of the more common eastern religions:

- Baha'i
- Buddhism (Classical and Zen Buddhism)
- Hinduism (many eastern religions have their roots in Hinduism)

NOTE: Hinduism had a major impact on Hubbard when he developed Scientology as a religion.

We will address the three beliefs mentioned above in this work for two reasons. First, they are the most recognized eastern religions that are still growing. Second, all three have become westernized and have begun to pull those who have some Biblical belief into their belief systems.

Most Eastern Religions:

- Do not believe that God created the world.
- Do not believe in the Christian God.
- Believe that God is more essence or in all things.
- Believes that there is more than one God!
- Do not consider Christ to be Deity. Christ was just another good man.
- Do not believe that the Bible is God's final truth.
- Believe in some form of Reincarnation or Rebirth.
- Believe that good deeds improve circumstances in the future (next life).
- Salvation is ultimate liberation from life-death cycle.
- There is no Heaven. Heaven is not a place.
- There is no Hell or Eternal Punishment
- There is no Devil or Satan!

Overview of Various Beliefs and the History of Change

Section Three

A Brief History of Established Religions

Western Religions

- **Armstrongism (Worldwide Church of God, renamed itself Grace Communion International)**
- **Catholicism**
- **Christian Science**
- **Islam**
- **Jehovah Witness**
- **Judaism**
- **Mormonism**
- **Scientology**
- **Seventh-day Adventists**
- **Unification Church (Moonies)**
- **Unity Church (Unity or Silent Unity)**
- **Universal Unitarianism**

Eastern Religions that have a Different View of God and Afterlife

- **Baha'i**
- **Buddhism**
- **Hinduism**

A Brief History of Established Religions

Date	Place Established	Founder	Church Name	Key Fact
33 AD	Israel, Jerusalem	Jesus Christ	Christ's Church Church of Christ Church of God	Started on Pentecost.
606 AD	Italy, Rome	Boniface III	Roman Catholic	Pope has infallible, ultimate say regarding doctrine or church beliefs.
610 AD Speculated	Saudi Arabia, Mecca	Muhammad	Islam	Received revelation from Gabrial the Angel. Originated in Mecca.
1520 AD	Germany	Martin Luther	Lutheran	He came to reject several teachings and practices of the Roman Catholic Church. 95 Thesis! Frederick the Wise and several German Princes protected Luther from the Catholic Church.
1523 AD	Switzerland	Ulrich Zwingli	Swiss Reformation	A priest who broke from the Catholic Church and started preaching the Bible. Didn't believe in the traditions of the Catholic Church. Taught that it was ok to eat meat during lent, Priests and nuns married and much more. Replaced Mass with a simple service where the Bible was preached. Believed in infant baptism and strongly opposed the Anabaptist teaching of adult baptism.
1525 AD	Switzerland	Conrad Grebel and Felix Mantz were the early 'leaders' of the movement	Anabaptists	Wanted the church to return to first century teaching. Also sought a self-governing church ruled by the Holy spirit instead of focusing on hierarchy and political systems that the Catholic Church was based on. Believed in adult baptism!
1534 AD	England	Henry VIII	Episcopalian	The Anglican church originated when King Henry Split from Roman Catholic Church because the Pope would not Grant him an annulment.
1536 AD	Switzerland	John Calvin	Presbyterian	By 1536, Calvin had disengaged himself from the Roman Catholic Church because of theological disagreements. Taught TULIP: Total depravity, Unconditional election, Limited atonement, Irresistible grace, and Perseverance of the saints.
1550 AD	England	Robert Browne	Congregational	Browne was one of the original proponents of the Separatist, or Free Church, movement among Nonconformists that demanded separation from the Church of England.

1607 AD	Holland	John Smythe	Baptist	English religious libertarian and Nonconformist minister, called "the Se-baptist" (self-baptizer), who is generally considered the founder of the organized Baptists of England.
1739 AD	England	John Wesley	Methodist	Wesley's writings provided a core of standard doctrine and interpretation to guide the new Methodist movement. In 1784, he sent instructions to America for the formation of a separate Methodist church for the United States.
1774 AD	England	John Biddle (1615-62), and the first Unitarian congregation came into being in 1774 at Essex Chapel in London,	Universal Unitarianism	All works are accepted that help lead members to spiritual growth, e.g., Bible, Qur'an.
1830 AD	America	Joseph Smith	Latter Day Saints or Mormonism	Joseph Smith found golden plates that had the book or Mormon inscribed on them. They claim that this is God's new revelation to man.
1830 AD	America	Ellen Gould White	Adventists (Seven-day)	Sabbath Worshipers
1866 AD	America	Mary Baker Eddy	Christian Scientist	There is no matter, no illness, no death.
1872 AD	America	Charles T. Russell	Jehovah's Witnesses	144,000 will go to heaven. Good remains on New Earth and evil is annihilated.
1889 AD	America	Charles Sherlock Filmore and Myrtle Fillmore	Unity, a church within the New Thought movement	Learned to repeat, "I am a child of God and therefore I do not inherit sickness." The Fillmore's learned they could heal their own physical problems using the above mentioned statement, along with prayer.
1933-4 AD	America	Herbert Armstrong	Worldwide Church of God	Bible Is coded. Must understand the code to truly understand the Bible.
1953 AD	America	L. Ron Hubbard	Scientology	Scientology begins with the concept that man is 'basically good, and that his spiritual salvation depends upon himself, his fellows and his attainment of brotherhood with the universe."
1954 AD	South Korea	Sun Myung Moon	Unification Church	Moon claimed that he was the second coming of Christ. He came to fulfill Christ's mission on earth—the perfect marriage.

Comparative Doctrine

Churches that were Formed in Reaction to Catholicism or to get back to Bible Teaching

Many religions claim that their religion is the one that started at Pentecost. However, most of those religions have begun as a result of someone altering doctrine or by rebelling against the Catholic Church. What most do not realize is that the Catholic Church actually altered the organization of the church and in several ways the doctrine of the original church. Several men who studied the Bible came to similar beliefs that the true church had been altered to become something other than what the New Testament design suggested it should be. When you look at the above chart you can see that many religions were developed or sought to return to the basic truths of the Bible as a result of doctrinal disagreements. The problem encountered was that the men who wanted to return the church to its roots often had some of their own opinions or beliefs interspersed with true Biblical teachings. Lutheranism, Presbyterian (Calvinism), Episcopalian, Congregational and Methodist reformers sprung from disagreements with Catholic doctrines, traditions or in some cases with the organizational system the Catholic Church had imposed on Christendom. Many of these 'rebellious' churches were trying to find their way back to what the Bible taught. Some had some success. Others ended up promoting doctrine that was questionable.

God's New Revelation to Muhammad

Islam traces its beginning back to Abraham, but the Qur'an was not written by Muhammad until around 610 AD. Muhammad stated that he received revelation from Gabriel the Angel and from it the Qur'an was written. The Muslim belief originated in Mecca. Their teaching states that the Qur'an is God's (Allah's) new revelation to men and is God's last word. This appears to be the first major religion where someone reports that God gave further revelation that took precedent over the Bible.

New Faces in the New World

Multiple new beliefs attempted to return to Biblical truth in American starting in the 1800's. The problem was that many of these new attempts at communicating Biblical truth ended up being redefined based on personal beliefs or interests. Joseph Smith, William Miller, Herbert Armstrong, Mary Baker Eddy, Charles T. Russell, Charles Sherlock Fillmore, L. Ron Hubbard, Sun Myung Moon and others have proposed new revelations or understandings regarding God's plan for us today and in many instances what that plan looks like after our physical death.

As a result of what these men and women proposed through analysis, revelation from God, etc. multiple churches with a variety of doctrines became a reality. Each of these religious beliefs have taught and promoted varying types of doctrine that are in direct conflict with Biblical truths. That is one of the big issues that we all face. What does the Bible really say about specific doctrine? Are you going to believe what the Bible says, or do you want to believe what man has written?

Information in this work is meant to help you take a better look at Scriptures so that Biblical truth can be found. Our challenge to you is to search out and believe what you read in the Bible, not what any man or woman has written. It doesn't matter if you are a Catholic, a Lutheran, a Methodist, a Baptist, an Episcopalian or a member of any other church. We just want you to look at the Bible and determine what the Bible says about specific doctrines. The Scripture does say, "Therefore, my beloved, as you have always obeyed, so now, not only as in my presence but much more in my absence, work out your own salvation with fear and trembling" (Philippians 2:12). Don't let men tell you what to believe. The Bible clearly teaches you what your spiritual life should be like. Make sure you are in a church that teaches Biblical truth for doctrine, not opinions, traditions of man or something that comes from 'new' revelation from God. God has already revealed what you need to know to be his follower. It's called the BIBLE!

Western Religions that have a Belief in a Higher Power

The focus in this portion of the book is to give you a look at some of the Western religions that have in several ways adapted Christianity. Churches are claiming new revelations, new apostles with greater understanding of God's will, direct communication with God and such like. Such religions have produced a variety of churches that minimize the Bible, add to, take away from or misinterpret God's Holy Word. It is impossible to look at every religious institution that has done any of the above. However, the list shown below shows some of the more well-known 'churches' that have altered God's will in some way. Like we said at the beginning, you will be surprised at how some religions have altered God's Word. You may even be surprised that some churches are on this short list.

- Armstrongism (Worldwide Church of God renamed itself Grace Communion International)
- Catholicism
- Christian Science
- Islam
- Jehovah's Witnesses
- Judaism
- Mormonism
- Scientology
- Seventh-day Adventists
- Unification Church (Moonies)
- Unity Church (Unity or Silent Unity)
- Universal Unitarianism

Armstrongism

Worldwide Church of God, Grace Communion International

Founder: Herbert W. Armstrong. With his books, Armstrong defined his theology.

Beginning Date: The Worldwide Church of God, originally the Radio Church of God, was established in Eugene, Oregon, in 1933-1934 through the evangelistic efforts of Herbert W. Armstrong. The name was changed to Worldwide Church of God in 1968.

Now: Over the years there have been multiple splinter groups. Until 2009 the most recognized evolution of Armstrongism is the Worldwide Church of God. It was later changed to the Grace Communion International Church.

NOTE: Because of the many splinter groups that have different theological beliefs this work will focus on the original beliefs taught by the 'Apostle' Herbert W. Armstrong. There are many splinter groups that still follow his teachings and some that only follow selected teachings.

Key Statement: The Bible as the only standard of faith and practice for Christians.

Doctrinal Books

- Bible
- Mystery of the Ages
- The Plain Truth

Armstrong Unique or Core Beliefs	
Topic	**Belief**
Leader or Prophet that Defines Beliefs.	Herbert Armstrong considers himself to be an Apostle and his writings are revelations from God. His works define theology. *
Bible Inspiration. Uses Works other than the Bible.	State that they teach the Bible, but their beliefs are based on Herbert W. Armstrong's interpretations. Armstrong's interpretation of Bible content is found in his book titled, 'Mystery of the Ages'.*
Scriptures Taken Out of Context.	"The paramount mysteries confronting all humanity. The revelation of these mysteries was lost, even to the Church of God, although the revelation of them has been preserved in the writings of the Bible. Why, then, has the world not clearly understood? Because the Bible was a coded book, not intended to be understood until our day in this latter half of the twentieth century (Mystery of the Ages, 1995).
Multiple gods	"The false Trinity teaching does limit God to three persons. But God is not limited. As God repeatedly reveals, his purpose it to reproduce himself into what well may become billions of God persons. It is the false Trinity teaching that limits God, denies God's purpose and has palpably deceived the whole Christian world" (Armstrong, Mystery of the Ages, 1995). "The ones who accept Jesus will receive the immortal resurrection of a spirit-body. Hence, they become God Beings and finish creating the many planets in the universe" (Armstrong, The Plain Truth, October/November, 1977).
Begotten or Born of God.	Armstrong Born of God (BOG) "When we are converted, our sins are forgiven, we receive the Holy Spirit, we are then BEGOTTEN of God – not yet BORN of God….even as Christ was BORN AGAIN, born of God by his resurrection, even so as WE – the brethren- shall be BORN AGAIN as sons of God, through the RESURRECTION OF THE DEAD…" (Herbert W. Armstrong, "Was Jesus Born Again?" in The Plain Truth, February 1963, p. 40). "Armstrong taught that God's purpose in creating mankind was to "reproduce Himself", and that the process of being "born again" was not instantaneous — that the believer (as a result of baptism by immersion) was only "begotten" until reborn as a spirit being at the return of Jesus. Those 'begotten' will then be instantaneously 'born anew' (John 3:3) but not again, "a second time", as "perishable" flesh and blood mortals (1 Cor. 15:53) but as "imperishable", immortal Spirit 'God' beings. He concluded that; "Until the resurrection, therefore, we cannot see, enter into or inherit the Kingdom of God. WE CANNOT BE BORN AGAIN UNTIL THE RESURRECTION!" (Armstrong, Herbert. "Just What Do You Mean Born Again?", 1972). "The Holy Spirit also is the divine 'spiritual sperm' that impregnates with immortal God-life" (Armstrong, Confusion, 6).

Comparative Doctrine

Jesus Son of God at Birth	"Jesus did not become the Son of God until about 4 BC, when he was born in human flesh of the virgin Mary" (Armstrong, The Plain Truth, February, 1979, 41).
Jesus' Resurrection	Armstrong teaches that Jesus Christ rose from the dead as a spirit without a physical form. "Now notice carefully, God the Father did not cause Jesus Christ to get back into the body that had died….And the resurrected body was no longer human---it was the Christ resurrected immortal, once again changed! As he had been changed, converted into mortal human flesh and blood, subject to death, and for the purpose of dying for your sins, now by a resurrection from the dead, he was again changed, converted into immortality (Armstrong, What Christ Died and Rose Again, The Plain Truth, April 1982, Pg. 20). "Because they knew what Jesus had looked like – and in his born again, resurrected body he looked the same, except he now was composed of spirit instead of matter!...He was born in a spirit body, which was manifested to his apostles in the same apparent size and shape as when he died" (Armstrong, The Plain Truth, January, 1978, 44).
Christians Become God Beings	A Christian will become a god being after salvation. "Those 'begotten' will then be instantaneously 'born anew' (John 3:3) but not again, "a second time", as "perishable" flesh and blood mortals (1 Cor. 15:53) but as "imperishable", immortal Spirit 'God' beings." (Armstrong, Herbert. "Just What Do You Mean Born Again?", 1972). Armstrong also teaches that men can become Gods. We can rise in the school of advancement, by following Armstrong, and become a God. Those who believe will be given immortal spirit bodies at the resurrection. They will then become God beings and help finish creating many planets in the universe (Just What Do You Mean—Born Again, 1962, Pg. 19).
No Consciousness at Death	Armstrong did not accept the concept of eternal judgment in this life. He believed that those who die as unbelievers prior to the return of Christ, exist in a state of "unconsciousness" until after the 'Millennium' at the second resurrection, during which they will be offered the choice to submit to God's government (Herbert Armstrong, Mystery of the Ages, p.352).
Death	"The 'wages of sin is death' (Rom. 6:23), and that death, which is the absence of life, is for all eternity. It is eternal punishment by remaining dead for all eternity — not remaining alive and being tortured in a fictitious burning hell fire (Do You have an Immoral Soul--Booklet, Pasadena, CA: Ambassador College Press, 1973).

Hell is not Eternal	"Even so, it will be with the Gehenna fire. It will be unquenched – but it will finally burn itself out" (Herbert Armstrong, Ambassador College Correspondence Course, Lesson 6, P. 14). All those incorrigibly wicked, those who refuse to accept God's government and laws being judged guilty of rebellion against God to rise in a third resurrection, and thrown into 'Gehenna' fire. Including persons who had committed the "unpardonable sin". Such persons suffering eternal death. Armstrong identified such as being the "second death" mentioned in the Book of Revelation (Herbert Armstrong, Mystery of the Ages, p. 354).
Holy Spirit	"When you receive the Holy Spirit, you don't receive a full measure of the Holy Spirit all at once, but you increase in the spirit of God as you grow and develop" (Armstrong, H. World Tomorrow Telecast; What is the Holy Spirit?). The Holy Spirit is God's spirit. It is the impregnation of immortal life, or the life of God. It is the love of God. Is the faith of Christ. Armstrong's description of Holy Spirit does not account for the Holy Spirit being an independent entity or personality. It is simply God's spirit (Armstrong, H. World Tomorrow Telecast; What is the Holy Spirit?).
Kingdom Proclaimed/Established	"Armstrong taught that a reason for Jesus Christ's presence on earth was to proclaim the Gospel message of a literal Kingdom of God that will be established on earth at Christ's 'second coming', and that the message of the Kingdom should be the focus of the gospel rather than the person of Christ (Armstrong, Herbert (1955). What is the True Gospel (PDF) (1972 ed.). Pasadena, California: Ambassador College). He made the extraordinary claim that the gospel Christ brought (of the Kingdom) had "not been proclaimed to the world" for about 1,900 years "until the first week in 1953" when he began preaching it again on Radio Luxembourg (Armstrong, Herbert. "Mystery of the Ages". Chapter 7 "Mystery of the Kingdom of God"). Jesus came, over 1,900 years ago, to announce the future kingdom of God. He's coming this time to establish that kingdom. That end-time last warning message is now going out worldwide in amplified power (Armstrong, 1985). "Since God's purpose is to reproduce himself—expand the God Family—and since it shall be the world-ruling family, then the Kingdom of God is the born family of God ruling the entire world" (Armstrong, A World Held Captive, The Plain Truth, June 1984, 6, 39).
Old Law Still in Effect	Armstrong taught the adherence to Levitical food regulations and the observance of the 'Holy Days' of the Mosaic Law (Herbert W. Armstrong, Pagan Holidays – Or God's Holy Days – Which, p.26).
Sabbath Keeping	"Sunday observance – this is the Mark of the Beast...If in your forehead and your hand, you shall be tormented by Gods plagues without mercy, yes, you!" (Herbert Armstrong, The Mark of the

	Beast, Pasadena: Ambassador College Press, 1957, Pg. 10, 11). The Worldwide Church of God conducted its worship Services during that period, accordingly, on Saturdays. Armstrong further explained that Christ is "Lord of the Sabbath" (Matthew 12:8) for it is He who 'made' it for mankind, thus it is a "blessing... to be ENJOYED, to spiritually REFRESH, in blessed fellowship and communion with CHRIST!" (Armstrong, Herbert. "Which Day Is The Christian Sabbath?", Chapter 8) Armstrong taught a form of Sabbatarianism, explaining that; by creating the Sabbath (on the seventh day of creation, through resting – not working) God "HALLOWED the Seventh-day of every week (Ex. 20:11)" and therefore made "future TIME holy!" Resting on the Sabbath day is thus commanded for all mankind and should be kept holy from Friday sunset to sunset on Saturday (Armstrong, Herbert W. Which Day Is The Christian Sabbath? Chapter 2).
Salvation after Death	The Armstrongites do not seem concerned about the salvation of lost sinners now. They think people will have a better chance 'at the great white throne of judgment' of Revelation 20:11-15. All will have a chance to be saved after death (Armstrong, The Plain Truth, October/November, 1977, 3ff).*
Second Coming of Christ	Armstrong preached that Jesus Christ will return to earth to "rescue" humanity from the brink of self-annihilation, resulting in the establishment of "God's government" upon earth, during a 'Millennium' period, under the rulership of Christ and first-resurrected saints. After His return, those surviving the "great tribulation" will be given the chance to voluntarily accept "God's way of life." (Herbert Armstrong, Mystery of the Ages, p. 344-345).* Christ is in heaven "until" the "times of restitution" (Acts 3:19–21) when God's government, world peace and utopian conditions shall be restored to this earth (Armstrong, Herbert. "Mystery of the Ages". Chapter 7 "Mystery of the Kingdom of God").
Revelation	In 1979 Armstrong proclaimed the book titled, "The Incredible Human Potential" was actually written by Jesus Christ and he was simply a stenographer. He stated, "I feel with deep conviction that I myself did not author this book—that the living Jesus Christ is its real author. I was merely like a stenographer writing it down. And with that understanding, I feel I may say that this is the most important—the most tremendously revealing—book since the Bible" (Armstrong, 1979). When he introduced the book Mystery of the Ages in 1985, he said, "I candidly feel it may be the most important book since the Bible" (Flurry, G. "Personal," The Philadephhia Trumpet, February 1997, 1). "I know of no other who has ever become founder of a religion, or a religious leader of any kind, who ever came into the truth in the way God brought me into it...God brought me through a process that erased former misknowledge—and, as it were, gave me a clear start

	from "scratch." I wonder if you realize that every truth of God, accepted as truth doctrine and belief in the Worldwide Church of God, came from Christ through me, or was finally approved and made official through me...I was appointed by Jesus Christ, the head of the Church" (Armstrong, End Vietnam War Now!" The Plain Truth, February, 1967, 47). Armstrong credited himself with restoring "at least eighteen basic essential truths...to the true Church" (Armstrong, Mystery of the Ages).
Current Day Apostle	Armstrong claimed that he was, "His [Jesus'] one apostle for this twentieth century" (Armstrong, The Plain Truth, July 1977, 1; and February 1978, 43).
Bible has Coded Message	"All these mysteries were....a coded message not allowed to be revealed and decoded until our time" (Mystery of the Ages, 1995).
No Trinity	But the theologians and "higher Critics" have blindly accepted the heretical and false doctrine introduced by pagan false prophets who crept in, that the Holy Spirit is a third Person—the heresy of the "Trinity." This limits God to "Three Persons" (Armstrong, Just What Do You Mean—Born Again. Pasadena: Radio Church of God, 1962,19).
Prophecy	See False Prophecy and Armstrongism. There are multiple prophecies that were found to be false.

The Prophet Test

False Prophecies in Armstrongism

Prophecy	Fulfillment	Prophecy True	False
Day of the Lord Prophecy of 1934: The present world-chaos Tribulation, to be followed by, or quickly after 1936, but the heavenly signs, which shall be followed by the "Day of the Lord"….to the time-sequences fixed by these prophecies, the Revelation story-flow agrees exactly (Armstrong, The Plain Truth, June/July 1934, 5).	This did not happen!		X
Catholic Church Comes to an End Prophecy of 1938: Thus shall the Catholic Church come to her final end. Thus saith the lord (Armstrong, The Plain Truth, March 1938, 8).	This did not happen!		X
Hitler and the Invasion of Russia: Hitler is the "Beast" of Revelation….There, Bible prophecy does indicate that Hitler must be the victor in his present Russian invasion (Armstrong, The Plain Truth, October, 1941, 7).	This did not happen!		X
One third of Population will Die. Prophecy of 1957: Within the next fifteen years [by 1972], fully one third of our whole population will die of disease and famine (Armstrong, The Plain Truth, December 1957, 23).	This did not happen!		X
The Day of the Eternal Prophecy of 1967: A time foretold in more than thirty prophecies---is going to strike between five and ten years [by 1977] from now! You will know, then, how real it is….I am not writing foolishly, but very soberly, on authority of the living Christ (Armstrong, The Plain Truth, February 1967, 47).	This did not happen!		X
"…we are to have soon (probably in about four years) such drought, and famine, that disease epidemics will follow, taking millions of lives….that condition is coming! And I do not mean in 400 years- nor in 40 years- but in the very next FOUR to FIVE" (Herbert W. Armstrong, The United States and British Commonwealth in Prophecy, p. 184).	This did not happen!		X

Note: There are many more failed prophecies that Armstrong made.

Catholicism

Founder: The Catholic Church claims that it is the continuation of the early Christian community established by Jesus Christ. They teach that their bishops are the successors to Jesus's apostles, and the Bishop of Rome, also known as the Pope, is the sole successor to Saint Peter who they believe was appointed by Jesus in the New Testament as head of the church and ministered in Rome.

Key Statement: The Bible as the only standard of faith and practice for Christians.

Beginning Date: The Catholic Church teaches that Peter was the first Pope.

Doctrinal Books

- Catholic Bible: Works found in the Catholic Bible, but not in the Protestant Bible are as follows.
  - ➢ Tobit
  - ➢ Judith
  - ➢ 1 Maccabees
  - ➢ 2 Maccabees
  - ➢ Wisdom of Solomon
  - ➢ Wisdom of Sirach (also called Ecclesiasticus)
  - ➢ Baruch including the Letter of Jeremiah
  - ➢ Additions to Esther
  - ➢ Additions to Daniel:
  - ➢ Prayer of Azariah and Song of the Three Holy Children (Septuagint Daniel 3:24–90)
  - ➢ Susanna (Septuagint prologue, Vulgate Daniel 13)
  - ➢ Bel and the Dragon (Septuagint epilogue, Vulgate Daniel 14)
- Catechism

The Split in the Catholic Church

Roman Catholic and Eastern Orthodox split for a multitude of reasons. Eastern Orthodox would not acknowledge the Roman Catholic Pope and ultimately the two 'Popes' excommunicated each other.

The Eastern Orthodox Church also claims to have roots back to the Apostles.

The Head of the Eastern Orthodox Church is called the: Ecumenical Patriarch of Constantinople. He is referred to as: His All Holiness

They state that the first holder of this title was Andrew the Apostle of Jesus. He was a Bishop in the Church. Alexander was the archbishop. Anatolius was the first named patriarch.

Established: 38

In 451 the title of patriarch was granted.

There has been conflict between the two, almost from their inception.

F. Russell Crites, Jr. and Derek Russell Crites

Catholic Beliefs and the Catechism

What is the Catechism and what does it have to do with Doctrine?

"The Catechism of the Catholic Church is intended primarily to explain the teachings of the Catholic faith. It is an excellent reference for the Catholic faithful. It is also a great resource for non-Catholics interested in learning what the Church really teaches. Many misunderstandings about the Church's teachings on controversial issues can be resolved by looking at what the Catechism says about Catholic beliefs" (http://www.aboutcatholics.com).

Who started it

The first Catholic catechism was written after the Council of Trent. It was published in 1566 and was called the Roman Catechism. It was reviewed and rewritten in 1994.

The Purpose of the Catechism

"The Catechism serves several important functions:

- It conveys the essential and fundamental content of Catholic faith and morals in a complete and summary way.
- It is a point of reference for national and diocesan catechisms.
- It is a positive, objective and declarative exposition of Catholic doctrine.
- It is intended to assist those who have the duty to catechize, namely promoters and teachers of catechesis" (http://www.usccb.org/).

Brief History of the Catechism

1566 Catechism: This catechism was a reaction to Martin Luther's documents that were published showing his disagreement with the Catholic Church.   It became evident that the Catholic Church had to write something that would explain to the people what the Catholic Church believed. Over a series of years Catholic leaders discussed what the Roman Catechism should have in it. "The first Catholic catechism was written after the Council of Trent. It was published in 1566 and called the Roman Catechism. A new catechism was not created until 1994 called The Catechism of the Catholic Church" (http://www.aboutcatholics.com).

1994 Catechism: "The 1994 Catechism of the Catholic Church originated with a recommendation made at the Extraordinary Synod of Bishops in 1985. In 1986 Pope John Paul II appointed a Commission of Cardinals and Bishops to develop a compendium of Catholic doctrine. In 1989 the Commission sent the text to all the Bishops of the world for consultation. In 1990 the Commission examined and evaluated over 24,000 amendments suggested by the world's bishops. The final draft is considerably different from the one that was circulated in 1989. In 1991 the Commission prepared the text for the Holy Father's official approval. On June 25, 1992 Pope John Paul II officially approved the definitive version of the Catechism of the Catholic Church. On December 8, 1992 Pope John Paul II promulgated the Catechism with an apostolic constitution" (http://www.usccb.org/).

NOTE: We will be looking at how closely the Catechism follows Biblical truth.

Comparative Doctrine

Catholic Unique or Core Beliefs	
Topic	**Belief**
Bible Study	According to the official teaching of the Catholic Church, Catholic men and women are not allowed to believe what they read in the Bible without checking it out with the Catholic Church. They are required to find out how the bishops of the Church interpret a passage and they are to accept what the bishops teach as if it came from Jesus Christ Himself. They are not allowed to use their own judgment or follow their own conscience. They are required to believe whatever the bishops teach without questioning it (Catechism 85, 87, 100, 862, 891, 939, 2034, 2037, 2041, 2050).
Interpreting God's Word	"The task of interpreting the Word of God authentically has been entrusted solely to the magisterium of the Church, that is, to the Pope and to the bishops in communion with him" (Catechism, 100).
Infant Baptism	"Born with a fallen human nature and tainted by original sin, children also have need of the new birth in Baptism to be freed from the power of darkness and brought into the realm of the freedom of the children of God, to which all men are called. The sheer gratuitousness of the grace of salvation is particularly manifest in infant Baptism. The Church and the parents would deny a child the priceless grace of becoming a child of God were they not to confer Baptism shortly after birth" (Catechism 1250). They must be baptized to receive forgiveness for all past sins (original sin). "Born with a fallen human nature and tainted by original sin, children also have need of the new birth in Baptism to be freed from the power of darkness and brought into the realm of the freedom of the children of God, to which all men are called. The sheer gratuitousness of the grace of salvation is particularly manifest in infant Baptism. The Church and the parents would deny a child the priceless grace of becoming a child of God were they not to confer Baptism shortly after birth" (Catechism, 1250). "The practice of infant Baptism is an immemorial tradition of the Church. There is explicit testimony to this practice from the second century on..." (Catechism, 1252).
Baptism	Pouring water for baptism: "The essential rite of Baptism consists in immersing the candidate in water or pouring water on his head, while pronouncing the invocation of the Most Holy Trinity: the Father, the Son, and the Holy Spirit" (Catechism 1278). Baptism of Blood: "The Church has always held the firm conviction that those who suffer death for the sake of the faith without having received Baptism are baptized by their death for and with Christ. This Baptism of blood, like the desire for Baptism, brings about the fruits of Baptism without being a sacrament" (Catechism 1259). "For catechumens who die before their Baptism, their explicit desire to receive it, together with repentance for their sins, and charity, assures them the salvation that they were not able to receive through the sacrament" (Catechism 1259).

Catholics are Christ!	"Lets us rejoice then and give thanks that we have become not only Christians, but Christ himself. Marvel and rejoice; we have become Christ" (Catechism, 795). "For the Son of Man became a man so that we might become God" (Catechism, 460). "The only-begotten Son of God, wanting to make us sharers in his divinity, assumed our nature, so that he, made man, might make men gods" (Catechism, 460).
Praying to Saints. They intercede for us and care for those left on earth.	"The witnesses who have preceded us into the kingdom, especially those whom the Church recognizes as saints, share in the living tradition of prayer by the example of their lives…They contemplate God, praise him and constantly care for those who they have left on earth. Their intercession is their most exalted service to God's plan. We can and should ask them to intercede for us and for the whole world" (Catechism, 2683). "Being more closely united to Christ, those who dwell in heaven fix the whole Church more firmly in holiness….they do not cease to intercede with the Father for us, as they proffer the merits which they acquired on earth through the one mediator between God and men, Christ Jesus….So by their fraternal concern is our weakness greatly helped" (Catechism, 956, See 493).
Communion/ Transubstantiation	Catholicism and Transubstantiation: The Council of Trent summarizes the Catholic faith by declaring: "Because Christ our Redeemer said that it was truly his body that he was offering under the species of bread, it has always been the conviction of the Church of God, and this holy Council now declares again, that by the consecration of the bread and wine there takes place a change of the whole substance of the bread into the substance of the body of Christ our Lord and of the whole substance of the wine into the substance of his blood. This change the holy Catholic Church has fittingly and properly called transubstantiation" (Catechism, 1376).
Celibacy	"All the ordained ministers of the Latin Church, with the exception of permanent deacons, are normally chosen from among men of faith who live a celibate life and who intend to remain celibate 'for the sake of the kingdom of heaven'….Celibacy is a sign of this new life to the service of which the Church's minister is consecrated; accepted with a joyous heart celibary radiantly proclaims the Reign of God" (Catechism, 1579).
Virgin Mary a Perpetual virgin…no other children	"Mary remained a virgin in conceiving her Son, a virgin in giving birth to him, a virgin in carrying him, a virgin in nursing him at her breast, always a virgin" (Catechism,510). "And so the liturgy of the Church celebrates Mary as Aeiparthenos, the 'Ever-virgin'" (Catechism, 499). "The Church has always understood these passages [Matthew 13:55; Mark 6:3; Galatians 1:19] as not referring to other children of the Virgin Mary. In fact James and Joseph, 'brothers of Jesus,' are the sons of another Mary, a disciple of Christ..." (Catechism, 500).

	"Jesus is Mary's only son, but her spiritual motherhood extends to all men whom indeed he came to save: "The Son whom she brought forth is he whom God placed as the first-born among many brethren, that is, the faithful in whose generation and formation she co-operates with a mother's love" (Catechism, 501).
Mary Lived a Sinless Life from Birth	"By the grace of God Mary remained free of Every personal sin her whole life long" (Catechism, 493). "Through the centuries the Church has become ever more aware that Mary, 'full of grace' through God, was redeemed from the moment of her conception" (Catechism, 491). "Espousing the divine will for salvation wholeheartedly, without a single sin to restrain her, she gave herself entirely to the person and to the work of her son..." (Catechism 494). "Mary is the most excellent fruit of redemption (SC 103): From the first instant of her conception, she was totally preserved from the stain of original sin and she remained pure from all personal sin throughout her life" (Catechism, 508...See also 722). Mary, "the All-Holy," lived a perfectly sinless life (Catechism 411, 493).
Salvation is through Mary	"Taken up to heaven she (Mary) did not lay aside this saving office but by her manifold intercession continues to bring us the gifts of eternal salvation..." Catechism, 969). "Being obedient she (Mary) became the cause of salvation for herself and for the whole human race" (Catechism, 494). "She (Mary) is inseparably linked with the saving work of her Son" (Catechism, 1172).
Mary the Model and source of Holiness	"From the Church he learns the example of holiness and recognizes its model and source in the all-holy Virgin Mary..." Catechism, 2030).
Mary Intercedes for Us	""Therefore the Blessed Virgin is invoked in the Church under the titles of Advocate, Helper, Benefactress, and Mediatrix" (Catechism, 969).
Mary Receives Our Prayers and Prays for Us	"....we can entrust all our cares and petitions to her; she prays for us as she prayed for herself: "Let it be to me according to your word." By entrusting ourselves to her prayer, we abandon ourselves to the will of God together with her: Thy will be done. "By asking Mary to pray for us, we acknowledge ourselves to be poor sinners and we address ourselves to the 'Mother of Mercy,' the All-Holy One. We give ourselves over to her now, in the Today of our lives. And our trust broadens further, already at the present moment, to surrender 'the hour of our death' wholly to her care. May she be there as she was at her son's death on the cross. May she welcome

	us as our mother at the hour of our passing to lead us to her son, Jesus, in paradise" Catechism, 2677). "...We can pray with and to her. The prayer of the Church is sustained by the prayer of Mary and united with it in hope" (Catechism, 2679).
Mary is Queen Over All Things	"Finally the Immaculate Virgin, preserved free from all stain of original sin, when the course of her earthly life was finished, was taken up bodily and soul into heavenly glory, and exalted by the Lord as Queen over all things" (Catechism, 966).
Praying for the Dead	"Communion with the dead. In full consciousness of this communication of the whole Mystical Body of Jesus Christ, the Church in its pilgrim members, from the earliest days of the Christian religion, has honored with great respect the memory of the dead; and because it is a holy and wholesome thought to pray for the dead that they may be loosed from their sins, she offers her suffrages for them. Our prayer for them is capable not only of helping them, but also of making the intercession for us effective" (Catechism, 958).

Elder/Bishop Qualifications	"Technically, celibacy is the commitment not to marry. In the Latin (Roman) Catholic Church, it is a prerequisite for ordination to the priesthood. The candidate must freely assume this obligation publicly and for life. Because church teaching reserves sexual activity to marriage, celibacy also requires abstinence" (US Catholic: Why are priests celebate?).
	
	Qualifications to be a Catholic bishop [Bishop is used interchangeably with Elder in the New Testament].
	
	Steps to becoming a Bishop
	
	  1. You must complete a theology degree.
	  2. You must attend a seminary for 4 - 5 years.
	  3. You must serve the current priest as a deacon.
	  4. You must work as an ordained priest.
	  5. You must wait until a bishop position opens.
	  6. You must accept the bishop position if you are chosen.
	
	When you complete all six steps you will become a Bishop in the Catholic church (See References and Recommended Readings under Catholicism and look for http references).

Bishops and Priests can Forgive Sins	"The Church, who through the bishop and his priests forgives sins in the name of Jesus Christ..." (Catechism, 1448). "Indeed bishops and priests, by virtue of the sacrament of Holy Orders, have the power to forgive all sins 'in the name of the Father, and of the Son, and of the Holy Spirit' " (Catechism, 1461). "For this reason the Eucharist cannot unite us to Christ without at the same time cleansing us from past sins and preserving us from future sins" (Catechism, 1393).

	"By the same charity that it enkindles in us, the Eucharist preserves us from future mortal sins" (Catechism, 1395).
Indulgences and the forgiveness of sin for those alive and dead **NOTE: Indulgences are basically good works that can be done.**	"Through indulgences the faithful can obtain the remission of temporal punishment resulting from sin for themselves and also for the souls in Purgatory" (Catechism, 1498). "An indulgence is a remission before God of the temporal punishment due to sins whose guilt has already been forgiven, which the faithful Christian who is duly disposed gains under certain prescribed conditions through the actions of the Church which, as the minister of redemption, dispenses and applies with authority the treasury of the satisfactions of Christ and the saints" (Catechism, 1471). "Since the faithful departed now being purified are also members of the same communion of saints, one way we can help them is to obtain indulgences for them, so that they temporal punishments due for their sins may be remitted" (Catechism, 1479).
Infallibility and the Pope	"The Roman Pontiff... enjoys this infallibility in virtue of his office, when, as supreme pastor and teacher of all the faithful - who confirms his brethren in the faith - he proclaims by a definitive act a doctrine pertaining to faith or morals... This infallibility extends as far as the deposit of divine Revelation itself" (Catechism, 891). The Catholic Church teaches that when the bishops officially teach doctrine relating to faith and morals, then God super naturally prevents them from making any errors. This is called "infallibility". It applies to official councils, such as the Second Vatican Council. It also applies to other teachings, as long as the bishops and the Pope are in agreement about them. (Catechism 890, 891, 939, 2033, 2034, 2049). The Pope is said to be infallible whenever he makes an official decree on matters of faith and morals. According to Catholic doctrine, it is impossible for the Pope to teach false doctrine. Catholics are expected to obey the Pope without question even when he is not making an "infallible" statement about doctrine. They are expected to submit their wills and minds to the Pope without question (Catechism, 892, 2037, 2050).
All men are born sinners...Original Sin	The Catholics also teach that all men are born sinners as a result of Adam's sin. "...it is a sin "contracted" and not "committed"—a state and not an act" (Catechism, 404).
In Mass during the Celebration of the Eucharist, the work of our redemption is carried out.	"In this divine sacrifice which is celebrated in the Mass, the same Christ who offered himself once in a bloody manner on the altar of the cross is contained and is offered in an unbloody manner" (Catechism, 1367). "When the Church celebrates the Eucharist, she commemorates Christ's Passover, and it is made present. As often as the sacrifice of the Cross by which Christ our Pasch has been sacrificed is celebrated on the altar, the work of our redemption is carried out" (Catechism, 1364).

Priests and Confessing Sins	"One who desires to obtain reconciliation with God and with the Church, must confess to a priest all the unconfessed grave sins he remembers after having carefully examined his conscious" (Catechism, 1493). "Confession to a priest is an essential part of the sacrament of Penance" (Catechism, 1456). "It is called the sacrament of confession, since the disclosure or confession of sins to a priest is an essential element of this sacrament" (Catechism, 1424). "Only priests who have received the faculty of absolving from the authority of the Church can forgive sins in the name of Christ" (Catechism, 1495). "The Fathers of the Church present this sacrament as the second plank [of salvation]..." (Catechism, 1446). "According to the Church's command, 'after having attained the age of discretion, each of the faithful is bound by an obligation faithfully to confess serious sins at least once a year'" (Catechism, 1457). "In its document on the ministry of priests, Vatican II says, "The priest receives a special Sacrament by which, through the anointing of the Holy Spirit, he is conformed to Christ the Priest in such a way that he can act, in Persona Christi, that is, in the very Person of Jesus Christ" (In Persona Christi by FATHER RICHARD REGO). ". . . He that despiseth the priest despiseth God; he that hears him hears God. The priest remits sins as God, and that which he calls his body at the alter is adored as God by himself and by the congregation. . . Wherefore they are justly called not only angels, but also God, holding as they do among us the power and authority of the immortal God" (Catholic Doctrine as defined by the Council of Trent, by the Rev. Anampon, S.J.).
Purgatory a place of purification after death	"All who die in God's grace and friendship, but still imperfectly purified, are indeed assured of their eternal salvation; but after death they undergo purification, so as to achieve the holiness necessary to enter the joy of heaven" (Catechism, 1030). "The Church gives the name Purgatory to this final purification of the elect..." (Catechism, 1031). "The Church formulated her doctrine of faith on Purgatory especially at the Councils of Florence and Trent" (Catechism, 1031). "But at the present time some of his disciples are pilgrims on earth. Others have died and are being purified, while still others are in glory..." (Catechism, 954).

Comparative Doctrine

Current Day Revelation	"The Roman Pontiff... enjoys this infallibility in virtue of his office, when, as supreme pastor and teacher of all the faithful - who confirms his brethren in the faith - he proclaims by a definitive act a doctrine pertaining to faith or morals... This infallibility extends as far as the deposit of divine Revelation itself" (Catechism, 891).
Salvation through the Catholic Church alone.	"The Second Vatican Council's Decree on Ecumenism explains: 'For it is through Christ's Catholic Church alone, which is the universal help toward salvation, that the fullness of the means of salvation can be obtained'" (Catechism, 816).
Confirmation Necessary for Salvation.	"Confirmation perfects Baptismal grace; it is the sacrament which gives the Holy Spirit in order to root us more deeply in the divine filiation, incorporate us more firmly into Christ, strengthen our bond with the Church…" (Catechism, 1316). "Confirmation, like Baptism, imprints a spiritual mark or indelible character on the Christian's soul…" (Catechism, 1317). "For by the sacrament of Confirmation, [the baptized] are more perfectly bound to the Church…(Catechism, 1295).
Statues or Images to be Venerated	"Sacred images in our churches and homes are intended to awaken and nourish our faith, in the mystery of Christ. Through the icon of Christ and his works of salvation, it is he whom we adore. Through sacred salvation, it is he whom we adore. Through sacred images of the holy Mother of God, of the angels and of the saints, we venerate the persons represented" (Catechism, 1192). "Following the divinely inspired teaching of or holy Fathers and the tradition of the Catholic Church (for we know that this tradition comes from the Holy Spirit who dwells in her) we rightly define with full certainty and correctness that, like the figure of the precious and life-giving cross, venerable and holy images of our Lord and God and Savior, Jesus Christ, our inviolate Lady, the holy Mother of God, and the venerated angels, all the saints and the just, whether painted or made of mosaic or another suitable material, are to be exhibited in the holy churches of God, on sacred vessels and vestments, walls and panels, in houses and on streets" (Catechism, 1161). NOTE: Definition of Venerate by Merriam-Webster "To regard with reverential respect or with admiring deference. To honor (an icon, a relic, etc.) with a ritual act of devotion."
Catholic Prayer	"Prayer cannot be reduced to spontaneous outpouring of interior impulse; in order to pray, one must have the will to pray. Nor is it enough to know what the Scriptures reveal about prayer; one must also learn how to pray. Through a living transmission (Sacred Tradition) within 'the believing and praying Church,' the Holy Spirit teaches the children how to pray" (Catechism, 2650).
Penance	"Absolution takes away sin, but it does not remedy all the disorders sin has caused. Raised up from sin, the sinner must still recover his full spiritual health by doing something more to make amends for the sin: he must 'make satisfaction for' or 'expiate' his sins. This satisfaction is also called 'penance'" (Catechism, 1459).

	"The penance the confessor imposes must take into account the penitent's personal situation and must seek his spiritual good. It must correspond as far as possible with the gravity and nature of the sins committed" (Catechism, 1460a). "It [Penance] can consist of prayer, an offering, works of mercy, service of neighbor, voluntary self-denial, sacrifices, and above all the patient acceptance of the cross we must bear" (Catechism, 1460b). "The Church also commends almsgiving, indulgences, and works of penance undertaken on behalf of the dead:" (Catechism, 1032).
Reconciliation	"Forgiveness of sins brings reconciliation with God, but also with the Church" (Catechism, 1462).
Salvation through Works	"Even though incorporated into the Church, one who does not however persevere in charity is not saved" (Catechism, 837).
The Catholic Church Forgives Sins	"There is no offense, however serious, that the Church cannot forgive" (Catechism, 982). "By Christ's will the Church possesses the power to forgive the sins of the baptized and exercises it through bishops and priests normally in the sacrament of Penance." (Catechism, 986). "The Church, who through the bishop and his priests forgives sins in the name of Jesus Christ…" (Catechism, 1448). "Indeed bishops and priests, by virtue of the sacrament of Holy Orders, have the power to forgive all sins 'in the name of the Father, and of the Son, and of the Holy Spirit" (Catechism, 1461). "The Church must be able to forgive all penitents their offenses, even if they should sin until the last moment of their lives" (Catechism, 979).
Church Governed by Peter's Successors	"The sole Church of Christ (is that) which our Savior, after his Resurrection, entrusted to Peter's pastoral care, commissioning him and the other apostles to extend and rule it… This Church, constituted and organized as a society in the present world, subsists in (subsist it in) the Catholic Church, which is governed by the successors of Peter and by the bishops in communion with him" (Catechism, 816).

Christian Science

Founder: Mary Eddy

Key Statement: The physical world, death, disease are all false or untrue. There is no matter.

Beginning Date: 1879   On August 23, the Church of Christ (Scientist) was incorporated and given a charter.

Doctrinal Books:

- Eddy, M. B. Miscellaneous Writing. Boston: Trustees, 1924.
- Eddy, M. B. Retrospection and Introspection. Boston: Trustees, 1920.
- Eddy, M. B. Science and Health with Key to the Scriptures, Boston: Trustees, 1934.
- Eddy, M. B. The Peoples Ideal About God. Boston, MA: 1936.

History

1843   In December Mary Married George Washington Glover
1844   In Jun Mr. Glover died of Yellow Fever.
1853   Mary wed Dr. Daniel Patterson. Dr. Patterson later eloped with one of his patients and Mary got a divorce
1862   Mary wrote Dr. Phineas P Quimby appealing for him to help her
1866   On February 3, Mary had a fall. She had to go to a hospital.
1867   Mary moved in with the Craft family.
1870   Mary was teaching pupils her system of healing for a fee of 300.00.
1875   Mary finished the writing of Science and Health, which is the textbook of Christian Science.
1877   Organization of a society was effected, a public hall was rented and Mary was employed as a preacher
1879   On August 23, the Church of Christ (Scientist) was incorporated and given a charter.
1881   Mary founded the "Massachusetts Metaphysical College" in her home.
1882   Mrs. Eddy's third husband, Asa Gilbert Eddy, died from organic heart disease
1886   The National Christian Scientist's Association was organized
1892   Mrs. Eddy organized the mother church in Boston and called it the First Church of Christ Scientist
1910   Mrs. Eddy, who stated that there is no death, died.

Tenets of Christian Science

- As adherents of Truth, we take the inspired Word of the Bible as our sufficient guide to eternal Life.
- We acknowledge and adore one supreme and infinite God.
- We acknowledge His Son, one Christ; the Holy Ghost or divine Comforter; and man in God's image and likeness.
- We acknowledge God's forgiveness of sin in the destruction of sin and the spiritual understanding that casts out evil as unreal. But the belief in sin is punished so long as the belief lasts.
- We acknowledge Jesus' atonement as the evidence of divine, efficacious Love, unfolding man's unity with God through Christ Jesus the Way-shower; and we acknowledge that

man is saved through Christ, through Truth, Life, and Love as demonstrated by the Galilean Prophet in healing the sick and overcoming sin and death.

- We acknowledge that the crucifixion of Jesus and his resurrection served to uplift faith to understand eternal Life, even the allness of Soul, Spirit, and the nothingness of matter.
- And we solemnly promise to watch, and pray for that Mind to be in us which was also in Christ Jesus; to do unto others as we would have them do unto us; and to be merciful, just, and pure (Taken from www.christianscience.com Beliefs and Teachings).

Christian Science Unique or Core Beliefs	
Topic	**Belief**
God did not create a physical world	God did not create a physical world for there is no matter. "Did infinite Mind create matter, and call it light? Spirit is light, and the contradiction of Spirit is matter, darkness, and darkness obscures light. Material sense is nothing but a supposition of the absence of Spirit. No solar rays nor planetary revolutions from the day of Spirit."

"Knowing the Science of creation, in which all is Mind and it's ideas, Jesus rebuked the material thought of his fellow-countrymen: "Ye can discern the face of the sky; but can ye not discern the signs of the times?"

"Spirit, God, gathers unformed thoughts into their proper channels, and unfolds these thoughts, even as He opens the petals of a holy purpose in order that the purpose may appear" (Science and Health, Pg. 506).

Matter is an illusion. All creation consists of spiritual ideas and identities that are reflected from God's mind. The physical is not real, concrete, it is a reflection (Science and Health, Pg. 503). |
| **Bible Inspiration** | "The literal rendering of the Scriptures [Bible] makes them nothing valuable, but often is the foundation of unbelief and helplessness. The metaphysical rendering [Science and Health] is health and peace and hope for all" (Miscellaneous Writings, Pg. 169).

The Science and truth of divine creation have been presented in the verses already considered (those of Genesis 1), and now the opposite error, a material view of creation, is to be set forth. The second chapter of Genesis contains a statement of this material view of God and the universe, a statement which is the exact opposite of scientific truth as before recorded" (Science and Health, Pg. 521). |
Angels	Angels are simply, "God's thoughts passing to man", (Science and Health, Pg. 581).
Devil	The Devil is "evil"; "a lie"; "error" (Science and Health, Pg. 584).
Christian Science and Health	"Health is not a condition of matter, but of Mind; nor can the material senses bear reliable testimony on the subject of health. The Science of Mind-healing shows it to be impossible for aught but Mind to testify truly or to exhibit the real status of man. Therefore the divine Principle of Science, reversing the testimony of the physical senses, reveals man as harmoniously existent in Truth, which is the only basis of health; and thus Science denies all disease, heals the sick, overthrows false evidence, and refutes materialistic logic" (Science and Health, Pg. 120).

Christian Science on Matter	Man has no body...there is no matter; he is not made up of brain, blood, bones, and other material elements. The Scripture inform us that man is made in the image and likeness of God. Matter is not that likeness...Man is spiritual and perfect...He is...the reflection of God, or Mind, and therefore is eternal; that which has no separate mind from God; that which has not a single quality underived from Deity; that which possesses no life, intelligence, nor creative power of his own, but reflects spiritually all that belongs to his Maker (Science and Health, Pg. 475). Christian Science on matter: "....the cardinal point in Christian Science, that matter and evil (including all inharmony, sin, disease, death) are unreal" (Miscellaneous Writings, Pg. 27).
Evil is a false belief	"It (evil) never originated or existed as an entity. It is but a false belief" (Miscellaneous Writings, Pg. 454).
Man cannot die	Man is incapable of sin, sickness and death. The real man cannot depart from holiness..." (Science and Health, Pg. 475).
Birth or the physical creation of life is not real.	"The belief that life can be in matter or soul in body, and that man springs from....an egg, is the result of....mortal error" (Science and Health, Pg. 485).
Christian Science on Mortality or Immortality	"...Let us remember that harmonious and immortal man has existed forever, and is always beyond and above the mortal illusion of any life, substance, and intelligence as exist in matter" (Science and Health, Pg. 302).
Christian Science on the Soul or Spirit	The Soul or Spirit means only one Mind, and cannot be rendered in the plural. It means Deity (Science and Health, Pg. 466).
Christian Science on Jesus Christs Ascension	"The eternal Christ and the corporeal Jesus manifest in flesh, continued until the Master's ascension, when the human, material concept, or Jesus, disappeared, while the spiritual self, or Christ's, continues to exist to the eternal order of divine Science, taking away the sins of the world..." (Science and Health, Pg. 334).
Jesus a result of Mary's self-conscious communion with God	"Jesus was the offspring of Mary's self-conscious communion with God" (Science and Health, Pg. 29-30). "Mary's conception of him was spiritual, for only purity could reflect Truth and Love, which were plainly incarnate in the good and pure Christ Jesus" (Science and Health, Pg. 332).
God is a divine principle from which everything flows	"God is all.... The soul or mind of the spiritual man is God, the divine principal of all being" (Science and Health, Pg. 302). There is no difference between the created and the Creator. Man is God's reflection, thus man is part of God (Science and Health, pp. 302, 337, 475).
Jesus did not die	Jesus did not die...he was alive while in the tomb, (Science and Health, Pg. 44).

Jesus was not resurrected from the dead	Jesus was experiencing thought for the days he was in the grave, so he wasn't dead: "Our Master reappeared to his students, -- to their apprehension he rose from the grave, -- on the third day of his ascending thought, and so presented to them the certain sense of eternal life" (Science and Health, 509:4-8).
Baptism is purification of the mind or error	"Christian Science has one faith, one Lord, one baptism; and this faith builds on Spirit, not matter; and this baptism is the purification of the mind, --- not an ablution of the body, but tears of repentance, an overflowing love, washing away the motives for sin; yea, it is love leaving self for God (The Peoples Idea of God, 1936). "Our baptism is a purification from all error" (Science and Health, Pg. 35).
Jesus' blood unnecessary for salvation	"The material blood of Jesus was no more efficacious to cleanse from sin when it washed upon 'the accursed tree' than when it was flowing in his veins as he went daily about his Father's business" (Science and Health, Pg. 25:6-8).
Death is not real	Mrs. Eddy believes that Death is not real, and heaven and hell are states of mind. "Any material evidence of death is false, for it contradicts the spiritual facts of being" (Science and Health, Pg. 380). "....man is incapable of sin, sickness and death" (Science and Health, Pg. 475).
God is mind	God is Mind, (Science and Health 330:20-21; 469:13).
Heaven is a divine state of mind	"Heaven is not a locality, but a divine state of Mind in which all the manifestations of Mind are harmonious and immortal..." (Science and Health, Pg. 291).
No such thing as Hell	"The olden opinion that hell is fire and brimstone, has yielded somewhat to the metaphysical fact that suffering is a thing of the mortal mind instead of the body; so, in place of material flames and odor, mental anguish is generally accepted as the penalty for sin" (Miscellaneous Writings, p. 237). Christian Science's Hell, which doesn't exist, lasts until the belief in mortal life and its pleasures and pain is gone. "The period required for this dream of material life, embracing its so-called pleasures and pains, to vanish from consciousness, "knoweth no man.....neither the Son, but the Father. This period will be of longer or shorter duration according to the tenacity of error (Science and Health, Pg. 77).
Spiritual progression after death	"Man's probation after death is the necessity of his immortality, for good dies not and evil is self-destructive, therefore evil must be mortal and self-destroyed. If man should not progress after death, but should remain in error, he would be inevitably self-annihilated" (Miscellaneous Writings, Pg. 2).

	Christian Science teaches that some kind of spiritual progress is made after 'death' and continues until the error of believing in matter is totally discarded. "Man is not annihilated nor does he lose his identify, but passing through the belief called death. After the momentary belief of dying passes from mortal mind, this mind is still in a conscious state of existence..." (Miscellaneous Writings, Pg. 47). "The period required for this dream of material life, embracing its so-called pleasures and pains, to vanish from consciousness. "Knoweth no man.....neither the Son, but the Father." This period will be of longer or shorter duration according to the tenacity of error" (Science and Health, Pg. 77).
Holy Spirit is power	The Holy Spirit is divine science, he is impersonal power (Science and Health, 331:31)
Jesus was not the Christ	Jesus was not the Christ. He was a man who displayed the Christ idea. Christ meaning perfection, not a person (Science and Health 333:3-15; 334:3). "The spiritual Christ was infallible; Jesus, the material manhood, was not the Christ" (Miscellaneous Writings, Pg. 84). The Christian who believes in the First commandments a monotheist. Thus he virtually unites with the Jew's belief in one God and recognizes that Jesus Christ is not God as Jesus Christ himself declared, but is the Son of God (Science and Health 152).
Jesus is not God nor was He Creator	"There is only one God.....All things are created spiritually. Mind, not matter, is the creator (Science and Health, Pg. 256). "Infinite Mind [God] is the creator, infinite image or idea emanating from this Mind (Science and Health, Pg. 257). Jesus is not mentioned regarding Creation. God as the Infinite Mind and it is from His mind that creation exists. "Jesus is not God..." (Science and Health, Pg. 361).
Jesus was not eternal, not Christ	The word Christ is not properly a synonym for Jesus, though it is commonly so used. Jesus was a human name, which belonged to him in common with other Hebrew boys and men, for it is identical with the name of Josua.......On the other hand, Christ is not a name so much as the divine title of Jesus. ,,,,,The divine image, idea, or Christ was, is, and ever will be inseparable from the divine Principle, God" (Science and Health, Pg. 333-334). To sum it up Jesus was a mortal man and no longer exists, he was not eternal. Christ (the spiritual idea) is simply a reflection of God.
Jesus was fallible	"He (Jesus) knew the mortal error which constitute the material body, and could destroy those errors; but at the time when Jesus felt our infirmities, he had not conquered all the beliefs of the flesh or his sense of material life, nor had he risen to his final demonstrations of spiritual power" (Science and Health, Pg. 53).

There is no final judgment.	"No final judgment awaits mortals, for the judgment-day of wisdom comes hourly and continually, even the judgment by which mortal man is divested of all material error" (Science and Health, 291).
Revelation in 1866	"In the year 1866, I discovered the Christ Science or divine laws of Life, Truth, and Love, and named my discovery Christian Science. God had been graciously preparing me during many years for the reception of this final revelation of the absolute divine Principle of scientific mental healing (Science and Health, Pg.107).
Salvation through Christian Science	"To get rid of sin through Science, is to divest sin of any supposed mind or reality, and never to admit that sin can have intelligence or power, pain or pleasure. You conquer error by denying its verity" (Science and Health, Pg. 399). In other words YOU must believe that there is no such thing as sin and that where there is no sin there is 'salvation'. Other than a Jesus has nothing to do with your 'salvation'.
No devil or satan	There is no devil, (Science and Health 469:13-17).
Second Coming Christ will not literally come back	Christ will not literally come back. Mrs. Eddy writes, "The second appearing of Jesus is, unquestionably, the spiritual advent of the advancing idea of God, as in Christian Science" (Retrospection and Introspection, Pg. 70). "It is authentically said that one expositor of Daniel's dates fixed the year 1866 or 1867 for the return of Christ – the return of the spiritual idea to the material earth or antipode of heaven. It is a marked coincidence that those dates were the first two years of my discovery of Christian Science" (The First Church of Christ, Scientist, and Miscellany, Pg. 181).
No such thing as sin	There is no sin, it is not real. It is an illusion, (Science and Health, Pg. 71, 480). Jesus "...came to destroy the belief of sin" (Science and Health, Pg. 473). "Therefore, the only reality of sin, sickness, or death is the awful fact that unrealities seem real to human, erring belief, until God strips off their disguise" (Science and Health, Pg. 472). "Nothing unspiritual can be real, harmonious, or eternal. Sin, sickness and mortality are the suppositional antipodes of Spirit and must be contradictions of reality" (Science and Health, Pg. 335).
No Trinity	"The theory of three persons in one God (that is, a personal Trinity or Tri-unity) suggests polytheism, rather than the one ever-present I AM" (Science and Health, Pg. 256). The Trinity is Life, Truth, and Love, (Science and Health, Pg. 331:26). "Life, Truth, and Love constitute the triune Person called God, -- that is, the triply divine Principle, Love. They represent a trinity in unity,

	three in one, -- the same in essence, though multiform in office: God the Father-Mother, Christ the spiritual ideal of sonship; divine Science or the Holy comforter" (Science and Health, Pg. 331-332). "Jesus is not God…" (Science and Health, Pg. 361).
Man is God's Reflection	You can teach that there is no difference between the created and the Creator. Man is God's reflection, thus man is part of God (Science and Health, pp. 302, 337, 475).

Comparative Doctrine

Islam

Founder: Muhammad was born an Arab in the city of Mecca in A.D. 570. He died in 632.

Key Statement: The Koran, Qur'an is God's (Allah's) new revelation to man. When the Bible conflicts with the Qur'an, the belief Muslims have is that the Bible is incorrect.

Beginning Date: 610, following the first revelation of Allah's will to the prophet Muhammad at the age of 40. The revelation was given through the angel Gabriel.

Doctrinal Books

- Qur'an or Koran
- Imam Bukhari, Bengali: Sahih Al-Bukhari - Vol. Set. Houston, TX: Dar-Us-Salam Publications, 2012 edition.

Most **Muslims** believe that **Islam** is the complete and universal version of a primordial faith that was revealed many times before through prophets including Adam, Abraham, Moses and Jesus. **Muslims** consider the Qur'an in its original Arabic to be the unaltered and final revelation of God (Allah).

Islam is the Arabic term for the name of the religion that came into being as a result of the revelations and teachings of Muhammad. Qur'an or Koran is the Arabic term used for the collection of revelations reportedly given from Allah (God) through his archangel to Muhammad. It is now Islamic scripture.

Muslims believe in the Laws of Moses, the Psalms of David and the Gospel of Christ. They also believe that those works have been distorted. Islam teaches that the Koran supersedes all of those works as a new revelation from God to Muhammad.

Quotes from the Koran (Qur'an)

Do they not ponder on the Qur'an? Had it been from other than Allah, they would surely have found therein much discrepancy (Surah 4:82).

Marriage to one's daughter-in-law is prohibited (Surah 4:31).

Muhammad was given a new revelation that ordered Zaid, Muhammad's adopted son, to divorce his wife so Muhammad could marry her by God's command Surah 33:36-40

Surah 11:42-43 Noah had a son who died in the Flood.

Surah 3:41 Zechariah was speechless for three days.

Islam Limits the number of wives a man can have to four Surah 4:3.

But the Qur'an itself teaches that Muhammad changed some of its verses and that his followers shredded the Qur'an (Qur'an 2:106; 16:101; 15:90–91). However, it also teaches that Allah's words cannot be changed (Qur'an 6:115; 18:27).

Islam Unique or Core Beliefs	
Topic	**Belief**
New Prophet	Muhammad is God's final prophet. Surah 48:29 says, Muhammad is the messenger of Allah. And those who are with him are severe against disbelievers, and merciful among themselves.
No Right to Question the Prophet	The Qur'an states that people have no right to question the prophet and his successors at all (Qur'an 33:36; 59:7).
One GOD	God is One and his name is Allah.
Jesus is not the Christ	The Qur'an declares Jesus to be a mere man—albeit a prophet—but not the Son of God (Qur'an 9:30).
Bible Inspiration	The Qu'ron is the most recent revelation from God (Allah) to man. In Qur'an, Allah says: "And we have sent down to thee the Book explaining all things, a guide, a mercy and glad tidings to Muslims" (Qur'an, 16:89). Allah says in Qur'an: "We have without doubt, sent down the message; and We will assuredly guard it (from corruption)" (Qur'an, 15:9). This is part of the tidings of the unseen which we reveal unto thee (O Messenger) by inspiration" (Qur'an, 3:44).
Jesus was not Crucified and did not die on the cross.	The Qu'ran teaches that Jesus was not crucified and did not die on the cross. "And because of their saying (in boast), "We killed Messiah 'Iesa (Jesus), son of Maryam (Mary), the Messenger of Allâh," – but they killed him not, nor crucified him, but the resemblance of 'Iesa (Jesus) was put over another man (and they killed that man), and those who differ therein are full of doubts. They have no (certain) knowledge, they follow nothing but conjecture. For surely; they killed him not [i.e. 'Iesa (Jesus), son of Maryam (Mary)]" (Surah 4:157-58).
God called the best of creators.	The Qur'an uses twice the phrase that Allah is "the best of creators" (Surah 23:14, 37:125). What other creators are in mind? On the other hand, many verses make clear that Allah alone is "the creator of all things" (Surah, 39:62).
Forbidden foods.	"Forbidden to you is that which dies of itself, and blood, and flesh of swine, and that on which any other name than that of Allah has been invoked, and the strangled (animal) and that beaten to death, and that killed by a fall and that killed by being smitten with the horn, and that which wild beasts have eaten, except what you slaughter, and what is sacrificed on stones set up (for idols) and that you divide by the arrows; that is a transgression. This day have those who disbelieve despaired of your religion, so fear them not, and fear Me. This day have I perfected for you your religion and completed My favor on you and chosen for you Islam as a religion; but whoever is compelled by hunger, not inclining willfully to sin, then surely Allah is most-Forgiving, most-Merciful" *(Surah 5: 3).*

	"He hath only forbidden you dead meat, and blood, and the flesh of swine, and that on which any other name hath been invoked besides that of Allah. But if one is forced by necessity, without willful disobedience, nor transgressing due limits – then is he guiltless. For Allah is Oft-Forgiving, Most Merciful" (Surah 2:173).
Giving essential	"Save yourself from hellfire even by giving half a date-fruit in charity" (Surah 2:498; Bkhari 2.24.498). "Those who believe, and do deeds of righteousness, and establish regular prayers and give zakat*, will have their reward; on them shall be no fear nor shall they grieve" (Surah 2:277). Note: Muslims are expected to give 2.5 percent (zakat) of their overall estate each year to the poor. [* Zakat is a form of obligatory charity.] "The Prophet said, "Do not withhold your money by counting it (that is, hording it), for if you did so, Allah would also withhold His blessings from you"" (Surah 2:514; Bukhari 2.24.513).
Adam was Created Using	A blood clot [96:1-2], water [2*1:30, 24:45, 25:54], "sounding" (i.e. burned) clay [15:26], dust [3:59, 30:20, 35:11], nothing [19:67] and this is then denied in 52:35, earth [11:61], a drop of thickened fluid [16:4, 75:37]
Man Created in Toil and Trouble	The Qur'an states that Allah created man in toil and trouble (Qur'an 90:4).
God cause some men to go astray.	Allah guides not those whom he makes to go astray.....and they will have no helpers (Surah 16:37). "Allah leads astray whom he pleases, and he guides whom He pleases, ..." (Surah 14:4). O you who believe! Whoever from among you turns back from his religion, Allah will bring a people whom He will love and he will love Him, humble towards the believers, stern toward the disbelievers, fighting in the Way of Allah, and never fear of the blame of the blamers. That is the Grace of Allah which He bestows on whom he wills (Surah 5:54). "If you reject, truly Allah has no need of you" (Surah 39:7).
Heaven	"The smallest reward for the people of paradise is an abode where there are 80,000 servants and 72 wives, over which stands a dome decorated with pearls, aquamarine, and ruby, as wide as the distance from Al-Jabiyyah [a Damascus suburb] to Sana'a [Yemen]" (Surah Al-Rahman (55), verse 72). "He it is Who created for you all that is in the earth. Then turned He to the heaven, and fashioned it as seven heavens. And He is Knower of all things" (Surah 2:29, emp. added); "Say: Who is Lord of the seven heavens, and Lord of the Tremendous Throne? They will say: Unto Allah (all that belongeth). Say: Will ye not then keep duty (unto Him)?" (Surah 23:86-87, emp. added);

	"The seven heavens and the earth and all that is therein praise Him" (Surah 17:44).
	In regards to creation the following is found in the Qur'an. "Then He ordained them seven heavens in two Days and inspired in each heaven its mandate; and we decked the nether heaven with lamps, and rendered it inviolable" (Surah 41:12).
	"As to the Righteous (they will be) in a position of Security, Among Gardens and Springs; Dressed in fine silk and in rich brocade, they will face each other; So; and We shall join them to Companions with beautiful, big, and lustrous eyes. Three can they call for every kind of fruit in peace and security;" (Surah 44:51-55; see Surah 76:11-22).
	"See ye not how Allah hath created seven heavens in harmony, and hath made the moon a light therein, and made the sun a lamp? (Surah 71:15-16, see also 23:17; 65:12; 67:3; 78:12).
	Seven Heavens **Here are two of several explanations about the seven heavens. This can be found in Ahlul Bayt Digital Islamic Library Project (Al-Islam.org)** 1. "Here by seven is meant to be multiplication (to be more). It means that He has created many heavens, i.e. He has created a number of times." 2. 3. "Still, according to the views of some great intellectuals, those small stars, galaxies and Milky Way, which are seen, all are part of the first heaven and beyond that six still bigger worlds are there. And by seven heavens the Holy Qur'an means all those seven worlds, which exist in the Universe."
Heavenly Deception	"And (the unbelievers) plotted and planned, and Allah too planned, and the best of planners is Allah" (Surah 3:54). Allah lies to lead some astray. "O my People! I fear a Day when there will be mutual wailing. No one shall defend you against Allah. Any whom Allah causes to err, there is no guide. That is how Allah leads the skeptic astray" (Surah 40:32). Telling flattering lies to make peace is OK! "He who makes peace between the people by inventing good information or saying good things, is not a liar" (Bukhari Vol.3 book 49 ch.2 no.857 p.533). "And (the unbelievers) plotted and planned, and Allah too planned, and the best of planners is Allah" (Surah 3:54). The Qur'an states that lying is legitimate under certain circumstances (Qur'an 2:225; 3:28; 16:106).

Hell	What will be the food for the people in Hell? The food for the people in Hell will be only "Dhari"* (Surah 88:6), or only foul pus from the washing of wounds (Surah 69:36). A different perspective on food. "Is that the better entertainment or the Tree of Zaqgoum*? For We have truly made it (as) a trial for the wrongdoers. For it is a tree that springs out of the bottom of Hellfire; The shoots of its fruit-stalks are like the heads of devils; Truly they will eat thereof and fill their bellies therewith. Then on top of that they will be given a mixture made of boiling water. Then shall their return be to the (blazing) fire" (Surah 37:62-68). [* A cursed tree that springs our of the bottom of Hell.] On the Day of Judgment, unbelievers will be "dragged into the Fire upon their faces, ...'Taste ye the touch of hell'" (Surah 54:48). "(They will be) in the midst of a fierce Blast of Fire and in Boiling Water, and in the shades of Black smoke: nothing (will there be) to refresh, nor to please" (Surah 56:42-43). "...For the wrongdoers We have prepared a Fire whose (smoke and flames), like the walls and roof of a tent, will hem them in: if they implore relief they will be granted water like melted brass, that will scald their faces. How dreadful the drink! How uncomfortable a couch to recline on!" (Surah 18:29). "Will there be food for the Sinful – Like molten brass; it will boil in their insides, Like the boiling of scalding water. (A voice will cry) 'Seize ye him and drag him into the midst of the Blazing Fire!" (Surah 44:43-46). The Qur'an states that hell has "keepers" or "angels of punishment" (Surah 40:49; 96:18). Apparently, the angel Malic is mostly in charge of hell. He presides over the torments that are inflicted on unbelievers: "The sinners will be in the punishment of Hell, to dwell therein (for aye).... They will cry: 'O Malik! Would that your Lord put an end to us!' He will say, 'Nay, but you shall abide!' " (Surah 43:74,77).
Jesus' Birth	So, she conceived him, and she retired with him to a remote place. And the pains of childbirth drove her to the trunk of a palm-tree: She cried (in her anguish): "Ah! would that I had died before this! would that I had been a thing forgotten and out of sight!" But (a voice) cried to her from beneath the (palm-tree): "Grieve not! for thy Lord hath provided a rivulet beneath thee; "And shake towards thyself the trunk of the palm-tree: It will let fall fresh ripe dates upon thee. "So, eat and drink and cool (thine) eye. And if thou dost see any man, say, 'I have vowed a fast to (God) Most Gracious, and this day will I enter into not talk with any human being'" (Surah 19:22-26).
Relationships with non-Muslims	Surah 60:1 says, O you who believe! Take not My enemies and your enemies as friends showing affection toward then, while they have disbelieved in what has come to you of the truth....and have driven out the Messenger and yourselves because you believe in Allah your Lord!

	Surah 5:14 call Jews people "who will listen to any lie" and states that Christians are enemies. Surah 5:51 says that Muslims are not to have Christians and Jews as friends.
Jesus Blood Not Sufficient	"Centered on an external entity – the mystical body of Christ in which the Christian must participate in order to be saved" while in Islam he sees that "the redemptive potential is centered in the individual himself" (Yasien Mohamed, Human Nature in Islam).
Jesus was just one of many prophets	Jesus is just one of the many prophets of Allah (Surah 4:171; 5:74). Such (was) Jesus the son of Mary: (it is) a statement of truth, about which they (vainly) dispute. It is not befitting to (the majesty of) God that He should beget a son. Glory be to Him! when He determines a matter, He only says to it, "Be", and it is (Surah 19:34-35). "Christ, the son of Mary, was no more than a messenger; many were the messengers that passed away before him. His mother was a woman of truth" (Surah 5:75; cf. 5:116-120).
Jesus was created	"The similitude of Jesus before Allah is as that of Adam; He created him from dust, then said to him; 'Be': and he was" (Qur'an 3:59). This suggests that Jesus was created. He was not God and as a result could not have helped with creation.
Jesus was not God, not deity, simply a human messenger	The Qur'an teaches that Jesus was not God....that he was a human prophet much like many other prophets. "The Messiah ['Iesa (Jesus)], son of Maryam (Mary), was no more than a Messenger; many were the Messengers that passed away before him. His mother [Maryam (Mary)] was a Siddiqah [i.e. she believed in the words of Allâh and His Books (see Verse 66:12)]. They both used to eat food (as any other human being, while Allâh does not eat). Look how We make the Ayât (proofs, evidences, verses, lessons, signs, revelations, etc.) clear to them, yet look how they are deluded away (from the truth)" (Qur'an 5:75).
Salvation after death is God's (Allah's) choice	"There will be no one of you who will not enter it (Hell). This was an inevitable decree of your Lord. Afterwards he may save some of the pious, God-fearing Muslims out of the burning fire" (Surah 19:71).
The Qu'ron is the most recent revelation from God (Allah) to man	At the age of 40, Muhammad is said to have been visited by the angel Gabriel. It was here that he received the beginnings of revelation that would become the Qur'an. This process of revelation, which was sometimes mediated through Gabriel and other times came directly to his heart, lasted approximately 23 years, and ended shortly before his death (Muslim Information Service of Australia. "Beginning of Revelation". Missionislam.com. Retrieved 2015-07-24). The Qur'an teaches abrogation. This is a legal term that suggests the "destruction or annulling of a former law by an act of the legislative power, by constitutional authority, or by usage' (Black, 1983). Surah 2:100 ff says, "And for whatever verse we abrogate or cast into oblivion, we bring one better or like it." In Surah 13:39 is

	says, "Every term has a Book. God blots out, and he establishes whatsoever he will;' and with him is the Mother of all Books."
	The Qur'on is the most recent revelation from God (Allah) to man. In Qur'an, Allah says: "And we have sent down to thee the Book explaining all things, a guide, a mercy and glad tidings to Muslims" (Qur'an, 16:89)
	Allah says in Qur'an: "We have without doubt, sent down the message; and We will assuredly guard it (from corruption)" (Qur'an, 15:9).
	This is part of the tidings of the unseen which we reveal unto thee (O Messenger) by inspiration". (Qur'an, 3:44)
	"Those who reject the Book and the (revelations) with which we sent Our messengers; but soon shall they know – When the yokes (shall be) round their necks, and the chains; they shall be dragged along – in boiling fetid fluid, then in the Fire shall they be burned" (Surah 40:70-72).
	"O you who have been given the Scripture! Believe in what We have revealed confirming what is (already) with you..."Qur'an 4:47
Punish, fight or slay Idolaters or those who wage war	Surah 9:5 says, "Fight and slay the idolaters wherever you find them, and seize them, and besiege them and lie in wait for them."
	Surah 5:33 says, "The punishment of those who wage war against God and His Apostle, and strive with might and main for mischief through the land is: execution, or crucifixion, or the cutting off of hands and feet from opposite sides, or exile from the land."

Jehovah's Witnesses

Founder: Charles Taze Russell (1852-1916)

Key Statement: The Bible as the only standard of faith and practice for Christians.

Beginning Date: On December 13, 1881, the Zion Watch Tower Tract Society was established as an unincorporated body. Most recognized this as the beginning date of the Jehovah's Witness movement.

Doctrinal Books

- Bible (New World Translation of the Bible)
- Let God Be True
- The Truth Shall Make Your Free
- Religion for Mankind
- Reasoning from the Scriptures
- Studies in the Scriptures (7 Volumes)
- And much more!

Watchtower Warning: The Watchtower, May 1, 1922, page 132, "To abandon or repudiate the Lord's chosen instrument [Russell] means to abandon or repudiate the Lord himself, upon the principle that he who rejects the servant sent by the Master thereby rejects the Master ... Brother Russell was the Lord's servant. Then to repudiate him and his work is equivalent to a repudiation of the Lord, upon the principle heretofore announced."

The Bible: "Jehovah Witness state that the Bible is their source for truth. To let God be found true means to let God have the say as to what is the truth that sets men free. It means to accept his Word, the Bible, as the truth.   Hence, in this book, our appeal is said herein by quotations from the Bible for proof of truthfulness and reliability" (What has Religion Done for Mankind? Brooklyn: Watchtower Bible and Tract Society, 1951, p. 9.)

Books and booklets published since 1942 are considered authoritative doctrinal guides. These replace earlier doctrinal guides.

HOWEVER: Instead of following Scripture (the Bible) they have taken their doctrine taught in their writings and with biased intent have incorporated it into 'their Bible' (New World Translation of the Bible)

Other Teachings

Governing Body: "The governing body of the Jehovah's Witnesses has unquestioned power. Members reveal new truths, such as revisions to previous claims about the end of the world, and have organizational power, such as choosing elders in local congregations" ("How Does Jehovah Direct His Organization?" Watchtower ONLINE LIBRARY.

Also, that some who saw the events of 1914 will also witness the end of the world: '...that some who saw the events of 1914 will also see the complete destruction of the present wicked world' Reasoning from the Scriptures, p.200, Watch Tower Bible and Tract Society of Pennsylvania, 1989. As we learned in Chapter 7 [Revelation], the apostle John was given a vision where he saw Jesus as King in heaven with 144,000 other kings. Who are the 144,000? John explains that they "have [Jesus'] name and the name of his Father written on their foreheads." And he adds:

"These are the ones who keep following the Lamb [that is, Jesus] no matter where he goes. These were bought from among mankind." (Read Revelation 14:1, 4.) The 144,000 are faithful Christians whom God has chosen "to rule as kings over the earth" with Jesus. When they die, they are resurrected to life in heaven. (Revelation 5:10) Since the time of the apostles, Jehovah has been choosing faithful Christians to be part of that group of 144,000 kings.

God's Name: "The name "Jehovah's Witnesses" was taken as the moniker for the religious group in 1931. It draws on Isaiah 43:10, which reads: "'You are my witnesses,' declares the Lord." The word "Jehovah" is a transliteration of the Hebrew name for God, YHWH. In the Witnesses' translation of the Bible" (the New World Translation of the Scriptures), the word "Jehovah" is inserted into the New Testament 237 times.

We belong to NO earthly organization. We adhere only to that heavenly organization. All the saints not living or that ever lived during this age, belong to OUR CHURCH ORGANIZATION: such are all ONE CHURCH and there is NO OTHER recognized by the Lord (Watchtower, March 1, 1979, p. 16).

"Adam brought death not only to himself but on all the race descended from him" (New Heavens and a New Earth, Pg. 89).

Other results of Adam's fall included inborn sin, imperfection, and disease (Religion for Mankind, Pg. 63).

Teach that most men will be saved. 144,000 will go to heaven and reign with God as joint heirs and co-rulers. All others, the sheep, who believe will live on an earthly paradise (New Heaven and a New Earth, Pg. 360).

Jehovah's Witnesses
Unique or Core Beliefs

Topics	Belief
Bible Inspiration	"If the six volumes of 'Scripture Studies' are practically the Bible, topically arranged with Bible proof texts given, we might not improperly name the volumes 'the Bible in an arranged form,' that is to say, they are not mere comments on the Bible, but they are practically the Bible itself. Furthermore, not only do we find that people cannot see the divine plan in studying the Bible by itself, but we see, also, that if anyone lays the Scripture Studies aside, even after he has used them, after he has become familiar with them, after he has read them for ten years—if he then lays them aside and ignores them and goes to the Bible alone, though he has understood his Bible for ten years our experience shows that within two years he goes into darkness. On the other hand, if he had merely read the Scripture Studies with their references and had not read a page of the Bible as such, he would be in the light at the end of two years, because he would have the light of the Scriptures" (Charles Taze Russell, The Watchtower, September 15, 1910). People are condemned if they say it is sufficient to only read the Bible. By just reading the Bible such individuals have reverted back to the apostate doctrines that Christendom's clergy were teaching 100 years ago (Watchtower, August 15, 1981, pp. 28-29).
Jesus was First the Archangel Michael	Jehovah's Witnesses hold that the Archangel Michael is Jesus Christ, and they are not at all alone or unique in doing so"(w58 9/15 p. 559 - The Watchtower—1958; New Heavens and a New Earth, Pg. 27, 30).
God Created Jesus	Instead, he [Jesus] was the first of Jehovah's creations, and subsequently created everything else." (Watch Tower Bible and Tract Society of Pennsylvania, "Michael," Watchtower ONLINE LIBRARY. The Kingdom is at Hand, 46-47, 49; See JW.Org Bible Teachings).
Jesus is not God	Jehovah's Witnesses believe that when Jesus was born on earth, he was a mere human and not God in human flesh. "That the Son of God born on earth was no mighty spirit person clothing himself with a baby's fleshly form and pretending to be absolutely ignorant like a new born infant is proved by one Scripture (Philippians 2:5-8), which shows he laid aside complete his spirit existence..." (The Truth Shall Make Your Free, Pg. 246). Jehovah's Witnesses deny the full deity of Jesus Christ, and his complete equality with Jehovah. He may be called a god, but not Jehovah God; he is a mighty one but not almighty as Jehovah God is (Let God Be True, Pg. 32-33; See Hoekema, 1976 p. 257).
Jesus was tortured on a stake	"He was executed on a torture stake, not crucified." (Watch Tower Bible and Tract Society of Pennsylvania, "Michael," Watchtower ONLINE LIBRARY.

Jesus was not Bodily Resurrected	"Rather than experiencing a bodily resurrection, Jesus was raised as a spirit, becoming the Archangel Michael again" (Watch Tower Bible and Tract Society of Pennsylvania, "Michael," Watchtower ONLINE LIBRARY. The Harp of God, 1928, Pg. 173; Religion for Mankind, Pg. 259).
Mary Impregnated with Life force of the Archangel Michael	Jehovah then placed the 'life force' of Michael [Archangel] in the womb of the virgin Mary so Jesus could be born a human being (Watchtower Book, The Kingdom at Hand).
Holy Spirit is Just a Force	The Holy Spirit is "the invisible active force of Almighty God which moves his servants to do his will" (Let God Be True, Pg. 108).
There is no trinity	"God through His Word, appeals to our reason. The Trinity doctrine is a negation of both the scriptures and reason" (Should You Believe in the Trinity, 1989). "The obvious conclusion is, therefore, that Satan is the originator of the Trinity doctrine" (Let God Be True, Pg. 101).
Established Kingdom in 1914	As soon as Jesus became King, he threw Satan and his wicked angels out of heaven and down to the locality of the earth. That is why things have become so bad here on earth since 1914.' What does God require of us, p.12 Watch Tower Bible and Tract Society of Pennsylvania, 1996.
144,000 become Kings over the New Earth	The 144,000 are faithful Christians whom God has chosen "to rule as kings over the earth" with Jesus. When they die, they are resurrected to life in heaven. (Revelation 5:10) Since the time of the apostles, Jehovah has been choosing faithful Christians to be part of that group of 144,000 kings. The 144,000 in heaven may also be called "associate kings" and "royal priests," since the power of judging has been given them. As a result, they may be called "associate judges" (This Means Everlasting Life, Pg.275; You May Survive Armageddon, Pg. 353; Make Sure of all Things, Pg. 221).
99.9 % of mankind destroyed	Jehovah's Witnesses doctrine regarding the last days, the Millennium and Final judgement suggests that 99.9 percent of mankind will be destroyed (The Watchtower, October 15, 1958; What does God require of us, Pg.12 Watch Tower Bible and Tract Society of Pennsylvania, 1996).
Blood Transfusion Sinful	Witnesses believe a blood transfusion "may result in the immediate and very temporary prolongation of life, but at the cost of eternal life for a dedicated Christian (Blood, Medicine, and the Law of God. Brooklyn: Watchtower Bible and Tract Society, 1961, p. 55).
Celebration of Holidays Forbidden	"Aside from their teachings about cosmology and theology, Jehovah's Witnesses are also known for a number of unique practices that separate them from the culture at large. For example, Witnesses do not celebrate any holidays, including birthdays. They note that many of the celebrations that are a part of the Christian calendar have their roots in pagan festivals" (Watch Tower Bible

	and Tract Society of Pennsylvania, "Celebrations That Displease God," Watchtower.
No Consciousness after Death	"The Grave, simply put, is where humans go when they die; it is a symbolic place or condition where any consciousness or activity ceases" (What Happens After Death?, Jehovah's Witnesses officially web site)
Heaven	Jehovah's Witnesses believe there are two peoples of God: (1) the Anointed Class (144,000) will live in heaven and rule with Christ; and (2) the "other sheep" (all other believers) will live forever on a paradise earth. This is an actual heavenly government with a King—Jesus Christ—and 144,000 co-rulers, who are "bought from the earth." (Revelation 5:9, 10; 14:1, 3, 4; Daniel 2:44; 7:13, 14) They will rule over the earth, which will be cleansed of all wickedness and will be inhabited by many millions of God-fearing humans (Proverbs 2:21, 22--See JW.Org Bible Teachings). Earth Becomes a Paradise. Anyone else who is saved – those who prove themselves to be loyal subjects of Jesus – will live in an eternal earthly paradise. Only the 144,000 faithful Jehovah's Witnesses will go to heaven.
No Eternal Hell	"The doctrine of a burning hell where the wicked are tortured eternally after death cannot be true mainly for four reasons: (1) It is wholly unscriptural; (2) It is unreasonable; (3)it is contrary to God's love; and (4) it is repugnant to justice" (Let God Be True). "However, those who become so wicked that they are beyond reform will not be resurrected. When such ones die, they suffer permanent destruction with no hope of a return to life—Matthew 23:33; Hebrews 10:26, 27" (See JW.Org Bible Teachings). No eternal hell, only non-existence.
God's Kingdom	Bible chronology indicates that God's Kingdom was established in heaven in 1914. This is shown by a prophecy recorded in chapter 4 of the Bible book of Daniel (Bible Teachings: What Does Bible Chronology Indicate About the Year 1914? Jehovah's Witnesses Official Web Site). "The fulfillment of Bible prophecy shows that in 1914, Christ became King and God's heavenly Kingdom began to rule. Hence, we are living in the "short period of time" that Satan has left. (Revelation 12:12; Psalm 110:2) We can also say with certainty that soon God's Kingdom will act to cause God's will to be done on earth" (Bible Teachings: What Does Bible Chronology Indicate About the Year 1914? Jehovah's Witnesses Official Web Site).
Revelation	Jehovah's Witnesses leaders claim that both the holy spirit and angels communicate information to them (Watchtower, March 1, 1972, p. 155 & August 1, 1987, p. 19). In the Watchtower it is stated, "It [the Watchtower] is God's sole collective channel for the flow of Biblical truth to men on earth (The Watchtower, July 16, 1960).

Salvation	To receive everlasting life in the earthly paradise we must identify that organization and serve God as part of it (Watchtower, February 15, 1983, p. 12).
Second Coming of Christ	Jehovah's Witnesses believe that the second coming of Jesus was an invisible, spiritual event that occurred in the year 1914. On October 1 of the year 1914, it is contended, the "appointed times of the nations" ended, and God's heavenly kingdom, with Christ enthroned as King, began (Paradise Lost, PG. 178, 203). Second Coming has already happened: On October 1, 1914 the "appointed times of the nations" ended, and God's heavenly kingdom began with Christ enthroned as King (Paradise Lost, Pg. 173-174).
Works and Salvation	Jehovah's Witnesses believe that salvation requires faith in Christ, association with God's organization (i.e., their religion), and obedience to its rules. Anyone may become one of sheep people who will gain everlasting life on a paradise earth. They just have to hear the voice of the Right Shephard and come into the New World Society (Paradise Lost, Pg. 195-169).

The Prophet Test

False Prophecies in Jehovah's Witnesses

Prophecy	Fulfillment	Prophecy True	False
Coming of Christ in 1874	Failed		X
Also, that some who saw the events of 1914 will also witness the end of the world: '…that some who saw the events of 1914 will also see the complete destruction of the present wicked world' Reasoning from the Scriptures, p. 200, Watch Tower Bible and Tract Society of Pennsylvania, 1989.	Failed		X
Watchtower was predicting that God's Kingdom was to be established on earth in 1914 (not in heaven). "The times of the Gentile' extent to 1914. "And the Heavenly Kingdom will not have full sway till then, but as a 'stone' the Kingdom of God is set up 'in the days of these Kings' and by consummating them it becomes a universal Kingdom – a 'great mountain and fills the whole earth" (Watchtower Reprints, Vol. I, March, 1880, p. 82).	Failed		X
Abraham, Isaac and Jacob resurrected in 1915	Failed		X
Establishment of God's Kingdom on Earth in 1925	Failed		X
Abraham in Jerusalem to resurrect loved ones in 1925	Failed		X
End of world in 1975	Failed		X

Alterations in Biblical Text
Examples

English Standard Bible	Scripture	New World Translation Bible (Jehavah's Witnesses)
"In the beginning was the Word, and the Word was with God, and the Word was God."	John 1:1	"In the beginning was the Word, and the Word was with God, and the Word was a god."
"Jesus said to them, "Truly, truly, I say to you, before Abraham was, I am."	John 8:58	Jesus said to them: "Most truly I say to you, before Abraham came into existence, I have been."
Pay careful attention to yourselves and to all the flock, in which the Holy Spirit has made you overseers, to care for the church of God, which he obtained with his own blood.	Acts 20:28	Pay attention to yourselves and to all the flock, among which the holy spirit has appointed you overseers, to shepherd the congregation of God, which he purchased with the blood of his own Son.
And he is before all things, and in him all things hold together.	Colossians 1:17	7 Also, he is before all other things, and by means of him all other things were made to exist,
For in him the whole fullness of deity dwells bodily,	Colossians 2:9	Because it is in him that all the fullness of the divine quality dwells bodily.
Declare these things; exhort and rebuke with all authority. Let no one disregard you.	Titus 2:13	while we wait for the happy hope and glorious manifestation of the great God and of our Savior, Jesus Christ,
But of the Son he says, "Your throne, O God, is forever and ever, the scepter of uprightness is the scepter of your kingdom."	Hebrews 1:8	But about the Son, he says: "God is your throne forever and ever, and the scepter of your Kingdom is the scepter of uprightness."

Comparative Doctrine

Judaism

Founder: God through his prophets and earthly leaders. Judaism is the religion of people of God, the Israelites, in the Old testament.

Key Statement: Judaism believes in God's law that was given to them by Abraham. They do not believe that Jesus was God's son who came to earth.

Beginning Date: In about 1812 BC Jewish history begins with a covenant that was established between God and Abraham. The Torah (Jewish Law), the primary document of Judaism, was given to the Jews by the Prophet Moses.

Doctrinal Books

Torah: Jewish people believe in the Torah, which was the whole of the laws given to the Israelities at Sinai. The five books of Moses which includes the 10 Commandments. Is usually printed with the rabbinic commentaries.

Talmud: An important collection of Jewish writings. Written about 2000 years ago, it is a recording of the rabbis discussion of the way to follow the Torah at that time.

Thirteen Principles of Faith Written by Rambam

These principles, which Rambam thought were the minimum requirements of Jewish belief, are:

- G-d exists (Jewish law generally limits the prohibition of erasing G-d's name to the Hebrew names of G-d--His original names. They would therefore be able to erase an English word such as G-d even if they were to spell it properly.)
- G-d is one and unique
- G-d is incorporeal
- G-d is eternal
- Prayer is to be directed to G-d alone and to no other
- The words of the prophets are true
- Moses' prophecies are true, and Moses was the greatest of the prophets
- The Written Torah (first 5 books of the Bible) and Oral Torah (teachings now contained in the Talmud and other writings) were given to Moses
- There will be no other Torah
- G-d knows the thoughts and deeds of men
- G-d will reward the good and punish the wicked
- The Messiah will come
- The dead will be resurrected

There are several sects in Judaism, which include:

Orthodox Judaism: Orthodox Jews are typically known for their strict observance of traditional Jewish law and rituals. For instance, most believe Shabbat shouldn't involve working, driving or handling money. It is a diverse sect that includes several subgroups, including Hasidic Jews. This form started in the 18th century in Eastern Europe and holds different values than traditional or ultra-Orthodox Judaism. Hasidic Jews emphasize a mystical experience with God that involves direct communion through prayer and worship. Chabad is a well-known Orthodox Jewish, Hasidic movement.

Reform Judaism: Reform Judaism is considered a liberal category of the religion that values ethical traditions over strict observance of Jewish laws. Followers promote progressive ideas and adaptation. Most of the Jews living in the United States follow Reform Judaic traditions.

Conservative Judaism: Many people consider this form of Judaism somewhere in between Orthodox and Reform Judaism. Typically, conservative Jews honor the traditions of Judaism while allowing for some modernization.

Reconstructionist Judaism: Reconstructionism dates back to 1922 when Mordecai Kaplan founded the Society for the Advancement of Judaism. This sect believes that Judaism is a religious civilization that's constantly evolving.

Humanistic Judaism: Rabbi Sherwin Wine founded this denomination of Judaism in 1963. Humanistic Jews celebrate Jewish history and culture without an emphasis on God.

Messianic Judaism: This modern movement combines the beliefs of Judaism and Christianity. Messianic Jews believe that Jesus Christ was the Messiah but still follow Jewish traditions.

Jewish Holidays

Passover: This holiday lasts seven or eight days and celebrates Jewish freedom from slavery in Egypt. Specifically, Passover refers to the biblical story of when the Hebrew God "passed over" houses of Jewish families and saved their children during a plague that was said to have killed all other first-born babies in Egypt.

Rosh Hashanah: Jews celebrate the birth of the universe and humanity during this holiday, which is also known as the Jewish New Year.

Yom Kippur: This "Day of Atonement" is considered the holiest day of the year for Jews who typically spend it fasting and praying.

High Holy Days: The 10 days starting with Rosh Hashanah and ending with Yom Kippur are also known as the High Holidays, the Days of Awe or Yamim Noraim. The High Holy Days are considered a time of repentance for Jewish people.

Hanukkah: This Jewish celebration, also known as the "Festival of Lights," lasts eight days. Hanukkah commemorates the rededication of the Jewish Temple in Jerusalem after the Maccabees defeated the Syrian-Greeks over 2,000 years ago.

Purim: This is a joyous holiday that celebrates a time when the Jewish people in Persia were saved from extermination.

Unique or Core Beliefs

Topic	Belief
There is only One God	"Belief in one God is one of Judaism's defining characteristics" (my jewish learning: God 101). Online!
Jesus is not Deity	"The New Testament also include numerous verses testifying to Jesus as equal to God and as divine — a belief hard to reconcile with Judaism's insistence on God's oneness' (my jewish learning: What Do Jews Believe About Jesus?). Online!
Jesus was not the Messiah	"Other Jews, recently, have come to regard him as a Jewish teacher. This does not mean, however, that they believe, as Christians do, that he was raised from the dead or was the messiah" (my jewish learning: What Do Jews Believe About Jesus?). Online!
Jesus was not Raised from the Dead	"This does not mean, however, that they believe, as Christians do, that he was raised from the dead" (What Do Jews Believe About Jesus?). Online!
Kingdom Established	Christianity emerged as a separate religion only in the centuries after Jesus' death" (What Do Jews Believe About Jesus?). Online!
Heaven—Garden of Eden or Gan Eden	"There are two paths before me, one leading to Gan Eden and the other to Gehinnom (Berakhot 28b)."
Hell	References to Gehinnom as a fiery place of judgment can be found in the apocalyptic literature of the Second Temple period. The Talmud embellished this idea, claiming that Gehinnom is 60 times hotter than earthly fire (Berakhot 57b). "There are two paths before me, one leading to Gan Eden and the other to Gehinnom (Berakhot 28b)."
Bible Inspiration	The New Testament is not God's will: Those who believe in Judaism focus on the Tora for their belief. The Torah usually refers to the Torah she'bi'ktav, the written Torah, also known as the chumash (the five volumes or Pentateuch, sometimes referred to as the Five Books of Moses).The Jewish people only believe in the Torah which is the first five books of the Old Testament; Genesis, Exodus, Leviticus, Numbers, and Deuteronomy. This includes the laws given to the Israelites at Sinai. "Torah" can refer to all of traditional Jewish learning (Summarized from my jewish learning: The Torah). Online!
Trinity	Jehovah God or Yahwa is the only God. There are no others. "The New Testament also include numerous verses testifying to Jesus as equal to God and as divine — a belief hard to reconcile with Judaism's insistence on God's oneness" (taken from myjewishlearning.com website). Online!

Jewish Customs	Minhag: Minhag identifies many customs that Jewish people follow closely. Though often widely practiced, customs are not considered mandatory by traditional Jews.
Halacha or the Jewish Legal Tradition and the 613 Mitzvot or (commandments)	Halacha, from the Hebrew word for "walking" or "path," is the rabbinic interpretation of Jewish law. The word "halakhah" is usually translated as "Jewish Law," This is often found in the Torah. It is the collective body of Jewish religious laws derived from the written and Oral Torah. A List of the 613 Mitzvot (Commandments). Today, spiritual descendants of both traditionalists and reformers interpret Jewish law according to their respective principles for their communities.
Work for Salvation	Halacha or the Jewish Legal Tradition and the 613 Mitzvot or commandments. This is the rabbinic interpretation of Jewish law. The word "halakhah" is usually translated as "Jewish Law." This is often found in the Torah. It is the collective body of Jewish religious law as derived from the written and Oral Torah. A list of the 613 Mitzvot (commandments). Today, spiritual descendants of both traditionalists and reformers interpret Jewish law according to their respective principles for their communities.
Myjewishlearning.com is a website dedicated to Jewish teachings and has a massive amount of information about the Jewish faith.	

Mormonism

Founder: Joseph Smith, Jr. (1805-1844) He and his brother Hyrum were shot and killed by a mob in Carthage, Illinois while awaiting trial in the town jail. After some competition by several men, Brigham Young took on the role of leading the Latter Day Saint movement.

Key Statement: The Book of Mormon is the true Gospel. They believe in the Bible as long as it does not conflict with the Book of Mormon.

Beginning Date: Beginning in 1830, Joseph Smith professed that the Book of Mormon was now the 'Complete Gospel' for those who would follow Mormonism.

Doctrinal Books

- Bible
- Book of Mormon
- Doctrine and Covenants
- Pearl of Great Price
- Mormon Doctrine
- And several other works.

Mormon Beginnings:

Here is a quick overview of how The Book of Mormon was revealed to Joseph Smith, Jr. and how Mormonism began.

- In 1820, Joseph Smith, Jr. claimed to have a major vision where he reported that he was chosen to be the Lord's anointed prophet for this dispensation.
- In 1825, the Angel Moroni, who was the glorified son of Mormon (this is the name of the man that The Book of Mormon is titled after) appeared to Joseph Smith, Jr. while he was in bed. This is where Joseph found out about the 'Golden Plates' that had The text of the Book of Mormon. This extraordinary revelation is recorded in The Pearl of Great Price (Joseph Smith History), 1:29-54).
- In 1827, Smith unearthed the Golden Plates in the hill Cumorah, near Palmyra, New York.
- Smith begin to translate the 'reformed Egyptian' hieroglyphics using the 'Urim and Thummim' (special spectacles that were given to Joseph by the angel Moroni).
- Smith began to dictate their translation to his wife Emma, Hale Smith and other associates including Martin Harris.
- During the time that Smith was translating the plates Oliver Cowdery, an itinerant schoolteacher, visited him and ultimately became one of the scribes who wrote down what Smith was translating.
- Martin Harris' wife wanted to see the translated document. After multiple requests Joseph Smith agreed to let him take the translation to his wife so she could see it. While in his possession the 116 pages containing the Book of Lehi were lost.
- Smith stated that he did not retranslate the material that Harris had lost because he said that if he did, evil men would alter the manuscript in an effort to discredit him. Smith said that instead, he had been divinely ordered to replace the lost material with Nephi's account of the same events (D&C 10: 17-18, 31).
- Smith completed The Book of Mormon without retranslating the Book of Lehi, replacing it with what he said was an abridgment taken from the Plates of Nephi.

- In 1830, Joseph Smith, Jr. had the translation placed in book form and The Book of Mormon became the 'Complete Gospel' for those who would follow Mormonism.

> "The day will come – and it is not far distant, either – when the name of the Prophet Joseph Smith will be coupled with the name of Jesus Christ of Nazareth, the Son of God, as his representative, as his agent whom he chose, ordained and set apart to lay anew the foundations of the Church of God in the world, which is indeed the Church of Jesus Christ, possessing all the powers of the gospel, all the rites and privileges, the authority of the Holy Priesthood, and every principle necessary to fit and qualify both the living and the dead to inherit eternal life, and to attain to exaltation in the kingdom of God" (Gospel Doctrine, 5th ed. [1939], 134). President Joseph F. Smith

Mormonism
Unique or Core Beliefs

Topic	Belief
Man can Become a God	God was once a man who lived on another world. There have been many worlds that were created by 'new' gods. There are many gods (Journal of Discourses, Vol. 7, Pg. 333).
Bible Inspiration	The Mormon church believes that the Book of Mormon is True Restored Gospel (2 Nephi 29:1-4). The Mormon Church believes that the Bible has changed, that errors in translation have been made through the years. As a result, they only believe in it "as far as it is correctly translated" (Articles of Faith, 8). The Mormon church believes that the Book of Mormon is True Restored Gospel. "Many Gentiles will reject the Book of Mormon—They will say, We need no more Bible—The Lord speaks to many nations—He will judge the world out of the books which will be written. About 559–545 B.C. 1 But behold, there shall be many—at that day when I shall proceed to do a marvelous work among them, that I may remember my covenants which I have made unto the children of men, that I may set my hand again the second time to recover my people, which are of the house of Israel; 2 And also, that I may remember the promises which I have made unto thee, Nephi, and also unto thy father, that I would remember your seed; and that the words of your seed should proceed forth out of my mouth unto your seed; and my words shall hiss forth unto the ends of the earth, for a standard unto my people, which are of the house of Israel; 3 And because my words shall hiss forth—many of the Gentiles shall say: A Bible! A Bible! We have got a Bible, and there cannot be any more Bible. 4 But thus saith the Lord God: O fools, they shall have a Bible; and it shall proceed forth from the Jews, mine ancient covenant people. And what thank they the Jews for the Bible which they receive from them? Yea, what do the Gentiles mean? Do they remember the travails, and the labors, and the pains of the Jews, and their diligence unto me, in bringing forth salvation unto the Gentiles?" (2 Nephi 29:1-4). Mormons also believe that Jesus spoke additional words for other books that would be written. "9 And I do this that I may prove unto many that I am the same yesterday, today, and forever; and that I speak forth my words according to mine own pleasure. And because that I have spoken one word ye need not suppose that I cannot speak another; for my work is not yet finished; neither shall it be until the end of man, neither from that time henceforth and forever. 10 Wherefore, because that ye have a Bible ye need not suppose that it contains all my words; neither need ye suppose that I have not caused more to be written. 11 For I command all men, both in the east and in the west, and in the north, and in the south, and in the islands of the sea, that they shall write the words which I speak unto them; for out of the books which shall be written I will judge the world, every man according to their works, according to that which is written. 12 For behold, I shall speak unto the Jews

	and they shall write it; and I shall also speak unto the Nephites and they shall write it; and I shall also speak unto the other tribes of the house of Israel, which I have led away, and they shall write it; and I shall also speak unto all nations of the earth and they shall write it. 13 And it shall come to pass that the Jews shall have the words of the Nephites, and the Nephites shall have the words of the Jews; and the Nephites and the Jews shall have the words of the lost tribes of Israel; and the lost tribes of Israel shall have the words of the Nephites and the Jews" (2 Nephi 29:9-13).
One Heaven	There are three different heavens. The highest of the highest is reserved for good Mormons who become gods and goddesses (Mormon Doctrine, Pg. 348).
Baptize for the Dead	Salvation can be obtained after death through Baptism for the dead (Doctrine and Covenants 124:28-36).
No Mention of Leaving, Eternal, Everlasting	Eternal damnation does not mean that a person cannot go to a lesser heaven. It means that the individual is barred, or denied privileges of progression and ultimately to becoming a god (Doctrines of Salvation, Joseph F. Smith, Vol. 2, Pg.227).
Live once	Satan, his angels and those who are Sons of Perdition (people who had a sure and perfect knowledge of the truth and left the faith, i.e., Mormonism) are denied the privilege of eternal progression to godhood. Ultimately, they will be dissolved to their original state and they must then be reorganized to begin life again in another god's universe (Journal of Discourses 1:118; Evidence and Reconciliations, Pg. 213-214).
Second Coming	Second Coming: There are specific signs that must be fulfilled before Jesus can return (Doctrine and Covenants 29:14; 34:9; 45:24).
Council of Gods Created the World	Council of Gods Created the World, (Abraham 4:1-13; Doctrine of Covenants 121:32).
Elders and Bishops Different	The offices of Elder and Bishop are two different offices. The detailed duties of the ordained elders in the Church today have been defined by latter-day revelation (Doctrine and Covenants 20:42–45; 42:44–52; 46:2; 107:12). Bishop is a man who has been ordained and set apart as the presiding high priest for a ward, or congregation. He has overall responsibility for ministering the temporal and spiritual affairs of the congregation (Doctrine and Covenants 72; 84:112; 107:68–76).
Foods Prohibited	The Mormons teach that wine, strong drinks, and hot drinks are to be abstained from (Doctrine and Covenants, 89).
Tithing Commanded	23 Behold, now it is called today until the becoming of the Son of Man, and verily it is a day of sacrifice, and a day for the tithing of my people; for he that is tithed shall not be burned at his coming (Doctrine and Covenants 64:23).

	8 Will a man rob God? Yet ye have robbed me. But ye say, Wherein have we robbed thee? In tithes and offerings. 9 Ye are cursed with a curse: for ye have robbed me, even this whole nation. 10 Bring ye all the tithes into the storehouse, that there may be meat in mine house, and prove me now herewith, saith the Lord of hosts, if I will not open you the windows of heaven, and pour you out a blessing, that there shall not be room enough to receive it (Malachi 3: 8-10).
Baptism	"Under the direction of the presiding authority, a worthy priest or Melchizedek Priesthood holder may perform the ordinance of baptism. To do so, he: 1. Stands in the water with the person to be baptized. 2. Holds the person's right wrist with his left hand (for convenience and safety); the person being baptized holds the priesthood holder's left wrist with his or her left hand. 3. Raises his right arm to the square. 4. States the person's full name and says, "Having been commissioned of Jesus Christ, I baptize you in the name of the Father, and of the Son, and of the Holy Ghost. Amen" (D&C 20:73). 5. Has the person hold his or her nose with the right hand (for convenience). The priesthood holder places his right hand high on the person's back and immerses the person completely, including the person's clothing. 6. Helps the person come up out of the water. Two priests or Melchizedek Priesthood holders witness each baptism to make sure it is performed properly. The bapism must be repeated if the words are not spoken exactly as given in Doctrine and Covenants" (Missionary Handbook, 2006).
God has a Physical Body	God has a physical body (Doctrines of Salvation, Vol. 1, p. 98).
God Progresses from mortal to Immortal	"Remember that God, our heavenly Father, was perhaps once a child, a mortal like we ourselves, and rose step by step in the scale of progress, in the school of advancement; has moved forward and overcome, until He has arrived at the point where He now is" (Journal of Discourses, Vol. 7, p. 333). We too may ascend to the status of Godhood by obedience to all principals and ordinances of the Gospel (The Gospel Through the Ages, pp. 114-117).
Three Different Heavens	There are three levels of heaven: telestial, terrestrial, and celestial, (Mormon Doctrine, p. 348). Only those who are worthy LDS members will attain the highest level: **Telestial Kingdom:** This 'heaven' is where unbelievers go: "These are they who received not the gospel of Christ, neither the testimony of Jesus...who receive not his fullness in the eternal world", but shall be "redeemed from the devil [at] the last resurrection" (Doctrine and Covenants 76: 82-86).

	Terrestrial Kingdom: This 'heaven' is for religious people who have not become Mormons and for Mormons who have not met the requirements of the Church, i.e., "Honorable men of the earth who are blinded by the craftiness of men and who therefore do not accept and live the gospel law" (Mormon Doctrine, p. 784). This level of heaven is not as desirable as the Celestial Kingdom, but the Son visits there: "These are they who receive of his glory but not of his fulness... the presence of the Son, but not the fullness of the Father...who are not valiant in the testimony of Jesus...they obtain not the crown over the kingdom of God" (Doctrine and Covenants 76: 76-79). **Celestial Kingdom:** This is the desired level of heaven where Mormons who have kept ALL of the laws and ordinances of their church can attain to. "These are they who received the testimony of Jesus, and believed on his name and were baptized...in the water...keeping the commandments that they might be washed and cleansed from all their sins, and receive the Holy Spirit ..." (Doctrine and Covenants 76: 51-57). "They are gods, even the sons of God...these shall dwell in the presence of God and his Christ forever...whose names are written in heaven" (Doctrine and Covenants 76: 58-68). The men become Gods and the women become their wives. They begin to have spirit children and the process of a new world/universe begins again for each God. **REWARD:** When a Mormon attains to the Celestial Kingdom he then can begin his own creation, just as the god they know started this world and populated it with his spiritual children.
Hell is Temporary	Hell is temporary (Mormon Doctrine, Pg. 349-351; Doctrine of Salvation 2:133-134). Joseph Smith stated, "Is it the duty of men in this life to repent. Every man who hears the gospel message is under obligation to receive it. If he fails, then in the spirit world he will be called upon to receive it..." (Doctrines of Salvation, Vol. 2, Pg. 183). Joseph Smith and others will teach those in spirit prison. Most people will then accept the 'Mormon Gospel' and will go to paradise and ultimately to a heavenly realm. Hell of fire and brimstone is reserved for Satan and his followers who rebelled in the Spirit World and for the Sons of Perdition; Those that leave the Mormon church once they have become a member, when you commit murder, when you assent to the murder of Jesus Christ or rebel to the point that you crucify him anew. (Mormon Doctrine, Pg. 816-817). A form of Reincarnation: "The ultimate punishment for the Sons of Perdition may be that they, having their spiritual bodies disorganized, must start over again, must begin anew the long journey of existence, repeating the steps that they took in the eternities before the Great Council was held (Evidence and Reconciliations, Pg. 213-214).

Jesus was not Eternal	"Among the spirit-children of Elohim the firstborn was and is Jehovah or Jesus Christ to whom all others are Juniors. . . Jesus Christ is not the Father of the spirits who have taken or yet shall take bodies upon this earth, for He is one of them. He is the Son as they are sons or daughters of Elohim" (Articles of Faith, pp. 471-473). Jesus was Created (Mormon Doctrine, Pg. 322-323).
Two Resurrections	Mormons believe that there will be two resurrections: one at the beginning and one at the end of the millennium (Doctrine and Covenants 88:96-98).
Christ will reign on Earth during millennium	This reign will occur during the millennium (Doctrine and Covenants 88:96-98).
There are Many Gods	"In the Heaven where our spirits were born, there are many Gods, each one of whom has his own wife or wives which were given to him previous to his redemption, while yet in his mortal state (The Seer, by Orson Pratt, pp. 37-38). "Each of these gods, including Jesus Christ and his Father, being in possession of not merely an organized spirit, but a glorious body of flesh and bones" (Parley P. Pratt, Key to the Science of Theology [1973 Edition] , Pg. 44; See also Doctrine and Covenants, 130:22.
Only those holding Priesthood have authority to administer the ordinances of the Gospel	"Under the direction of the presiding authority, a worthy priest or Melchizedek Priesthood holder may perform the ordinance of baptism." (Missionary Handbook, 2006).
Salvation after Death Can Repent and Leave spirit world after death	"...spirit world....is divided into two parts; paradise which is the abode of the righteous, and hell which is the abode of the wicked...when the wicked spirits repent, they leave their prison-hell and join the righteous in paradise" (Mormon Doctrine, Pg. 762). "It is the duty of men in this life to repent. Every human who hears the gospel message is under obligation to receive it. If he fails, then in the spirit world he will be called upon to receive it..." (Doctrines of Salvation, Vol. 2, Pg.183).
Dissolved spirits can start over for another chance	Brigham Young taught that their bodies and spirits would ultimately be dissolved to their original state and that they must then be reorganized to begin life again in another god's universe (Journal of Discourses 1:118). John Widtsoe clarified the teaching further, explaining that "the ultimate punishment of the Sons of Perdition may be that they, having their spiritual bodies disorganized, must start over again, must begin anew the long journey of existence, repeating the steps that they took in the eternities before the Great Council was held" (Evidence and Reconciliations, pp. 213-214).

Multiple Revelations	The Angel Moroni appeared to Joseph smith on September 21, 1823 and told him of a book that deposited, written upon gold plates, giving an account of the former inhabitants of this continent,. This book contained the fullness of the Gospel that was delivered to the inhabitants by Jesus Christ himself. Once translated, this became the Book of Mormon (Pearl of Great Price, Joseph Smith History).
	Mormons believe that God speaks to them today through revelation. "We believe in the gift of tongues, prophecy, revelation, visions, healing, interpretation of tongues, etc." (Articles of Faith, 7).
	Current Day Revelation proclaimed! (HJS 1:15-20, 30-32; 2 Nephi 28:30-31; 2 Nephi 29:11-14).
Hell is not Forever	Eternal damnation is a state that does not allow man to progress to godhood. "Eternal punishment is, thus, the kind of punishment imposed by God who is Eternal, and those subject to it may suffer there for either a short or a long period. After their buffetings and trials cause them to repent, they are freed from this type of eternal damnation" (Mormon Doctrine, Pg. 236, 1966).
Must have Joseph Smiths consent to get to Celestial Heaven	". . . no man of woman in this dispensation will ever enter into the celestial kingdom of God without the consent of Joseph Smith . . . every man and woman must have the certificate of Joseph Smith, junior, as a passport to their entrance into the mansion where God and Christ are-- . . . I cannot go there without his consent. . . He reigns there as supreme a being in his sphere, capacity, and calling, as God does in heaven" (Journal of Discourses, Vol. 7, p. 289).
Most people will go to one of the three heavens	Most people will go to one of the three heavens god had prepared. Only Satan, his fallen angels and the 'Son's of Perdition' will be thrown into the lake of fire (Doctrine and Covenants, 76:44). However, Brigham Young stated that their bodies and spirits would ultimately be dissolved to their original state and that they must then be reorganized to begin life again [reincarnation of sorts] in another god's universe (Journal of Discourses 1:118)
Will be Signs that Christ is about to Return	**Signs of Christ's Return:** Signs that Must be Fulfilled
	"14 But, behold, I say unto you that before this great day shall come the sun shall be darkened, and the moon shall be turned into blood, and the stars shall fall from heaven, and there shall be greater signs in heaven above and in the earth beneath; 15 And there shall be weeping and wailing among the hosts of men; 16 And there shall be a great hailstorm sent forth to destroy the crops of the earth" (Doctrine and Covenants, 29:14-16).
	"24 And this I have told you concerning Jerusalem; and when that day shall come, shall a remnant be scattered among all nations; 25 But they shall be gathered again; but they shall remain until the times of the Gentiles be fulfilled. 26 And in that day shall be heard of wars and rumors of wars, and the whole earth shall be in commotion, and men's hearts shall fail them, and they shall say

	that Christ delayeth his coming until the end of the earth" (Doctrine and Covenants, 45:24). "6 To lift up your voice as with the sound of a trump, both long and loud, and cry repentance unto a crooked and perverse generation, preparing the way of the Lord for his second coming. 7 For behold, verily, verily, I say unto you, the time is soon at hand that I shall come in a cloud with power and great glory. 8 And it shall be a great day at the time of my coming, for all nations shall tremble. 9 But before that great day shall come, the sun shall be darkened, and the moon be turned into blood; and the stars shall refuse their shining, and some shall fall, and great destructions await the wicked" (Doctrine and Covenants, 34:6-9). "40 And they shall see signs and wonders, for they shall be shown forth in the heavens above, and in the earth beneath. 41 And they shall behold blood, and fire, and vapors of smoke. 42 And before the day of the Lord shall come, the sun shall be darkened, and the moon be turned into blood, and the stars fall from heaven. 43 And the remnant shall be gathered unto this place; 44 And then they shall look for me, and, behold, I will come; and they shall see me in the clouds of heaven, clothed with power and great glory; with all the holy angels; and he that watches not for me shall be cut off" (Doctrine and Covenants, 45:40-44).
God the Father in physical form impregnated Mary	God the Father came to earth in his physical form and had sexual intercourse with Mary to produce Jesus. (Journal of Discourses, V. 8, pp. 115, 211).
God will judge you by your works	11 For I [Jesus] command all men, both in the east and in the west, and in the north, and in the south, and in the islands of the sea, that they shall write the words which I speak unto them; for out of the books which shall be written I will judge the world, every man according to their works, according to that which is written. 2 Nephi 29:11.

F. Russell Crites, Jr. and Derek Russell Crites

The Prophet Test

False Prophecies in Mormonism

Prophecy	Fulfillment	Prophecy True	False
In Doctrine and Covenants 84:1-5 Joseph prophesies that, "the New Jerusalem and its Temple are to built in Missouri in this generation."	This was prophesied in 1832 and has not occurred.		X
In Doctrine and Covenants 124:56-60 Joseph Smith prophesied that, "Nauvoo House was to be built and that it would belong in the Smith family forever."	The house no longer belongs to the Smith family.		X
In History of the Church (vol. 2, p. 182), Joseph prophesied that, "The coming of the Lord which was nigh . . . even 56 years should wind up the scene."	It's been much more than 56 years and Jesus has not returned.		X
The Lord gave Joseph Smith a misleading revelation in Doctrine and Covenants 114:1. D. W. Patten was told that he was to go on a mission in the spring of 1839.	Patten died in the fall of 1838 and did not go on the mission.		X
Brigham Young prophesied that the slaves would never be set free in the Journal of Discourses, Vol. 10, p. 250.	History confirms that slaves were set free.		X

There are many other false prophecies that could be noted, but only one is necessary. Whenever you are dealing with a member of a church that has its own "prophet," give him God's Prophet Test. To do this you would need to understand what has been prophesied by someone in that particular church or cult.

Scientology

Founder: L. Ron Hubbard

Date: May 1952

Key Statement: The ultimate goal of Scientology is true spiritual enlightenment and freedom for all. (What is Scientology? As found on the Official Scientology website).

Some of the Works:

- Dianetics: The Original Thesis
- Dianetics: The Evolution of a Science
- Dianetics: The Modern Science of Mental Health
- Scientology: A New Slant on Life, Self-Analysis
- Scientology: The Fundamentals of Thought.

What is Scientology?

Developed by L. Ron Hubbard, Scientology is a religion that offers a precise path leading to a complete and certain understanding of one's true spiritual nature and one's relationship to self, family, groups, Mankind, all life forms, the material universe, the spiritual universe and the Supreme Being.

Scientology addresses the spirit—not the body or mind—and believes that Man is far more than a product of his environment, or his genes.

Scientology Terms

Auditing: Auditing provides a precise path by which any individual may walk an exact route to higher states of spiritual awareness (Scientology Website, What is Auditing?).

Pre-Clear: A person who is not yet clear. "A pre-clear is a precise thing, part animal, part pictures, and part God" (Scientology Clear Procedure, Issue One – 1969, Pg. 21).

Clear: "Clear is the name of a state achieved through auditing and describes a being who no longer has his own reactive mind, the hidden source of irrational behavior, unreasonable fears, upsets and insecurities. Without a reactive mind, individuals regain their basic personality, self-determinism and, in essence, become much, much more themselves" (Scientology Website: What is the State of Clear?).

Dianetics: Means "through thought" or "Through the soul".

Electronic Galvanometer: "The auditor asks questions that eventually leads to erasing engrams" (Scientology Website, Glossary of Scientology and Dianetics Terms).

Engrams: Mental picture images held in the mind of past experiences. These are apparently the "single source of aberrations and psychosomatic ills" (Dianetics, Pg. 577).

Theta: "Energy peculiar to life which acts upon material in the physical universe and animates it, mobilizes it and changes it; natural creative energy of a being which he is free to direct toward survival goals. The term comes from the Greek letter theta (Theta), which the Greeks used to represent thought" (Scientology Website, Glossary of Scientology and Dianetics Terms).

Thetan: "An immortal spiritual being; the human soul. The term soul is not used because it has developed so many other meanings from use in other religions and practices that it doesn't describe precisely what was discovered in Scientology. We use the term thetan instead, from the Greek letter theta (Theta), the traditional symbol for thought or life. One does not have a thetan, something one keeps somewhere apart from oneself; one is a thetan. The thetan is the person himself, not his body or his name or the physical universe, his mind or anything else. It is that which is aware of being aware; the identity which IS the individual" (Scientology Website, Glossary of Scientology and Dianetics Terms).

Time Track: "The consecutive record of mental image pictures which accumulates through a person's life. It is a very accurate record of a person's past. As a rough analogy, the time track could be likened to a motion-picture film — if that film were three-dimensional, had fifty-seven perceptions and could fully react upon the observer" (Scientology Website, Glossary of Scientology and Dianetics Terms).

TRs: "Abbreviation for training routines, practical drills which can greatly increase a student's ability in essential auditing skills, such as communication" (Scientology Website, Glossary of Scientology and Dianetics Terms).

Scientology
Unique or Core Beliefs

Topics	Belief
Evolutionary Belief that man evolves from photon converter to 'Homo Novis'	Evolution: In Scientology: History of Man, Hubbard describes his version of Darwinian evolution for man. The first stage of life was a photon converter which converted light into energy. Then there was jellyfish, a clam, a shellfish, and continued until he became a two-legged up right 'man'. He also taught that the Piltdown man was part of the evolutionary process (the Piltdown Man was determined to be a hoax after he wrote the book). This continues and now man must seek to become 'Homo Novis' which is the ultimate goal. Man will become godlike (Scientology: History of Man).
Bible a Product of Hindu teachings	The Bible, God is a byproduct of Hindu teachings or scriptures (Phoenix Lectures, Pg. 27,31; Staff, A World Religion, Pg. 5).
No Dogma Concerning God	"Unlike religions with Judeo-Christian origins, the Church of Scientology has no set dogma concerning God that it imposes on its members. As with all its tenets, Scientology does not ask individuals to accept anything on faith alone. Rather, as one's level of spiritual awareness increases through participation in Scientology auditing and training, one attains his own certainty of every dynamic. Accordingly, only when the Seventh Dynamic (spiritual) is reached in its entirety will one discover and come to a full understanding of the Eighth Dynamic (infinity) and one's relationship to the Supreme Being" (Scientology Website, Does Scientology Have a Concept of God?).
There are gods above other gods	"There are gods above all other gods.....There is no argument here against the existence of a supreme Being or an devaluation intended. It is that amongst the gods, there are many false gods elected to power and position.....There are gods above other gods, and gods beyond the gods of the universe" (Scientology, 8-8008,1967 Pg. 73).
Creation Account	The following was written about creation by Hubbard in his book titled, Factors. It is a summation of what he stated. "Before the beginning was a Cause and the entire purpose of the Cause was the creation of effect...In the beginning and forever is the decision and the decision is TO BE.....The first action of beingness is to assume a viewpoint......The second action of beingness is to extend from the viewpoint, points to view, which are dimension points...Thus there is space created, for the definition of space is: viewpoint of dimension. And the purpose of a dimension point is space and a point to view....The action of a dimension point is reaching and withdrawing....And from the viewpoint to the dimension points there are connection and interchange: thus new dimension points are made: thus there is communication....And thus there is LIGHT....And thus there is energy....And thus there is life" (Factors, 2007).
Christ preexisted Earth Life on another Planet	Christ is a legend that preexisted earth-life on other planets and was implanted into humans on earth (Professional Auditor's Bulletin 31, quoted by Anderson, Reort,130).

Jesus was no greater than Buddha	Jesus was just a shade above "clear" and was no greater than Buddha or Moses (Christianity Magazine, 5:10, as quoted by Anderson, Report, 150). "But what I am telling you is that these people handed on a torch of wisdom, of information, generation to generation. It was handed along geographical routes and one of those geographical routes was the Middle East. And one of the people who handed it on was a man named Moses. And again it was handed on to a man named Christ. And he handed it on and even the Arab nations benefited from this through their own prophet, Muhammad" (Scientology Web Site: What is Scientology's View of Moses, Jesus, Muhammad, the Buddha and Other Religious Figures of the Past?).
Pre-Clear	A pre-clear is a precise thing, part animal, part pictures, and part God" (Scientology Clear Procedure, Issue One – 1969, Pg. 21).
Forgiveness is not needed	"It is despicable and utterly beneath contempt to tell a man he must repent, that he is evil" (Hubbard, Auditor's Bulletin, Pg. 31).
Death	Martin summarizes that, "The Thetan (spirit) has some amazing characteristics, according to Hubbard. It is more than eighty trillion years old and dwells somewhere within the skull of an individual (Hubbard, Scientology: The fundamentals of thoughts, 1972). When the individual organism dies, the Thetan reports to an implant station (one is on Mars) before being shot down to earth. This is the 'Between lives area'. Here he 'reports in,' is given a strong forgetter implant, known to fight other Thetans over inhabiting a body. They communicate by telepathy, move objects by kinetics, and travel at high rates of speed. Thetans can be packed in ice and frozen, or they may be dumped into the ocean from a flying saucer. This, Hubbard assures us, "is quite authentic" (Hubbard, History of Man, Pg. 20, 43, 64-66). "Given the Scientology tenet that the body is mortal but the spirit is immortal, and given the minister's role in comforting those bereaved by loss, a funeral ceremony serves to end the cycle of the life passed and focus on the future. Even more significantly, a Scientology funeral ceremony helps the departed end this chapter of life and move forward to the next. Scientology is rich in knowledge which can help a person live a happier, more productive life. When that life draws to a close, the religion can also help ensure the being is in the best condition possible and is helped on their way to a new life. It is true that bodies wear out and pass away. But it is also true that the being never does. Scientology funeral ceremonies recognize this truth and impart a profound understanding of the nature of Man. The Scientology funeral service celebrates the life of the person who has departed his body. Friends and family have the opportunity to say goodbye, to acknowledge and thank the person for what he has done in this lifetime and to wish him well as he moves on to his next. The service is a reaffirmation of the knowledge that we are immortal spiritual beings" (Scientology Web Site: What is the Scientology Funeral Service?).

Man is Basically Good	"A fundamental tenet of Scientology is that Man is basically good; that he is seeking to survive; and that his survival depends upon himself and upon his fellows and his attainment of brotherhood with the universe. However, his experiences in the physical universe, through many lifetimes, have led him into evil, where he has committed harmful acts or sins, causing him to become aberrated (departing from rational thought or behavior). These harmful acts further reduce Man's awareness and innate goodness as a spiritual being. Through Scientology, one confronts these acts, erases the ignorance and aberration which surrounds them, and comes to know and experience truth again. All religions seek truth. Freedom of the spirit is only to be found on the road to truth. Sin is composed, according to Scientology, of lies and hidden actions and is therefore untruth" (Scientology Web Site: Does Scientology Believe Man is Sinful?).
Outside the Body Experiences	"Before entering Scientology many people experience the feeling of looking down on one's body, but they do not understand what is happening. Once they have achieved greater spiritual awareness through Scientology auditing and training they find that this experience becomes nothing out of the ordinary. In Scientology, this phenomenon is called exteriorization—the detachment of one's spirit from the body while yet fully conscious and aware. Scientology believes that Man is not his body, his mind or his brain. He, a spiritual force, energizes the physical body. Indeed, through the discovery of exteriorization, Scientology proved, for the first time, that Man is a spiritual being" (Scientology Web Site: Does Scientology Believe One can Exist Outside of the Body?).
No Heaven or Hell	"The manifestation that our Hereafter is our 'next life' entirely alters the general concept of spiritual destiny. There is no argument whatever with the tenets of any faith, since it is not precisely stated uniformly by all religions that one immediately goes to a Heaven or Hell. It is certain that an individual experiences the effect of the civilization, which he has had part in creating, in his next lifetime. In other words, the individual comes back. He has a responsibility for what goes on today since he will experience it tomorrow" (Scientology Website, Does Scientology have Doctrines Concerning Heaven or Hell?).
There is no real judgment	According to Scientology beliefs, "the individual comes back. He has a responsibility for what goes on today since he will experience it tomorrow" ("Position on Reincarnation & Past Lives: Official Church of Scientology". scientology.org. January 0001).
Reincarnation or Rebirth	"The vast majority of the world's population believes in reincarnation and only in the last few hundred years, with the rise of the physical sciences, did a strictly materialistic view begin to eclipse the spiritual. More recently, the traditional definition of reincarnation has been altered from its original meaning. The word has come to mean "to be born again in different life forms" (such as an animal, an insect, etc.) whereas its actual definition is "to be born again into the flesh or into another body." So what is commonly thought of as reincarnation is a definite system and is not part of Scientology. Rather, the Church ascribes to the latter, original definition.

	It is a fact that unless one begins to handle aberration built up in past lives, he doesn't progress. In Scientology, one is given the tools to handle upsets and aberrations from past lives that adversely affect the individual in the present, thus freeing one to live a much happier life. "Today in Scientology, many people have certainty that they have lived lives prior to their current one. These are referred to as past lives, not as reincarnation. Past lives is not a dogma in Scientology, but generally Scientologists, during their auditing, experience a past life and then know for themselves that they have lived before. To believe one had a physical or other existence prior to the identity of the current body is not a new concept— but it is an exciting one" (Does Scientology Believe in Reincarnation or Past Lives?, As found on the Official Scientology website). "All these people [Gautama Buddha, Jesus, Mohammad] were saying something that was much more important than 'There is a spiritual side to life.' They were saying, 'There is hope. They can come to you and they can tell you that all is lost and that you are dead, you are trapped, and that there's no hope for you. They can come to you and say this, but this is not true. There is hope. You do go on living. This life is not all there is. There is some future life in which you can do better, succeed more worthily than you have.' That is all these men said...." (The Hope of Man, a lecture given on June 3, 1955, Mr. Hubbard). Man continues to be reborn until he reaches something akin to deity. "Man is an immortal spiritual being.....His experience extends well beyond a single lifetime" (Does Scientology have a Concept of God? As found on the Official Scientology website). "The manifestation that our Hereafter is our 'next life' entirely alters the general concept of spiritual destiny. There is no argument whatever with the tenets of any faith, since it is not precisely stated uniformly by all religions that one immediately goes to a Heaven or Hell. It is certain that an individual experiences the effect of the civilization, which he has had part in creating, in his next lifetime. In other words, the individual comes back. He has a responsibility for what goes on today since he will experience it tomorrow."
Salvation is being free of rebirth (Reincarnation)	Salvation is being free of the endless cycle of birth and rebirth (Reincarnation or Rebirth). "Scientology further holds Man to be basically good, and that his spiritual salvation depends upon himself, his fellows and his attainment of brotherhood with the universe" (Does Scientology have a Concept of God? As found on the Official Scientology website).
Will Eventually become godlike and be called "homo novis'	Man is basically good and through reincarnation (rebirth) he will ultimately be godlike and will be called "homo novis" (Hubbard, Dianetics, Pg. 26). Hubbard goes on to say that the next step in the evolution of man is called homo novis. At this point man becomes a "godlike' being (History of Man, Pg. 5-6, 27-34, 38).
Works..Help Yourself	"Scientologists take the maxim quite to heart that God helps those who help themselves. They believe that each person has the answers to the mysteries of life. All one requires is awareness of these answers, and this is what Scientology helps one achieve" (Scientology Website, Can't God Be the Only One to Help Man?).

Seventh-day Adventists

Founder: Ellen G. White

Beginning Date: May 21, 1863 in Battle Creek, Michigan

Key Statement: Seventh-day Adventists accept the Bible as their only creed and hold certain fundamental beliefs to be the teaching of the Holy Scriptures. These beliefs, as set forth here, constitute the church's understanding and expression of the teaching of Scripture.

Some of the Works

- The Bible
- Writings of Ellen G White

General Conference of Seventh-day Adventists meets and changes or keeps the teachings they have established 2015).

Beliefs:

In Seventh-day Adventist theology, there will be an end time remnant of believers who are faithful to God.

The Seventh-day Adventists wear a name that was decided and determined by men. Seventh-day Adventists have decided to name themselves after doctrine.

Ellen Gould White (**Ellen Gould Harmon**; November 26, 1827 – July 16, 1915) was an author and an American Christian pioneer. Along with other Sabbatarian Adventist leaders such as Joseph Bates and her husband James White, she was instrumental within a small group of early Adventists who formed what became known as the Seventh-day Adventist Church.

White claimed to have received over 2,000 visions and dreams from God in public and private meetings throughout her life, which were witnessed by Adventist pioneers and the general public. She verbally described and published for public consumption the content of the alleged visions. The Adventist pioneers viewed these experiences as the Biblical gift of prophecy as outlined in Revelation 12:17 and Revelation 19:10 which describe the testimony of Jesus as the "spirit of prophecy." Her *Conflict of the Ages* series of writings endeavor to showcase the hand of God in Biblical history and in church history. This cosmic conflict, referred to by Seventh-day Adventist theologians as the "Great Controversy theme," became foundational to the development of Seventh-day Adventist theology. Her book on successful Christian living, *Steps to Christ*, has been published in more than 140 languages.

Some of her other notable books include *The Desire of Ages* and *The Great Controversy*.

Seventh-day Adventists Unique or Core Beliefs	
Topics	**Belief**
Bible Inspiration	"Finally, in the reception of members into our churches, we desire on this subject to know two things: 1. That they believe the Bible doctrine of spiritual gifts; 2. That they will candidly acquaint themselves with the visions of Sr. White which have ever held so prominent a place in this work. We believe that every person standing thus and carrying out this purpose will be guided in the way of truth and righteousness. And those who occupy this ground, are never denied all the time they desire to decide in this matter (Ellen White's Writings, Believe His Prophets).
Consciousness After Death	"The wages of sin is death. But God, who alone is immortal, will grant eternal life to His redeemed. Until that day death is an unconscious state for all people" (Fundamental Beliefs, 25)

Ellen G. White believed and taught that God would simply annihilate the souls of those who did not follow him. "But I saw that God would not shut them up in hell to endure endless misery, neither will He take them to heaven; for to bring them into the company of the pure and holy would make them exceedingly miserable. But He will destroy them utterly and cause them to be as if they had not been; then His justice will be satisfied. He formed man out of the dust of the earth, and the disobedient and unholy will be consumed by fire and return to dust again" (The Great Controversy, 1958). |
| **Foods Prohibited** | Hoekema summarizes their belief by saying, "Under the 'unclean foods' from which the candidates for baptism must promise to abstain are included such beverages as coffee and tea, and such meats as pork, ham, shrimp, lobster, and clams" (Questions on Doctrine, Pg. 623; See Hoekema, 1976 p. 34). |
| **Hell is not forever or Eternal** | Ellen G. White wrote, "How repugnant to every emotion of love and mercy, and even to our sense of justice, is the doctrine that the wicked dead are tormented with fire and brimstone in an eternally burning hell; that for the sins of a brief, earthly life they are to suffer torture as long as God shall live" (The Great Controversy, 1958)."

"But I saw that God would not shut them up in hell to endure endless misery, neither will He take them to heaven; for to bring them into the company of the pure and holy would make them exceedingly miserable. (The Great Controversy, 1958). |
| **Unbelievers destroyed by fire...annihilated** | Ellen G. White believed and taught that God would simply annihilate the souls of those who did not follow him. "But He will destroy them utterly and cause them to be as if they had not been; then His justice will be satisfied. He formed man out of the dust of the earth, and the disobedient and unholy will be consumed by fire and return to dust again" (The Great Controversy, 1958). |

Kingdom Established when Christ Returns	Kingdom Established when Christ Returns. The Adventists believe that when Jesus returns He will then set up His kingdom and begin His 1,000 year reign (Official website of the Seventh-day Adventist Church).

That He (Christ) will return in a premillennial, personal, imminent second advent. (Seventh-day Adventists Answer Questions on Doctrine, an Explanation of Certain Major Aspects of Seventh-day Adventist Belief).

The Kingdom will be established when Christ returns. The Adventists believe that when Jesus returns He will then set up His kingdom and begin His 1,000 year reign (Official website of the Seventh-day Adventist Church).

Thousand Year Reign & Second Resurrection. The second resurrection, the resurrection of the unrighteous, will take place a thousand years later (General Conference of Seventh-day Adventists, 2015).

Millennium or Thousand Year Reign. Christ with His saints in heaven between the first and second resurrections (General Conference of Seventh-day Adventists, 2015).

Millennium on Earth. The wicked dead will be judged; the earth will be utterly desolate, without living human inhabitants, but occupied by Satan and his angels (General Conference of Seventh-day Adventists, 2015).

End of Millennium. Christ with His saints and the Holy City will descend from heaven to earth. The unrighteous dead will then be resurrected, and with Satan and his angels will surround the city; but fire from God will consume them and cleanse the earth. The universe will thus be freed of sin and sinners forever (General Conference of Seventh-day Adventists, 2015).

The New Earth. On the new earth, in which righteousness dwells, God will provide an eternal home for the redeemed and a perfect environment for everlasting life, love, joy, and learning in His presence. For here God Himself will dwell with His people, and suffering and death will have passed away. The great controversy will be ended, and sin will be no more. All things, animate and inanimate, will declare that God is love; and He shall reign forever (General Conference of Seventh-day Adventists, 2015). |
| **Keep Old Law of Commandments and Sabbath.** | "Lo, here are the people of God mentioned in Revelation 12, having the "testimony of Jesus," which is the "spirit of prophecy" (December, 1844), and keeping the commandments—all ten of them—the Seventh-day Sabbath included. Here the remnant church was born, and these two significant truths identify it" (Ellen White's Writings, Believe His Prophets)

"It was on the first Sabbath in April, 1847, that she had her first vision regarding the Sabbath. By putting together Testimonies for the Church 1:75 ff., and a letter to Joseph Bates written April 7, 1847, now appearing in Early Writings, 32-35, we get the whole story of what she saw and heard. She seemed to be transferred from earth to heaven, and in vision she was taken through the heavenly sanctuary, where she saw the most holy place and the ark containing the law. She was amazed to see the fourth commandment shining above all the others in glory, with a sort of halo of light all around it. She was told of the change of the Sabbath, of |

	the significance of its acceptance and observance, especially in the troublous times ahead, when it will become a sign or a mark for the people who have chosen to obey God rather than man" (Ellen White's Writings, Believe His Prophets). ". . . in the last days the Sabbath test will be made plain. When this time comes anyone who does not keep the Sabbath will receive the mark of the beast and will be kept from heaven" (The Great Controversy, p. 449). Assemble together on the Sabbath (Saturday). The fourth commandment of God's unchangeable law requires the observance of this Seventh-day Sabbath as the day of rest, worship, and ministry in harmony with the teaching and practice of Jesus, the Lord of the Sabbath (General Conference of Seventh-day Adventists, 2015).
Men are Born Sinners	"Sin...is an inheritance. Men are born sinners. Through disobedience, Adam's nature became changed. He was no longer a holy and righteous being, but a sinful being. And this sinful nature must, of necessity, be transmitted to his children as an inheritance" (Branson, Pg. 43).
Revelation: Ellen G. White was the Lord's Messenger and the SDA church believes in current day prophecy	"Lo, here are the people of God mentioned in Revelation 12, having the "testimony of Jesus," which is the "spirit of prophecy" (December, 1844), and keeping the commandments—all ten of them—the Seventh-day Sabbath included. Here the remnant church was born, and these two significant truths identify it" (Ellen White's Writings, Believe His Prophets). The 18th of the **28 Fundamentals** states the Adventists viewpoint on the Gift of Prophecy: "One of the gifts of the Holy Spirit is prophecy. This gift is an identifying mark of the remnant church and was manifested in the ministry of Ellen. G. White. As the Lord's messenger, her writings are a continuing and authoritative source of truth which provide for the church comfort, guidance, instruction, and correction. SDA church had a dynamic concept of what they called present truth, opposed to creedal rigidity, and had an openness to new theological understandings that built upon the landmark doctrines, or Pillars of Adventism that had made them a people (Knight, 2000). A Search for Identity. Review and Herald Pub.) The 18 of the 28 Fundamentals states the Adventists viewpoint on the Gift of Prophecy: "One of the gifts of the Holy Spirit is prophecy. This gift is an identifying mark of the remnant church and was manifested in the ministry of Ellen. G. White . As the Lord's messenger, her writings are a continuing and authoritative source of truth which provide for the church comfort, guidance, instruction, and correction. They also make clear that the Bible is the standard by which all teaching and experience must be tested. (Joel 2:28, 29; Acts 2:14-21; Heb. 1:1-3; Rev. 12:17; 19:10.). Ellen G White stated, "I have had no claims to make, only that I am instructed that I am the Lord's messenger.... Early in my work I was asked several times, Are you a prophet? I have ever responded, "I am the Lord's messenger." I know that many have called me a prophet, but I have made no claim to this title. My Savior declared me to be His messenger. "Your work," He instructed me, "is to bear My word. Strange things will arise; and in your youth I set you apart to bear the message to the erring ones, to carry the word before unbelievers, and with pen and voice to reprove from the Word actions that are not right. Exhort from the Word. I will make My Word open to you.... My spirit and My power shall

	be with you" (1 October 1904, while preaching in the Battle Creak Tabernacle, reported by D.E. Rebox in the book titled, Believe His Prophets).
Sabbath Keeping	"Lo, here are the people of God mentioned in Revelation 12, having the "testimony of Jesus," which is the "spirit of prophecy" (December, 1844), and keeping the commandments—all ten of them—the Seventh-day Sabbath included. Here the remnant church was born, and these two significant truths identify it" (Ellen White's Writings, Believe His Prophets). "It was on the first Sabbath in April, 1847, that she had her first vision regarding the Sabbath. By putting together Testimonies for the Church 1:75 ff., and a letter to Joseph Bates written April 7, 1847, now appearing in Early Writings, 32-35, we get the whole story of what she saw and heard. She seemed to be transferred from earth to heaven, and in vision she was taken through the heavenly sanctuary, where she saw the most holy place and the ark containing the law. She was amazed to see the fourth commandment shining above all the others in glory, with a sort of halo of light all around it. She was told of the change of the Sabbath, of the significance of its acceptance and observance, especially in the troublous times ahead, when it will become a sign or a mark for the people who have chosen to obey God rather than man" (Ellen White's Writings, Believe His Prophets). ". . . in the last days the Sabbath test will be made plain. When this time comes anyone who does not keep the Sabbath will receive the mark of the beast and will be kept from heaven" (The Great Controversy, p. 449).
Second Coming of Jesus	Jesus failed to come as they had expected. "Let us now project ourselves in imagination back to the year 1844. Many, with William Miller in the lead, were fervently preaching that the coming of Christ and the end of the world would be on October 22, 1844. Excitement ran high. Thousands upon thousands were seriously preparing to meet Christ as He would come in the clouds of heaven. Hundreds of thousands stood by a bit restless and uncertain, but hoping to make the right decision by the fateful day, afraid that He might come, and at the same time hoping that He would not come..... I could almost feel myself among that group on October 22, looking at the sky, watching for the appearance of Christ, as a small cloud, which would come closer and closer. But the sun went down that fateful evening and He did not come. I could actually sense the disappointment of that early Advent group. My heart went out to them in their bitter disappointment" (Ellen White's Writings, Believe His Prophets) When He returns, the righteous dead will be resurrected, and together with the righteous living will be glorified and taken to heaven, but the unrighteous will die (General Conference of Seventh-day Adventists, 2015). The "remnant church" is understood to act as a catalyst for the formation of this group. The eschatological remnant will consist of some (but not all) constituents of the present "remnant church", together with a cohort of believers from other (that is, non-Adventist) churches. Only members of the eschatological remnant will be saved through the end-times (Official website of the Seventh-day Adventist Church). Only the Righteous Resurrected. The resurrected righteous and the living righteous will be glorified and caught up to meet their Lord (General Conference of Seventh-day Adventists, 2015).

Jesus Bore the Weight of the Sins of mankind	Satan bore not only the weight and punishment of his own sins, but also of the sins of the redeemed host, which had been placed upon him.... (Ellen G. White, Early Writings, p. 294,295).

The Prophet Test

False Prophecies in Seventh-day Adventism

Prophecy	Fulfillment	Prophecy True	False
Ellen G. White's stated in 1856 that, 'There are some here who will be alive to see the coming of the Lord, and there are some here who will be food for worms'?"	Did not happen! No one alive in 1856 is alive today.		X
Ellen G. White 1850: "Some of us have had time to get the truth and to advance step by step, and every step we have taken has given us strength to take the next. But now time is almost finished, and what we have been years learning, they will have to learn in a few months. They will also have much to unlearn and much to learn again. Those who would not receive the mark of the beast and his image when the decree goes forth, must have now to say, Nay, we will not regard the institution of the beast" (Ellen G. White, Early Writings, p.67).	Did not happen! The decree to receive the mark of the beast has not been issued well past a few months.		X

Comparative Doctrine

Unification Church
(Moonies)

Founder: Sun Myung Moon

Date Founded: May 1, 1954, Seoul, South Korea

Headquarters: Seoul, South Korea

Key Statement: Moon is the Second coming of Christ who has come to fulfill Jesus Christ's mission.

Major Works

- Bible
- Divine Principle
- An Introduction to Theology.
- Unification Theology
- Master Speaks
- New Hope: Twelve Talks
- The New Future of Christianity
- Christianity in Crisis
- God's Warning to the World
- Unification Church 120 Day Training Manual
- The Divine Principle Study Guide.
- And more!

The Unification Church is one of the most controversial religious movements of the past century. Founded in Seoul in the 1950s by the Rev Moon.

Multiple revisions have been made to correct errors of transcribers and translators including theological problems within the book (Yamoto).

Communication with the Spirit-World (Spiritual/occult) endorsed. DP p.163 "Any Christian who, in spiritual communication, can see John the Baptist directly in the spirit world will be able to understand the authenticity of all these things."

Moon is involved in spiritism (MS. 2/20/1973 p.7 DP p.529ff). Famed occultic spiritist Arthur Ford mentions Moon as a friend who has practiced the occultic arts with him. (Ford's book, Unknown But Known. Signet Mystic, 1968.)

DP p.529 "Therefore, countless men of religion are receiving very clear revelations concerning the Lord's Second Coming in Korea in many different ways, by contacting many spirit men of various levels : from the realm of miscellaneous spirits to the realm of the paradise level spirits. Nevertheless, the leaders of the present Christian world, due to their spiritual ignorance, are still unresponsive, and have refused to pay heed to such things. This is similar to what happened in Jesus' day, when the chief priests and rabbis, who should have been the first to know of the coming of the Messiah, were entirely unaware of the fact due to their spiritual ignorance, while, on the other hand, the astrologers and shepherds knew of the message through revelations."

The Unification Church is much smaller now that Reverend Moon passed away.

Unification Church Unique or Core Beliefs	
Topic	**Belief**
Bible Inspiration	Moon stated that New Truth was needed. In regard to Bible Inspiration Moon stated that, "Jesus did not say that His word was the truth but that he himself was the truth, way and the life (John 14:6). This is because His words were only a means of expressing himself as the truth... We can understand that the New Testament was given as a textbook for the teaching of truth to the people of 2,000 years ago... In consequence, today the truth must appear with a higher standard and with a scientific method of expression in order to enable intelligent modern men to understand it" (Divine Principle, Pg. 131). "The Bible, however, is not the truth itself, but a textbook teaching the truth. Naturally the quality of teaching and the method and extent of giving the truth must vary according to each age, for the truth is given to people of different ages, who are at different spiritual and intellectual levels. Therefore, we must not regard the textbook as absolute in every detail" (Divine Principle, Pg. 9). "The New Testament was a textbook given for the teaching of the truth to the people of 2,000 years ago, people whose spiritual and intellectual standards were then very low compared to today. . . In consequence, today the truth must appear with higher standards . . . we call this the New Truth" (Divine Principle, Pg. 167, 168). The Divine Principle also states that Moon is a messenger of God. He is supposed to be the fulfillment of the Judeo-Christian religion, bringing to us the "completed testament" (Divine Principle, Pg. 137, 232-238; Divine Principle Study Guide, Pg. 5-6 163-173). "Innumerable Christians of today are dashing on the way which they think will lead them to the Kingdom of Heaven. Nevertheless, this road is apt to lead them into Hell" (Divine Principle, Pg. 535). In Time magazine Moon stated that, "God is now throwing Christianity away and is establishing a new religion" (Time, September 30, 1974, Pg. 68). "Consequently, the most important matter of all is the viewpoint from which one interprets the Bible.....since it is absolutely incomprehensible to the intellect of modern men that the Lord would come on the clouds, it is necessary for us to consider the Bible in detail a second time..." (Divine Principle, Pg. 500).
Original Sin and the Fall of Man	"The inherited sin of man has been inherited from the first man and the first woman . . . original sin remains in the flesh and is transmitted continuously from generation to generation" (Divine Principle, Pg. 66, 148). According to Moon, man's fall was twofold. First, the spiritual fall, then the physical fall. Both falls were the result of illicit sexual intercourse (Divine Principle, Pg. 77). Eve was tempted and then sinned by having sexual intercourse with Satan. Her sin resulted in the spiritual fall of man (Divine Principle, Pg. 78-79).

	As a result of Eve's sexual union with Satan she bore Cain (Divine Principle, Pg. 242).

Eve tempted Adam into premature sexual union. His sin resulted in the physical fall of man (Divine Principle, Pg. 26).

There were **two falls of man**, not one. "Eve's fall consisted of two kinds of illicit love affairs. The first one was the spiritual fall through love with the archangel [Lucifer]. The second was the physical fall through love with Adam" (Divine Principle, Pg. 241).

"Therefore, all the saints since the resurrection of Jesus through the present day have enjoyed the benefit of the providence of spiritual salvation only. Even in devout men of faith, the original sin remains in the flesh and is transmitted continuously from generation to generation. The more devout a saint becomes in his faith, therefore, the more severe becomes his fight against sin. Thus, Christ (Moon) must come again on the earth to accomplish the purpose of the providence of the physical, as well as the spiritual salvation, by redeeming the original sin which has not been liquidated even through the cross" (Divine Principle, Pg. 148). |
| **Moon Sacrificed more than Christ** | Moon stated that, "During my first 3 years of public ministry, just as Jesus did, I had to go through severe hardships culminating in the torture of prison life, which was more for me than Jesus' cross. I had to accomplish all left unaccomplished by my predecessor....When you think of that, you must feel indebted to me and you cannot lift your face before me" (Master Speaks, 27 May,1973, Pg. 13; 4 March,1973, Pg. 10). |
| **The Creation is the Creator** | According to Moon creation "...is the creator, God, projecting himself into a substantial form" (A Prophet Speaks Today, Pg. 3).

"Underlying God and creation are dualities, such as positive & negative, external form & internal character (Divine Principle, Pg. 21), male & female (Divine Principle Pg. 24), or yang & yin (Divine Principle, Pg. 26) as the I Ching talks about."

The universe is God's "external feminine object" (Divine Principle, Pg. 25) which God as subject gives love as an emotional force to. |
| **Jesus was not the Creator** | "We can understand that the Bible (John 1:10) only clarifies the fact that Jesus was a man who had perfected the purpose of creation, and does not signify that he was the Creator Himself" (Divine Principle, Pg. 211). |
| **God and Man are One** | "Man is God's substantial object," (Divine Principle, Pg. 26).

"God and man are one. Man is incarnate God" (Christianity in Crisis, Pg. 5). |
| **Jesus was Born of a Father and Mother** | Jesus was the son of Zechariah, not born of a virgin. "Jesus was born of a father and a mother, just as anyone is, but in his case the Spirit of God was working also" (Master Speaks, Pg. 9). |
| **Jesus' Death** | Jesus' ". . . body was invaded by Satan and he was killed" (Divine Principle, Pg. 148).' |

Christs Sacrifice was not Intended	"We, therefore, must realize that Jesus did not come to die on the cross" (Divine Principle, Pg. 435).
Christ Failed His Mission	Christ did not fulfill his mission on earth (Divine Principle and its Application, Pg. 64-65). "The crucifixion of Jesus was a secondary choice....after it became obvious that he would not be able to fulfill his mission" (Kim, Principle, Pg. 60-61). Moon believed that Jesus had a primary mission from God. He stated that, "there had to be a bride, a Mother---another Eve. So God intended for this perfected Adam---Jesus Christ---to restore his bride, the perfected Eve" (Moon, The New Future of Christianity, Pg. 171-172). Moon states that, "I am Jesus who came 2000 years ago. My mission still remains to be accomplished. In order to realize God's will, you must be responsible for a great mission" (120 Day Training Manual, p. 324). A major part of Christ's mission was to establish the perfect marriage while he was on earth (Divine Principle, pp. 140-141). Jesus came not to die, but to accomplish both salvations. (DP p.147). However, because John the Baptist failed God, the Jews rejected Jesus. As a result, Christ could only save us spiritually by giving Satan His body and dying for mankind (DP p.148) Any who have perfect goodness have deity, so Jesus may well be called God. Jesus on earth was identical to us, except he was without original sin (DP p.101,210-212).
Jesus' Blood is Insufficient	"Today the Christian gospel preaches salvation by the blood of Jesus. How ridiculous that is in the sight of God!" (Moon, Master Speaks, April 8,1978, Pg. 12).
Jesus is not God	"It is plain that Jesus is not God himself" (Divine Principle, p. 211). Moon stated that, "...Jesus, being one body with God, may be called a second God (image of God), but can by no means be God Himself" (Divine Principle, Pg. 210-211). "...Jesus, as a man having fulfilled the purpose of creation, is one body with God. ... Nevertheless, he can by no means be God Himself. ... Jesus, being one body with God, may be called a second God (image of God), but he can by no means be God Himself. Jesus is not God" (Divine Principle, Pg. 210-212).
Christ was a man	Christ was a man (Divine Principle, Pg. 258).
The Trinity is God, The Lord of the Second Advent (Moon) and Moons Wife	Rhodes summarized Moon's belief regarding the Trinity by writing, "According to Moon, it was God's original intention in creating Adam and Eve to form a Trinity by uniting them into one body with himself (that is God, the "True Father" [Adam], and the "true Mother" [Eve]). This plan was foiled because Adam and Even did not perfect themselves and fell into sin. Because of the fall, a Satanic trinity was formed with Satan, Adam, and Eve (false parents). Later, once Jesus perfected himself spiritually, God formed a spiritual Trinity with Jesus and the Holy Spirit (who is a female spirit; hence Jesus and the Holy Spirit supposedly took

	the roles of "second Adam' and "second Eve"). But because Jesus died on the cross before getting married, God could not form a physical trinity with Jesus and the woman he might have married. Moon claims that the members of the physical Trinity will be God, the Lord of the Second, and the Lord of the Second Advent's wife. Moon teaches that when this physical Trinity is formed, the kingdom of heaven will be established on earth" (Divine Principle, 519; Yamamoto, 1974; Rhodes, 2001). "Accordingly, in order to fulfill the purpose of creation, Jesus and the Holy Spirit must establish the four position foundation centered on God, by becoming one body in unity through the action of give and take, each as the object of God, substantially divided from His dual essentialities. In this manner, Jesus and the Holy Spirit become one body centered on God; this is called 'Trinity.'" However, due to the fall, Adam and Eve established the four position foundation centered on Satan, thus resulting in a trinity centered on Satan" (Divine Principle, Pg. 217). Since Christ's death, God has prepared the world for "his" return. Abel-type democracies will conquer Cain-type communism in a 3rd World War. Then the "Lord of the Second Advent" will publicly appear and set up the Kingdom of Heaven on earth (Divine Principle p.430-496).
Revelations by Moon	"With the fullness of time, God has sent one person to this earth to resolve the fundamental problems of human life and the universe. His name is Sun Myung Moon. For several decades he wandered through the spirit world so vast as to be beyond imagining. He trod a bloody path of suffering in search of the truth, passing through tribulations that God alone remembers. Since he understood that no one can find the ultimate truth to save humanity without first passing through the bitterest of trials, he fought alone against millions of devils, both in the spiritual and physical worlds, and triumphed over them all. Through intimate spiritual communion with God and by meeting with Jesus and many saints in Paradise, he brought to light all the secrets of Heaven" (Divine Principle (translated 1966). "There are many who receive revelations indicating that the Holy Spirit is a female spirit. . . this is the age in which man can communicate directly with God...there are many people today who can communicate with the spirit world. God gives him (man) the revelation that he is lord" (Divine Principle, pp. 215, 177-178). "You may again want to ask me, 'With what authority do you weigh these things?' I spoke with Jesus Christ in the spirit world. And I spoke with John the Baptist. This is my (Sun Myung Moon) authority. If you cannot at this time determine that my words are the truth, you will surely discover that they are in the course of time. These hidden truths presented to you as a new revelation. You have heard me speak the Bible. If you believe the Bible, you must believe what I am saying" (Christianity in Crisis, p. 98). "Until our mission with the Christian church is over, we must quote the Bible and use it to explain the Divine Principle. After we receive the inheritance of the Christian church we will be free to teach without the Bible" (Master Speaks, March and April, 1965, MS-7, p. 1).

	"The Divine Principle. . . is truth in its fullest meaning, but not the Bible word for word. The Divine Principle clearly shows how the Bible is symbolic and how it is parabolic. . . the Bible is based upon the truth. The Divine Principle gives the true meaning of the secret behind the verse" (Master Speaks, March and April, 1965, MS-7, p. 1).
The Messiah has come and his Name is Moon	"Then they can understand that Reverend Moon is Messiah, the Lord of the Second Advent....If only they can understand the fall of man they can understand that Father is the Messiah....Father is visible God" (120 Day Training Manal, Pg. 160, 222, 352). Jesus was the second Adam. For 2000 years Christians are have supposed to prepare for the coming of the second Messiah. That Messiah will be born somewhere in the east. Korea is the only logical place for people there have a strong faith in God. Moon is the second coming of the Messiah (Divine Principle, 519; Yamamoto, 1974). "I (Moon) am Jesus who came 2000 years ago. My mission still remains to be accomplished. In order to realize God's will, you must be responsible for a great mission" (120 Day Training Manual, p. 324). "Adam and Eve were supposed to be the True Parents of mankind in God's plan. When they failed, God intended Jesus to be the True Parent of mankind. When he was crucified on the cross, God promised another messiah. He is coming to consummate the ideal of God-centered True Parents. He will generate a new family of God through restoring the family unit under God's ideal. When we have True Parents of God, we can all become true brothers and sisters" (Reverend Moon, cited in Frederic Sontag, Sun Myung Mood and the Unification Church, 142-143).
Pray in the Name of the True Parents	"As Christians, we prayed in the name of the Father, the Son, and the Holy Ghost or Holy Spirit. Now we should pray in the name of the True Parents" (Master Speaks, March and April, 1965, MS-3, p.2).
Moon and His Family are Sinless	". . . Father (Moon) is sinless, Mother (Moon's wife) is sinless, and their children are sinless. . . This is called the Messiah's family; this was established in 1967, on December 31. The sinless family was established on earth" (120 Day Training Manual, p. 236).
Heavenly Deception	Heavenly Deception' is acceptable—lying to get money for the Unification Church movement (Master Speaks, p.6). "You must be able to manipulate those people" in order to get what you need from the general populace (Master Speaks, p.6).
Cannot Eat Unclean Foods	Hoekema summarizes their belief by saying, "Under the 'unclean foods' from which the candidates for baptism must promise to abstain are included such beverages as coffee and tea, and such meats as pork, ham, shrimp, lobster, and clams" (Questions on Doctrine, Pg. 623; See Hoekema, 1976 p. 34).
Holy Spirit is Female	"Since the Holy Spirit is a female Spirit, we cannot become the 'bride' of Jesus unless we receive the Holy Spirit" (Divine Principle, Pg. 215). Holy Spirit is female in nature: "....according to Divine Principle, since God possesses polarity, there is a sense in which it is legitimate to refer

	to the feminine activity of the Holy Spirit. Because the Spirit carries out maternal functions of comforting, nourishing and nurturing individual Christians, it serves as a mother spirit. The Holy Spirit is a feminine spirit who works beside Jesus in the spirit world" (An Introduction to Theology, 1983). In the same paper the Holy Spirit is described differently: "In Unification theology the main point is that the Holy Spirit is not a separate entity, a being different from God the Father. The Holy Spirit simply refers to God's redemptive activity. Hence in Genesis the Spirit is defined as God's breath: The Lord God breathed His Spirit into Adam, making him a living soul" (Kim, 1980).
Kingdom to Be Established by Moon	Moon teaches that when this physical Trinity is formed, the kingdom of heaven will be established on earth" (Divine Principle, 519; Yamamoto, 1974; Rhodes, 2001). "...to meet the Lord in the air signifies that the saints will receive the Lord in the world of good sovereignty when Christ [Moon] comes again and restores the Kingdom of Heaven on earth by overthrowing the Satanic sovereignty" (Divine Principle Pg. 117).
God is Abolishing Hell	"Men of evil nature have established evil homes, societies, and an evil world, by multiplying children of evil. This is the Hell on earth in which fallen men have been living," (Divine Principle, Pg.102-103, 216). "The ultimate purpose of God's providence of restoration is to save all mankind. Therefore, it is God's intention to abolish Hell completely, after the lapse of the period necessary for the full payment of all indemnity" (Divine Principle, Pg. 190).
Moon is God, Lord of the Second Advent	"Father [Moon] is visible God" 120 Day Training Manual, Pg. 135-136). "Then they can understand that Rev. Moon is Messiah, the Lord of the Second Advent. . . If only they can understand the fall of man they can understand that Father is the Messiah. . .Father is visible God" (120 Day Training Manual, Pg. 160, 222, 362). Jesus' return in the sky is only symbolic; actually a "Lord of the Second Advent" will be born on earth. He will fulfill physical salvation by ridding believers of original sin. Without being Jesus, he will have Jesus' Spirit and complete Jesus' "unsuccessful" mission so this counts as Christ's return (Divine Principle p.187-188). He should have been born in Korea (Divine Principle p.520-532) soon after 1918 (Divine Principle p.449,499). This "True Parent" will rule the ideal world of one great family (Divine Principle p. 536).
Forgiveness of Sins through Moon	Moon's shed blood drawn during his persecution provides for the forgiveness of man's sins. Without Moon there is no forgiveness of sin (Unification Church 120 Day Training Manual, pp. 135-136). "Through father [Moon] and Mother [his wife] we can be born anew, sinlessly" (120 Day Training Manual, Pg. 41-42).

Salvation Through Moon	"Therefore, all the saints since the resurrection of Jesus through the present day have enjoyed the benefit of the providence of spiritual salvation only. Even in devout men of faith, the original sin remains in the flesh and is transmitted continuously from generation to generation. The more devout a saint becomes in his faith, therefore, the more severe becomes his fight against sin. Thus, Christ (Moon) must come again on the earth to accomplish the purpose of the providence of the physical, as well as the spiritual salvation, by redeeming the original sin which has not been liquidated even through the cross" (Divine Principle, p. 148).
Four Basic Spirit Worlds After Death	According to Moon there are four basic spirit worlds. Evil men go to a place of darkness or what's called hell. Men who attain to only the form stage go to a place of darkness, those who attain to the life-spirit stage (through faith in the Gospel) go to paradise, those who reach the perfection or divine-spirit stage (by serving the Lord in person) go to the Kingdom of Heaven when they die (Divine Principle, pp. 174-175).
Spirit World at Death	At death you will go to a spirit world. Human ancestors will help you progress to the highest stage where you "...will become divine, like God, and exist in the highest level of heaven" (Speeches, Pg. 14-15).
No Judgment after Death	According to Moon there will be no judgment as Christianity has traditionally believed, rather man will be restored to the original position God intended. There will be no destruction by fire, "Therefore, it is God's intention to abolish Hell completely" (Divine Principle, Pg. 190). Judgment according to the Unification thought has three stages. "The three stages of judgment are the judgment of words, the judgment of personality and the judgment of heart....The kingdom of heaven is the dwelling place for those that have won and overcome these three stages of judgment" (New Hope, Pg. 3-4).
Spiritual Progress until you Reach Deity	Man will spiritually advance, even after death, until he reaches deity....to even become a god (Speeches, Pg. 14-15). Can progress after death (Divine Principle, Pg. 181-182). All mankind get to progress; even after death. Four stages of progression from Hell to Heaven (Divine Principle, Pg. 174-175). **Hell:** Reserved for evil men. Evil men who have died must torment sinful people on earth, eventually leading them to the formation stage of development. **Place of Darkness--Formation Stage:** Reserved for good men who followed laws and commandments. Must influence those living to believe in Jesus and the Lord of the Second Advent [Moon]. **Paradise—Growth Stage:** Reserved for those who believed in Jesus while on earth. Must influence saints that they must serve and believe in Moon. **Kingdom of Heaven—Perfection Stage:** Reserved for those who believe in and serve Moon. No further progression is needed, they are one with God!

Eternal Life	Everyone will eventually be perfected and as a result saved (Divine Principle, Pg. 187, 190, 511-512). There are three stages of progression; the Formative Stage, the Growth Stage and the Perfection Stage (Divine Principle, Pg. 174-175).
Disembodied Spirits Help	Disembodied spirit, (dead ancestors) descend on Moonies and work with them. The disembodied spirit gains another level in the spirit world. Their goal is to progress in order to become divine like God and finally get to the highest level of heaven (Kim, Speeches Pg. 14-15; Moon, New Heaven, Pg. 72; Kim, Theology Pg. 154).

The Prophet Test

False Prophecies in the Unification Church

Prophecy	Fulfillment	Prophecy True	False
Moon's idea of the "True Family" promised willing couples they would help reinstitute a perfect line of humanity.	Failed		X

Comparative Doctrine

Unity Church

(Unity or Silent Unity)

Founder: **Charles and Myrtle Fillmore**

Date: 1889, Kansas City, MO

Headquarters: Unity Village, MO

Key Statement: Unity has its roots in the New Thought movement. It is a blend of Christianity, positive thinking, eastern religions, and spiritism.

Major Works

- Jesus Christ Heals
- Metaphysical Bible Dictionary
- Christian Healing
- The Revealed Word
- Teach Us to Pray
- And More!

Incorporated: As the Unity School of Christianity in 1914
It's business names are Unity, Unity Church, or Silent Unity.

Web site: Unity.org.

Type of Religion: It is one of the largest Gnostic cults in Christendom

Unity
Unique or Core Beliefs

Scripture	Belief
Bible is Fallible. One of many texts	"The Bible is the greatest of many sacred texts. It is not inspired by a personal God and it is not infallible" (What Unity Teaches, 1952; Unity, 1896). "…spiritual principle is embodied in the sacred books of the world's living religions. Christians hold to the Bible as the supreme exponent of spiritual principle. They believe that the Bible is the greatest and most deeply spiritual of all the Scriptures, though they realize that other scriptures, such as the Zend-Avesta and the Upanishads, as well as the teachings of Buddha, the Koran, the Tao of Lao-tse and the writings of Confucius, contain expressions of eminent spiritual truths" (What Unity Teaches, 1952). "…Scripture may be a satisfactory authority for those who are not themselves in direct communion with the Lord" (Unity, 1986).
God Does Not Love	"Yet God does not love anybody or anything. God is the love in everybody and everything. God is love; man becomes loving by permitting that which God is to find expression in word and act" (Fillmore, Jesus Christ Heals).
No Belief in God	Belief in a personal God has retarded the progress of the race! (Scott, The True Character of God).
Trinity a Stumbling Block	The doctrine of the trinity is often a stumbling block, because we find it difficult to understand how three persons can be one. Three persons cannot be one, and theology will always be a mystery until theologians become metaphysicians" (The Fillmore Fellowship).
Christ's Atonement is a pagan Idea	"These theories of the sin offering of Jesus are conceived with the personal God idea. They carry out the pagan concept of a big god who becomes very angry with his disobedient children and can be mollified only with a human sacrifice. A correct understanding by man of God as the supreme creative reveals how broken law may be mended by one who is willing to make certain sacrifices" (Fillmore, Teach Us to Pray).
Jesus Resurrected His Own Body	"Jesus spent whole nights in prayer, according to the Gospels, and it is quite evident that He was resurrecting His body by realizing, as we do in our prayers, that God was His indwelling life." (Fillmore, Jesus Christ Heals).
Deity of Christ the same as all humans	"Christ is the only begotten son of God with one complete idea of perfect mind and divine Mind. This Christ, or perfect-man idea, existing eternally in divine Mind is the true spirit and higher self of every individual" (Filmore, Metaphysical Bible Dictionary). Unity Church followers believe in the divinity of Jesus, but only in the sense that all humans are the children of God and share that divine potential. They believe that Jesus was a master teacher who expressed this divine potential and sought to show others how to do the same. Unity uses the term "Christ" to mean the divinity in all people. For them Jesus is the great example of the Christ in physical form (Teach Us to Pray, 1997).

Salvation by using Creative Principles	Being 'born-again' or 'born from above' is not a miraculous change that takes place in man; it is the establishment of that which has always existed as the perfect man idea of divine Mind" (Christian Healing, Pg. 24). "We have thought that we were to be saved by Jesus' making personal petitions and sacrifices for us, but now we see that we are to be saved by using the creative principles that he developed in himself and that He is ever ready to cooperate with us in developing in ourselves by observing the law as He observed it. 'I in them, and thou in me, that they may be perfected into one" (Jesus Christ Heals, Pg. 162).
Jesus is the reincarnation of David	See Matthew 22:41-42 "...Jesus asked them a question, 42 saying, "What do you think about the Christ? Whose son is he?" They said to him, "The son of David." "....Jesus demands of the pharisees, 'What think ye of Christ? Whose son is he?' They answered, not as one might ordinarily expect, 'The son of Joseph,' but 'The son of David.' In other words He was the reincarnation of David" (Wilson, Have We lived Before).
Holy Spirit	"Do not be misled by the personality of the Holy Spirit and the reference to it as 'he.' This was the bias of the Oriental mind, making God and all forms of the Deity masculine" (Jesus Christ Heals, Pg. 183). "The Spirit of wholeness quickens and heals me. The Spirit of wholeness is called the Holy Spirit in the New Testament. In classical mythology it is called Hygeria. Modern medical men refer to it as the restorative power of nature. It has been recognized by savage and civilized in every land and age. It has many names, and they all identify it as a universal urge toward perfection in man and the universe and toward keeping things going regardless of any retarding or interfering force" (Jesus Christ Heals, Pg. 183).
Trinity is a stumbling block	The Father is Principle, the Son is that Principle revealed in the creative plan, the Holy Spirit is the executive power of both Father and Son carrying out the plan" (Metaphysical Bible Dictionary,1931). "The doctrine of the trinity is often a stumbling block, because we find it difficult to understand how three persons can be one. Three persons cannot be one...God is the name of the all-encompassing Mind, Christ is the name of the all-loving Mind. Holy Spirit is the all-active manifestations. These three are one fundamental Mind in its three creative aspect" (The Revealed Word,1959).
Forgiveness of Sins	"The forgiveness of sin is an erasure of mortal thoughts from consciousness. The joy which comes to the converted Christian is the inflow of Divine Love after the mind has been cleansed. By denial of sin" (Fillmore, Christian Healing).
Sin is failure to express attributes of being	"Sin is man's failure to express the attributes of Being—life, love, intelligence, wisdom, and the other God qualities" (The Revealing Word, Pg. 180).
Evil denied	"I deny all belief in evil, for God made all that really is and pronounced it good" (Fillmore, Christian Healing).

Pain, Sickness, Death	"Pain, sickness, poverty, old age and death are not real, and they have no power over me. There is nothing in all the universe for me to fear" (Cady, Lessons in Truth).
Heaven/Hell	"Heaven and hell are symbols, not places for people to go. Knowing this should be a relief, but there are many who want to believe in them as places. Mystically they represent states of consciousness. Hell is the consciousness of error based on mistaken views about God, man, and the universe. It isn't a consciousness created by God, but is one formed by man through his misuse of the power of thought. Satan is a ruling belief in consciousness that motivates much of our negative behavior. He was considered to be a fallen angel and, mystically, he was. There is only one power—God power. The power of negative thought is a fallen angel; it has the possibility of good, but can be very destructive when used negatively" (Filmore Fellowship, Heaven and/or Hell Metaphysically Interpreted).
Reincarnation	"Eventually all souls reincarnate on the earth as babes and in due time take up their problems where they left off at death" (Fillmore, Teach Us to Pray). "...Jesus demands of the Pharisees, 'What think ye of Christ? Whose son is he?' They answered, not as one might ordinarily expect, 'The son of Joseph,' but 'The son of David.' In other words, He was the reincarnation of David" (Have We Lived Before, 1936).

Comparative Doctrine

Unitarian Universalist Church

Founder: Members of American Unitarian Association and Universalist Church of America via consolidation

Date: May 1961

Headquarters: Autonomous

Key Statement: Unitarian Universalists assert no creed, but instead are unified by their shared search for spiritual growth. As such, their congregations include many atheists, agnostics, and theists within their membership.

Major Works: No specific works that identify creed or beliefs. However, they accept all works that lead to spiritual growth, e.g., Bible, Qur'an, Poetry (insights/beliefs from most world religions).

Incorporated:

"The Unitarians and Universalists talked for many years about merging, and although their theologies were close, they were kept apart by class differences. The Unitarians tended to come from the educated, upper-middle class, and tended to be more cerebral in their worship style than the Universalists, who were mainly rural and less well educated. They decided in 1961, at last, to merge and now the faith is known as Unitarian Universalist" (Official website for Unitarian Universalist Association   uua.org).

Official Web Site: uua.org

Who attends: "...atheists and Christians, Muslims, Jews, Hindus and Buddhists, people of faith and no faith, straight and gay, lesbian, bisexual, transgender;" (Official website for Unitarian Universalist Association   uua.org).

Statement on Website: "We are called to bring a teaching of hope, to bring a saving message, to welcome all in our doors: the joyful, the heartbroken, atheists and Christians, Muslims, Jews, Hindus and Buddhists, people of faith and no faith, straight and gay, lesbian, bisexual, transgender; all who are searching, seeking, looking for more: more meaning, more service, more love..." (Official website for Unitarian Universalist Association   uua.org).

Unique or Core Beliefs

Topics	Belief
Doctrinal Books	Specific Doctrine: "To become a Unitarian Universalist, you make no doctrinal promises, but you are required to do much more. You are required to choose your own beliefs — you promise, that is, to use your reason and your experience and the dictates of your conscience to decide upon your own theology, and then you are asked to actually live by that theology. You are asked to take your chosen faith very seriously" (Official website for Unitarian Universalist Association uua.org).
	"We are a free religious faith, and so have no creed….Our faith, of course, does have requirements. To become a Unitarian Universalist, you make no doctrinal promises, but you are required to do much more. You are required to choose your own beliefs" (Official website for Unitarian Universalist Association uua.org).
	"And as freedom is wont to do, our faith invites a certain degree of wackiness and abuse. But if that's the price of freedom, then I still choose freedom" (Official website for Unitarian Universalist Association uua.org).
	"One might say that life is our scripture. While Unitarianism and Universalism both have roots in the Protestant Christian tradition, where the Bible is the sacred text, we now look to additional sources for religious and moral inspiration. Over two centuries, our religious tradition, a "living tradition," has branched out from its roots. We celebrate the spiritual insights of the world's religions, recognizing wisdom in many scriptures" (Official website for Unitarian Universalist Association uua.org).
	"…..regularly use readings from a wide range of sources, including Native American, ancient Chinese, the Hebrew Bible, Rumi, as well as a lot of contemporary poetry. Truth is where you find it. There is no single scripture that holds all the truth" (Official website for Unitarian Universalist Association uua.org).
God	"Unitarian Universalists have many ways of naming what is sacred. Some believe in a God; some don't believe in a God. Some believe in a sacred force at work in the world, and call it "love," "mystery," "source of all" or "spirit of life." We are thousands of individuals of all ages, each influenced by our cultures and life experiences to understand "the ground of our being" in our own way. Unitarian Universalists are agnostic, theist, atheist, and everything in between" (Official website for Unitarian Universalist Association uua.org).
	"Our universe, from the smallest particles to the galaxies beyond our galaxy, fills us with profound wonder. Why life exists and for what purpose—humans have struggled to answer that question for millennia. In a day and age when so much is revealed to us by science, "God" may or may not be part of our worldview" (Official website for Unitarian Universalist Association uua.org).
	"If God is One, then the God of the Jews and the God of the Muslims and the God of the Christians is One. God is One" (Official website for Unitarian Universalist Association uua.org).

Comparative Doctrine

Pro Evolution	"People with atheist and agnostic beliefs find a supportive community in our congregations. We are pro-science, pro-reason, and pro-Evolution" (Official website for Unitarian Universalist Association uua.org). "…we believe in evolution — not only evolution of life forms, but evolution of thought and evolution of moral and ethical understanding" (Official website for Unitarian Universalist Association uua.org).
No specific Doctrine	Creed or Beliefs: "The lack of formal creed has been a cause for criticism among some who argue that Unitarian Universalism is thus without religious content. "We know there is no "one right answer" when it comes to belief, and we don't let that stop us from taking action for a better world. We build a community that welcomes us in our wholeness, cherishes our doubts, and invites our ongoing search for truth" (Official website for Unitarian Universalist Association uua.org). All sources are accepted, and none are required. Their members are welcome to believe and act on their own preferred literature or resources. "We know there is no "one right answer" when it comes to belief, and we don't let that stop us from taking action for a better world. We build a community that welcomes us in our wholeness, cherishes our doubts, and invites our ongoing search for truth" The lack of formal creed has been a cause for criticism among some who argue that Unitarian Universalism is thus without religious content. "We know there is no "one right answer" when it comes to belief, and we don't let that stop us from taking action for a better world. We build a community that welcomes us in our wholeness, cherishes our doubts, and invites our ongoing search for truth" (Official website for Unitarian Universalist Association uua.org).
Original Sin	"We are not predestined by God before our births, to be saved or unsaved. We are not mired in original sin by the very fact of our birth…" (Official website for Unitarian Universalist Association uua.org).
Baptism	We do not "…have to go through a ceremony called baptism, even as babies, to cleanse ourselves of that sin [original sin]" (Official website for Unitarian Universalist Association uua.org).
Jesus was a prophet much like other prophets	"We believe that Jesus was a prophet of God, and that other prophets from God have risen in other faith traditions" (Official website for Unitarian Universalist Association uua.org). "UUs may view Jesus as a moral exemplar, practicing the compassion, generosity, and mercy that he preached" (Official website for Unitarian Universalist Association uua.org). "For some, Jesus is a prophetic leader and an instrument of the divine. They may or may not believe Jesus was the son of God or was resurrected but share with Christians a conviction that his witness has the spiritual power to redeem mistakes and save lives" (Official website for Unitarian Universalist Association uua.org).

Christ's Mission	"Unitarian Universalist theology is of this world, not of the next. Jesus, in fact, taught that the realm of God is within and, contrary to most Christian practice, his teachings were centered on relationship, not salvation" (Official website for Unitarian Universalist Association uua.org)
Purpose of Life	"Our universe, from the smallest particles to the galaxies beyond our galaxy, fills us with profound wonder. Why life exists and for what purpose—humans have struggled to answer that question for millennia" (Unitarian Universalist Community of Casper, web page).
Holy Spirit	"Do not be misled by the personality of the Holy Spirit and the reference to it as 'he.' This was the bias of the Oriental mind, making God and all forms of the Deity masculine" (Jesus Christ Heals, Pg. 183).
Kingdom of God	"For one reason, we simply don't know anything about it. No one as yet has come back to report. But we do know about suffering and injustice on this earth, and so we try to create the Kingdom of Heaven here and now, with real people" (Official website for Unitarian Universalist Association uua.org).
Trinity	"…The concept of the trinity was found to be confusing for our Catholic forebears, and they disagreed with their colleagues in the church hierarchy. But when the vote was taken in 325, the Nicene Creed was adopted, and the doctrine of the trinity was established. Note that the trinity is not a Biblical concept — it originated in the power structure of the Catholic Church. Basically, the Unitarians lost the vote" (Official website for Unitarian Universalist Association uua.org).
Jesus Sacrifice Essential	"He also rejected the idea that Jesus's death on the cross saved us — he taught that what saved us was Jesus's embodiment of love and justice" (Official website for Unitarian Universalist Association uua.org).
Paradise	"Historically, paradise for the Universalist was a place where people struggle with injustice and where they are called upon to develop wisdom and our capacity to love" (Official website for Unitarian Universalist Association uua.org).
Afterlife	"Unitarian Universalists do not emphasize an afterlife. For one reason, we simply don't know anything about it. No one as yet has come back to report" (Official website for Unitarian Universalist Association uua.org).
Consciousness after Death	"Unitarian Universalist views about life after death are informed by both science and spiritual traditions. Many of us live with the assumption that life does not continue after death, and many of us hold it as an open question, wondering if our minds will have any awareness when we are no longer living" (Official website for Unitarian Universalist Association uua.org).
Judgment	"Few of us believe in divine judgment after death." (Official website for Unitarian Universalist Association uua.org).
Hell	"It's in our religious DNA: the Universalist side of our tradition broke with mainstream Christianity by rejecting the idea of eternal damnation" (Official website for Unitarian Universalist Association uua.org).

Heaven and Hell	"The American Universalist preacher Hosea Ballou told his followers that heaven and hell are not found in any kind of afterlife, but simply in the life we create on this earth" (Official website for Unitarian Universalist Association uua.org).
Revelation	"So the truth that I embrace today may not be the truth I embrace tomorrow. Revelation is not static, but is ever unfolding. More and more will be revealed" (Official website for Unitarian Universalist Association uua.org).

Eastern Religions that have a Different View of God and Afterlife

The focus in this portion of the book is to give you a look at some of the Eastern religions that are totally contrary to the teachings of the Bible. However, they do have some basic teachings that are similar to what Christianity teaches.

- Baha'i
- Buddhism
- Hinduism

Baha'i

Founder: Baha'u'llah born Mirza Husayn-Ali Nuri

The Bahá'í Faith began with the mission entrusted by God to two Divine Messengers—the Báb and Bahá'u'lláh. Today, the distinctive unity of the Faith They founded stems from explicit instructions given by Bahá'u'lláh that have assured the continuity of guidance following His passing. This line of succession, referred to as the Covenant, went from Bahá'u'lláh to His Son 'Abdu'l-Bahá, and then from 'Abdu'l-Bahá to His grandson, Shoghi Effendi, and the Universal House of Justice, ordained by Bahá'u'lláh. A Bahá'í accepts the divine authority of the Báb and Bahá'u'lláh and of these appointed successors.

Key Statement: The Bahá'í Faith teaches the essential worth of all religions.

Beginning Date: Established by Bahá'u'lláh in 1863

Doctrinal Books or Materials

- Star of the West Brochure, 1913
- Baha'u'llah and Shoghi Effendi Gleanings from the Writings of Bahá'u'lláh, 2005.
- Schaefer, Udo The Light that Shineth in the Darkness
- The official Bahai website

Key Individuals in Baha'i

The Báb   (1819-1850)

The Báb is the Herald of the Bahá'í Faith. In the middle of the 19th century, he announced that he was the bearer of a message destined to transform humanity's spiritual life. His mission was to prepare the way for the coming of a second Messenger from God, greater than himself, who would usher in an age of peace and justice.

Bahá'u'lláh   (1817-1892)

Bahá'u'lláh, the "Glory of God", is the Promised One foretold by the Báb and all of the Divine Messengers of the past. Bahá'u'lláh delivered a new Revelation from God to humanity. Thousands of verses, letters and books flowed from his pen. In His Writings, he outlined a framework for the development of a global civilization which takes into account both the spiritual and material dimensions of human life. For this, he endured 40 years of imprisonment, torture and exile.

Abdu'l-Bahá   (1844-1921)

In His will, Bahá'u'lláh appointed His oldest son, 'Abdu'l-Bahá, as the authorized interpreter of His teachings and Head of the Faith. Throughout the East and West, 'Abdu'l-Bahá became known as an ambassador of peace, an exemplary human being, and the leading exponent of a new Faith.

Shoghi Effendi (1897-1957)

Appointed Guardian of the Bahá'í Faith by 'Abdu'l-Bahá, His eldest grandson, Shoghi Effendi, spent 36 years systematically nurturing the development, deepening the understanding, and strengthening the unity of the Bahá'í community, as it increasingly grew to reflect the diversity of the entire human race.

Current Leader: The Universal House of Justice (established 1963) The development of the Bahá'í Faith worldwide is today guided by the Universal House of Justice. In His book of laws, Bahá'u'lláh instructed the Universal House of Justice to exert a positive influence on the welfare of humankind, promote education, peace and global prosperity, and safeguard human honor and the position of religion.

Baha'i
Unique or Core Beliefs

Topic	Belief
Bible Inspiration	"You must realize that many of the things written in the New Testament were written long after Jesus died, hence it is impossible to have absolute accuracy in everything. It would be natural for His followers to assert such things, but the revelation of Baha'u'llah supersedes such claims" (Baha'i apologist and teacher Udo Schaefer as quoted in The Kingdom of the Cults by Walter Martin). "The revelation of Jesus was for His own dispensation, that of the Son, and now it is no longer the point of guidance to the world. Baha'is must be severed from all and everything that is past—things both good and bad—everything.....Now all is changed. All the teachings of the past are past" (Star of the West Brochure, 1913).
Jesus' Resurrection May not be True	"The alleged resurrection of Jesus and His ascension into heaven may or may not be true depending upon your point of view. As I said before, we are concerned with Baha'u'llah and the new era or age, and while we reverence Jesus as we do the great prophets of other religions, we do not believe that it is necessarily important that the Baha'i Faith recognize ever tenet of a specific religion. We believe that Jesus conquered death, that He triumphed over the grave, but these are things that are in the realm of the spirit and must receive spiritual interpretation. The revelation of Baha'u'llah supersedes such claims" (Baha'i apologist and teacher Udo Schaefer as quoted in The Kingdome of the Cults by Walter Martin).
Jesus is Only One of Nine Manifestations	"Jesus was only one of nine manifestations of the divine being and appeared in His era of time.....today Baha'u'llah is the source of revelation" (Baha'i apologist and teacher Udo Schaefer as quoted in The Kingdome of the Cults by Walter Martin). "God has sent Divine Messengers known as Manifestations of God—among them Abraham, Krishna, Zoroaster, Moses, Buddha, Jesus Christ, Muhammad, and, in more recent times, the Báb and Bahá'u'lláh—to cultivate humanity's spiritual, intellectual and moral capacities" (the official Bahai website). "They believe that Jesus was just one of nine manifestations of the divine being and He appeared in his era of time. Today the Ba'u'llah is the source of revelation" (Martin, 2003)
Christ's Sacrifice Not Essential for Salvation	"A Christian may find spiritual peace in believing in a substitutionary atonement. In Baha'ism this is unnecessary. That age is past. The new age of spiritual maturity has dawned through Baha'u'llah, and we are to listen to his word" (Baha'i apologist and teacher Udo Schaefer as quoted in The Kingdome of the Cults by Walter Martin).
Heaven is Not a Place	"The Bahá'í teachings state that there is no such physical place as heaven or hell, and emphasize the eternal journey of the soul towards perfection. They explain that references to "heaven" and "hell" in the Holy Scriptures of other religions are to be understood symbolically, describing states of nearness to and distance from God in this world and in the realms beyond. 'Abdu'l-Bahá has said

	that when human beings "become illuminated with the radiance of the sun of reality, and ennobled with all the virtues, they esteem this the greatest reward, and they know it to be the true paradise" (bahai'.org The Human Soul-Heaven and Hell). "We do believe in the paradise of God, which will be the abode of the righteous and in the resurrection and the final righting of all things" (Baha'i apologist and teacher Udo Schaefer as quoted in The Kingdom of the Cults by Walter Martin).
No Such thing As Hell and Eternal Flames	"We know nothing of eternal flames where sinners will be confined forever without respite" (Baha'i apologist and teacher Udo Schaefer as quoted in The Kingdom of the Cults by Walter Martin).
Baha'u'llah is the Coming of the Holy Spirit	"I believe it is your gospel of John that Jesus promised another Comforter who would abide always. We understand this to be the coming of Baha'u'llah, a direct fulfillment of the words of Jesus" (Baha'i apologist and teacher Udo Schaefer as quoted in The Kingdom of the Cults by Walter Martin).
Judgment	"The Baha'i faith recognizes divine judgment, though not in the graphic terms that Christians portray it. We know nothing of eternal flames where sinners will be confined forever without respite. We do believe in the paradise of God, which will be the abode of the righteous and in the resurrection and the final righting of all things (Baha'i apologist and teacher Udo Schaefer as quoted in The Kingdom of the Cults by Walter Martin).
Revelation	"The revelation of Jesus was for His own dispensation that of the Son, and now is no longer the point of guidance to the world. Baha'is must be severed from all and everything that is past---things both good and bad---everything. Now all is changed. All the teaching of the past are past" (Baha'i apologist and teacher Udo Schaefer as quoted in The Kingdom of the Cults by Walter Martin). "...the revelation of Baha'u'llah supersedes such claims (Baha'i apologist and teacher Udo Schaefer as quoted in The Kingdom of the Cults by Walter Martin). "The writings of Baha'u'llah, since they are the last manifestation, are to be considered the final authority in matters of religion so far as the Baha'i faith is concerned" (Baha'i apologist and teacher Udo Schaefer as quoted in The Kingdom of the Cults by Walter Martin). "It's robe is the Revelation vouchsafed unto it by God. Whenever this robe hath fulfilled its purpose, the Almighty will assuredly renew it. For every age requireth a fresh measure of the light of God. Every Divine Revelation hath been sent down in a manner that befitted the circumstances of the age in which it hath appeared" (Gleanings from the Writings of Bahá'u'lláh, XXXIV). "Many, unable to examine the claim of the Tah'a'u'llah objectively because they are not sufficiently unbiased and detached from their old-fashioned traditional doctrines, nevertheless pass judgment on the Cause of God" (55:2). (The Light that Shineth in the Darkness, Udo Schaefer).

Salvation after Death	"The Bahá'í teachings state that there is no such physical place as heaven or hell, and emphasize the eternal journey of the soul towards perfection. They explain that references to "heaven" and "hell" in the Holy Scriptures of other religions are to be understood symbolically, describing states of nearness to and distance from God in this world and in the realms beyond. 'Abdu'l-Bahá has said that when human beings "become illuminated with the radiance of the sun of reality, and ennobled with all the virtues, they esteem this the greatest reward, and they know it to be the true paradise" (bahai'.org The Human Soul-Heaven and Hell).
Salvation is Not Through Christ	"We accept the fact that no one is perfect, but by the practice of principles laid down by Bahu'u'llah and by making every effort through prayer and personal sacrifice to live in accord with the character of the divine being revealed in him, we can arrive at eventual salvation as you like to term it" (Martin, 1977 p. 256).
Believes in Reincarnation and Multiple Lives	"Baha'is believe that "afterlife" isn't just a static place, but rather a progression toward God.....Baha'is definitely believe in progress. The Baha'i teachings say that we human beings each progress spiritually in this world through our own actions and efforts; and that the human race itself progresses, too, moving from one stage of collective knowledge, education and understanding to the next" (Bahaiteachings.org Volume 4, p. 189). What this suggests is that all men eventually understand what needs to be done to progress toward god.
No Satan or the Devil	There is no entity that is Satan. "The reality underlying this question is that the evil spirit, Satan or whatever is interpreted as evil, refers to the lower nature in man. This baser nature is symbolized in various ways. In man there are two expressions, one is the expression of nature, the other the expression of the spiritual realm.... God has never created an evil spirit; all such ideas and nomenclature are symbols expressing the mere human or earthly nature of man. It is an essential condition of the soil of earth that thorns, weeds and fruitless trees may grow from it. Relatively speaking, this is evil; it is simply the lower state and baser product of nature" (Abdu'l-Baha, Promulgation of Universal Peace, Pg. 294–295). "The reality underlying this question is that the evil spirit, Satan or whatever is interpreted as evil, refers to the lower nature in man. This baser nature is symbolized in various ways. In man there are two expressions, one is the expression of nature, the other the expression of the spiritual realm.... God has never created an evil spirit; all such ideas and nomenclature are symbols expressing the mere human or earthly nature of man. It is an essential condition of the soil of earth that thorns, weeds and fruitless trees may grow from it. Relatively speaking, this is evil; it is simply the lower state and baser product of nature" (Abdu'l-Baha, Promulgation of Universal Peace, Pg. 294–295). "The meaning of the serpent is attachment to the human world" (Abdu'l-Baha, Some Answered Questions, Pg. 123).

Baha'u'llah is the Second Coming of Christ	The Baha'is claim that Baha'u'llah is the fulfillment of the Biblical prophecies of the return of Christ (Selections from the Writings of Abdu'l-Baha, 110-12). "Know that the return of Christ for a second time doth not mean what the people believe, but, rather, signifieth the One promised to come after Him. He shall come with the Kingdom of God and His power which hath surrounded the world. This power (or reign) is in the world of hearts and spirits and not in that of matter (or bodies). For the material world is not comparable to a single wing of a fly, or rather less in the sight of thy Lord, wert thou of those who know! Verily Christ came with His Kingdom from the beginning which hath no beginning and will come with His Kingdom to the eternity of eternities, inasmuch as in this sense Christ is an expression of the divine reality, the simple essence and heavenly entity which hath no beginning or ending. It hath appearance, arising and manifestation and setting in each of the cycles." (Abdu'l-Baha, Tablets of Abdu'l-Baha v1, Pg. 137).
No Trinity	Believes that God is one person as does Judaism and Islam. Cannot accept the idea that God is both three and one (Martin's Interview with Udo Schaefer, a well known Baha'i apologist and teacher).
Work for Salvation	"We accept the fact that no one is perfect, but by the practice of principles laid down by Baha'u'llah and by making every effort through prayer and personal sacrifice to live in accord with the character of the divine being revealed to him, we can arrive at eventual salvation as you like to term it" (Baha'i apologist and teacher Udo Schaefer as quoted in The Kingdom of the Cults by Walter Martin).

Buddhism

Founder: Siddhartha Gautama, the Buddha. He was born about 560 B.C. in northeastern India. in a place called Lumbini near the Himalayan foothills (present-day Nepal). His father was a raja or ruler. His family name was Gautama and he was given he name Siddhartha. Buddhism is an offshoot of Hinduism and is a Dharmic religion. Siddhartha Gautama became enlightened at Bodhgaya, India and delivered his first set of teachings at a deer park in Sarnath, India. He was not a god, a prophet or any kind of supernatural being.

Key Statement: The path to enlightenment is attained by utilizing morality, meditation and wisdom.

Beginning Date: Around the 5th century B.C.

Types of Buddhism: Buddhism can be broken down into three main schools. They are Theravada Buddhism, Mahayana Buddhism, and Vajrayana Buddhism. Most of their beliefs are similar with some varients.

Doctrinal Books

- Most consider the Pali Tripitaka text to be the most reliable reaching of Buddha. Pali canon, also called Tipitaka (Pali: "Triple Basket") or Tripitaka (Sanskrit), the complete canon, first recorded in Pali, of the Theravada ("Way of the Elders") branch of Buddhism. ... The Pali texts constitute the entire surviving body of literature in that language.

Calling story: Buddhism is centered upon the life and teachings of Gautama Buddha

God: Believes in a universal cosmic consciousness sometimes called the void. It is a non-personal essence. All Buddhists seek the state of Nirvana where they become one with the void.

Supreme Creator: Buddhism is a nontheistic religion, i.e., it does not believe in a supreme creator being a.k.a. God.

Salvation Obtained by: Salvation is achieved by following the Middle Path, the Four Noble Truths and the Eightfold Path. The goal is to attain enlightenment and be released from the cycle of rebirth and death, thus attaining Nirvana

The Middle Path or Way: "...the Middle Way refers to the Buddha's enlightened view of life and also the actions or attitudes that will create happiness for oneself and others; it is found in the ongoing, dynamic effort to apply Buddhist wisdom to the questions and challenges of life and society" (Soka Gakkai International Website).

Four Noble Truths: "The Four Aryan (or Noble) Truths are perhaps the most basic formulation of the Buddha's teaching. They are expressed as follows:

1. All existence is dukkha. The word dukkha has been variously translated as 'suffering', 'anguish', 'pain', or 'unsatisfactoriness'. The Buddha's insight was that our lives are a struggle, and we do not find ultimate happiness or satisfaction in anything we experience. This is the problem of existence.

2. The cause of dukkha is craving. The natural human tendency is to blame our difficulties on things outside ourselves. But the Buddha says that their actual root is to be found in the mind

itself. In particular our tendency to grasp at things (or alternatively to push them away) places us fundamentally at odds with the way life really is.

3. The cessation of dukkha comes with the cessation of craving. As we are the ultimate cause of our difficulties, we are also the solution. We cannot change the things that happen to us, but we can change our responses.

4 There is a path that leads from dukkha. Although the Buddha throws responsibility back on to the individual he also taught methods through which we can change ourselves, for example the Noble Eightfold Path" (the buddhist centre website).

Eightfold Path

"1. * Samma-Ditthi — Complete or Perfect Vision, also translated as right view or understanding. Vision of the nature of reality and the path of transformation.

2. Samma-Sankappa — Perfected Emotion or Aspiration, also translated as right thought or attitude. Liberating emotional intelligence in your life and acting from love and compassion. An informed heart and feeling mind that are free to practice letting go.

3. Samma-Vaca — Perfected or whole Speech. Also called right speech. Clear, truthful, uplifting and non-harmful communication.

4. Samma-Kammanta — Integral Action. Also called right action. An ethical foundation for life based on the principle of non-exploitation of oneself and others. The five precepts.

5. Samma-Ajiva — Proper Livelihood. Also called right livelihood. This is a livelihood based on correct action the ethical principal of non-exploitation. The basis of an Ideal society.

6. Samma-Vayama — Complete or Full Effort, Energy or Vitality. Also called right effort or diligence. Consciously directing our life energy to the transformative path of creative and healing action that fosters wholeness. Conscious evolution.

7. Samma-Sati — Complete or Thorough Awareness. Also called "right mindfulness". Developing awareness, "if you hold yourself dear watch yourself well". Levels of Awareness and mindfulness - of things, oneself, feelings, thought, people and Reality.

8. Samma-Samadhi — Full, Integral or Holistic Samadhi. This is often translated as concentration, meditation, absorption or one-pointedness of mind. None of these translations is adequate. Samadhi literally means to be fixed, absorbed in or established at one point, thus the first level of meaning is concentration when the mind is fixed on a single object. The second level of meaning goes further and represents the establishment, not just of the mind, but also of the whole being in various levels or modes of consciousness and awareness. This is Samadhi in the sense of enlightenment or Buddhahood" (Buddhist studies website).

FUNDAMENTAL BUDDHISTIC BELIEFS

The following beliefs were identified and agreed upon by the great Buddhistic teachers of the day. These beliefs are shown below:

1. Buddhists are taught to show the same tolerance, forbearance, and brotherly love to all men, without distinction; and an unswerving kindness towards the members of the animal kingdom.
2. The universe was evolved, not created; and it functions according to law, not according to the caprice of any God.

3. The truths upon which Buddhism is founded are natural. They have, we believe, been taught in successive kalpas, or world-periods, by certain illuminated beings called BUDDHAS, the name BUDDHA meaning Enlightened.

4. The fourth Teacher in the present kalpa was Sakya Muni, or Gautama Buddha, who was born in a Royal family in India about 2,500 years ago. He is an historical personage and his name was Sidhartha Gautama.

5. Sakya Muni taught that ignorance produces desire, unsatisfied desire is the cause of rebirth, and rebirth, the cause of sorrow. To get rid of sorrow therefore, it is necessary to escape rebirth ; to escape rebirth, it necessary to extinguish desire ; and to extinguish desire, it is necessary to destroy ignorance.

6. Ignorance fosters the belief that rebirth is a necessary thing. When ignorance is destroyed the worthlessness of every such rebirth, considered as an end in itself, is perceived, as well as the paramount need of adopting a course of life by which the necessity for such repeated rebirths can be abolished. Ignorance also begets the illusive and illogical idea that there is only one existence for man, and the other illusion that ~this -one life is followed by states of -unchangeable pleasure or torment.

7. The dispersion of all this ignorance can be attained by the perservering practice of an all embracing altruism in conduct, development of intelligence, wisdom in thought, and destruction of desire for the lower personal pleasures.

8. The desire to live being the cause of rebirth, when that is extinguished rebirths cease and the perfected individual attains by meditation that highest state of peace called Nirvana.

9. Sakya Muni taught that ignorance can be dispelled and sorrow removed by the knowledge of the four Noble Truths:
   - The miseries of existence ;
   - The cause productive of misery, which is the desire ever renewed of satisfying oneself without being able ever to secure that end ;
   - The destruction of that desire, or the estranging of oneself from it ;
   - The means of obtaining this destruction of desire. The means which he pointed out is called the Noble Eightfold Path:
     - Right Belief
     - Right Thought
     - Right Speech
     - Right Action
     - Right Means of Livelihood
     - Right Exertion
     - Right Remembrance
     - Right Meditation.

10. Right Meditation leads to spiritual enlightenment, or the development of that Buddha-like faculty which is latent in every man.

11. The essence of Buddhism, as summed up by the Tathagatha (Buddha) himself, as :
    - To cease from all sin,
    - To get virtue,
    - To purify the heart.

12. The universe is subject to a natural causation known as Karma. The merits and demerits of a being in past existences determine his condition in the present one. Each man, therefore, has prepared the causes of the effects which he now experiences.

13. The obstacles to the attainment of good karma may be removed by the observance of the following precepts, which are embraced in the moral code of Buddhism:
    (1) Kill not
    (2) Steal not
    (3) Indulge in no forbidden sexual pleasure
    (4) Lie not

14. Take no intoxication or stupefying drug or liquor.

15. Buddhism discourages superstitious credulity. Gautama Buddha taught it to be the duty of a parent to have his child educated in science and literature. He also taught that no

one should believe what is spoken by any sage, written in any book, or affirmed by tradition, unless it accord with reason.

Drafted as a common platform upon which all Buddhists can agree (The Buddhist Catechism by Henry S. Olcott).   Publication Division MINISTRY OF CULTURAL AFFAIRS 135, Dharmapala Mawatha, Colombo 7 SRI LANKA 1903.

Approved and recommended for use in Buddhist Schools by H. SUMANGALA, Pradhana Nayaka Sthavira, High Priest of Sripada and the Western Province and Principal of the Vidyodaya Pirrftna.

Good Karma, Bad Karma

Good karma. Actions which create good wholesome karma are set out as:

- Generosity
- Morality
- Reverence
- Meditation
- Service to the community
- Transference of merit
- Rejoicing about other's good fortune
- Hearing the teaching
- Explaining the teaching
- Understanding the teaching correctly

Some of the benefits of good karma are birth in fortunate circumstances, opportunity to live according to the Dhamma and happiness.

Bad karma. Actions which create bad unwholesome karma are set out in three sections as:

Three caused by actions:
- Harming living beings (killing)
- Stealing (defined as taking what is not one's own)
- Misuse of the senses (sexual misconduct)

Four caused by speech:
- Lying
- Slander
- Harsh speech
- Frivolous talk (i.e. gossip etc.)

Three caused by mind:
- Attachment
- Ill will (anger)
- Ignorance

The above information on Karma show above is taken from, The Buddhist Society website, Karma - Actions and Results.

Buddhism Unique or Core Beliefs	
Topics	**Belief**
Inspiration of Bible	"Buddhists do not believe in the Bible. The Tripitaka (Pali Canon), Mahayana Sutras and the Tibetan Book of the Dead are three major noncanonical Buddhist texts" (The Buddhist Society Website).
The Universe Evolved	"The universe was evolved, not created; and it functions according to law, not according to the caprice of any God" (Fundamental Buddhistic Beliefs).
There is no creator	Hinayana Buddhism, consistently rejects the notion of a creator deity. If here is no creator, then he obviously cannot change. "The Buddha did not teach that a God created the Universe" (The Buddhist Society at(The Buddhist Society Website).
Levels of hell depending on Karma	According to Theravada Buddhism. there are 31 planes, or forms of beings, 6 floors of heaven. and 7 floors of hell. They are: 1) 20 planes of Brahmas. or higher spiritual beings; 2)6 planes of Nats or Devas. or lower spiritual beings; 3) Human existence; 4) Animals; 5) Peta. Apaya beings-in-woe; 6) Asuraka. Apaya beings in-semi-woe; 7) Hell. beings-in-torment. composed of 8 floors. (Source: Myanmar Travel Information; Facts and Details Website, Buddhism Cosmology, Death, Heaven and Hell).
No heaven instead Nirvana.	"Heaven has traditionally been viewed as a stop on the way to enlightenment not an end to itself. Beings in heaven have not yet achieved enlightenment and are subject to rebirth (Facts and Details Website, Buddhism Cosmology, Death, Heaven and Hell). The bhikshu, full of delight, who is calm in the doctrine of Buddha will reach the quiet place (Nirvana), cessation of natural desires, and happiness (Dhammapada V. 381).
No God	First, there is the more predominant belief of a "Creator God" in major religions. That concept is of course in direct contradiction with not only Buddha Dhamma, but also with modern science. Both Buddha Dhamma and modern science are based on the Principle of Causality: There must be a cause(s) for each and every effect (What Does Buddha Dhamma Say about Creator, Satan, Angels, and Demons? puredhamma.net). Thus there is no "Creator God" or a "Satan". It is each person acting on his/her own free will that is committing good or bad acts. But it is a complex issue, because what we are today is the kind of "cumulative result" of all our actions in the deep past through our previous lives. These can be condensed as our character (or "gati" or "gathi") or sansaric habits (or "āsavas")" (What Does Buddha Dhamma Say about Creator, Satan, Angels, and Demons? puredhamma.net).
No Devil or Satan	Thus there is no "Creator God" or a "Satan". It is each person acting on his/her own free will that is committing good or bad acts. But it is a complex issue, because what we are today is the kind of "cumulative result" of all our actions in the deep past through our previous lives.

	These can be condensed as our character (or "gati" or "gathi") or sansaric habits (or "āsavas")" (What Does Buddha Dhamma Say about Creator, Satan, Angels, and Demons? puredhamma.net).
	There is no entity that is Satan. "The reality underlying this question is that the evil spirit, Satan or whatever is interpreted as evil, refers to the lower nature in man. This baser nature is symbolized in various ways. In man there are two expressions, one is the expression of nature, the other the expression of the spiritual realm.... God has never created an evil spirit; all such ideas and nomenclature are symbols expressing the mere human or earthly nature of man. It is an essential condition of the soil of earth that thorns, weeds and fruitless trees may grow from it. Relatively speaking, this is evil; it is simply the lower state and baser product of nature" (Abdu'l-Baha, Promulgation of Universal Peace, Pg. 294–295).
	"The reality underlying this question is that the evil spirit, Satan or whatever is interpreted as evil, refers to the lower nature in man. This baser nature is symbolized in various ways. In man there are two expressions, one is the expression of nature, the other the expression of the spiritual realm.... God has never created an evil spirit; all such ideas and nomenclature are symbols expressing the mere human or earthly nature of man. It is an essential condition of the soil of earth that thorns, weeds and fruitless trees may grow from it. Relatively speaking, this is evil; it is simply the lower state and baser product of nature" (Abdu'l-Baha, Promulgation of Universal Peace, Pg. 294–295).
	"The meaning of the serpent is attachment to the human world" (Abdu'l-Baha, Some Answered Questions, Pg. 123).
Rebirth (Similar to Reincarnation)	"The universe is subject to a natural causation known as Karma. The merits and demerits of a being in past existences determine his condition in the present one. Each man, therefore, has prepared the causes of the effects which he now experiences" (Fundamental Buddhistic Beliefs).
	Rebirth is another key doctrine in Buddhism and it goes hand in hand with karma. There is a subtle difference between rebirth and reincarnation as expounded in Hinduism. Buddhism rejects the theory of a transmigrating permanent soul, whether created by a god or emanating from a divine essence.
Salvation Not Through Christ	"The bhikshu, full of delight, who is calm in the doctrine of Buddha will reach the quiet place (Nirvana), cessation of natural desires, and happiness" (Dhammapada V. 381).
Soul	"Buddhists do not believe that there is anything everlasting or unchangeable in human beings, no soul or self in which a stable sense of 'I' might anchor itself" (The Buddhist Society at www.thebuddhistsociety.org).
Work for Salvation	"The bhikshu, full of delight, who is calm in the doctrine of Buddha will reach the quiet place (Nirvana), cessation of natural desires, and happiness" (Dhammapada Vs. 381).

Karma and the Mind	"Mind foreruns all conditions [....] they are mind made. If one speaks or acts with a wicked mind, because of that, pain follows one. If one speaks or acts with a good mind, because of that, happiness follows one" (The Dhammapada, Vs. 1 and 2).

Hinduism

Founder: Hinduism does not have a definite founder associated with it. It is called Santana dharma.

Key Statement: The goal is to reach nirvana and become one with 'god'.

Beginning Date: Those that follow Hinduism believe it to be the oldest of all the living religions. It is a religion that has always existed. However, most scholars believe it started between 2300 B.C. and 1500 B.C. in the Indus Valley. This is near current day Pakistan.

Deity: Krishna is a Hindu deity, usually worshiped as the supreme god or as the eighth incarnation of Vishnu the Preserver, depending on the specific Hindu tradition.

Doctrinal Books

According to the Hindu American Foundation (HAF) the following works are important for understanding Hinduism.

Shruti

► Vedas: The word Veda means "knowledge". There are four Vedas: Rig, Sama, Yajur and Atharva, of which the Rig Veda is the oldest.

► Upanishads: These texts, numbering over 100, contain an extensive exploration of the methods of understanding the self, God, and the nature of the world.

Smriti

► Upavedas: The Upavedas consist of four main texts, including:

- Ayurveda - science of health and life
- Dhanurveda - science of warfare
- Gandharvaveda - the study of aesthetics, and delineates art forms
- Arthashastra - guidance on public administration, governance, economy, and politics

► Puranas: Stories in the Puranas translate the meanings of the ancient Shruti scriptures and teach them to the masses by explaining the teachings of the Vedas and Upanishads through stories and parables. There are 18 major Puranas (Mahapuranas) and many minor ones (upapuranas).

► Ramayana: This popular epic tells the life story the noble prince named Rama, whom Hindus believe to be an incarnation of the Divine. Prince Rama suffers fourteen years of exile and many hardships while destroying powerful demons before returning to rule his kingdom. There are numerous versions of the Ramayana, of which the most well-known are those by the original author Sage Valmiki and the poet-saint Tulsidas.

► Mahabharata: With over 100,000 verses, the Mahabharata is a historical epic, and is the longest poem the world has known. Based on an extended conflict between two branches of the Kaurava family, the Mahabharata is a trove of stories and discourses on the practice of Dharma, including the importance of truth, justice, self sacrifice, and the upholding of Dharma, the need for complete devotion to God, and the ultimate futility of war

▶ Bhagavad Gita: The Bhagavad Gita is a primary scripture for Hindus. Although it is a tiny part of the Mahabharata and technically classed as a Smriti text, it is traditionally accorded the rank of an Upanishad. It is meant to help one understand that upholding dharma can be challenging, especially in situations where there is not a clear right or wrong.

▶ Agama Shastras: Ancient and numerous, including many that have been lost over the centuries, these texts deal with practical aspects of devotion and worship, including personal and temple rituals and practices.

- Hinduism has multiple gods: Brahma, Vishnu, Siva, Rama, and Krishna.
- Hinduism believes in polytheism, pantheism, and the use of images.
- Hinduism believes in reincarnation
- Hinduism believes in nirvana.

The term Hinduism refers to the religious and social institutions of India. The highest written authorities in Hinduism are the Vedas.

Lesser authorities include the epic poems Ramayana and Mahabhrata. The latter includes the Bhagavad-gita (BG, p. 24). These are not considered quite as high in authority as the Vedas, yet in practice they have had greater popular influence.

"The Absolute Truth is contained in the Vedas, the oldest scriptures in the world. The essence of the Vedas is found in the Bhagavad-gita, a literal record of Krishna's words" - (Back, inside front cover; cf. BG, p. 13).

The Brahmanas are authoritative commentaries on the basic Vedas. Upanishads and Aranyakas are more recent writings generally considered authoritative.

In addition, the highest caste called the Brahmans (religious teachers) are considered authorities.

Hindus do not claim these authorities were all revealed by a direct, deliberate act of God (as the Bible claims to have been). In general Hindus believe God is everywhere in nature, and godly men can perceive the truth revealed within or around them. These Scriptures are viewed as truths these godly men have perceived from their own study. The Bhagavad-gita, however, does claim to be the very words of Krishna.

"The recommended means for achieving the mature stage of love of God ... is to chant the holy names of the Lord. The easiest method for most people is to chant the Hare Krishna mantra: Hare Krishna, Hare Krishna, Krishna Krishna, Hare Hare Hare Rama, Hare Rama, Rama Rama, Hare Hare" (Back - inside front cover).

Karma: "Karma is the universal principle of cause and effect. Our actions, both good and bad, come back to us in the future, helping us to learn from life's lessons and become better people" (www.Hinduismtoday.com   Hinduism Magazine). The individual soul passes through a cycle of successive lives and its next incarnation is always dependent on how the previous life was lived (good or bad karma). Hinduism explains that the soul reincarnates until all karmas are resolved and God Realization is attained. By ending the cycle, the individual will no longer endure the pain and suffering of earthly existence performed countless times over. (Go to hinduismtoday.com or look at the books listed in this work). Also see Reincarnation and Death on page 148-149.

Cows and Hinduism: "The only cow-question for Hindus is, "Why don't more people respect and protect this remarkable creature?" Mahatma Gandhi once said, "One can measure the greatness of a nation and its moral progress by the way it treats its animals. Cow protection to me is not mere protection of the cow. It means protection of all that lives and is helpless and weak in the world. The cow means the entire subhuman world" (www.Hinduismtoday.com   Hinduism Magazine).

Hinduism Unique or Core Beliefs	
Topic	**Belief**

Creation	The creation account from the Vishnu Purana, wherein Vishnu, lying on an ocean of milk atop the serpent Sesha, sprung a lotus from his naval that contained the god Brahma. Having been sprung from Vishnu's navel, Brahma creates all living beings, as well as the sun, moon, planets, etc. and a number of other gods and demigods. Following Brahma's creative acts, it is then said that Vishnu expanded himself into Ksirodakasayi Visnu (Paramatma) and entered into everything that exists in the material and immaterial spheres" (Patheos Library of World Faiths & Religions: What is the creation story in Hinduism?).
	
	"...most Hindu creation accounts articulate a fundamental nondualism, wherein the material world-which is either fully divine or is, at least, infused with divinity-emanates from (as opposed to being created by) the principal deity. Two popular Hindu creations stories come from the Brihadaranyaka Upanishad and the Vishnu Purana. Both accounts demonstrate the fundamental nondualism typical of most Hindu creation accounts.
	
	   1) Brhadaryanka Upanishad 1.4: the world is said to have come into existence because the Primeval One, having become bored being the only being in existence, split Itself into a variety of forms and manifestations (i.e., the material world and all of its beings) so that, through them, It could experience a loving and playful relationship with Itself.
	
	   2) The creation account from the Vishnu Purana, wherein Vishnu, lying on an ocean of milk atop the serpent Sesha, sprung a lotus from his naval that contained the god Brahma. Having been sprung from Vishnu's navel, Brahma creates all living beings, as well as the sun, moon, planets, etc. and a number of other gods and demigods. Following Brahma's creative acts, it is then said that Vishnu expanded himself into Ksirodakasayi Visnu (Paramatma) and entered into everything that exists in the material and immaterial spheres" (Patheos Library of World Faiths & Religions: What is the creation story in Hinduism?).

Bible Inspiration	"The Absolute Truth is contained in the Vedas, the oldest scriptures in the world. The essence of the Vedas is found in the Bhagavad-gita, a literal record of Krishna's words" - (Back, inside front cover; cf. BG, p. 13).
Good Deeds to improve circumstances in the future (next life)	By doing good deeds in this life, therefore, one can improve his circumstances in the future, especially in future reincarnations (Bhagavad Gita, p. 9,10). "Each soul is free to find his own way, whether by devotion, austerity, meditation, yoga or selfless service ... Hindus believe that no religion teaches the only way to salvation above all others, but that all genuine paths are facets of God's Light, deserving tolerance and understanding." Hinduism Today

Salvation is ultimate liberation from life death cycle	"Hindus believe that the soul reincarnates, evolving through many births until all karmas have been resolved, and moksha, liberation from the cycle of rebirth, is attained. Not a single soul will be deprived of this destiny." (www.Hinduismtoday.com Hinduism Magazine). "Salvation, for the Hindu, can be achieved in one of three ways: the way of works, the way of knowledge, or the way of devotion. The Way of Works- karma marga, is the path to salvation through religious. duty. The Way of Knowledge- another way of achieving salvation in the Hindu sense is the way of knowledge. The way of devotion- bhakti, is chronologically the last of the three ways of salvation. It is that devotion to a deity which may be reflected in acts of worship, both public and private" (HINDUISM AND CONCEPT OF SALVATION {With special reference to The Bhagavad Gita} Tahira Basharat. "All performance of dharma is meant for ultimate liberation (moksha). It should not be performed for material gain. Furthermore, one who is engaged in the ultimate occupational service (dharma) should not use material gain (artha) simply for sense gratification (karma)" (Bhagavat Purana 1.2.9). To explain, dharma or righteousness. Artha is economic development. Karma is sensual enjoyment. Moksha is the liberation or the ultimate goal man. Salvation for a Hindu is called Moksha. Moksha is achieved through union with God. Moksha occurs when an enlightened human being is freed from the cycle of life-and-death (the endless cycle of death and reincarnation) and comes into a state of completeness. He then becomes one with God.
Reincarnation and Death	On Reincarnation: "Yes, we believe the soul is immortal and takes birth time and time again. Through this process, we have experiences, learn lessons and evolve spiritually…[reincarnation] continues its long pilgrimage until it is one with God." (www.Hinduismtoday.com Hinduism Magazine). Hinduism teaches Reincarnation which states that our actions, both good and bad, come back to us in the future, helping us to learn from life's lessons and become better people. After many lifetimes of following dharma, the soul is fully matured in love, wisdom and knowledge of God. There is no longer a need for physical birth, for all lessons have been learned, all karmas fulfilled. That soul is then liberated, freed from the cycle of birth, death and rebirth. Evolution then continues in the more refined spiritual worlds….Hindus believe that the soul reincarnates, evolving through many births until all karmas have been resolved, and moksha, liberation from the cycle of rebirth, is attained. Not a single soul will be deprived of this destiny." (www.Hinduismtoday.com Hinduism Magazine). "Hinduism explains that the soul reincarnates until all karmas are resolved and God Realization is attained. All souls, without exception, will attain this highest spiritual summit, though it may take many lives. This is a mystical religion ... finally reaching the pinnacle of consciousness where man and God are forever one" (Hinduism Today).

	At Death: "At death the soul leaves the physical body. But the soul does not die. It lives on in a subtle body called the astral body. The astral body exists in the nonphysical dimension called the astral plane, which is also the world we are in during our dreams at night when we sleep. Here we continue to have experiences until we are reborn again in another physical body as a baby" (www.Hinduismtoday.com Hinduism Magazine). All men will eventually be released from the cycle of birth and death to merge with the One Soul (Brahma). "Moksha comes when all extraneous karmas have been resolved and God has been fully realized. This means that before Moksha, the soul must have gone through all the experiences of life in the physical world. Once having faced in the spirit of love and understanding all of these various and varies experiences, Moksha comes and marks the way-station where the liberated soul is free from rebirth. When our soul has sufficiently evolved and undergone all necessary karmas in this physical universe and God-Realization has been attained, it will not return to the First World (KARMA AND REINCARNATION: Insights on Two Fundamental Hindu Concepts From the Teachings of Sivaya Subramuniyaswami, Hinduism Today Magazine, July 1987).
Heaven or Eternal Life. Heaven is not a place. Eternal life is ceasing to exist and become part of an impersonal 'God'	To the Hindu, therefore, punishment consists of continuing to exist on earth. "Eternal life" consists of ceasing to exist in a bodily form and becoming part of the impersonal God. There is no concept of a bodily resurrection, and no ultimate punishment of the wicked. In fact, there is no ultimate spirit being who opposes God or urges men to do evil. So, all will eventually progress, after a sufficient number of lives, to liberation, (Bhagavad Gita, p. 19-28; WR142-144; EB-III, 1014; EB-XI, 580; cf. Renou, 40-44).
Hell or Eternal Punishment	"There is no eternal hell, no damnation in Hinduism, and no intrinsic evil--no satanic force that opposes the will of God" (Hinduism Today, 9/2011).
Foods Prohibited	"Hindus teach vegetarianism as a way to live with a minimum of hurt to other beings. But in today's world not all Hindus are vegetarians...... Priests and religious leaders are definitely vegetarian, so as to maintain a high level of purity and spiritual consciousness to fulfill their responsibilities, and to awaken the refined areas of their nature" (www.Hinduismtoday.com Hinduism Magazine).
God is more essence or all things	Brahman is 'world soul' or 'cosmic soul'. It is the eternal essence of the universe and the ultimate divine reality. It is God in a sense, but nothing like the God of Christians. In the Brihadaranyaka Upanishad 1.4.10 it means, 'I am Brahman'. In the Chandogya Upanishad 3.14.1 it is communicated as 'All this is Brahman'. In the Chandogya Upanishad 6.2.1 it means 'That [Brahman] is one, without a second'. In the Itareya Upanishad 3.3.7 it means, 'Knowledge is Brahman'. So, the essence of 'God' can be seen everywhere in everything. It's not a matter of God changing. It's a matter of God being multiple things depending on the source you read. So, it appears that within Hinduism 'God' has changed and been defined in multiple ways,

No Devil or Satan	"In fact, there is no ultimate spirit being who opposes God or urges men to do evil. So, all will eventually progress, after a sufficient number of lives, to liberation, (Bhagavad Gita, p. 19-28; WR142-144; EB-III, 1014; EB-XI, 580; cf. Renou, 40-44). "There is no....satanic force that opposes the will of God" (Hinduism Today, 9/2011).
More than one God	"Hindus all believe in one Supreme God who created the universe. He is all-pervasive. He created many Gods, highly advanced spiritual beings, to be His helpers" (www.Hinduismtoday.com Hinduism Magazine). Idols: "Hindus do not worship a stone or metal "idol" as God. We worship God through the image. We invoke the presence of God from the higher, unseen worlds, into the image so that we can commune with Him and receive His blessings......The stone or metal deity images in Hindu temples and shrines are not mere symbols of the Gods. They are the form through which their love, power and blessings flood forth into this world" (www.Hinduismtoday.com Hinduism Magazine).

Contradictions Between the Bible and Various Beliefs or Interpretations

Section Four
* Identifies Specific False Doctrines being Taught
Note: Spaces have been included for each doctrine that allow you to add scriptures if desired.

Baptism (BAP)
Baptism for the Dead (BD)*
Bible Inspiration (BI)
Born of God (BOG)*
Consciousness or Life After Death (LAD)
Death (DE)
Elder Qualifications (EQ)
Foods Prohibited (FP)*
Forgiveness of Sins (FOS)
God Created the World (GCW)
God Is Spirit (GS)
God and Creation Separate (GCS)
God and Man Separate (GMS)
God Causes Some to Go Astray (GCA)*
God Never Changes   (GNC)
Heavenly Deception   (HD)*
Heaven Is A Place (HAP)
Hell is Eternal (EH)
Holy Spirit (HS)
Infallibility (INF)*
Infant Baptism   (IB)
Jesus' Birth (JB)
Jesus' Blood Sufficient (JBS)
Jesus Is The Christ—Deity   (JIC)
Jesus Is Eternal   (JE)
Jesus' Mission   (JM)
Jesus' Physical Death   (JPD)
Jesus' Physical Resurrection (JPR)
Jesus was Sinless (JS)
Judged By Grace through Faith (JGF)

Judgment Day (JMT)
Kingdom Established (KE)
Lord's Supper or Communion (LS)
Mary: Perpetual Virgin (MPV)*
Mary was Sinless (MS)*
Old Law Void (OLV)
Once Saved Always Saved (OSAS)
One Christ   (OC)
One God   (OG)
One Heaven (OH)
One Mediator   (OM)
Original Sin   (OS)
Priests   (PR)
Purgatory   (PUR)*
Reincarnation/Rebirth/Reorganization (RN)*
Relationship with Unbelievers (RU)
Revelation--Current Day Prophecy (RV)*
Sabbath or Sunday   (SOS)
Saints   (STS)*
Salvation before Death (SBD)
Salvation-Most Men Lost (MML)
Salvation Through Christ (STC)
Satan-Devil (SAT)
Second Coming   (SC)
Sin (SIN)
Tithing or Giving (TI)
Trinity Or Godhead   (TR)
Unconditional Election (UE)
Virgin Birth   (VB)

Baptism

Biblical Code: BAP

Bible: The following scriptures state that, "He saved us, not because of works done by us in righteousness, but according to his own mercy, by the washing of regeneration and renewal of the Holy Spirit" (Titus 3:5). This Scripture shows that God regenerates or makes us righteous through baptism….and the Holy Spirit now renews us as He works in our lives. Those who believe, put on Christ at baptism (Galatians 3:26-27). In 1 Peter 3:21 we are told that baptism saves us. If we simply look at the Scriptures, they clearly say that baptism is part of the salvation process…it is part of the God process that changes us. We can also see that baptism was initiated by those who had chosen to believe in Jesus Christ (Mark 16:16). The book titled, Grace and Salvation, by this author, addresses this issue in multiple ways. Last, the conversion examples of baptism by immersion are clearly seen in Acts (See conversion examples below).

Scripture	Content
Acts 2:38	And Peter said to them, "**Repent and be baptized** every one of you in the name of Jesus Christ for the forgiveness of your sins, and you will receive the gift of the Holy Spirit."
Matthew 28:18-20	And Jesus came and said to them, "All authority in heaven and on earth has been given to me. Go therefore and make disciples of all nations, **baptizing them in the name of the Father and of the Son and of the Holy Spirit**, teaching them to observe all that I have commanded you. And behold, I am with you always, to the end of the age."
Mark 16:15-16	And he said to them, "Go into all the world and proclaim the gospel to the whole creation. Whoever **believes and is baptized will be saved**, but whoever does not believe will be condemned.
John 3:5	Jesus answered, "Truly, truly, I say to you, unless one is **born of water and the Spirit,** he cannot enter the kingdom of God."
2 Corinthians 5:17	17 Therefore, if anyone is in Christ, he **is a new creation**. The old has passed away; behold, the new has come.
1 Peter 3:21	**Baptism, which corresponds to this, now saves** you, not as a removal of dirt from the body but as an appeal to God for a good conscience, through the resurrection of Jesus Christ.
Acts 22:16	And now why do you wait? **Rise and be baptized** and wash away your sins, calling on his name.
Romans 6:3	Do you not know that all of us who have **been baptized into Christ Jesus were baptized into his death**?
1 Corinthians 12:13	For in one Spirit we were all **baptized into one body**—Jews or Greeks, slaves or free—and all were made to drink of one Spirit.
Galatians 3:26-27	For in Christ Jesus you are all sons of God, through faith. For as many of you as were **baptized into Christ have put on Christ**.

Titus 3:5	He saved us, not because of works done by us in righteousness, but according to his own mercy, by the **washing of regeneration** and renewal of the Holy Spirit.
Conversion Examples	Acts 2:37-41; 8:12; 8:13; 8:26-40; 10:34-48; 16:14-15; 16:25-34; 18:8; 19:1-7; 22:1-16 (See appendix for chart and chain if desired.)

Catholicism

Pouring water for baptism: "The essential rite of Baptism consists in immersing the candidate in water or pouring water on his head, while pronouncing the invocation of the Most Holy Trinity: the Father, the Son, and the Holy Spirit" (Catechism 1278).

Baptism of Blood: "The Church has always held the firm conviction that those who suffer death for the sake of the faith without having received Baptism are baptized by their death for and with Christ. This Baptism of blood, like the desire for Baptism, brings about the fruits of Baptism without being a sacrament" (Catechism 1259).

"For catechumens who die before their Baptism, their explicit desire to receive it, together with repentance for their sins, and charity, assures them the salvation that they were not able to receive through the sacrament" (Catechism 1259).

Christian Science

"Christian Science has one faith, one Lord, one baptism; and this faith builds on Spirit, not matter; and this baptism is the purification of the mind, --- not an ablution of the body, but tears of repentance, an overflowing love, washing away the motives for sin; yea, it is love leaving self for God (The Peoples Idea of God, 1936).

"Our baptism is a purification from all error" (Science and Health, Pg. 35).

Mormonism

"Under the direction of the presiding authority, a worthy priest or Melchizedek Priesthood holder may perform the ordinance of baptism. To do so, he:
1. Stands in the water with the person to be baptized.
2. Holds the person's right wrist with his left hand (for convenience and safety); the person being baptized holds the priesthood holder's left wrist with his or her left hand.
3. Raises his right arm to the square.
4. States the person's full name and says, "Having been commissioned of Jesus Christ, I baptize you in the name of the Father, and of the Son, and of the Holy Ghost. Amen" (D&C 20:73).
5. Have the person hold his or her nose with the right hand (for convenience). The priesthood holder places his right hand high on the person's back and immerses the person completely, including the person's clothing.
6. Helps the person come up out of the water.

Two priests or Melchizedek Priesthood holders witness each baptism to make sure it is performed properly. The baptism must be repeated if the words are not spoken exactly as given in Doctrine and Covenants" (Missionary Handbook, 2006).

Baptism for the Dead

Biblical Code: BD

Bible: In Hebrews 9:27 it makes it abundantly clear that you cannot change a person's state once he is dead. It says, "And just as it is appointed for man to die once, and after that comes judgment." You die and then there is judgment. There are no second chances. If you are not a Christian you must repent of your sinful lifestyle (Romans 3:23), confess the name of Jesus (Romans 10:9-10) and then be baptized for the Remission of your sins (Acts 2:38). No one can do that for another person. The following scriptures state that the individual must take actions to be saved. Repentance and being baptized in one. Believing and being baptized is another. Belief and confession is another. In all cases the words were given to a living person or group of people in order to explain what needed to be done if they were to be saved and become one of God's children.

Scripture	Content
Acts 2:38	And Peter said to them, "**Repent and be baptized** every one of you in the name of Jesus Christ for the forgiveness of your sins, and you will receive the gift of the Holy Spirit."
Hebrews 9:27	"And just as it is appointed for man to **die once, and after that comes judgment,**"
Revelation 20:11-15	"Then I saw a great white throne and him who was seated on it. From his presence earth and sky fled away, and no place was found for them. And I saw the dead, great and small, standing before the throne, and books were opened. Then another book was opened, which is the book of life. **And the dead were judged by what was written in the books, according to what they had done.** And the sea gave up the dead who were in it, Death and Hades gave up the dead who were in them, and they were judged, each one of them, according to what they had done. Then Death and Hades were thrown into the lake of fire. This is the second death, the lake of fire. And if anyone's name was not found written in the book of life, he was thrown into the lake of fire."
2 Corinthians 6:1-2	Working together with him, then, we appeal to you not to receive the grace of God in vain. For he says, "In a favorable time I listened to you, and in a day of salvation I have helped you. "Behold, now is the favorable time; behold, **now is the day of salvation."**
Mark 16:16	"Whoever **believes and is baptized will be saved**, but whoever does not believe will be condemned."
Romans 10:8-17	"But what does it say? "The word is near you, in your mouth and in your heart" (that is, the word of faith that we proclaim); because, if you confess with your mouth that Jesus is Lord and believe in your heart that God raised him from the dead, you will be saved. For with the heart one believes and is justified, and with the mouth one confesses and is saved. For the Scripture says, "Everyone who believes in him will not be put to shame." For there is no distinction between Jew and Greek; for the same Lord is Lord of all, bestowing his riches on all who call on him. **For "everyone who calls on the name of the Lord will be saved." How then will**

	they call on him in whom they have not believed? And how are they to believe in him of whom they have never heard? And how are they to hear without someone preaching? And how are they to preach unless they are sent? As it is written, "How beautiful are the feet of those who preach the good news!" But they have not all obeyed the gospel. For Isaiah says, "Lord, who has believed what he has heard from us?" So faith comes from hearing, and hearing through the word of Christ."

Catholicism

Baptism of Blood: "The Church has always held the firm conviction that those who suffer death for the sake of the faith without having received Baptism are baptized by their death for and with Christ. This Baptism of blood, like the desire for Baptism, brings about the fruits of Baptism without being a sacrament" (Catechism 1259).

"For catechumens who die before their Baptism, their explicit desire to receive it, together with repentance for their sins, and charity, assures them the salvation that they were not able to receive through the sacrament" (Catechism 1259).

Mormonism

28 "For there is not a place found on earth that he may come to and restore again that which was lost unto you, or which he hath taken away, even the fulness of the priesthood. 29 For a baptismal font there is not upon the earth, that they, my saints, may be baptized for those who are dead—30 For this ordinance belongeth to my house, and cannot be acceptable to me, only in the days of your poverty, wherein ye are not able to build a house unto me. 31 But I command you, all ye my saints, to build a house unto me; and I grant unto you a sufficient time to build a house unto me; and during this time your baptisms shall be acceptable unto me. 32 But behold, at the end of this appointment your baptisms for your dead shall not be acceptable unto me; and if you do not these things at the end of the appointment ye shall be rejected as a church, with your dead, saith the Lord your God. 33 For verily I say unto you, that after you have had sufficient time to build a house to me, wherein the ordinance of baptizing for the dead belongeth, and for which the same was instituted from before the foundation of the world, your baptisms for your dead cannot be acceptable unto me; 34 For therein are the keys of the holy priesthood ordained, that you may receive honor and glory. 35 And after this time, your baptisms for the dead, by those who are scattered abroad, are not acceptable unto me, saith the Lord. 36 For it is ordained that in Zion, and in her stakes, and in Jerusalem, those places which I have appointed for refuge, shall be the places for your baptisms for your dead" (Doctrine and Covenants, 124:28-36).

Bible Inspiration

Biblical Code: BI

Bible: The following scriptures tell us that prophecy of Scripture occurred as a result of men being moved by the Holy Spirit spoke from God (2 Peter 1:20-21). We are also told that, "All Scripture is breathed out by God…" (2 Timothy 3:16-17). In addition, the New Testament writers were "…taught by the Spirit, combining spiritual thoughts with spiritual words."

Scripture	Content
2 Peter 1:3	His divine power has **granted to us all things that pertain to life and godliness**, through the knowledge of him who called us to his own glory and excellence,
John 14:26	But the Helper, the Holy Spirit, whom the Father will send in my name, he will **teach you all things and bring to your remembrance** all that I have said to you.
John 16:12-15	I still have many things to say to you, but you cannot bear them now. When the Spirit of truth comes, **he will guide you into all the truth,** for he will not speak on his own authority, but whatever he hears he will speak, and he will declare to you the things that are to come. He will glorify me, for he will take what is mine and declare it to you. All that the Father has is mine; therefore I said that he will take what is mine and declare it to you.
1 Corinthians 2:13	which things we also speak, not in words taught by human wisdom, but in **those taught by the Spirit**, combining spiritual thoughts with spiritual words.
2 Timothy 3:16-17	All Scripture is breathed out by God and profitable for teaching, for reproof, for correction, and for training in righteousness, **that the man of God may be competent, equipped for every good work**.
Hebrews 1:1-2	God, after He spoke long ago to the fathers in the prophets in many portions and in many ways, **in these last days has spoken to us in His Son**, whom He appointed heir of all things, through whom also He made the world.
2 Peter 1:20-21	But know this first of all, that no prophecy of Scripture is a matter of one's own interpretation, for no prophecy was ever made by an act of human will, but **men moved by the Holy Spirit spoke from God.**

Armstrongism

"The paramount mysteries confronting all humanity. The revelation of these mysteries was lost, even to the Church of God, although the revelation of them has been preserved in the writings of the Bible. Why, then, has the world not clearly understood? Because the Bible was a coded book, not intended to be understood until our day in this latter half of the twentieth century (Mystery of the Ages, 1995).

Baha'i

"You must realize that many of the things written in the New Testament were written long after Jesus died, hence it is impossible to have absolute accuracy in everything. It would be natural for His followers to assert such things, but the revelation of Baha'u'llah supersedes such claims (Baha'i apologist and teacher Udo Schaefer as quoted in The Kingdome of the Cults by Walter Martin).

Catholicism

"It is clear therefore that, in the supremely wise arrangement of God, sacred Tradition, Sacred Scripture, and the Magisterium of the Church are so connected and associated that one of them cannot stand without the others. Working together, each in its own way, under the actions of the one Holy Spirit, they all contribute effectively to the salvation of souls" (Catechism, 95).

"The task of giving an authentic interpretation of the Word of God, whether in its written form or in the form of Tradition, has been entrusted to the living, teaching office of the Church alone. This means that the task of interpretation has been entrusted to the bishops in communion with the successor of Peter, the Bishop of Rome" (Catechism, 85).

Christian Science

"The literal rendering of the Scriptures [Bible] makes them nothing valuable, but often is the foundation of unbelief and helplessness. The metaphysical rendering [Science and Health] is health and peace and hope for all" (Miscellaneous Writings, Pg. 169).

The Science and truth of divine creation have been presented in the verses already considered (those of Genesis 1), and now the opposite error, a material view of creation, is to be set forth. The second chapter of Genesis contains a statement of this material view of God and the universe, a statement which is the exact opposite of scientific truth as before recorded" (Science and Health, Pg. 521).

Islam

The Qur'on is the most recent revelation from God (Allah) to man. In Qur'an, Allah says: "And we have sent down to thee the Book explaining all things, a guide, a mercy and glad tidings to Muslims" (Qur'an, 16:89).

Allah says in Qur'an: "We have without doubt, sent down the message; and We will assuredly guard it (from corruption)" (Qur'an, 15:9).

This is part of the tidings of the unseen which we reveal unto thee (O Messenger) by inspiration". (Qur'an, 3:44)

Jehovah's Witnesses

"If the six volumes of 'Scripture Studies' are practically the Bible, topically arranged with Bible proof texts given, we might not improperly name the volumes 'the Bible in an arranged form,' that is to say, they are not mere comments on the Bible, but they are practically the Bible itself. Furthermore, not only do we find that people cannot see the divine plan in studying the Bible by itself, but we see, also, that if anyone lays the Scripture Studies aside, even after he has used them, after he has become familiar with them, after he has read them for ten years—if he then lays them aside and ignores them and goes to the Bible alone, though he has understood his Bible for ten years our experience shows that within two years he goes into darkness. On the other hand, if he had merely read the Scripture Studies with their references and had not read a page of the Bible as such, he would be in the light at the end of two years, because he would have the light of the Scriptures" (Charles Taze Russell, The Watchtower, September 15, 1910).

People are condemned if they say it is sufficient to only read the Bible. By just reading the Bible such individuals have reverted back to the apostate doctrines that Christendom's clergy were teaching 100 years ago (Watchtower, August 15, 1981, pp. 28-29).

Judaism

Those who believe in Judaism focus on the Tora for their belief. The Torah usually refers to the Torah she'bi'ktav, the written Torah, also known as the chumash (the five volumes or Pentateuch, sometimes referred to as the Five Books of Moses).The Jewish people only believe in the Torah which is the first five books of he Old Testament; Genesis, Exodus, Leviticus, Numbers, and Deuteronomy. This includes the laws given to the Israelites at Sinai. The concept of "Torah " is much broader than the books themselves, the delimited concept of the Torah. "Torah" can refer to all of traditional Jewish learning (Summarized from my jewish learning: The Torah).

Mormonism

The Mormon Church believes that the Bible has changed, that errors in translation have been made through the years. As a result, they only believe in it "as far as it is correctly translated" (Articles of Faith, 8).

The Mormon church believes that the Book of Mormon is True Restored Gospel. "Many Gentiles will reject the Book of Mormon—They will say, We need no more Bible—The Lord speaks to many nations—He will judge the world out of the books which will be written. About 559–545 B.C. 1 But behold, there shall be many—at that day when I shall proceed to do a marvelous work among them, that I may remember my covenants which I have made unto the children of men, that I may set my hand again the second time to recover my people, which are of the house of Israel; 2 And also, that I may remember the promises which I have made unto thee, Nephi, and also unto thy father, that I would remember your seed; and that the words of your seed should proceed forth out of my mouth unto your seed; and my words shall hiss forth unto the ends of the earth, for a standard unto my people, which are of the house of Israel; 3 And because my words shall hiss forth—many of the Gentiles shall say: A Bible! A Bible! We have got a Bible, and there cannot be any more Bible. 4 But thus saith the Lord God: O fools, they shall have a Bible; and it shall proceed forth from the Jews, mine ancient covenant people. And what thank they the Jews for the Bible which they receive from them? Yea, what do the Gentiles mean? Do they remember the travails, and the labors, and the pains of the Jews, and their diligence unto me, in bringing forth salvation unto the Gentiles?" (2 Nephi 29:1-4).

Mormons also believe that Jesus spoke additional words for other books that would be written. "9 And I do this that I may prove unto many that I am the same yesterday, today, and forever; and that I speak forth my words according to mine own pleasure. And because that I have spoken one word ye need not suppose that I cannot speak another; for my work is not yet finished; neither shall it be until the end of man, neither from that time henceforth and forever. 10 Wherefore, because that ye have a Bible ye need not suppose that it contains all my words; neither need ye suppose that I have not caused more to be written. 11 For I command all men, both in the east and in the west, and in the north, and in the south, and in the islands of the sea, that they shall write the words which I speak unto them; for out of the books which shall be written I will judge the world, every man according to their works, according to that which is written. 12 For behold, I shall speak unto the Jews and they shall write it; and I shall also speak unto the Nephites and they shall write it; and I shall also speak unto the other tribes of the house of Israel, which I have led away, and they shall write it; and I shall also speak unto all nations of the earth and they shall write it. 13 And it shall come to pass that the Jews shall have the words of the Nephites, and the Nephites shall have the words of the Jews; and the Nephites and the Jews shall have the words of the lost tribes of Israel; and the lost tribes of Israel shall have the words of the Nephites and the Jews" (2 Nephi 29:9-13).

Scientology

The Bible and God is a byproduct of Hindu teaching of scriptures (Phoenix Lectures, Pg. 27, 31; Staff, A world Religion, Pg. 5).

Seventh-day Adventists

"Finally, in the reception of members into our churches, we desire on this subject to know two things: 1. That they believe the Bible doctrine of spiritual gifts; 2. That they will candidly acquaint themselves with the visions of Sr. White which have ever held so prominent a place in this work. We believe that every person standing thus and carrying out this purpose will be guided in the way of truth and righteousness. And those who occupy this ground, are never denied all the time they desire to decide in this matter (Ellen White's Writings, Believe His Prophets).

Unification Church

"The Bible, however, is not the truth itself, but a textbook teaching the truth. Naturally the quality of teaching and the method and extent of giving the truth must vary according to each age, for the truth is given to people of different ages, who are at different spiritual and intellectual levels. Therefore, we must not regard the textbook as absolute in every detail" (Divine Principle, Pg. 9).
"The New Testament was a textbook given for the teaching of the truth to the people of 2,000 years ago, people whose spiritual and intellectual standards were then very low compared to today. . . In consequence, today the truth must appear with higher standards . . . we call this the New Truth" (Divine Principle, Pg. 167, 168).

The Divine Principle also states that Moon is a messenger of God. He is supposed to be the fulfillment of the Judeo-Christian religion, bringing to us the "completed testament" (Divine Principle, Pg. 137, 232-238; Divine Principle Study Guide, Pg. 5-6 163-173).

"Innumerable Christians of today are dashing on the way which they think will lead them to the Kingdom of Heaven. Nevertheless, this road is apt to lead them into Hell" (Divine Principle, Pg. 535).

In Time magazine Moon stated that, "God is now throwing Christianity away and is establishing a new religion" (Time, September 30, 1974, Pg. 68).

Unity

"...spiritual principle is embodied in the sacred books of the world's living religions. Christians hold to the Bible as the supreme exponent of spiritual principle. They believe that the Bible is the greatest and most deeply spiritual of all the Scriptures, though they realize that other scriptures, such as the Zend-Avesta and the Upanishads, as well as the teachings of Buddha, the Koran, the Tao of Lao-tse and the writings of Confucius, contain expressions of eminent spiritual truths" (What Unity Teaches, 1952).

"...Scripture may be a satisfactory authority for those who are not themselves in direct communion with the Lord" (Unity, 1986).

Born of God

Biblical Code: BOG

Bible: The following scriptures tell us that when we become Christians we are born of God (1 John 5:1). The Bible goes on to state that everyone who practices righteousness is born of God while living.

Scripture	Content
John 3:3-5	Jesus answered him, "Truly, truly, I say to you, unless one **is born again he cannot see the kingdom of God.**" Nicodemus said to him, "How can a man be born when he is old? Can he enter a second time into his mother's womb and be born?" Jesus answered, "Truly, truly, I say to you, unless one is **born of water and the Spirit,** he cannot enter the kingdom of God.
1 Jn. 2:29	If you know that he is righteous, you may be sure that everyone who practices righteousness **has been born of him**.
1 Jn. 3:9	No one **born of God** makes a practice of sinning, for God's seed abides in him, and he cannot keep on sinning because he has been **born of God**.
1 Jn. 4:7	Beloved, let us love one another, for love is from God, and whoever loves has been **born of God and knows God**.
1 Jn. 5:1	**Everyone who believes that Jesus is the Christ has been born of God,** and everyone who loves the Father loves whoever has been born of him.

Armstrongism

Armstrong Born of God (BOG) "When we are converted, our sins forgiven, we receive the Holy Spirit, we are then BEGOTTEN of God – not yet BORN of God....even as Christ was BORN AGAIN, born of God by his resurrection, even so as WE – the brethren- shall be BORN AGAIN as sons of God, through the RESURRECTION OF THE DEAD..." (Herbert W. Armstrong, "Was Jesus Born Again?" in The Plain Truth, February 1963, p. 40).

"Armstrong taught that God's purpose in creating mankind was to "reproduce Himself", and that the process of being "born again" was not instantaneous — that the believer (as a result of baptism by immersion) was only "begotten" until reborn as a spirit being at the return of Jesus. Those 'begotten' will then be instantaneously 'born anew' (John 3:3) but not again, "a second time", as "perishable" flesh and blood mortals (1 Cor. 15:53) but as "imperishable", immortal Spirit 'God' beings. He concluded that; "Until the resurrection, therefore, we cannot see, enter into or inherit the Kingdom of God. WE CANNOT BE BORN AGAIN UNTIL THE RESURRECTION!" (Armstrong, Herbert. "Just What Do You Mean Born Again?", 1972).

"The Holy Spirit also is the divine 'spiritual sperm' that impregnates with immortal God-life" (Armstrong, Confusion, 6).

Consciousness or Life after Death

Biblical Code: CAD

Bible: The following scriptures suggest that It is the body that is raised to life in the resurrection (Matt. 27:52). The spirit remains consciously alive. Not only so, the dead are "in Christ" (1 Thess. 4:16; Rev. 14:13)...."51 Jesus preached to the dead. He preached to those in hades which is the same as sheol in the Old Testament. It is the place where the lost dead go. Abraham also spoke to the 'rich man' (Luke 16:19-28). In addition, the Book of Revelation also draws attention to the conscious life and blessing enjoyed by those who are in heaven or what some believe is paradise (a place where Christians initially go after death).

Scripture	Content
Matthew 17:1-3	And after six days Jesus took with him Peter and James, and John his brother, and led them up a high mountain by themselves. And he was transfigured before them, and his face shone like the sun, and his clothes became white as light. And behold, **there appeared to them Moses and Elijah, talking with him.**
Luke 16:25	**But Abraham replied**, 'Son, remember that in your lifetime you received your good things, while Lazarus received bad things, but now he is comforted here, and you are in agony."
Revelation 5:9	**And they sang a new song, saying**: "You are worthy to take the scroll and to open its seals, because you were slain, and with your blood you purchased for God persons from every tribe and language and people and nation.
Revelation 6:9-11	When he opened the fifth seal, I saw under the altar the souls of those who had been slain because of the word of God and the testimony they had maintained. **They called out in a loud voice**, "How long, Sovereign Lord, holy and true, until you judge the inhabitants of the earth and avenge our blood?" Then each of them was given a white robe, and they were told to wait a little longer, until the full number of their fellow servants, their brothers and sisters, were killed just as they had been.
Revelation 7:9-10	After this I looked, and there before me was a great multitude that no one could count, from every nation, tribe, people and language, standing before the throne and before the Lamb. They were wearing white robes and were holding palm branches in their hands. **And they cried out in a loud voice: "Salvation belongs to our God, who sits on the throne, and to the Lamb."**
Revelation 14:11-13	And **the smoke of their torment will rise for ever and ever**. There will be no rest day or night for those who worship the beast and its image, or for anyone who receives the mark of its name." This calls for patient endurance on the part of the people of God who keep his commands and remain faithful to Jesus. Then I heard a voice from heaven say, "Write this: Blessed are the dead who die in the Lord from now on." "Yes," says the Spirit, "they will rest from their labor, for their deeds will follow them."

Revelation 20:10	And the devil, who deceived them, was thrown into the lake of burning sulfur, where the beast and the false prophet had been thrown. They will be **tormented day and night** for ever and ever.
Revelation 20:11-14	Then I saw a great white throne and him who was seated on it. The earth and the heavens fled from his presence, and there was no place for them. **And I saw the dead, great and small, standing before the throne,** and books were opened. Another book was opened, which is the book of life. The dead were judged according to what they had done as recorded in the books. The sea gave up the dead that were in it, and death and Hades gave up the dead that were in them, and each person was judged according to what they had done. Then death and Hades were thrown into the lake of fire. The lake of fire is the second death.

Armstrongism

Armstrong did not accept the concept of eternal judgment in this life. He believed that those who die as unbelievers prior to the return of Christ, exist in a state of "unconsciousness" until after the 'Millennium' at the second resurrection, during which they will be offered the choice to submit to God's government (Herbert Armstrong, Mystery of the Ages, p.352).

Jehovah's Witnesses

5 Jehovah knows what happens to us when we die, and he has told us that when a person dies, his life ends. Death is the opposite of life. So when someone dies, his feelings and memories do not keep on living somewhere else. * When we die we can't see, we can't hear, and we can't think anymore (Bible Questions Answered: Where Do We Go When We Die? From Jehovah's Witnesses Officially Web Site).

"The Grave, simply put, is where humans go when they die; it is a symbolic place or condition where any consciousness or activity ceases" (What Happens After Death?, Jehovah's Witnesses officially web site)

Seventh-day Adventists

"The wages of sin is death. But God, who alone is immortal, will grant eternal life to His redeemed. Until that day death is an unconscious state for all people" (Fundamental Beliefs, 25)

Ellen G. White believed and taught that God would simply annihilates the souls of those who did not follow him. "But I saw that God would not shut them up in hell to endure endless misery, neither will He take them to heaven; for to bring them into the company of the pure and holy would make them exceedingly miserable. But He will destroy them utterly and cause them to be as if they had not been; then His justice will be satisfied. He formed man out of the dust of the earth, and the disobedient and unholy will be consumed by fire and return to dust again" (The Great Controversy, 1958).

Unitarian Universalist

"Unitarian Universalist views about life after death are informed by both science and spiritual traditions. Many of us live with the assumption that life does not continue after death, and many of us hold it as an open question, wondering if our minds will have any awareness when we are no longer living" (Official website for Unitarian Universalist Association uua.org).

Death

Biblical Code: DE

Bible: The following scriptures suggest that, "...it is appointed for man to die once, and after that comes judgment" (Hebrews 9:27). The spirit of man returns to God, while the body returns to dust (Ecclesiastes 12:7) then we will begiven a new imperishable body (1 Corinthians 15:42-45).

Scripture	Content
Hebrews 9:27	27 "And just as it is appointed for **man to die once, and after that comes judgment,**"
1 Corinthians. 15:52-57	in a moment, in the twinkling of an eye, at the last trumpet. For the trumpet will sound, and the **dead will be raised imperishable**, and we shall be changed. For this perishable body must put on the imperishable, and this mortal body must put on immortality. When the perishable puts on the imperishable, and the mortal puts on immortality, then shall come to pass the saying that is written: "Death is swallowed up in victory." "Where, O death, is your victory? Where, O death, is your sting?" The sting of death is sin, and the power of sin is the law. But thanks be to God! He gives us the victory through our Lord Jesus Christ.
Revelation 21:4	"He will wipe every tear from their eyes. There will be **no more death'** or mourning or crying or pain, for the old order of things has passed away."
Ecclesiastes 12:7	"And the dust returns to the earth as it was, and **the spirit returns to God** who gave it."

Armstrongism

"The 'wages of sin is death' (Rom. 6:23), and that death, which is the absence of life, is for all eternity. It is eternal punishment by remaining dead for all eternity — not remaining alive and being tortured in a fictitious burning hell fire (Do You have an Immoral Soul--Booklet, Pasadena, CA: Ambassador College Press, 1973).

Christian Science

Mrs. Eddy believes that Death is not real, and heaven and hell are states of mind. "Any material evidence of death is false, for it contradicts the spiritual facts of being" (Science and Health, Pg. 380).

"....man is incapable of sin, sickness and death" (Science and Health, Pg. 475).

Hinduism

At Death: "At death the soul leaves the physical body. But the soul does not die. It lives on in a subtle body called the astral body. The astral body exists in the nonphysical dimension called the astral plane, which is also the world we are in during our dreams at night when we sleep. Here we continue to have experiences until we are reborn again in another physical body as a baby" (www.Hinduismtoday.com   Hinduism Magazine).

Scientology

Martin summarizes that, "The Thetan (spirit) has some amazing characteristics, according to Hubbard. It is more than eighty trillion years old and dwells somewhere within the skull of an individual (Hubbard, Scientology: The fundamentals of thoughts, 1972).   When the individual organism dies, the Thetan reports to an implant station (one is on Mars) before being shot down to earth. This is the 'Between lives area'. Here he 'reports in,' is given a strong forgetter implant, known to fight other Thetans over inhabiting a body. They communicate by telepathy, move objects by kinetics, and travel at high rates of speed. Thetans can be packed in ice and frozen, or they may be dumped into the ocean from a flying saucer. This, Hubbard assures us, "is quite authentic" (Hubbard, History of Man, Pg. 20, 43, 64-66).

Unification Church (Moonism)

At death you will go to a spirit world.   Human ancestors will help you progress to the highest stage where you "...will become divine, like God, and exist in the highest level of heaven" (Speeches, Pg. 14-15).

Unity

"Pain, sickness, poverty, old age and death are not real, and they have no power over me. There is nothing in all the universe for me to fear" (Lessons in Truth, Pg. 35).

Unitarian Universalist

"Unitarian Universalist views about life after death are informed by both science and spiritual traditions. Many of us live with the assumption that life does not continue after death, and many of us hold it as an open question, wondering if our minds will have any awareness when we are no longer living" (Official website for Unitarian Universalist Association   uua.org).

Elder Qualifications

Biblical Code: EQ

Bible: The following scriptures discuss the description of the role of an elder and the qualifications that are required for a man to become an elder. The designation overseers, bishops and elders are used interchangeably by various interpretations of the Bible. Elders should be married to one wife, have believing children, are shepherds of the church, are to have specific qualities or characteristics and should not have others, and should "...encourage others by sound doctrine and refute those who oppose it" (Titus 1:5-9).

Scripture	Content
Acts 20:28-31	Pay careful attention to yourselves and to all the flock, in which the **Holy Spirit has made you overseers,** to care for the church of God, which he obtained with his own blood. I know that after my departure fierce wolves will come in among you, not sparing the flock; and from among your own selves will arise men speaking twisted things, to draw away the disciples after them. Therefore be alert, remembering that for three years I did not cease night or day to admonish every one with tears.
1 Timothy 3:1-7	"Here is a trustworthy saying: **Whoever aspires to be an overseer desires a noble task**. Now the overseer is to be above reproach, faithful to his wife, temperate, self-controlled, respectable, hospitable, able to teach, not given to drunkenness, not violent but gentle, not quarrelsome, not a lover of money. He must manage his own family well and see that his children obey him, and he must do so in a manner worthy of full respect. (If anyone does not know how to manage his own family, how can he take care of God's church?) He must not be a recent convert, or he may become conceited and fall under the same judgment as the devil. He must also have a good reputation with outsiders, so that he will not fall into disgrace and into the devil's trap."
Titus 1:5-9	"The reason I left you in Crete was that you might put in order what was left unfinished and **appoint elders in every town**, as I directed you. An elder must be blameless, faithful to his wife, a man whose children believe and are not open to the charge of being wild and disobedient. Since an overseer manages God's household, he must be blameless—not overbearing, not quick-tempered, not given to drunkenness, not violent, not pursuing dishonest gain. Rather, he must be hospitable, one who loves what is good, who is self-controlled, upright, holy and disciplined. He must hold firmly to the trustworthy message as it has been taught, so that he can encourage others by sound doctrine and refute those who oppose it."

Catholicism

"Technically, celibacy is the commitment not to marry. In the Latin (Roman) Catholic Church, it is a prerequisite for ordination to the priesthood. The candidate must freely assume this obligation publicly and for life. Because church teaching reserves sexual activity to marriage, celibacy also requires abstinence" (US Catholic: Why are priests celebate?).

Qualifications to be a Catholic bishop [Bishop is used interchangeably with Elder in the New Testament].

Steps to becoming a Bishop

1. You must complete a theology degree.
2. You must attend a seminary for 4 - 5 years.
3. You must serve the current priest as a deacon.
4. You must work as an ordained priest.
5. You must wait until a bishop position opens.
6. You must accept the bishop position if you are chosen.

When you complete all six steps you will become a Bishop in the Catholic church (See References and Recommended Readings under Catholicism and look for http references).

Mormonism

The offices of Elder and Bishop are two different offices. The detailed duties of the ordained elders in the Church today have been defined by latter-day revelation (Doctrine and Covenants 20:42–45; 42:44–52; 46:2; 107:12).

Bishop is a man who has been ordained and set apart as the presiding high priest for a ward, or congregation. He has overall responsibility for ministering the temporal and spiritual affairs of the congregation (Doctrine and Covenants 72; 84:112; 107:68–76).

Elder missionaries do not have to be married! "When young adults serve missions, they go out to serve in various parts of the world for 18 months (for women) or 2 years (for men). Then they come home and are encouraged to settle down and find a spouse. So yes, they get married. But they don't get married while they are serving missions" (Quote taken from Quora, not a Mormon Document, but written by a former Mormon Elder and Missionary).

Foods Prohibited

Biblical Code: FP

Bible: The following scriptures state that what you eat is not what defiles you. However, "You are to abstain from food sacrificed to idols, from blood, from the meat of strangled animals and from sexual immorality. You will do well to avoid these things" (Acts 15:29). Other than those specific items we are told, "For everything God created is good, and nothing is to be rejected if it is received with thanksgiving…" (1 Timothy 4:4).

Scripture	Content
Acts 15:28-29	"It seemed good to the Holy Spirit and to us not to burden you with anything beyond the following requirements: **You are to abstain from food sacrificed to idols, from blood, from the meat of strangled animals** and from sexual immorality. You will do well to avoid these things."
Acts 10:10-15	He became hungry and wanted something to eat, and while the meal was being prepared, he fell into a trance. He saw heaven opened and something like a large sheet being let down to earth by its four corners. It contained all kinds of four-footed animals, as well as reptiles and birds. Then a voice told him, "Get up, Peter. Kill and eat." "Surely not, Lord!" Peter replied. "I have never eaten anything impure or unclean." The voice spoke to him a second time, "**Do not call anything impure that God has made clean.**"
Romans 14:20 (1-23)	"Do not destroy the work of God for the sake of food. **All food is clean**, but it is wrong for a person to eat anything that causes someone else to stumble."
1 Timothy 4:3-4 (1-5)	"They forbid people to marry and order them to **abstain from certain foods, which God created to be received with thanksgiving** by those who believe and who know the truth. For everything God created is good, and nothing is to be rejected if it is received with thanksgiving,"
Colossians 2:16 (16-23)	"Therefore **do not let anyone judge you by what you eat or drink**, or with regard to a religious festival, a New Moon celebration or a Sabbath day."
Matthew 15:11	"**What goes into someone's mouth does not defile them**, but what comes out of their mouth, that is what defiles them."

Catholicism

The current practice of fast and abstinence is regulated by Canons 1250–1253 of the 1983 code.[22] They specify that all Fridays throughout the year, and the time of Lent are penitential times throughout the entire Church. All adults (those who have attained the 'age of majority', which is 21 years in canon law) are bound by law to fast on Ash Wednesday and Good Friday until the beginning of their sixtieth year. All persons who have completed their twenty-first year are bound by the law of abstinence on all Fridays unless they are solemnities, and again on Ash Wednesday; but in practice, this requirement has been greatly reduced by the Episcopal Conferences because under Canon 1253, it is these Conferences that have the authority to set down the local norms for fasting and abstinence in their territories. (However, the precept to both fast and abstain on Ash Wednesday and Good Friday is usually not dispensed from.)

Hinduism

Foods Prohibited: "Hindus teach vegetarianism as a way to live with a minimum of hurt to other beings. But in today's world not all Hindus are vegetarians...... Priests and religious leaders are definitely vegetarian, so as to maintain a high level of purity and spiritual consciousness to fulfill their responsibilities, and to awaken the refined areas of their nature" (www.Hinduismtoday.com Hinduism Magazine).

Islam

"Forbidden to you is that which dies of itself, and blood, and flesh of swine, and that on which any other name than that of Allah has been invoked, and the strangled (animal) and that beaten to death, and that killed by a fall and that killed by being smitten with the horn, and that which wild beasts have eaten, except what you slaughter, and what is sacrificed on stones set up (for idols) and that you divide by the arrows; that is a transgression. This day have those who disbelieve despaired of your religion, so fear them not, and fear Me. This day have I perfected for you your religion and completed My favor on you and chosen for you Islam as a religion; but whoever is compelled by hunger, not inclining willfully to sin, then surely Allah is most-Forgiving, most-Merciful" (Surah 5: 3).

"He hath only forbidden you dead meat, and blood, and the flesh of swine, and that on which any other name hath been invoked besides that of Allah. But if one is forced by necessity, without willful disobedience, nor transgressing due limits – then is he guiltless. For Allah is Oft-Forgiving, Most Merciful" (Surah 2:173).

Judaism

Judaism continues to abide by the old laws and commandments found in the Torah (the first 5 books of the Old Testament).

"And the pig, because it has a cloven hoof that is completely split, but will not regurgitate its cud; it is unclean for you. You shall not eat of their flesh, and you shall not touch their carcasses; they are unclean for you" (Leviticus 11:7–8).

"And the pig, because it has a split hoof, but does not chew the cud; it is unclean for you. You shall neither eat of their flesh nor touch their carcass" (Deuteronomy 14:8).

Cannot eat certain foods. Not to eat the flesh of unclean beasts (Lev. 11:4)

Mormonism

The Mormons teach that wine, strong drinks, and hot drinks are to be abstained from (Doctrine and Covenants, 89).

Seventh-day Adventists

Hoekema summarizes their belief by saying, "Under the 'unclean foods' from which the candidates for baptism must promise to abstain are included such beverages as coffee and tea, and such meats as pork, ham, shrimp, lobster, and clams" (Questions on Doctrine, Pg. 623; See Hoekema, 1976 p. 34).

Forgiveness of Sins

Biblical Code: FOS

Bible: The following scriptures states that only "...the Son of Man [Jesus] has the authority to forgive sins" (Mark 2:10). And Peter stated, "Repent and be baptized every one of you in the name of Jesus Christ for the forgiveness of your sins..." (Acts 2:38).

Scripture	Content
Mark 2:10	"But that you may know that the Son of Man has authority on earth to **forgive sins**."
Acts 2:38	And Peter said to them, "Repent and be baptized every one of you in the name of Jesus Christ **for the forgiveness of your sins,** and you will receive the gift of the Holy Spirit."
Acts 10:43	"To him all the prophets bear witness that everyone who believes in him receives **forgiveness of sins** through his name."
Acts 13:38	"Let it be known to you therefore, brothers, that through this man **forgiveness of sins** is proclaimed to you,"
Ephesians 1:7	"In him we have redemption through his blood, **the forgiveness of our trespasses**, according to the riches of his grace..."
Colossians 1:13-14	"He has delivered us from the domain of darkness and transferred us to the kingdom of his beloved Son, in whom we have redemption, **the forgiveness of sins**."
1 John 1:8-10	"If we say we have no sin, we deceive ourselves, and the truth is not in us. If we confess our sins, **he is faithful and just to forgive us our sins and to cleanse us from all unrighteousness**. If we say we have not sinned, we make him a liar, and his word is not in us."

Catholicism

"The Church, who through the bishop and his priests forgives sins in the name of Jesus Christ..." (Catechism, 1448).

"Indeed bishops and priests, by virtue of the sacrament of Holy Orders, have the power to forgive all sins 'in the name of the Father, and of the Son, and of the Holy Spirit' " (Catechism, 1461).

"For this reason, the Eucharist cannot unite us to Christ without at the same time cleansing us from past sins and preserving us from future sins" (Catechism, 1393).

"By the same charity that it enkindles in us, the Eucharist preserves us from future mortal sins" (Catechism, 1395).

"Forgiveness of sins brings reconciliation with God, but also with the Church" (Catechism, 1462). "The Church must be able to forgive all penitents their offenses, even if they should sin until the last moment of their lives" (Catechism, 979).

"Communion with the dead. In full consciousness of this communication of the whole Mystical Body of Jesus Christ, the Church in its pilgrim members, from the earliest days of the Christian religion, has honored with great respect the memory of the dead, and because it is a holy and wholesome thought to pray for the dead that they may be loosed from their sins she offers her suffrages for them. Our prayer for them is capable not only of helping them, but also of making their intercession for us effective" (Catechism, 958).

"One who desires to obtain reconciliation with God and with the Church, must confess to a priest all the unconfessed grave sins he remembers after having carefully examined his conscious" (Catechism, 1493).

"Confession to a priest is an essential part of the sacrament of Penance" (Catechism, 1456).

"It is called the sacrament of confession, since the disclosure or confession of sins to a priest is an essential element of this sacrament" (Catechism, 1424).

"Only priests who have received the faculty of absolving from the authority of the Church can forgive sins in the name of Christ" (Catechism, 1495).

"In its document on the ministry of priests, Vatican II says, "The priest receives a special Sacrament by which, through the anointing of the Holy Spirit, he is conformed to Christ the Priest in such a way that he can act, in Persona Christi, that is, in the very Person of Jesus Christ" (In Persona Christi by FATHER RICHARD REGO).

". . . He that despiseth the priest despiseth God; he that hears him hears God. The priest remits sins as God, and that which he calls his body at the alter is adored as God by himself and by the congregation. . . Wherefore they are justly called not only angels, but also God, holding as they do among us the power and authority of the immortal God" (Catholic Doctrine as defined by the Council of Trent, by the Rev. Anampon, S.J.).

"There is no offense, however serious, that the Church cannot forgive" (Catechism, 982).

"By Christ's will the Church possesses the power to forgive the sins of the Baptized" (Catechism, 986).

"The Church, who through the bishop and his priests forgives sins in the name of Jesus Christ..." (Catechism, 1448).

Mormonism

Forgiveness consists of laws and ordinances. "As these sins are the result of individual acts it is just that forgiveness for them should be conditioned on individual compliance with prescribed requirements – obedience to the laws and ordinances of the Gospel" (Articales of Faith, P. 798).

"Jesus' sacrifice was not able to cleanse us from all our sins, (Murder and repeated adultry are exceptions)..." (Journal of Discourses, Vol. 3, 1956, P. 347).

Scientology

"It is despicable and utterly beneath contempt to tell a man he must repent, that he is evil" (Hubbard, Auditor's Bulletin, Pg. 31).

Unification Church

". . . Father (Moon) is given authority here on earth by God to forgive sins" (120 Day Training Manual, Pg. 41-42).

Moon's shed blood (drawn during his persecution) provides for the forgiveness of man's sins. Without Moon there is no forgiveness of sin (120 Day Training Manual, Pg. 135-136).

God Created the World

Biblical Code: GCW

Bible: God Created the World, man (Adam and Eve) and everything around it. The following scriptures suggest that, God ",,,made heaven, the heaven of heavens, with all their host, the earth and all that is on it, the seas and all that is in them" (Nehemiah 9:6). Then he placed man on earth, and told them to "....be fruitful and multiply and fill the earth and subdue it and have dominion over the fish of the sea and over the birds of the heavens and over every living thing that moves on the earth" (Genesis 1:28).

Scripture	Content
Genesis 1:1 (1-31)	In the beginning, **God created the heavens and the earth**.
Nehemiah 9:6	"You are the LORD, you alone. **You have made heaven, the heaven of heavens, with all their host, the earth** and all that is on it, the seas and all that is in them; and you preserve all of them; the host of heaven worships you."
Colossians 1:15-17	"He is the image of the invisible God, the firstborn of all creation. **For by him all things were created, in heaven and on earth,** visible and invisible, whether thrones or dominions or rulers or authorities--all things were created through him and for him. And he is before all things, and in him all things hold together."
Hebrews 11:3	"By faith we understand that **the universe was created by the word of God**, so that what is seen was not made out of things that are visible."
Genesis 2:2-3(1-25)	"And on the seventh day God finished his work that he had done, and he rested on the seventh day from all his work that he had done. So God blessed the seventh day and made it holy, because on it God rested from all **his work that he had done in creation**."

Armstrongism

"The ones who accept Jesus will receive the immortal resurrection of a spirit-body. Hence, they become God Beings and finish creating the many planets in the universe" (Armstrong, The Plain Truth, October/November, 1977).

Buddhism

"The universe was evolved, not created; and it functions according to law, not according to the caprice of any God" (Fundamental Buddhistic Beliefs).

Hianana Buddhism, consistently rejects the notion of a creator deity. If there is no creator, then he obviously cannot change. "The Buddha did not teach that God created the Universe" (The Buddhist Society at www.thebuddhistsociety.org).

Christian Science

God did not create a physical world for there is no matter. "Did infinite Mind create matter, and call it light? Spirit is light, and the contradiction of Spirit is matter, darkness, and darkness obscures light. Material sense is nothing but a supposition of the absence of Spirit. No solar rays nor planetary revolutions from the day of Spirit" (Science and Health, Pg. 504).

"Spirit, God, gathers unformed thoughts into their proper channels, and unfolds these thoughts, even as He opens the petals of a holy purpose in order that the purpose may appear" (Science and Health, Pg. 506).

Matter is an illusion. All creation consists of spiritual ideas and identities that are reflected from God's mind. The physical is not real, concrete, it is a reflection (Science and Health, Pg. 503).

Hinduism

"…most Hindu creation accounts articulate a fundamental nondualism, wherein the material world-which is either fully divine or is, at least, infused with divinity-emanates from (as opposed to being created by) the principal deity. Two popular Hindu creations stories come from the Brihadaranyaka Upanishad and the Vishnu Purana. Both accounts demonstrate the fundamental nondualism typical of most Hindu creation accounts.

1) Brhadaryanka Upanishad 1.4: the world is said to have come into existence because the Primeval One, having become bored being the only being in existence, split Itself into a variety of forms and manifestations (i.e., the material world and all of its beings) so that, through them, It could experience a loving and playful relationship with Itself (Patheos Library of World Faiths & Religions: What is the creation story in Hinduism?).

2) The creation account from the Vishnu Purana, wherein Vishnu, lying on an ocean of milk atop the serpent Sesha, sprung a lotus from his naval that contained the god Brahma. Having been sprung from Vishnu's navel, Brahma creates all living beings, as well as the sun, moon, planets, etc. and a number of other gods and demigods. Following Brahma's creative acts, it is then said that Vishnu expanded himself into Ksirodakasayi Visnu (Paramatma) and entered into everything that exists in the material and immaterial spheres" (Patheos Library of World Faiths & Religions: What is the creation story in Hinduism?). *

Islam

The Qur'an uses twice the phrase that Allah is "the best of creators" (Surah 23:14, 37:125). What other creators are in mind? On the other hand, many verses make clear that Allah alone is "the creator of all things" (Surah, 39:62).

Mormonism

Council of Gods Created the World, (Abraham 4:1-13; Doctrine of Covenants 121:32).

Scientology

The following was written about creation by Hubbard in his book titled, Factors. It is a summation of what he stated. "Before the beginning was a Cause and the entire purpose of the Cause was the creation of effect…In the beginning and forever is the decision and the decision is

TO BE….The first action of beingness is to assume a viewpoint……The second action of beingness is to extend from the viewpoint, points to view, which are dimension points…Thus there is space created, for the definition of space is: viewpoint of dimension. And the purpose of a dimension point is space and a point to view….The action of a dimension point is reaching and withdrawing….And from the viewpoint to the dimension points there are connection and interchange: thus new dimension points are made: thus there is communication….And thus there is LIGHT….And thus there is energy….And thus there is life" (Factors, 2007).

Evolution: In Scientology: History of Man, Hubbard describes his version of Darwinian evolution for man. He first stage of life was a photon converter which converted light into energy. Then there was jellyfish, a clam, a shellfish, and continued until he became a two-legged up right 'man'. He also taught that the Piltdown man was part of the evolutionary process (the Piltdown Man was determined to be a hoax after he wrote the book). This continues and now man must seek to become 'Homo Novis' which is the ultimate goal. Man will become godlike (Scientology: History of Man).

Unification Church

According to Moon creation "…is the creator, God, projecting himself into a substantial form" (A Prophet Speaks Today, Pg. 3).

"Underlying God and creation are dualities, such as positive & negative, external form & internal character (Divine Principle, Pg. 21), male & female (Divine Principle Pg. 24), or yang & yin (Divine Principle, Pg. 26) as the I Ching talks about. The universe is God's "external feminine object" (Divine Principle, Pg. 25) which God as subject gives love as an emotional force to.

Unitarian Universalist

"People with atheist and agnostic beliefs find a supportive community in our congregations. We are pro-science, pro-reason, and pro-Evolution" (Official website for Unitarian Universalist Association uua.org).

God is Spirit

Biblical Code: GS

Bible: The following scriptures show that, "God is spirit, and those who worship him must worship in spirit and truth" (John 4:24).

Scripture	Content
John 4:24	"**God is spirit**, and those who worship him must worship in spirit and truth."
Matthew 16:17	And Jesus answered him, "Blessed are you, Simon Bar-Jonah! **For flesh and blood has not revealed this to you, but my Father who is in heaven.**
2 Corinthians 3:17	"Now the **Lord is the Spirit,** and where the Spirit of the Lord is, there is freedom."
Genesis 1:2	"The earth was without form and void, and darkness was over the face of the deep. And the **Spirit of God** was hovering over the face of the waters."

Christian Science

God is Mind, (Science and Health 330:20-21; 469:13).

Mormonism

God has a physical body (Doctrines of Salvation, Vol. 1, p. 98).

"Therefore we know that both the Father and the Son are in form and stature perfect men, each of them possesses a tangible body...of flesh and bones..." (Articles of Faith, Talmage).

Scientology

"Unlike religions with Judeo-Christian origins, the Church of Scientology has no set dogma concerning God that it imposes on its members. As with all its tenets, Scientology does not ask individuals to accept anything on faith alone. Rather, as one's level of spiritual awareness increases through participation in Scientology auditing and training, one attains his own certainty of every dynamic. Accordingly, only when the Seventh Dynamic (spiritual) is reached in its entirety will one discover and come to a full understanding of the Eighth Dynamic (infinity) and one's relationship to the Supreme Being" (Scientology Website, Does Scientology Have a Concept of God?).

God and Creation Separate

Biblical Code: GCS

Bible: The following scriptures show that God and His Creation are separate. The universe was created by the word of God (Hebrews 11:3). We can also see that God made all things and then rested on the seventh day (Genesis 2:2-3).

Scripture	Content
Genesis 2:2-3	"And on the seventh day God finished his work that he had done, and he rested **on the seventh day from all his work that he had done**. So God blessed the seventh day and made it holy, because on it God rested from all his work that he had done in creation."
Hebrews 11:3	"By faith we understand that **the universe was created by the word of God,** so that what is seen was not made out of things that are visible."

Christian Science

Matter is an illusion. All creation consists of spiritual ideas and identities that are reflected from God's mind. The physical is not real, concrete, it is a reflection (Science and Health, Pg. 503).

Hinduism

"...most Hindu creation accounts articulate a fundamental nondualism, wherein the material world-which is either fully divine or is, at least, infused with divinity-emanates from (as opposed to being created by) the principal deity. Two popular Hindu creations stories come from the Brihadaranyaka Upanishad and the Vishnu Purana. Both accounts demonstrate the fundamental nondualism typical of most Hindu creation accounts.

1) Brhadaryanka Upanishad 1.4: the world is said to have come into existence because the Primeval One, having become bored being the only being in existence, split Itself into a variety of forms and manifestations (i.e., the material world and all of its beings) so that, through them, It could experience a loving and playful relationship with Itself.

2) The creation account from the Vishnu Purana, wherein Vishnu, lying on an ocean of milk atop the serpent Sesha, sprung a lotus from his naval that contained the god Brahma. Having been sprung from Vishnu's navel, Brahma creates all living beings, as well as the sun, moon, planets, etc. and a number of other gods and demigods. Following Brahma's creative acts, it is then said that Vishnu expanded himself into Ksirodakasayi Visnu (Paramatma) and entered into everything that exists in the material and immaterial spheres" (Patheos Library of World Faiths & Religions: What is the creation story in Hinduism?).

Brahman is 'world soul' or 'cosmic soul'. It is the eternal essence of the universe and the ultimate divine reality. It is God in a sense, but nothing like the God of Christians. In the Brihadaranyaka Upanishad 1.4.10 it means, 'I am Brahman'. In the Chandogya Upanishad 3.14.1 it is communicated as 'All this is Brahman'. In the Chandogya Upanishad 6.2.1 it means 'That [Brahman] is one, without a second'. In the Itareya Upanishad 3.3.7 it means, 'Knowledge is Brahman'. So, the essence of 'God' can be seen everywhere in everything. It's not a matter of God changing. It's a matter of God being multiple things depending on the source you read. So, it appears that within Hinduism 'God' has changed and been defined in multiple ways,

Unification Church

According to Moon creation "...is the creator, God, projecting himself into a substantial form" (A Prophet Speaks Today, Pg. 3).

God and Man Separate

Biblical Code: GMS

Bible: The following scriptures explain how God is separate from His Creation. The scriptures tell us that it was through Jesus, God's Son, that he created the world. The Genesis writer also states that God and Jesus created man and every animal that lives on the earth (Genesis 1:26-27). There is a direct differentiation between God, Jesus, man, creation and animals.

Scripture	Content
Genesis 1:26-27	**Then God said, "Let us make man in our image, after our likeness.** And let them have dominion over the fish of the sea and over the birds of the heavens and over the livestock and over all the earth and over every creeping thing that creeps on the earth." So **God created man in his own image**, in the image of God he created him; male and female he created them.
Numbers 23:19	"**God is not man,** that he should lie, or a son of man, that he should change his mind. Has he said, and will he not do it? Or has he spoken, and will he not fulfill it?"
Hosea 11:9	"I will not execute my burning anger; I will not again destroy Ephraim; for **I am God and not a man**, the Holy One in your midst, and I will not come in wrath."
Hebrews 1:2	"but in these last days **he has spoken to us by his Son**, whom he appointed the heir of all things, through whom also he created the world."

Christian Science

"God is all…. The soul or mind of the spiritual man is God, the divine principal of all being" (Science and Health, Pg. 302).

There is no difference between the created and the Creator. Man is God's reflection, thus man is part of God (Science and Health, pp. 302, 337, 475).

Scientology

"A pre-clear is a precise thing, part animal, part pictures, and part God" (Scientology Clear Procedure, Issue One – 1969, Pg. 21).

Unification Church

"Man is God's substantial object," (Divine Principle, Pg. 26).

"God and man are one. Man is incarnate God" (Christianity in Crisis, Pg. 5)

God Causes Some to Go Astray

Biblical Code: GCA

Bible: The following scriptures tell us that God loves everyone and that he is kind even to those who are ungrateful and evil (Luke 6:35).

Scripture	Content
Luke 6:35-36	"But love your enemies, and do good, and lend, expecting nothing in return, and your reward will be great, and you will be sons of the Most High, for **he is kind to the ungrateful and the evil. Be merciful, even as your Father is merciful.**"
Romans 5:8	"…but **God shows his love for us in that while we were still sinners**, Christ died for us."

Islam

Allah guides not those whom he makes to go astray…..and they will have no helpers (Surah 16:37).

O you who believe! Whoever from amount you turns back from his religion, Allah will bring a people whom He will love and he will love Him, humble towards the believers, stern toward the disbelievers, fighting in the Way of Allah, and never fear of the blame of the blamers. That is the Grace of Allah which He bestows on whom he wills (Surah 5:54).

"If you reject, truly Allah has no need of you" (Surah 39:7).

God Never Changes

Biblical Code: GNC

Bible: The Bible teaches us that God is the one God, that he is eternal, that He will always be the same and that he does not change. "For I the LORD do not change..." (Malachi 3:6).

Scripture	Content
Malachi 3:6	"For **I the LORD do not change;** therefore you, O children of Jacob, are not consumed."
Isaiah 40:28	"Do you not know? Have you not heard? **The LORD is the everlasting God,** the Creator of the ends of the earth. He will not grow tired or weary, and his understanding no one can fathom."
Isaiah 44:6-8	"This is what the LORD says— Israel's King and Redeemer, the LORD Almighty: **I am the first and I am the last; apart from me there is no God. Who then is like me?** Let him proclaim it. Let him declare and lay out before me what has happened since I established my ancient people, and what is yet to come— yes, let them foretell what will come. Do not tremble, do not be afraid. Did I not proclaim this and foretell it long ago? You are my witnesses. Is there any God besides me? No, there is no other Rock; I know not one."
Romans 1:20	"For **his invisible attributes, namely, his eternal power and divine nature, have been clearly perceived, ever since the creation of the world,** in the things that have been made. So they are without excuse."
1 Timothy 6:15-16	"which he will display at the proper time--he who is the blessed and only Sovereign, the King of kings and Lord of lords, who alone has immortality, who dwells in unapproachable light, whom no one has ever seen or can see. To him be honor and eternal dominion. Amen."

Buddhism

Hinayana Buddhism, consistently rejects the notion of a creator deity. If here is no creator, then he obviously cannot change.   "The Buddha did not teach that a God created the Universe" (The Buddhist Society at www.thebuddhistsociety.org).

Hinduism

Brahman is 'world soul' or 'cosmic soul'. It is the eternal essence of the universe and the ultimate divine reality. It is God in a sense, but nothing like the God of Christians.   In the

Brihadaranyaka Upanishad 1.4.10 it means, 'I am Brahman'. In the Chandogya Upanishad 3.14.1 it is communicated as 'All this is Brahman'. In the Chandogya Upanishad 6.2.1 it means 'That [Brahman] is one, without a second'. In the itareya Upanishad 3.3.7 it means, 'Knowledge is Brahman'. So, the essence of 'God' can be seen everywhere in everything. It's not a matter of God changing. It's a matter of God being multiple things depending on the source you read. So, it appears that within Hinduism 'God' has changed and been defined in multiple ways,

Mormonism

"Remember that God, our heavenly Father, was perhaps once a child, a mortal like we ourselves, and rose step by step in the scale of progress, in the school of advancement; has moved forward and overcome, until He has arrived at the point where He now is" (Journal of Discourses, Vol. 7, p. 333).

"God himself was once as we are now, and is an exalted man, and sits enthroned in yonder heavens!!!....We have imagined that God was God from all eternity. I will refute that idea and take away the veil, so that you may see…" (Times and Seasons Vol. 5; also see Teachings of the Prophet Joseph Smith and Mormon Doctrine).

We too may ascend to the status of Godhood by obedience to all principals and ordinances of the Gospel (The Gospel Through the Ages, pp. 114-117).

Heavenly Deception

Biblical Code: HD

Bible: The Bible teaches that lying is totally unacceptable for Christians. Those who practice lying are of the devil (John 8:44) for he is the father of lies. The New Testament writers communicated strongly that, "...all liars, their portion will be in the lake that burns with fire and sulfur, which is the second death" (Revelation 21:8). How can one even attempt to believe that lying for God is acceptable when it is stated so strongly that lying is totally unacceptable to God.

Scripture	Content
John 8:44	**"You are of your father the devil, and your will is to do your father's desires.** He was a murderer from the beginning, **and has nothing to do with the truth, because there is no truth in him**. When he lies, he speaks out of his own character, for he is a liar and the father of lies."
Colossians 3:9	**"Do not lie to one another,** seeing that you have put off the old self with its practices."
1 Timothy 1:10	"the sexually immoral, men who practice homosexuality, enslavers, **liars,** perjurers, and whatever else is contrary to sound doctrine,"
Revelation 21:8	"But as for the cowardly, the faithless, the detestable, as for murderers, the sexually immoral, sorcerers, idolaters, **and all liars, their portion will be in the lake that burns with fire and sulfur, which is the second death."**
Revelation 22:15	"Outside are the dogs, those who practice magic arts, the sexually immoral, the murderers, the idolaters and **everyone who loves and practices falsehood."**

Islam

"And (the unbelievers) plotted and planned, and Allah too planned, and the best of planners is Allah" (Surah 3:54).

Allah lies to lead some astray. "O my People! I fear a Day when there will be mutual wailing. No one shall defend you against Allah. Any whom Allah causes to err, there is no guide. That is how Allah leads the skeptic astray" (Surah 40:32).

Telling flattering lies to make peace is OK! "He who makes peace between the people by inventing good information or saying good things, is not a liar" (Bukhari Vol.3 book 49 ch.2 no.857 p.533).

Unification Church

Heavenly Deception' is acceptable—lying to get money for the Unification Church movement (Master Speaks, p. 6).

"You must be able to manipulate those people" in order to get what you need from the general populace (Master Speaks, p. 6).

> ### Question about Lying
>
> If God cannot Lie (Titus 1:2; Hebrews 6:18), and Satan is the father of lies (John 8:44) who is really suggesting to any man that it is good or acceptable to lie? And if you listen, who are you following?

Comparative Doctrine

Heaven is a Place

Biblical Code: HAP

Bible: The Bible teaches us that heaven is a place. Jesus stated that he was going to prepare a place for us (John 14:2). We have a building from God that's been prepared for us....we have citizenship in heaven.

Scripture	Content
John 14:1-3	"Let not your hearts be troubled. Believe in God; believe also in me. In **my Father's house are many rooms**. If it were not so, would I have told you that I go to prepare a place for you? And if I go and **prepare a place for you**, I will come again and will take you to myself, that where I am you may be also."
John 17:24	"Father, I desire that they also, whom you have given me, **may be with me where I am,** to see my glory that you have given me because you loved me before the foundation of the world."
2 Corinthians 5:1	"For we know that if the tent that is our earthly home is destroyed, **we have a building from God, a house not made with hands, eternal in the heavens."**
Philippians 3:20	"But **our citizenship is in heaven**, and from it we await a Savior, the Lord Jesus Christ,"
Colossians 1:5	"because of the **hope laid up for you in heaven**. Of this you have heard before in the word of the truth, the gospel,"
1 Thessalonians 4:17	"Then we who are alive, who are left, will be caught up together with them in the clouds to meet the Lord in the air, **and so we will always be with the Lord.**
Hebrews 11:16	"But as it is, they desire a better country, that is, a heavenly one. Therefore, God is not ashamed to be called their God, for he has **prepared for them a city**."
Revelation 21:1-7	"Then I saw **a new heaven and a new earth**, for the first heaven and the first earth had passed away, and the sea was no more. And I saw the holy city, new Jerusalem, coming down out of heaven from God, prepared as a bride adorned for her husband. And I heard a loud voice from the throne saying, "Behold, the dwelling place of God is with man. He will dwell with them, and they will be his people, and God himself will be with them as their God. He will wipe away every tear from their eyes, and death shall be no more, neither shall there be mourning, nor crying, nor pain anymore, for the former things have passed away." And he who was seated on the throne said, "Behold, I am making all things new." Also he said, "Write this down, for these words are trustworthy and true." And he said to me, "It is done! I am the Alpha and the Omega, the beginning and the end. To the thirsty I will give from the spring of the water of life without payment. The

	one who conquers will have this heritage, and I will be his God and he will be my son."
Psalm 11:4	"The Lord is in his holy temple; the **Lord's throne is in heaven**; his eyes see, his eyelids test the children of man."

Baha'i

"The Bahá'í teachings state that there is no such physical place as heaven or hell, and emphasise the eternal journey of the soul towards perfection. They explain that references to "heaven" and "hell" in the Holy Scriptures of other religions are to be understood symbolically, describing states of nearness to and distance from God in this world and in the realms beyond. 'Abdu'l-Bahá has said that when human beings "become illuminated with the radiance of the sun of reality, and ennobled with all the virtues, they esteem this the greatest reward, and they know it to be the true paradise" (bahai'.org   The Human Soul-Heaven and Hell).

"We do believe in the paradise of God, which will be the abode of the righteous and in the resurrection and the final righting of all things" (Baha'i apologist and teacher Udo Schaefer as quoted in The Kingdom of the Cults by Walter Martin).

Buddhism

There is not heave, only Nirvana.   "The Bhikshu, full of delight, who is calm in the doctrine of Buddha will reach the quiet place (Nirvana), cessation of natural desires, and happiness" (Dhammapada v. 381).

Christian Science

"Heaven is not a locality, but a divine state of Mind in which all the manifestations of Mind are harmonious and immortal…" (Science and Health, Pg. 291).

Islam

"The smallest reward for the people of paradise is an abode where there are 80,000 servants and 72 wives, over which stands a dome decorated with pearls, aquamarine, and ruby, as wide as the distance from Al-Jabiyyah [a Damascus suburb] to Sana'a [Yemen]" (Surah Al-Rahman (55), verse 72).

"He it is Who created for you all that is in the earth. Then turned He to the heaven, and fashioned it as seven heavens. And He is Knower of all things" (Surah 2:29, emp. added);

"As to the Righteous (they will be) in a position of Security, Among Gardens and Springs; Dressed in fine silk and in rich brocade, they will face each other; So; and We shall join them to Companions with beautiful, big, and lustrous eyes. Three can they call for every kind of fruit in peace and security;" (Surah 44:51-55; see Surah 76:11-22).

Comparative Doctrine

Hinduism

To the Hindu, therefore, punishment consists of continuing to exist on earth. "Eternal life" consists of ceasing to exist in a bodily form and becoming part of the impersonal God. There is no concept of a bodily resurrection, and no ultimate punishment of the wicked. In fact, there is no ultimate spirit being who opposes God or urges men to do evil. So, all will eventually progress, after a sufficient number of lives, to liberation, (Bhagavad Gita, p. 19-28; WR142-144; EB-III, 1014; EB-XI, 580; cf. Renou, 40-44).

Jehovah's Witnesses

Jehovah's Witnesses believe that when this world ends, there will be a separate heaven and an earthly paradise. 144,000 faithful Jehovah's Witnesses will reign with Jesus in heaven: 'God has purposed to associate a limited number of faithful humans with Jesus Christ in the heavenly Kingdom.' Reasoning from the Scriptures, p.76 Watch Tower Bible and Tract Society of Pennsylvania, 1989 Anyone else who is saved – those who prove themselves to be loyal subjects of Jesus – will live in an eternal earthly paradise.

Jehovah's Witnesses believe there are two peoples of God: (1) the Anointed Class (144,000) will live in heaven and rule with Christ; and (2) the "other sheep" (all other believers) will live forever on a paradise earth. This is an actual heavenly government with a King—Jesus Christ—and 144,000 co-rulers, who are "bought from the earth." (Revelation 5:9, 10; 14:1, 3, 4; Daniel 2:44; 7:13, 14) They will rule over the earth, which will be cleansed of all wickedness and will be inhabited by many millions of God-fearing humans (Proverbs 2:21, 22--See JW.Org Bible Teachings). Earth Becomes a Paradise. Anyone else who is saved – those who prove themselves to be loyal subjects of Jesus – will live in an eternal earthly paradise. Only the 144,000 faithful Jehovah's Witnesses will go to heaven.

God promises everlasting life on earth for most good people (Psalm 37:11, 29, 34--See JW.Org Bible Teachings).

Mormonism

There are three levels of heaven: telestial, terrestrial, and celestial, (Mormon Doctrine, p. 348). Only those who are worthy LDS members will attain the highest level:

Telestial Kingdom: This 'heaven' is where unbelievers go: "These are they who received not the gospel of Christ, neither the testimony of Jesus...who receive not his fullness in the eternal world", but shall be "redeemed from the devil [at] the last resurrection" (Doctrine and Covenants 76: 82-86).

Terrestrial Kingdom: This 'heaven' is for religious people who have not become Mormons and for Mormons who have not met the requirements of the Church, i.e., "Honorable men of the earth who are blinded by the craftiness of men and who therefore do not accept and live the gospel law" (Mormon Doctrine, p. 784). This level of heaven is not as desirable as the Celestial Kingdom, but the Son visits there: "These are they who receive of his glory but not of his fulness... the presence of the Son, but not the fullness of the Father...who are not valiant in the testimony of Jesus...they obtain not the crown over the kingdom of God" (Doctrine and Covenants 76: 76-79).

Celestial Kingdom: This is the desired level of heaven where Mormons who have kept ALL of the laws and ordinances of their church can attain to. "These are they who received the testimony of Jesus, and believed on his name and were baptized...in the water...keeping the commandments that they might be washed and cleansed from all their sins, and receive the Holy Spirit ..." (Doctrine and Covenants 76: 51-57). "They are gods, even the sons of God...these shall dwell in the presence of God and his Christ forever...whose names are written in heaven" (Doctrine and Covenants 76: 58-68). The men become Gods and the women become their wives. They begin to have spirit children and the process of a new world/universe begins again for each God.

REWARD: When a Mormon attains to the Celestial Kingdom he then can begin his own creation, just as the god they believe started this world and populated it with his spiritual children.

Scientology

"The manifestation that our Hereafter is our 'next life' entirely alters the general concept of spiritual destiny. There is no argument whatever with the tenets of any faith, since it is not precisely stated uniformly by all religions that one immediately goes to a Heaven or Hell. It is certain that an individual experiences the effect of the civilization, which he has had part in creating, in his next lifetime. In other words, the individual comes back. He has a responsibility for what goes on today since he will experience it tomorrow."

Unification Church

According to Moon there are four basic spirit worlds. Evil men go to a place of darkness or what's called hell. Men who attain to only the form stage go to a place of darkness, those who attain to the life-spirit stage (through faith in the Gospel) go to paradise, those who reach the perfection or divine-spirit stage (by serving the Lord in person) go to the Kingdom of Heaven when they die (Divine Principle, pp. 174-175).

Unitarian Universalist

"The American Universalist preacher Hosea Ballou told his followers that heaven and hell are not found in any kind of afterlife, but simply in the life we create on this earth" (Official website for Unitarian Universalist Association   uua.org).
"...paradise for the Universalist was a place where people struggle with injustice and where they are called upon to develop wisdom and our capacity to love" (Official website for Unitarian Universalist Association   uua.org).

Unity

"Heaven and hell are symbols, not places for people to go. Knowing this should be a relief, but there are many who want to believe in them as places. Mystically they represent states of consciousness. Hell is the consciousness of error based on mistaken views about God, man, and the universe. It isn't a consciousness created by God, but is one formed by man through his misuse of the power of thought. Satan is a ruling belief in consciousness that motivates much of our negative behavior. He was considered to be a fallen angel and, mystically, he was. There is only one power—God power. The power of negative thought is a fallen angel; it has the possibility of good, but can be very destructive when used negatively" (Filmore Fellowship, Heaven and/or Hell Metaphysically Interpreted).

Hell is Eternal

Biblical Code: EH

Bible: The following scriptures suggest that, 1) there is a hell, and 2) it is eternal in nature. This means that it lasts forever, just as heaven will. People who go to hell stay there forever. It is not just a short stop to pay for sins and then you go on to paradise or heaven. There are specific things that happen to those who go there. They will suffer the punishment of eternal fire for ever and ever (Revelation 20:10). Eternal means forever, not that it was established by God.

Scripture	Content
Matthew 25:45-46 (41-46)	"He will reply, 'Truly I tell you, whatever you did not do for one of the least of these, you did not do for me.' "Then they will go away to **eternal punishment**, but the righteous to eternal life."
Matthew 13:49-50 (47-50)	"This is how it will be at the end of the age. The angels will come and separate the wicked from the righteous and throw them into the **blazing furnace, where there will be weeping and gnashing of teeth.**"
Luke 16:22-23 (19-31)	"The time came when the beggar died and the angels carried him to Abraham's side. The rich man also died and was buried. **In Hades, where he was in torment,** he looked up and saw Abraham far away, with Lazarus by his side."
Revelation 14:9-11	"A third angel followed them and said in a loud voice: "If anyone worships the beast and its image and receives its mark on their forehead or on their hand, they, too, will drink the wine of God's fury, which has been poured full strength into the cup of his wrath. **They will be tormented with burning sulfur in the presence of the holy angels and of the Lamb. And the smoke of their torment will rise for ever and ever.** There will be no rest day or night for those who worship the beast and its image, or for anyone who receives the mark of its name."
Revelation 20:10	"And the devil, who deceived them, was thrown into the lake of burning sulfur, where the beast and the false prophet had been thrown. **They will be tormented day and night for ever and ever.**"
Revelation 21:8	"But the cowardly, the unbelieving, the vile, the murderers, the sexually immoral, those who practice magic arts, the idolaters and all liars—**they will be consigned to the fiery lake of burning sulfur.** This is the second death."
Matthew 25:46	"Then they will go away to **eternal punishment**, but the righteous to eternal life."
2 Thessalonians 1:8-9	"He will punish those who **do not know God and do not obey the gospel of our Lord Jesus. They will be punished with everlasting destruction** and shut out from the presence of the Lord and from the glory of his might."

Jude 7	"In a similar way, Sodom and Gomorrah and the surrounding towns gave themselves up to sexual immorality and perversion. They serve as an example of those who **suffer the punishment of eternal fire.**"
Revelations 20:11-15	"Then I saw a great white throne and him who was seated on it. From his presence earth and sky fled away, and no place was found for them. And I saw the dead, great and small, standing before the throne, and books were opened. Then another book was opened, which is the book of life. And the dead were judged by what was written in the books, according to what they had done. And the sea gave up the dead who were in it, Death and Hades gave up the dead who were in them, and they were judged, each one of them, according to what they had done. Then Death and Hades were thrown into the lake of fire. This is the second death, the lake of fire. **And if anyone's name was not found written in the book of life, he was thrown into the lake of fire.**"

Armstrongism

"Even so, it will be with the Gehenna fire. It will be unquenched – but it will finally burn itself out" (Herbert Armstrong, Ambassador College Correspondence Course, Lesson 6, P. 14).

All those incorrigibly wicked, those who refuse to accept God's government and laws being judged guilty of rebellion against God to rise in a third resurrection, & thrown into 'Gehenna' fire. Including persons who had committed the "unpardonable sin". Such persons suffering eternal death. Armstrong identified such as being the "second death" mentioned in the Book of Revelation (Herbert Armstrong, Mystery of the Ages, p. 354).

Baha'i

"The Bahá'í teachings state that there is no such physical place as heaven or hell.....spiritual punishment...is to be subjected to the world of nature; to be veiled from God; to be brutal and ignorant; to fall into carnal lusts; to be absorbed in animal frailties; to be characterized with dark qualities...these are the greatest punishments and tortures...", (bahai'.org   The Human Soul- Heaven and Hell).

"We know nothing of eternal flames where sinners will be confined forever without respite" (Baha'i apologist and teacher Udo Schaefer as quoted in The Kingdom of the Cults by Walter Martin).

Buddhism

"From the Buddhist point of view, those who go to hell can work themselves upward by making use of the merit that they had acquired previously. There are no locks on the gates of hell. Hell is a temporary place and there is no reason for those beings to suffer there forever" (The Buddhist Concept of Heaven and Hell. Venerable K. Sri Dhammananda Maha Thera www.budsas.org).

Hinduism

"There is no eternal hell, no damnation in Hinduism, and no intrinsic evil--no satanic force that opposes the will of God" (Hinduism Today, 9/2011).

To the Hindu, therefore, punishment consists of continuing to exist on earth. "Eternal life" consists of ceasing to exist in a bodily form and becoming part of the impersonal God. There is no concept of a bodily resurrection, and no ultimate punishment of the wicked. In fact, there is no ultimate spirit being who opposes God or urges men to do evil. So, all will eventually progress, after a sufficient number of lives, to liberation, (Bhagavad Gita, p. 19-28; WR142-144; EB-III, 1014; EB-XI, 580; cf. Renou, 40-44).

Christian Science

"The olden opinion that hell is fire and brimstone, has yielded somewhat to the metaphysical fact that suffering is a thing of the mortal mind instead of the body; so, in place of material flames and odor, mental anguish is generally accepted as the penalty for sin" (Miscellaneous Writings, p. 237).

Christian Science's Hell, which doesn't exist, lasts until the belief in mortal life and its pleasures and pain is gone. "The period required for this dream of material life, embracing its so-called pleasures and pains, to vanish from consciousness, "knoweth no man.....neither the Son, but the Father. This period will be of longer or shorter duration according to the tenacity of error (Science and Health, Pg. 77).

"Man's probation after death is the necessity of his immortality, for good dies not and evil is self-destructive, therefore evil must be mortal and self-destroyed. If man should not progress after death, but should remain in error, he would be inevitably self-annihilated" (Miscellaneous Writings, Pg. 2).

Islam

What will be the food for the people in Hell? The food for the people in Hell will be only "Dhari"* (Surah 88:6), or only foul pus from the washing of wounds (Surah 69:36).

A different perspective on food. "Is that the better entertainment or the Tree of zaqaqum? For We have truly made it (as) a trial for the wrongdoers. For it is a tree that springs out of the bottom of Hellfire; The shoots of its fruit-stalks are like the heads of devils; Truly they will eat thereof and fill their bellies therewith. Then on top of that they will be given a mixture made of boiling water. Then shall their return be to the (blazing) fire" (Surah 37:62-68).

On the Day of Judgment, unbelievers will be "dragged into the Fire upon their faces, ...'Taste ye the touch of hell'" (Surah 54:48).

"(They will be) in the midst of a fierce Blast of Fire and in Boiling Water, and in the shades of Black smoke: nothing (will there be) to refresh, nor to please" (Surah 56:42-43).

"...For the wrongdoers We have prepared a Fire whose (smoke and flames), like the walls and roof of a tent, will hem them in: if they implore relief they will be granted water like melted brass, that will scald their faces. How dreadful the drink! How uncomfortable a couch to recline on!" (Surah 18:29).

"Will there be food for the Sinful – Like molten brass; it will boil in their insides, Like the boiling of scalding water. (A voice will cry) 'Seize ye him and drag him into the midst of the Blazing Fire!" (Surah 44:43-46).

The Qur'an states that hell has "keepers" or "angels of punishment" (Surah 40:49; 96:18). Apparently, the angel Malic is mostly in charge of hell. He presides over the torments that are inflicted on unbelievers: "The sinners will be in the punishment of Hell, to dwell therein (for aye).... They will cry: 'O Malik! Would that your Lord put an end to us!' He will say, 'Nay, but you shall abide!' " (Surah 43:74,77).

Jehovah's Witnesses

"The doctrine of a burning hell where the wicked are tortured eternally after death cannot be true mainly for four reasons: (1) It is wholly unscriptural; (2) It is unreasonable; (3)it is contrary to God's love; and (4) it is repugnant to justice" (Let God Be True).

"Some Bible translations use the word "hell" for the Hebrew word "Sheol" and the matching Greek word "Hades," both of which refer to the common grave of mankind. (Psalm 16:10; Acts 2:27) Many people believe in a fiery hell…..However, the Bible teaches otherwise……Those in hell are unconscious and so cannot feel pain….Death, not torment in a fiery hell, is the penalty for sin (Bible Teachings: What Is Hell? Is It a Place of Eternal Torment? Official Jehovah's Witnesses Website).

"However, those who become so wicked that they are beyond reform will not be resurrected. When such ones die, they suffer permanent destruction with no hope of a return to life—Matthew 23:33; Hebrews 10:26, 27" (See JW.Org Bible Teachings). No eternal hell, only non-existence.

Mormonism

Hell is temporary (Mormon Doctrine, Pg. 349-351; Doctrine of Salvation 2:133-134).   Joseph Smith stated, "Is it the duty of men in this life to repent. Every man who hears the gospel message is under obligation to receive it. If he fails, then in the spirit world he will be called upon to receive it…" (Doctrines of Salvation, Vol. 2, Pg. 183). Joseph Smith and others will teach those in spirit prison. Most people will then accept the 'Mormon Gospel' and will go to paradise and ultimately to a heavenly realm.

Hell of fire and brimstone is reserved for Satan and his followers who rebelled in the Spirit World and for the Sons of Perdition; Those that leave the Mormon church once they have become a member, when you commit murder, when you assent to the murder of Jesus Christ or rebel to the point that you crucify him anew. (Mormon Doctrine, Pg. 816-817).

Eternal damnation does not mean that a person cannot go to a lesser heaven. It means that the individual; is barred, or denied privileges of progression and ultimately to become a god (Doctrines of Salvation, Joseph F. Smith, Vol. 2. Pg. 227).

Scientology

"The manifestation that our Hereafter is our 'next life' entirely alters the general concept of spiritual destiny. There is no argument whatever with the tenets of any faith, since it is not precisely stated uniformly by all religions that one immediately goes to a Heaven or Hell. It is certain that an individual experiences the effect of the civilization, which he has had part in creating, in his next lifetime. In other words, the individual comes back. He has a responsibility for what goes on today since he will experience it tomorrow."

Seventh-day Adventists

Ellen G. White wrote, "How repugnant to every emotion of love and mercy, and even to our sense of justice, is the doctrine that the wicked dead are tormented with fire and brimstone in an eternally burning hell; that for the sins of a brief, earthly life they are to suffer torture as long as God shall live" (The Great Controversy, 1958)."

Ellen G. White believed and taught that God would simply annihilates the souls of those who did not follow him. "But I saw that God would not shut them up in hell to endure endless misery, neither will He take them to heaven; for to bring them into the company of the pure and holy would make them exceedingly miserable. But He will destroy them utterly and cause them to be as if they had not been; then His justice will be satisfied. He formed man out of the dust of the earth, and the disobedient and unholy will be consumed by fire and return to dust again" (The Great Controversy, 1958).

Unification Church

"Men of evil nature have established evil homes, societies, and an evil world, by multiplying children of evil. This is the Hell on earth in which fallen men have been living," (Divine Principle, Pg.102-103, 216).

"Therefore, it is God's intention to abolish Hell completely" (Divine Principle, Pg. 190).

According to Moon there will be no judgment as Christianity has traditionally believed, rather man will be restored to the original position God intended there will be no destruction by fire (Divine Principle, Pg. 190).

Unitarian Universalist

"Unitarian Universalist views about life after death are informed by both science and spiritual traditions. Many of us live with the assumption that life does not continue after death, and many of us hold it as an open question, wondering if our minds will have any awareness when we are no longer living" (Official website for Unitarian Universalist Association uua.org).

Few of us believe in divine judgment after death. It's in our religious DNA: the Universalist side of our tradition broke with mainstream Christianity by rejecting the idea of eternal damnation" (Official website for Unitarian Univ*ersalist Association uua.org).

"The American Universalist preacher Hosea Ballou told his followers that heaven and hell are not found in any kind of afterlife, but simply in the life we create on this earth" (Official website for Unitarian Universalist Association uua.org).

Unity

"Heaven and hell are symbols, not places for people to go. Knowing this should be a relief, but there are many who want to believe in them as places. Mystically they represent states of consciousness. Hell is the consciousness of error based on mistaken views about God, man, and the universe. It isn't a consciousness created by God, but is one formed by man through his misuse of the power of thought. Satan is a ruling belief in consciousness that motivates much of our negative behavior. He was considered to be a fallen angel and, mystically, he was. There is only one power—God power. The power of negative thought is a fallen angel; it has the possibility of good, but can be very destructive when used negatively" (Filmore Fellowship, Heaven and/or Hell Metaphysically Interpreted).

Holy Spirit

Biblical Code: HS

Bible: The Bible teaches us that the Holy Spirit is a personality and can choose to take or not take action. He has a mind of his own and a will to do what is needed for the Christian. To accept Jesus is to accept the Holy Spirit into your life. He is there to guide you and help you mature in Christ. You cannot have one without the other.

Scripture	Content
Matthew 28:19	"Therefore go and make disciples of all nations, baptizing them in the name of the Father and of the Son and of **the Holy Spirit**,"
John 14:26	"But **the Advocate, the Holy Spirit,** whom the Father will send in my name, **will teach you** all things and **will remind you** of everything I have said to you."
John 15:26	"When the Advocate comes, whom I will send to you from the Father—the Spirit of truth who goes out from the Father—**he will testify about me.**"
John 16:13-14 (7-15)	"But when he, the Spirit of truth, comes, **he will guide you** into all the truth. He will not speak on his own; he will speak only what he hears, and **he will tell you what is yet to come**. He will glorify me because it is from me that he will receive what he will make known to you."
Acts 13:4	"The two of them, **sent on their way by the Holy Spirit**, went down to Seleucia and sailed from there to Cyprus."
Acts 8:29	"The **Spirit told Philip**, "Go to that chariot and stay near it."
Romans 8:26-27 (20-28)	"In the same way, **the Spirit helps us in our weakness**. We do not know what we ought to pray for, but the Spirit himself intercedes for us through wordless groans. And he who searches our hearts knows the mind of the Spirit, because **the Spirit intercedes for God's people** in accordance with the will of God."
1 Corinthians 12:11	"All these are the work of one and the same Spirit, **and he distributes them to each one, just as he determines.**"

Armstronism

"When you receive the Holy Spirit, you'd don't receive all, a full measure of the Holy Spirit all at once, but you increase in the spirit of God as you grow and develop" (Armstrong, H. World Tomorrow Telecast; What is the Holy Spirit?).

The Holy Spirit is God's spirit. It is the impregnation of immortal life, or the life of God. It is the love of God. Is the faith of Christ. Armstrong's description of Holy Spirit does not account for the Holy Spirit being an independent entity or personality. It is simply God's spirit (Armstrong, H. World Tomorrow Telecast; What is the Holy Spirit?).

Baha'i

"I believe it is your gospel of John that Jesus promised another Comforter who would abide always. We understand this to be the coming of Baha'u'llah, a direct fulfillment of the words of Jesus" (Baha'i apologist and teacher Udo Schaefer as quoted in The Kingdom of the Cults by Walter Martin).

Christian Science

The Holy Spirit is divine science, he is impersonal power (Science and Health, 331:31)

Jehovah's Witnesses

The Holy Spirit is "the invisible active force of Almighty God which moves his servants to do his will" (Let God Be True, Pg. 108).

Jehovah's Witnesses believe that the Holy Spirit is an impersonal force of God and not a distinct person. God's holy spirit operates only as he directs it. (Luke 11:13). The Bible shows that the holy spirit is not a person (Exodus 15:8, 10). The holy spirit is God's power in action, his active force (Micah 3:8; Luke 1:35) (See JW.Org Bible Teachings).

Unification Church

"Since the Holy Spirit is a female Spirit, we cannot become the 'bride' of Jesus unless we receive the Holy Spirit" (Divine Principle, Pg. 215).

Holy Spirit is female in nature: "....according to Divine Principle, since God possesses polarity, there is a sense in which it is legitimate to refer to the feminine activity of the Holy Spirit. Because the Spirit carries out maternal functions of comforting, nourishing and nurturing individual Christians, it serves as a mother spirit. The Holy Spirit is a feminine spirit who works beside Jesus in the spirit world" (An Introduction to Theology, 1983).

In the same paper the Holy Spirit is described differently: "In Unification theology the main point is that the Holy Spirit is not a separate entity, a being different from God the Father. The Holy Spirit simply refers to God's redemptive activity. Hence in Genesis the Spirit is defined as God's breath: The Lord God breathed His Spirit into Adam, making him a living soul" (Kim, 1980).

Unity

"Do not be misled by the personality of the Holy Spirit and the reference to it as 'he.' This was the bias of the Oriental mind, making God and all forms of the Deity masculine" (Jesus Christ Heals, Pg. 183).

"The Spirit of wholeness quickens and heals me. The Spirit of wholeness is called the Holy Spirit in the New Testament. In classical mythology it is called Hygeria. Modern medical men refer to it as the restorative power of nature. It has been recognized by savage and civilized in every land and age. It has many names, and they all identify it as a universal urge toward perfection in man and the universe and toward keeping things going regardless of any retarding or interfering force" (Jesus Christ Heals, Pg. 183).

Infallibility

Biblical Code: INF

Bible: The Bible teaches us that we have been given all that we need for life and godliness, which also tells us that we only need to follow what the Bible is teaching us (2 Peter 1:3). Any distorted interpretation of the Bible that adds to or takes away from the message of God cannot be accepted (Galatians 1:7-9). All other men sin or make mistakes in life (Romans 3:23). Because of this, no man no matter what his position is should claim to speak for or interpret God's word, for God has already shown us what His will is in the Holy Bible.

Scripture	Content
Galatians 1:7-9	"not that there is another one, but there are some who trouble you and want to distort the gospel of Christ. But **even if we or an angel from heaven should preach to you a gospel contrary to the one we preached to you, let him be accursed.** As we have said before, so now I say again: If anyone is preaching to you a gospel contrary to the one you received, let him be accursed."
Hebrews 1:1-2	"Long ago, at many times and in many ways, God spoke to our fathers by the prophets, but **in these last days he has spoken to us by his Son**, whom he appointed the heir of all things, through whom also he created the world."
Hebrews 13:20-21	"Now may the God of peace who brought again from the dead our Lord Jesus, the great shepherd of the sheep, by the blood of the eternal covenant, **equip you with everything good that you may do his will,** working in us that which is pleasing in his sight, through Jesus Christ, to whom be glory forever and ever. Amen."
2 Peter 1:3	**"His divine power has granted to us all things that pertain to life and godliness**, through the knowledge of him who called us to his own glory and excellence," Note: See section on Revelation. Any change, alteration, or communication of God's will that is not directly from the Bible is not from God.

Catholicism

"The Roman Pontiff... enjoys this infallibility in virtue of his office, when, as supreme pastor and teacher of all the faithful - who confirms his brethren in the faith - he proclaims by a definitive act a doctrine pertaining to faith or morals... This infallibility extends as far as the deposit of divine Revelation itself" (Catechism, 891).

The Catholic Church teaches that when the bishops officially teach doctrine relating to faith and morals, then God super naturally prevents them from making any errors. This is called "infallibility". It applies to official councils, such as the Second Vatican Council. It also applies to other teachings, as long as the bishops and the Pope are in agreement about them (Catechism 890, 891, 939, 2033, 2034, 2049).

The Pope is said to be infallible whenever he makes an official decree on matters of faith and morals. According to Catholic doctrine, it is impossible for the Pope to teach false doctrine. Catholics are expected to obey the Pope without question even when he is not making an "infallible" statement about doctrine. They are expected to submit their wills and minds to the Pope without question (Catechism 892, 2037, 2050).

Infant Baptism

Biblical Code: IB

Bible: Infant baptism is a result of a belief in original sin which asserts that human nature was corrupted due to the first sin by Adam and Eve and, therefore, all humans are inherently sinful. It was first taught by Augustine around the late 4th Century AD. Which in and of itself suggests that it was not taught by Jesus, the Apostles nor can it be found in the New Testament. Simply stated, the reason Infant baptism is so important to people who believe in Original Sin is that babies are already sinful when they are born and must be baptized to have their sins removed or they could not go to heaven. Scriptures suggest that in order to be baptized you must be capable of believing and you must be able to verbalize your desire to repent! This also presumes the necessity of knowing you need to repent. You must know what it means to sin. You must also be able to profess your faith. You must be able to confess or declare that you believe that Jesus is the Lord and that he was raised from the dead. In See Original Sin in this work.

Scripture	Content
Mark 16:15-16	"He said to them, "Go into all the world and preach the gospel to all creation. **Whoever believes and is baptized** will be saved, but whoever does not believe will be condemned."
Acts 2:38	"Peter replied, "**Repent and be baptized**, every one of you, in the name of Jesus Christ for the forgiveness of your sins. And you will receive the gift of the Holy Spirit."
Romans 10:9-10	"**If you declare with your mouth,** "Jesus is Lord," and believe in your heart that God raised him from the dead, you will be saved. For it is with your heart that you believe and are justified, and it is with your mouth that you profess your faith and are saved."
Galatians 3:26-27	"For in Christ Jesus **you are all sons of God, through faith.** For as many of you as were baptized into Christ have put on Christ."

Catholicism

"They must be baptized to receive forgiveness for all past sins (original sin). "Born with a fallen human nature and tainted by original sin, children also have need of the new birth in Baptism to be freed from the power of darkness and brought into the realm of the freedom of the children of God, to which all men are called. The sheer gratuitousness of the grace of salvation is particularly manifest in infant Baptism. The Church and the parents would deny a child the priceless grace of becoming a child of God were they not to confer Baptism shortly after birth" (Catechism, 1250).

"The practice of infant Baptism is an immemorial tradition of the Church. There is explicit testimony to this practice from the second century on..." (Catechism, 1252).

"Born with a fallen human nature and tainted by original sin, children also have need of the new birth in Baptism to be freed from the power of darkness and brought into the realm of the freedom of the children of God, to which all men are called. The sheer gratuitousness of the grace of salvation is particularly manifest in infant Baptism. The Church and the parents would deny a child the priceless grace of becoming a child of God were they not to confer Baptism shortly after birth" (Catechism 1250).

NOTE: Any church that accepts Calvin's teachings will teach that infants should be baptized at birth since they are tainted with original sin.

Jesus' Birth

Biblical Code: JB

Bible: The Bible clearly teaches us that Jesus was born of the virgin Mary (Matthew 1:23). He was born in Bethlehem, in Judea (Matthew 2:5), in a manger (Luke 2:12). It states that Jesus is deity, the Christ (Matthew 1:18) and he is the Son of God (Romans 8:3).

Scripture	Content
Matthew 1:18-25	"Now the birth of Jesus Christ took place in this way. When his mother Mary had been betrothed to Joseph, before they came together **she was found to be with child from the Holy Spirit**. And her husband Joseph, being a just man and unwilling to put her to shame, resolved to divorce her quietly. "But as he considered these things, behold, an angel of the Lord appeared to him in a dream, saying, "Joseph, son of David, do not fear to take Mary as your wife, for that which is **conceived in her is from the Holy Spirit**. She will bear a son, and you shall call his name Jesus, for he will save his people from their sins." All this took place to fulfill what the Lord had spoken by the prophet: "Behold, **the virgin shall conceive and bear a son, and they shall call his name Immanuel**"(which means, God with us). When Joseph woke from sleep, he did as the angel of the Lord commanded him: he took his wife, but knew her not until she had given birth to a son. And he called his name Jesus."
Matthew 2:1-12	"Now after **Jesus was born in Bethlehem of Judea** in the days of Herod the king, behold, wise men from the east came to Jerusalem, saying, "Where is he who has been born king of the Jews? For we saw his star when it rose and have come to worship him." When Herod the king heard this, he was troubled, and all Jerusalem with him; and assembling all the chief priests and scribes of the people, he inquired of them where the Christ was to be born. They told him, "In Bethlehem of Judea, for so it is written by the prophet: "'And you, O Bethlehem, in the land of Judah, are by no means least among the rulers of Judah; for from you shall come a ruler who will shepherd my people Israel.'" Then Herod summoned the wise men secretly and ascertained from them what time the star had appeared. And he sent them to Bethlehem, saying, "Go and search diligently for the child, and when you have found him, bring me word, that I too may come and worship him." After listening to the king, they went on their way. And behold, the star that they had seen when it rose went before them until it came to rest over the place where the child was. When they saw the star, they rejoiced exceedingly with great joy. And going into the house they saw the child with Mary his mother, and they fell down and worshiped him. Then, opening their treasures, they offered him gifts, gold and frankincense and myrrh. And being warned in a dream not to return to Herod, they departed to their own country by another way."

Luke 2:4-7	"And Joseph also went up from Galilee, from the town of Nazareth, to Judea, **to the city of David, which is called Bethlehem,** because he was of the house and lineage of David, to be registered with Mary, his betrothed, who was with child. And while they were there, the time came for her to give birth. **And she gave birth to her firstborn son** and wrapped him in swaddling cloths and laid him in a manger, because there was no place for them in the inn."
Luke 2:12-15	"And this will be a sign for you: you will find a baby wrapped in swaddling cloths and lying in a manger." And suddenly there was with the angel a multitude of the heavenly host praising God and saying, "Glory to God in the highest, and on earth peace among those with whom he is pleased!" When the angels went away from them into heaven, the shepherds said to one another, "Let us go **over to Bethlehem** and see this thing that has happened, which the Lord has made known to us."
Isaiah 7:13-14 Prophecy	"And he said, "Hear then, O house of David! Is it too little for you to weary men, that you weary my God also? Therefore the Lord himself will give you a sign. Behold, **the virgin shall conceive and bear a son, and shall call his name Immanuel.**"
Isaiah 9:6 Prophecy	"For to us a child is born, to us a son is given; and the government shall be upon his shoulder, and his name shall be called Wonderful Counselor, Mighty God, Everlasting Father, Prince of Peace."
Micah 5:2 (2-5) Prophecy	"But you, **O Bethlehem Ephrathah,** who are too little to be among the clans of Judah, from you shall come forth for me one who is to be ruler in Israel, whose coming forth is from of old, from ancient days."

Christian Science

"Jesus was the offspring of Mary's self-conscious communion with God" (Science and Health, Pg. 29-30).

"Mary's conception of him was spiritual, for only purity could reflect Truth and Love, which were plainly incarnate in the good and pure Christ Jesus" (Science and Health, Pg. 332).

Islam

So, she conceived him, and she retired with him to a remote place. And the pains of childbirth drove her to the trunk of a palm-tree: She cried (in her anguish): "Ah! would that I had died before this! would that I had been a thing forgotten and out of sight!" But (a voice) cried to her from beneath the (palm-tree): "Grieve not! for thy Lord hath provided a rivulet beneath thee; "And shake towards thyself the trunk of the palm-tree: It will let fall fresh ripe dates upon thee. "So, eat and drink and cool (thine) eye. And if thou dost see any human, say, 'I have vowed a fast to (Allah) Most Gracious, and this day will I enter into no talk with any human being'" (Surah 19:22-26).

Jehovah's Witnesses

Jehovah then placed the 'life force' of Michael [Archangel] in the womb of the virgin Mary so Jesus could be born a human being (Watchtower Book, The Kingdom at Hand).

Jesus' Blood/Sacrifice Sufficient

Biblical Code: JBS

Bible: The Bible teaches us that, "...we have now been justified by his blood" (Romans 5:9). We also "have been sanctified through the offering of the body of Jesus Christ once for all" (Hebrews 10:10) and "if we walk in the light, as he is in the light, we have fellowship with one another, and the blood of Jesus his Son cleanses us from all sin" (1 John 1:7). It also tells us that, "...we all have been sanctified through the offering of the body of Jesus Christ once for all" (Hebrews 10:10) and that "...the blood of Jesus, His son, cleanses us from all sin" (1 John 1:7). Without Jesus' sacrifice there would be no forgiveness of sins.

Scripture	Content
Hebrews 9:14-15 (9-28)	"how much more will **the blood of Christ**, who through the eternal Spirit offered himself without blemish to God, **purify our conscience from dead works to serve the living God.** Therefore he is the mediator of a new covenant, so that those who are called may receive the promised eternal inheritance, since a death has occurred that redeems them from the transgressions committed under the first covenant."
Romans 5:6-9	"For while we were still weak, at the right time Christ died for the ungodly. For one will scarcely die for a righteous person--though perhaps for a good person one would dare even to die--but God shows his love for us in that while we were still sinners, Christ died for us. Since, therefore, **we have now been justified by his blood,** much more shall we be saved by him from the wrath of God."
Matthew 26:27-28	"And he took a cup, and when he had given thanks he gave it to them, saying, "Drink of it, all of you, for **this is my blood of the covenant, which is poured out for many for the forgiveness of sins.**"
Hebrews 10:10-14	"And by that will we have been sanctified through the offering of **the body of Jesus Christ once for all.** And every priest stands daily at his service, offering repeatedly the same sacrifices, which can never take away sins. But when Christ had offered for all time a single sacrifice for sins, he sat down at the right hand of God, waiting from that time until his enemies should be made a footstool for his feet. For by a single offering he has perfected for all time those who are being sanctified."
1 John 1:7	"But if we walk in the light, as he is in the light, we have fellowship with one another, and **the blood of Jesus his Son cleanses us from all sin.**"
Revelation 1:5	"and from Jesus Christ the faithful witness, the firstborn of the dead, and the ruler of kings on earth. To him who loves us and has **freed us from our sins by his blood.**"

Ephesians 2:13 (11-18)	"But now in Christ Jesus you who once were far off have been **brought near by the blood of Christ.**"

Baha'i

"A Christian may find spiritual peace in believing in a substitutionary atonement. In Baha'ism this is unnecessary. That age is past. The new age of spiritual maturity has dawned through Baha'u'llah, and we are to listen to his word" (Baha'i apologist and teacher Udo Schaefer as quoted in The Kingdom of the Cults by Walter Martin).

Christian Science

"The material blood of Jesus was no more efficacious to cleanse from sin when it washed upon 'the accursed tree' than when it was flowing in his veins as he went daily about his Father's business" (Science and Health, Pg. 25:6-8).

Islam

"Centered on an external entity – the mystical body of Christ in which the Christian must participate in order to be saved" while in Islam he sees that "the redemptive potential is centered in the individual himself" (Yasien Mohamed, Human Nature in Islam).

"And they said we have killed the Messiah Jesus son of Mary, the Messenger of God. They did not kill him, nor did they crucify him, though it was made to appear like that to them; those that disagreed about him are full of doubt, with no knowledge to follow, only supposition: they certainly did not kill him. On the contrary, God raised him unto himself. God is almighty and wise" (Surah 4:157-158).

Judaism

Jesus was simply a Jewish teacher so him dying on the cross has nothing to do with salvation (My Jewish Learning: What Do Jews Believe About Jesus?).

Unification Church

Moon stated that, "During my first 3 years of public ministry, just as Jesus did, I had to go through severe hardships culminating in the torture of prison life, which was more for me than Jesus' cross. I had to accomplish all left unaccomplished by my predecessor....When you think of that, you must feel indebted to me and you cannot lift your face before me" (Master Speaks, 27 May,1973, Pg. 13; 4 March,1973, Pg. 10).

"Today the Christian gospel preaches salvation by the blood of Jesus. How ridiculous that is in the sight of God!" (Moon, Master Speaks, April 8,1978, Pg. 12).

"We, therefore, must realize that Jesus did not come to die on the cross" (Divine Principle, Pg. 435).

Unitarian Universalist

"He also rejected the idea that Jesus's death on the cross saved us — he taught that what saved us was Jesus's embodiment of love and justice" (Official website for Unitarian Universalist Association uua.org).

Jesus is The Christ—Deity

Biblical Code: JIC

Bible: The Bible teaches us that Jesus is the Christ and God's son (Matthew 16:16), that He and the Father are one (John 10:30) and that "...in him the whole fullness of deity dwells bodily" (Colossians 2:9).

Scripture	Content
Matthew 16:16	Simon Peter replied, "**You are the Christ**, the Son of the living God."
Mark 14:61-62	"But he remained silent and made no answer. Again the high priest asked him, "**Are you the Christ, the Son of the Blessed?**" **And Jesus said, "I am,** and you will see the Son of Man seated at the right hand of Power, and coming with the clouds of heaven."
John 1:1	"**In the beginning was the Word, and the Word was with God, and the Word was God.**"
John 1:14	"And the **Word became flesh** and dwelt among us, and we have seen his glory, glory as of the only Son from the Father, full of grace and truth."
Romans 8:3	"For God has done what the law, weakened by the flesh, could not do. By **sending his own Son** in the likeness of sinful flesh and for sin, he condemned sin in the flesh,"
Colossians 2:9	"**For in him the whole fullness of deity dwells bodily,**"
Hebrews 1:1-4 (1-14)	"Long ago, at many times and in many ways, God spoke to our fathers by the prophets, but in these last days he has spoken to us **by his Son,** whom he appointed the heir of all things, through whom also he created the world. He is the radiance of the glory of God and the exact imprint of his nature, and he upholds the universe by the word of his power. After making purification for sins, he sat down at the right hand of the Majesty on high, having become as much superior to angels as the name he has inherited is more excellent than theirs."
1 John 2:22	"Who is the liar but he who denies that **Jesus is the Christ**? This is the antichrist, he who denies the Father and the Son."
Revelation 1:17-18	"When I saw him, I fell at his feet as though dead. But he laid his right hand on me, saying, "Fear not, **I am the first and the last**, and the living one. I died, and behold I am alive forevermore, and I have the keys of Death and Hades."

Baha'i

Jesus was only one of nine manifestations of the divine being and appeared in His era of time.....today Baha'u'llah is the source of revelation (Baha'i apologist and teacher Udo Schaefer as quoted in The Kingdome of the Cults by Walter Martin).

God has sent Divine Messengers known as Manifestations of God—among them Abraham, Krishna, Zoroaster, Moses, Buddha, Jesus Christ, Muhammad, and, in more recent times, the Báb and Bahá'u'lláh—to cultivate humanity's spiritual, intellectual and moral capacities (the official Bahai website). They believe that Jesus was just one of nine manifestations of the divine being and He appeared in her era of time. Today the Ba'u'llah is the source of revelation (Martin, 2003)

Christian Science

Jesus was not the Christ. He was a man who displayed the Christ idea. Christ meaning perfection, not a person (Science and Health 333:3-15; 334:3).

"The spiritual Christ was infallible; Jesus, the material manhood, was not the Christ" (Miscellaneous Writings, Pg. 84).

The Christian who believes in the First commandments is a monotheist. Thus he virtually unites with the Jew's belief in one God and recognizes that Jesus Christ is not God as Jesus Christ himself declared, but is the Son of God (Science and Health 152).

Islam

Jesus is just one of the many prophets of Allah (Surah 4:171; 5:74).

Such (was) Jesus the son of Mary: (it is) a statement of truth, about which they (vainly) dispute. It is not befitting to (the majesty of) God that He should beget a son. Glory be to Him! when He determines a matter, He only says to it, "Be", and it is (Surah 19:34-35).
"Christ, the son of Mary, was no more than a messenger; many were the messengers that passed away before him. His mother was a woman of truth" (Surah 5:75; cf. 5:116-120).

"The similitude of Jesus before Allah is as that of Adam; He created him from dust, then said to him; 'Be': and he was" (Surah 3:59).
The Qur'an teaches that Jesus was not God...that he was a man prophet much like many other prophets. "The Messiah, son of Maryam, was no more than a Messenger; many were the Messengers that passed away before him. His mother was a Siddiqah [she believed in the words of Allah and His books—see Surah 66:12]. They both used to eat food as any other human being, while Allah does not eat). Look how We make the Ayat (proofs, evidences, verses, lessons, signs, revelations, etc.) clear to them, yet look how they are deluded away from the truth" (Surah 5:75).

Jehovah's Witnesses

Hoekema summarizes their belief. "Jehovah's Witnesses deny the full deity of Jesus Christ, and his complete equality with Jehovah. He may be called a god, but not Jehovah God; he is a mighty one but not almighty as Jehovah God is" (Let God Be True, Pg. 32-33; See Hoekema, 1976 p. 257).

Jehovah's Witnesses believe that when Jesus was born on earth, he was a mere human and not God in human flesh. "That the Son of God born on earth was no mighty spirit person clothing himself with a baby's fleshly form and pretending to be absolutely ignorant like a new born infant is proved by one Scripture (Philippians 2:5-8), which shows he laid aside complete his spirit existence…" (The Truth Shall Make Your Free, Pg. 246).

While on earth Christ only had the nature of man. "By this miracle [the virgin birth] he was born a man (Philippians 2:7…). He was not clothed upon with flesh over an invisible spirit person, but he WAS flesh (Religion for Mankind, Pg. 231).

They also teach that in his prehumen existence he was the Archangel Michael (New Heavens and a New Earth, Pg. 27, 30).

Judaism

Jews "…have come to regard him as a Jewish teacher. This does not mean, however, that they believe, as Christians do, that he was raised from the dead or was the messiah" (taken from myjewishlearning website What Do Jews Believe About Jesus?).

In the Mishneh Torah specific things Jews believe the messiah must accomplish in order to confirm his identity — among them restoring the kingdom of David to its former glory, achieving victory in battle against Israel's enemies, rebuilding the temple (which the Romans destroyed in 70 AD) and ingathering the exiles to the land of Israel. "And if he's not successful with this, or if he is killed, it's known that he is not the one that was promised by the Torah," Maimonides wrote. Jesus failed this 'test'. (Rambam, 1998).

"The New Testament also include numerous verses testifying to Jesus as equal to God and as divine — a belief hard to reconcile with Judaism's insistence on God's oneness" (taken from myjewishlearning website).

Scientology

"But what I am telling you is that these people handed on a torch of wisdom, of information, generation to generation. It was handed along geographical routes and one of those geographical routes was the Middle East. And one of the people who handed it on was a man named Moses. And again it was handed on to a man named Christ. And he handed it on and even the Arab nations benefited from this through their own prophet, Muhammad" (What is Scientology's View of Moses, Jesus, Muhammad, the Buddha and Other Religious Figures of the Past? As found on the Official Scientology website).

Jesus was just a shade above "clear" and was no greater than Buddha or Moses (Christianity Magazine, 5:10, as quoted by Anderson, Report, 150).

Unification Church

"Jesus was born of a father and a mother, just as everyone else is, but in his case the Spirit of God was working also" (Master Speaks, Pg. 9).
Christ was a man (Divine Principle, Pg. 258).

"Adam and Eve were supposed to be the True Parents of mankind in God's plan. When they failed, God intended Jesus to be the True Parent of mankind. When he was crucified on the cross, God promised another messiah. He is coming to consummate the ideal of God-centered True Parents. He will generate a new family of God through restoring the family unit under God's ideal. When we have True Parents of God, we can all become true brothers and sisters" (Reverend Moon, cited in Frederic Sontag, Sun Myung Mood and the Unification Church, 142-143).

Jesus was the second Adam. For 2000 years Christians have supposed to prepare for the coming of the second Messiah. That Messiah will be born somewhere in the east. Korea is the only logical place for people there have a strong faith in God. Moon is the second coming of the Messiah (Divine Principle, 519; Yamamoto, 1974).

"It is plain that Jesus is not God himself" (Divine Principle, p. 211).

Unity

"Unity Church followers believe in the divinity of Jesus, but only in the sense that all humans are the children of God and share that divine potential. They believe that Jesus was a master teacher who expressed this divine potential and sought to show others how to do the same. Unity uses the term "Christ" to mean the divinity in all people. For them Jesus is the great example of the Christ in physical form" (Teach Us to Pray, 1997).

Unitarian Universalist

"We believe that Jesus was a prophet of God, and that other prophets from God have risen in other faith traditions" (Official website for Unitarian Universalist Association uua.org).

Comparative Doctrine

Jesus is Eternal

Biblical Code: JE

Bible: The Bible teaches us that Jesus was with God in the very beginning of creation (John 1:1). In Hebrews 7:15-17 the writer says about Jesus, "You are a priest forever, after the order of Melchizedek."

Scripture	Content
John 1:1	**"In the beginning was the Word,** and the Word was with God, and the Word was God."
Colossians 1:17	"And he is before all things, and in him all things hold together."
Hebrews 7:3	**"He is without father or mother or genealogy, having neither beginning of days nor end of life,** but resembling the Son of God he continues a priest forever."
Hebrews 1:8-12	**But of the Son he says, "Your throne, O God, is forever and ever,** the scepter of uprightness is the scepter of your kingdom. You have loved righteousness and hated wickedness; therefore God, your God, has anointed you with the oil of gladness beyond your companions." And, "You, Lord, laid the foundation of the earth in the beginning, and the heavens are the work of your hands; they will perish, but you remain; they will all wear out like a garment, like a robe you will roll them up, like a garment they will be changed. But you are the same, and your years will have no end."

Christian Science

The word Christ is not properly a synonym for Jesus, though it is commonly so used. Jesus was a human name, which belonged to him in common with other Hebrew boys and men, for it is identical with the name of Josua.......On the other hand, Christ is not a name so much as the divine title of Jesus. ,,,,,The divine image, idea, or Christ was, is, and ever will be inseparable from the divine Principle, God" (Science and Health, Pg. 333-334). To sum it up Jesus was a mortal man and no longer exists, he was not eternal.   Christ (the spiritual idea) is simply a reflection of God.

Islam

The Qur'an teaches that Jesus was not God....that he was a human prophet much like many other prophets. "The Messiah ['Iesa (Jesus)], son of Maryam (Mary), was no more than a Messenger; many were the Messengers that passed away before him. His mother [Maryam (Mary)] was a Siddiqah [i.e. she believed in the words of Allâh and His Books (see Verse 66:12)]. They both used to eat food (as any other human being, while Allâh does not eat). Look how We make the Ayât (proofs, evidences, verses, lessons, signs, revelations, etc.) clear to them, yet look how they are deluded away (from the truth)" (Qur'an 5:75).

Jehovah's Witnesses

"He [Jesus] was a god, but not the Almighty God, who is Jehovah" (Let God Be True, Pg. 33; The Truth Shall Make You Free, Pg. 44).

Jesus was the first and direct creation of Jehovah God (The Kingdom is at Hand, 46-47, 49; See JW.Org Bible Teachings).

"Instead, he [Jesus] was the first of Jehovah's creations, and subsequently created everything else" (Watch Tower Bible and Tract Society of Pennsylvania. "Michael" Watfchtower Online Library. The Kingdom at Hand, 46-47,I 49; See JW.Org Bible Teachings).

The Jehovah's Witnesses believe that the Angel Michael was actually Jesus Christ in his pre-human form (New Heaven and New Earth, Pg. 27).

Jehovah's Witnesses believe that Jesus was created by Jehovah as the archangel Michael before the physical world existed, and is a lesser, though mighty, god. ...the archangel Michael is Jesus Christ... So the evidence indicates that the Son of God was known as Michael before he came to earth and is known also by that name since his return to heaven where he resides as the glorified spirit Son of God. (Reasoning from the Scriptures, Pg. 218 Watch Tower Bible and Tract Society of Pennsylvania, 1989 See JW.Org)

Mormonism

"Among the spirit-children of Elohim the firstborn was and is Jehovah or Jesus Christ to whom all others are Juniors. . . Jesus Christ is not the Father of the spirits who have taken or yet shall take bodies upon this earth, for He is one of them. He is the Son as they are sons or daughters of Elohim" (Articles of Faith, pp. 471-473). Jesus was Created (Mormon Doctrine, Pg. 322-323).

Scientology

Christ is a legend that preexisted earth-life on other planets and was implanted into humans on earth (Professional Auditor's Bulletin 31, quoted by Anderson, Reort,130).

Comparative Doctrine

Jesus' Mission

Biblical Code: JM

Bible: Luke writes that Jesus "…. came to seek and to save the lost" (Luke 19:10). His mission was to become the savior of the world and provide man a way to connect with the Father and ultimately have a place with Him in heaven.

Scripture	Content
Matthew 20:28	"**Jesus came** not to be served but to serve, and **to give his life as a ransom for many."**
Luke 4:43	but he said to them, "**I must preach the good news of the kingdom of God to the other towns as well; for I was sent for this purpose."**
Luke 19:10	**"For the Son of Man came to seek and to save the lost."**
John 12:27-33	"Now is my soul troubled. And what shall I say? 'Father, save me from this hour'? **But for this purpose I have come to this hour. Father, glorify your name."** Then a voice came from heaven: "I have glorified it, and I will glorify it again." The crowd that stood there and heard it said that it had thundered. Others said, "An angel has spoken to him." Jesus answered, "This voice has come for your sake, not mine. Now is the judgment of this world; now will the ruler of this world be cast out. And I, when I am lifted up from the earth, will draw all people to myself." He said this to show by what kind of death he was going to die.
1 John 4:14	"And we have seen and testify that **the Father has sent his Son to be the Savior of the world."**

Judaism

"More than 1,000 years after Jesus' crucifixion, the medieval sage Maimonides (also known as Rambam) laid out in his Mishneh Torah specific things Jews believe the messiah must accomplish in order to confirm his identity — among them restoring the kingdom of David to its former glory, achieving victory in battle against Israel's enemies, rebuilding the temple (which the Romans destroyed in 70 AD) and in gathering the exiles to the land of Israel. "And if he's not successful with this, or if he is killed, it's known that he is not the one that was promised by the Torah," Maimonides wrote" (My Jewish Learning: What Do Jews Believe About Jesus?).

Unification Church

"The crucifixion of Jesus was a secondary choice….after it became obvious that he would not be able to fulfill his mission" (Kim, Principle, Pg. 60-61).

Moon believed that Jesus had a primary mission from God. He stated that, "there had to be a bride, a Mother---another Eve. So God intended for this perfected Adam---Jesus Christ---to restore his bride, the perfected Eve" (Moon, The New Future of Christianity, Pg. 171-172).

"I am Jesus who came 2000 years ago. My mission still remains to be accomplished. In order to realize God's will, you must be responsible for a great mission" (120 Day Training Manual, p. 324).

A major part of Christ's mission was to establish the perfect marriage while he was on earth (Divine Principle, pp. 140-141).

Christ did not fulfill his mission on earth (Divine Principle and its Application, Pg. 64-65).

Unitarian Universalist

"Unitarian Universalist theology is of this world, not of the next. Jesus, in fact, taught that the realm of God is within and, contrary to most Christian practice, his teachings were centered on relationship, not salvation" (Official website for Unitarian Universalist Association   uua.org).

Jesus' Physical Death

Biblical Code: JPD

Bible: The following scriptures discuss Jesus' death. Jesus foretold his death and resurrection (Mark 8:31). A Roman centurion stated that Jesus was dead (Mark 15:45). His body was wrapped in a linen shroud and he was laid in a tomb (Luke 23:53).

Scripture	Content
Matthew 27:58-60	"He went to Pilate and asked for **the body of Jesus**. Then Pilate ordered it to be given to him. And Joseph took the body and wrapped it in a clean linen shroud and laid it in his own new tomb,"
Mark 8:31	"And he began to teach them that the **Son of Man must suffer many things** and be rejected by the elders and the chief priests and the scribes **and be killed,** and after three days rise again."
Mark 15:43-46	"Joseph of Arimathea, a respected member of the council, who was also himself looking for the kingdom of God, took courage and went to Pilate and asked for **the body of Jesus**. Pilate was surprised to hear that **he should have already died**. And summoning the centurion, he asked him whether he was already dead. And when he learned from the centurion that **he was dead**, he granted the corpse to Joseph. And Joseph bought a linen shroud, and taking him down, **wrapped him in the linen shroud and laid him in a tomb** that had been cut out of the rock. And he rolled a stone against the entrance of the tomb."
Luke 23:46	"Then Jesus, calling out with a loud voice, said, "Father, into your hands I commit my spirit!" **And having said this he breathed his last.**"
Luke 23:52-53	"This man went to Pilate and **asked for the body of Jesus**. Then he took it down and wrapped it in a linen shroud and laid him in a tomb cut in stone, where no one had ever yet been laid."
John 10:11-18	"I am the good shepherd. The good shepherd **lays down his life** for the sheep. He who is a hired hand and not a shepherd, who does not own the sheep, sees the wolf coming and leaves the sheep and flees, and the wolf snatches them and scatters them He flees because he is a hired hand and cares nothing for the sheep. I am the good shepherd. I know my own and my own know me, just as the Father knows me and I know the Father; and I lay down my life for the sheep. And I have other sheep that are not of this fold. I must bring them also, and they will listen to my voice. So there will be one flock, one shepherd. For this reason the Father loves me, because I lay down my life that I may take it up again. No one takes it from me, but I lay it down of my own accord. I have authority to lay it down, and I have authority to take it up again. This charge I have received from my Father."
John 19:33 (31-42)	"But when they came to Jesus and **saw that he was already dead**, they did not break his legs."

Rev. 1:18b	"...**I died,** and behold I am alive forevermore, and I have the keys of Death and Hades."
Mark 15:45-47	"And when he learned from the centurion **that he was dead**, he granted the corpse to Joseph. And Joseph bought a linen shroud, and taking him down, wrapped him in the linen shroud and laid him in a tomb that had been cut out of the rock. And he rolled a stone against the entrance of the tomb. Mary Magdalene and Mary the mother of Jesus saw where he was laid.

Christian Science

Jesus did not die...he was alive while in the tomb, (Science and Health, Pg. 44).

Islam

The Qu'ran teaches that Jesus was not crucified and did not die on the cross. "And because of their saying (in boast), "We killed Messiah 'Iesa (Jesus), son of Maryam (Mary), the Messenger of Allâh," – but they killed him not, nor crucified him, but the resemblance of 'Iesa (Jesus) was put over another man (and they killed that man), and those who differ therein are full of doubts. They have no (certain) knowledge, they follow nothing but conjecture. For surely; they killed him not [i.e. 'Iesa (Jesus), son of Maryam (Mary)]" (Qur'an 4:157)

Jehovah's Witnesses

"He was executed on a torture stake, not crucified" (Watch tower Bible and Tract Society of Pennsylvania, "Michael" Watchtower Online Library).

Unification Church

Jesus' ". . . body was invaded by Satan and he was killed" (Divine Principle, Pg. 148).

Jesus' Physical Resurrection

Biblical Code: JPR

Bible: The following scriptures suggest that Jesus was resurrected from the dead and that he spoke to different people, handled food, ate food in front of them, and individuals touched him. After his resurrection he came to his disciples several times.   In Luke 24:39 Jesus said, "See my hands and my feet, that it is I myself. Touch me, and see. For a spirit does not have flesh and bones as you see that I have."

Scripture	Content
Luke 24:13-29	(Summary) **Jesus spoke to two of his disciples on the Road to Emmaus after his resurrection.**
Luke 24:30-32	When he was at table with them, **he took the bread and blessed and broke it and gave it to them. And their eyes were opened, and they recognized him.** And he vanished from their sight. They said to each other, "Did not our hearts burn within us while he talked to us on the road, while he opened to us the Scriptures?"
Luke 24:38-43	And he said to them, "Why are you troubled, and why do doubts arise in your hearts? **See my hands and my feet, that it is I myself. Touch me, and see. For a spirit does not have flesh and bones as you see that I have."** And when he had said this, he showed them his hands and his feet. And while they still disbelieved for joy and were marveling, he said to them, "Have you anything here to eat?" They gave him a piece of broiled fish, and he took it and ate before them.
John 2:19-21	Jesus answered them, "Destroy this temple, and **in three days I will raise it up."** The Jews then said, "It has taken forty-six years to build this temple, and will you raise it up in three days?" But he was speaking about the temple of his body.
John 20:17	**Jesus said to her, "Do not cling to me, for I have not yet ascended to the Father;** but go to my brothers and say to them, 'I am ascending to my Father and your Father, to my God and your God.'"
John 21:12-14	Jesus said to them, "Come and have breakfast." Now none of the disciples dared ask him, "Who are you?" They knew it was the Lord. Jesus came and took the bread and gave it to them, and so with the fish. **This was now the third time that Jesus was revealed to the disciples after he was raised from the dead.**

Armstrongism

Armstrong teaches that Jesus Christ rose from the dead as a spirit without a physical form. "Now notice carefully, God the Father did not cause Jesus Christ to get back into the body that had died....And the resurrected body was no longer human---it was the Christ resurrected immortal, once again changed! As he had been changed, converted into mortal human flesh and blood, subject to death, and for the purpose of dying for your sins, now by a resurrection from the dead, he was again changed, converted into immortality (Armstrong, What Christ Died and Rose Again, The Plain Truth, April 1982, Pg. 20).

Baha'i

"The alleged resurrection of Jesus and His ascension into heaven may or may not be true depending upon your point of view. As I said before, we are concerned with Baha'u'llah and the new era or age, and while we reverence Jesus as we do the great prophets of other religions, we do not believe that it is necessarily important that the Baha'i Faith recognize ever tenet of a specific religion. We believe that Jesus conquered death, that He triumphed over the grave, but these are things that are in the realm of the spirit and must receive spiritual interpretation the revelation of Baha'u'llah supersedes such claims" (Baha'i apologist and teacher Udo Schaefer as quoted in The Kingdome of the Cults by Walter Martin).

Christian Science

Jesus was experiencing thought for the days he was in the grave, so he wasn't dead: "Our Master reappeared to his students, -- to their apprehension he rose from the grave, -- on the third day of his ascending thought, and so presented to them the certain sense of eternal life" (Science and Health, 509:4-8).

Islam

That they said (in boast), "We killed Christ Jesus the son of Mary, the Apostle of God";- but they killed him not, nor crucified him, but so it was made to appear to them, and those who differ therein are full of doubts, with no (certain) knowledge, but only conjecture to follow, for of a surety they killed him not:- Nay, God raised him up unto Himself; and God is Exalted in Power, Wise;- (Surah 4:157-158).

Jehovah's Witnesses

Jehovah's Witnesses believe that Jesus was resurrected spiritually from the dead, but not physically (The Harp of God, 1928, Pg. 173; Religion for Mankind, Pg. 259).

"Rather than experiencing a bodily resurrection, Jesus was raised as a spirit, becoming the Archangel Michael again" (Watch Tower Bible and Tract Society of Pennsylvania, "Michael," Watchtower Online Library).

Judaism

Do not believe that Jesus was the Messiah or that he rose from the dead (My Jewish Learning: What Do Jews Believe About Jesus?).

Unity

"Jesus spent whole nights in prayer, according to the Gospels, and it is quite evident that He was resurrecting His body by realizing, as we do in our prayers, that God was His indwelling life." (Jesus Christ Heals, Pg.13).

Comparative Doctrine

Jesus was Sinless

Biblical Code: JS

Bible: The Bible states that, "for all have sinned and fall short of the glory of God," (Romans 3:23) and that Jesus "...knew no sin" (2 Corinthians 5:21), even though he was "...tempted as we are..." (Hebrews 4:15).   No man or woman has ever been sinless except for Jesus.

Scripture	Content
2 Corinthians 5:21	"For our sake **he made him to be sin who knew no sin,** so that in him we might become the righteousness of God."
Hebrews 4:15	"For we do not have a high priest who is unable to sympathize with our weaknesses, but **one who in every respect has been tempted as we are, yet without sin."**
1 Peter 1:18-19	"knowing that you were ransomed from the futile ways inherited from your forefathers, not with perishable things such as silver or gold, **but with the precious blood of Christ, like that of a lamb without blemish or spot."**
1 Peter 2:22	"**He committed no sin,** neither was deceit found in his mouth."
1 John 3:5	"You know that he appeared to take away sins, **and in him there is no sin."**

Christian Science

Jesus was Fallible. "He (Jesus) knew the mortal error which constitute the material body, and could destroy those errors; but at the time when Jesus felt our infirmities, he had not conquered all the beliefs of the flesh or his sense of material life, nor had he risen to his final demonstrations of spiritual power" (Science and Health, Pg. 53).

Unification Church

". . . Father (Moon) is sinless, Mother (Moon's wife) is sinless, and their children are sinless. . . This is called the Messiah's family; this was established in 1967, on December 31. The sinless family was established on earth" (120 Day Training Manual, p. 236).

Judged by Grace Through Faith

Biblical Code: JGF

Bible: The Bible teaches us that we are saved by grace and that our works are the fruit or result of our Christianity. That does not mean that as individuals we do not need to follow the Biblical plan to obtain salvation or live a Christian life. Regardless, we are judged by grace through faith (Ephesians 2:8-10).

Scripture	Content
Ephesians 2:8-10	**"For by grace you have been saved through faith.** And this is not your own doing; it is the gift of God, not a result of works, so that no one may boast. For we are his workmanship, created in Christ Jesus for good works, which God prepared beforehand, that we should walk in them."
Romans 1:16	"For I am not ashamed of the gospel, **for it is the power of God for salvation to everyone who believes,** to the Jew first and also to the Greek."
Galatians 2:16-21	"yet we know that a person is not justified by works of the law **but through faith in Jesus Christ, so we also have believed in Christ Jesus, in order to be justified by faith in Christ** and not by works of the law, because by works of the law no one will be justified. But if, in our endeavor to be justified in Christ, we too were found to be sinners, is Christ then a servant of sin? Certainly not! For if I rebuild what I tore down, I prove myself to be a transgressor. For through the law I died to the law, so that I might live to God. I have been crucified with Christ. It is no longer I who live, but Christ who lives in me. And the life I now live in the flesh I live by faith in the Son of God, who loved me and gave himself for me. I do not nullify the grace of God, for if righteousness were through the law, then Christ died for no purpose."
Titus 3:4-8	"But when the goodness and loving kindness of God our Savior appeared, **he saved us, not because of works done by us in righteousness, but according to his own mercy, by the washing of regeneration and renewal of the Holy Spirit,** whom he poured out on us richly **through Jesus Christ our Savior,** so that being justified by his grace we might become heirs according to the hope of eternal life. The saying is trustworthy, and I want you to insist on these things, so that those who have believed in God may be careful to devote themselves to good works. These things are excellent and profitable for people."
John 6:29 (26-29)	Jesus answered them, **"This is the work of God, that you believe in him whom he has sent."**
James 2:24 (18-26)	"You see that **a person is justified by works and not by faith alone."**
Colossians 2:11-12	"In him also you were circumcised with a circumcision made without hands, by putting off the body of the flesh, by the circumcision of Christ, **having been buried with him in baptism, in which you were also raised with him through faith** in the powerful working of God, who raised him from the dead.

Romans 10:9-10	"You see that **a person is justified by works and not by faith alone.**"
Acts 2:38	And Peter said to them, "**Repent and be baptized every one of you in the name of Jesus Christ for the forgiveness of your sins,** and you will receive the gift of the Holy Spirit."

Armstrongism

Armstrong believed that repentance, faith and the indwelling of God's Holy Spirit enables true and full obedience to God's law, but stressed that keeping God's law (and repentance upon having sinned) is a requirement for salvation (Armstrong, Herbert (1961). What do you mean... Salvation? (PDF). Pasadena, California: Ambassador College Press).

Baha'i

"We accept the fact that no one is perfect, but by the practice of principles laid down by Baha'u'llah and by making every effort through prayer and personal sacrifice to live in accord with the character of the divine being revealed to him, we can arrive at eventual salvation as you like to term it" (Baha'i apologist and teacher Udo Schaefer as quoted in The Kingdom of the Cults by Walter Martin).

Buddhism

"The bhikshu, full of delight, who is calm in the doctrine of Buddha will reach the quiet place (Nirvana), cessation of natural desires, and happiness" (Dhammapada V. 381).

Catholicism

"Even though incorporated into the Church, one who does not however persevere in charity is not saved" (Catechism, 837).

Hinduism

The Hindi must evolve by working to get rid of all Kama has been resolved. It's only then that they can be 'saved'. "Hindus believe that the soul reincarnates, evolving through many births until all karmas have been resolved, and moksha, liberation from the cycle of rebirth, is attained. Not a single soul will be deprived of this destiny." (www.Hinduismtoday.com Hinduism Magazine).

Islam

In the preface of the Qur'an it shows that the central subject is man and what man must do to "succeed" in eternal life. Written by Abdullah Yusuf Ali.
The term Najat is found only once in the Qur'an (Surah 40:41). It simply means an escape from judgment. So instead of salvation Islam offers guidance to mankind and if you obey your chances of being forgiven are increased, but no guaranteed (see Abdullah Yusuf Ali's introduction to his classic translation and commentary on the Surah: The Glorious Surah).

Every Muslim must fulfill the works of the Five Pillars of the Faith to escape the judgment of Allah (Surah 10:10-9).

1. Recite the Shahada "There is no God but Allah, and Mohammad is the prophet of Allah"
2. Participate in five daily prayers
3. Almsgiving or Zakat: Giving income to help others.
4. Fasting: During Ramadan. Can eat or drink before sunrise or after sunset.
5. Pilgrimage to Mecca: At least once in a Muslim's lifetime.

Jehovah's Witnesses

Jehovah's Witnesses believe that salvation requires faith in Christ, association with God's organization (i.e., their religion), and obedience to its rules. Anyone may become one of sheep people who will gain everlasting life on a paradise earth. They just have to hear the voice of the Right Shephard and come into the New World Society (Paradise Lost, Pg. 195-169).
To receive everlasting life in the earthly paradise we must identify that organization [Jehovah's Witnesses] and serve God as part of it (Watchtower, February 15, 1983, P. 12).

Judaism

Halacha or the Jewish Legal Tradition and the 613 Mitzvot or commandments. This is the rabbinic interpretation of Jewish law. The word "halakhah" is usually translated as "Jewish Law." This is often found in the Torah. It is the collective body of Jewish religious law as derived from the written and Oral Torah. A list of the 613 Mitzvot (commandments). Today, spiritual descendants of both traditionalists and reformers interpret Jewish law according to their respective principles for their communities.

Mormonism

11 For I (Jesus) command all men, both in the east and in the west, and in the north, and in the south, and in the islands of the sea, that they shall write the words which I speak unto them; for out of the books which shall be written I will judge the world, every man according to their works, according to that which is written. 2 Nephi 29:11. *For clarification as to whom is speaking…not in text.

Unity

"We have thought that we were to be saved by Jesus' making personal petitions and sacrifices for us, but now we see that we are to be saved by using the creative principles that he developed in himself and that He is ever ready to cooperate with us in developing in ourselves by observing the law as He observed it. 'I in them, and thou in me, that they may be perfected into one" (Jesus Christ Heals, Pg. 162).

Comparative Doctrine

Judgment Day

Biblical Code: JMT

Bible: The Bible teaches us that "...on the day of judgment people will give account for every careless word they speak."   In Romans 2:16 we are told that, "On that day when, according to my gospel, God judges the secrets of men by Christ Jesus."

Scripture	Content
Matthew 12:36	"I tell you, **on the day of judgment people will give account for every careless word they speak,**"
Matthew 25:31-46	"When the Son of Man comes in his glory, and all the angels with him, then he will sit on his glorious throne. Before him will be gathered all the nations, and he will separate people one from another as a shepherd separates the sheep from the goats. **And he will place the sheep on his right, but the goats on the left. Then the King will say to those on his right, 'Come, you who are blessed by my Father, inherit the kingdom prepared for you from the foundation of the world.** For I was hungry and you gave me food, I was thirsty and you gave me drink, I was a stranger and you welcomed me, ...'"
John 12:48	"The one who rejects me and does not receive my words has a judge; **the word that I have spoken will judge him on the last day.**"
Acts 17:31	"because **he has fixed a day on which he will judge the world in righteousness** by a man whom he has appointed; and of this he has given assurance to all by raising him from the dead."
Romans 2:16	"On that day when, according to my gospel, **God judges the secrets of men by Christ Jesus.**"
2 Corinthians 5:10	**"For we must all appear before the judgment seat of Christ, so that each one may receive what is due for what he has done in the body, whether good or evil."**
2 Thessalonians 1:5-10	"This is evidence of the righteous judgment of God, that you may be considered worthy of the kingdom of God, for which you are also suffering— since indeed God considers it just to repay with affliction those who afflict you, and to grant relief to you who are afflicted as well as to us, **when the Lord Jesus is revealed from heaven with his mighty angels in flaming fire, inflicting vengeance on those who do not know God and on those who do not obey the gospel of our Lord Jesus.** They will suffer the punishment of eternal destruction, away from the presence of the Lord and from the glory of his might,"

2 Timothy 4:8	"Henceforth there is laid up for me the crown of righteousness, which **the Lord, the righteous judge, will award to me on that Day,** and not only to me but also to all who have loved his appearing."
Hebrews 9:27	"And just as it is appointed for man to die once, **and after that comes judgment,**"
2 Peter 2:4	**"For if God did not spare angels when they sinned, but cast them into hell and committed them to chains of gloomy darkness to be kept until the judgment;"**
2 Peter 2:9	"then the Lord knows how to rescue the godly from trials, and to keep the unrighteous under punishment **until the day of judgment,**"
Revelation 20:15	**"And if anyone's name was not found written in the book of life, he was thrown into the lake of fire."**

Baha'i

"The Baha'i faith recognizes divine judgment, though not in the graphic terms that Christians portray it. We know nothing of eternal frames where sinners will be confined forever without respite. We do believe in the paradise of God, which will be the abode of the righteous and in the resurrection and the final righting of all things (Baha'i apologist and teacher Udo Schaefer as quoted in The Kingdome of the Cults by Walter Martin).

Christian Science

There is no final judgment. "No final judgment awaits mortals, for the judgment-day of wisdom comes hourly and continually, even the judgment by which mortal man is divested of all material error" (Science and Health, 291).

Jehovah's Witnesses

The 144,000 in heaven may also be called "associate kings" and "royal priests," since the power of judging has been given them. As a result, they may be called "associate judges" (This Means Everlasting Life, Pg.275; You May Survive Armageddon, Pg. 353; Make Sure of all Things, Pg. 221).

Mormonism

Mormons believe that there will be two resurrections; one at the beginning and one at the end of the millennium (Doctrine and Covenants, 88:96-98).

Scientology

There is no real judgment. According to Scientology beliefs, "the individual comes back. He has a responsibility for what goes on today since he will experience it tomorrow" ("Position on Reincarnation & Past Lives: Official Church of Scientology". scientology.org. January 0001).

Unification Church

According to Moon there will be no judgment as Christianity has traditionally believed, rather man will be restored to the original position God intended there will be no destruction by fire (Divine Principle, p. 190).

Judgment according to the Unification thought has three stages. "The three stages of judgment are the judgment of words, the judgment of personality and the judgment of heart....The kingdom of heaven is the dwelling place for those that have won and overcome these three stages of judgment" (New Hope, Pg. 3-4).

Kingdom Established

Biblical Code: KE

Bible: The Bible teaches us that the kingdom has been established since the time of Christ and that we have been made "...a kingdom, priests to his God and Father, to him be glory and dominion forever and ever. Amen" (Revelation 1:6).

Scripture	Content
Colossians 1:12-13	"giving thanks to the Father, who has qualified you to share in the inheritance of the saints in light. He has delivered us from the domain of darkness and **transferred us to the kingdom of his beloved Son,**"
Acts 8:12	"But when they believed Philip as he proclaimed the good news of **the kingdom of God** and the name of Jesus Christ, they were baptized, both men and women."
Matthew 16:18-19	"And I tell you, you are Peter, and on this rock I will build my church, and the gates of hell shall not prevail against it. I will give you the keys of **the kingdom of heaven,** and whatever you bind on earth shall be bound in heaven, and whatever you loose on earth shall be loosed in heaven."
Matthew 16:28	"Truly, I say to you, there are some standing here who will not taste death until they see the Son of Man coming **in his kingdom.**"
Mark 9:1	"And he said to them, "Truly, I say to you, there are some standing here who will not taste death until they see **the kingdom of God** after it has come with power."
Luke 17:21	"nor will they say, 'Look, here it is!' or 'There!' for behold, **the kingdom of God is in the midst of you.**"
Revelation 1:6, 9	"and has **made us to be a kingdom and** priests to serve his God and Father—to him be glory and power for ever and ever! Amen..... I, John, your brother and companion in the suffering and kingdom and patient endurance that are ours in Jesus, was on the island of Patmos because of the word of God and the testimony of Jesus."
Revelation 5:10	"and you have **made them a kingdom** and priests to our God, and they shall reign on the earth."

Armstrongism

"Armstrong taught that a reason for Jesus Christ's presence on earth was to proclaim the Gospel message of a literal Kingdom of God that will be established on earth at Christ's 'second coming', and that the message of the Kingdom should be the focus of the gospel rather than the person of Christ (Armstrong, Herbert (1955). What is the True Gospel (PDF) (1972 ed.). Pasadena, California: Ambassador College).

He made the extraordinary claim that the gospel Christ brought (of the Kingdom) had "not been proclaimed to the world" for about 1,900 years "until the first week in 1953" when he began preaching it again on Radio Luxembourg (Armstrong, Herbert. "Mystery of the Ages". Chapter 7 "Mystery of the Kingdom of God").

Jesus came, over 1,900 years ago, to announce the future kingdom of God. He's coming this time to establish that kingdom. That end-time last warning message is now going out worldwide in amplified power (Armstrong, 1985).

"Since God's purpose is to reproduce himself—expand the God Family—and since it shall be the world-ruling family, then the Kingdom of God is the born family of God ruling the entire world" (Armstrong, A World Held Captive, The Plain Truth, June 1984, 6, 39).

Jehovah's Witnesses

Bible chronology indicates that God's Kingdom was established in heaven in 1914. This is shown by a prophecy recorded in chapter 4 of the Bible book of Daniel (Bible Teachings: What Does Bible Chronology Indicate About the Year 1914? Jehovah's Witnesses Official Web Site). Jehovah's Witnesses are convinced that Jesus began ruling as King of God's Kingdom in 1914 and that the last days began in that same year.

The 144,000 in heaven may also be called "associate kings" and "royal priests," since the power of judging has been given them. As a result, they may be called "associate judges" (This Means Everlasting Life, Pg. 275; You May Survive Armageddon, Pg. 353, Make sure of all Things, Pg. 221).

"The fulfillment of Bible prophecy shows that in 1914, Christ became King and God's heavenly Kingdom began to rule. Hence, we are living in the "short period of time" that Satan has left. (Revelation 12:12; Psalm 110:2) We can also say with certainty that soon God's Kingdom will act to cause God's will to be done on earth" (Bible Teachings: What Does Bible Chronology Indicate About the Year 1914? Jehovah's Witnesses Official Web Site).

Jehovah's Witnesses doctrine regarding the last days, the Millennium and Final judgement suggests that 99.9 percent of mankind will be destroyed (The Watchtower, October 15, 1958).

As soon as Jesus became King, he threw Satan and his wicked angels out of heaven and down to the locality of the earth. That is why things have become so bad here on earth since 1914 (What does God require of us, Pg.12 Watch Tower Bible and Tract Society of Pennsylvania, 1996).

"Jehovah's Witnesses understand the thousand years of Revelation 20 as pointing to a literal thousand-year period, beginning immediately after Armageddon, during which God's new world is to be established on earth. This period is referred to in their literature as that of Christ's millennial reign, or of his thousand-year reign" (Hoekema, 1976 Pg. 312; New Heavens and a New Earth, Pg. 321; Paradise Lost, Pg. 226).

As we learned in Chapter 7, the apostle John was given a vision where he saw Jesus as King in heaven with 144,000 other kings. Who are the 144,000? John explains that they "have [Jesus'] name and the name of his Father written on their foreheads." And he adds: "These are the ones who keep following the Lamb [that is, Jesus] no matter where he goes. These were bought from among mankind." (Read Revelation 14:1, 4.) The 144,000 are faithful Christians whom God has chosen "to rule as kings over the earth" with Jesus. When they die, they are resurrected to life in heaven. (Revelation 5:10) Since the time of the apostles, Jehovah has been choosing faithful Christians to be part of that group of 144,000 kings.

Mormonism

Mormonism was founded on April 6, 1830, Fayette, NY. President Gordon B. Hinckley has said: "It should be recognized that this church is not a social club. This is the kingdom of God in the earth. It is The Church of Jesus Christ of Latter-day Saints. Its purpose is to bring salvation and exaltation to both the living and the dead" (Ensign, May 1990, p. 97).

In 1991 Elder Howard W. Hunter said: "We represent and speak today for a worldwide church, the organized and established kingdom of God on earth" (Ensign, May 1991, p. 65).

Seventh-day Adventists

Kingdom Established when Christ Returns. The Adventists believe that when Jesus returns He will then set up His kingdom and begin His 1,000 year reign (Official website of the Seventh-day Adventist Church).

That He (Christ) will return in a premillennial, personal, imminent second advent. (Seventh-day Adventists Answer Questions on Doctrine, an Explanation of Certain Major Aspects of Seventh-day Adventist Belief).

The Kingdom will be established when Christ returns. The Adventists believe that when Jesus returns He will then set up His kingdom and begin His 1,000 year reign (Official website of the Seventh-day Adventist Church).

Thousand Year Reign & Second Resurrection. The second resurrection, the resurrection of the unrighteous, will take place a thousand years later (General Conference of Seventh-day Adventists, 2015).

Millennium or Thousand Year Reign. Christ with His saints in heaven between the first and second resurrections (General Conference of Seventh-day Adventists, 2015).

Millennium on Earth. The wicked dead will be judged; the earth will be utterly desolate, without living human inhabitants, but occupied by Satan and his angels (General Conference of Seventh-day Adventists, 2015).

End of Millennium. Christ with His saints and the Holy City will descend from heaven to earth. The unrighteous dead will then be resurrected, and with Satan and his angels will surround the city; but fire from God will consume them and cleanse the earth. The universe will thus be freed of sin and sinners forever (General Conference of Seventh-day Adventists, 2015).

The New Earth. On the new earth, in which righteousness dwells, God will provide an eternal home for the redeemed and a perfect environment for everlasting life, love, joy, and learning in His presence. For here God Himself will dwell with His people, and suffering and death will have passed away. The great controversy will be ended, and sin will be no more. All things, animate and inanimate, will declare that God is love; and He shall reign forever (General Conference of Seventh-day Adventists, 2015).

Unification Church

Moon stated that, "We will erect the heavenly kingdom on earth with our own hands" (New Hope, P. 41).

"The ideal of God is to restore the first God-centered family on earth. With this one model as a center, all the rest of mankind can be adopted into this family. We will become like the, and the first heavenly family will be expanded, multiplying into the tribal, national, and worldwide kingdom of God on earth" (A Prophet Speaks Today, P. 152).

Unitarian Universalist

"For one reason, we simply don't know anything about it. No one as yet has come back to report. But we do know about suffering and injustice on this earth, and so we try to create the Kingdom of Heaven here and now, with real people" (Official website for Unitarian Universalist Association uua.org).

Comparative Doctrine

Lord's Supper or Communion

Biblical Code: LS

Bible: The Bible describes in multiple places that Jesus instigated the Lord's supper and that the churches continued to follow what he had started. In Acts it discusses how the early Christians met on the first day of the week so they can break bread (Acts 20:7).

Scripture	Content
1 Corinthians 10:16	"The **cup of blessing that** we bless, is it not a participation in the blood of Christ? **The bread that we break**, is it not a participation in the body of Christ?"
Acts 20:7	"**On the first day of the week, when we were gathered together to break bread,** Paul talked with them, intending to depart on the next day, and he prolonged his speech until midnight."
1 Corinthians 11:20-34	**When you come together, it is not the Lord's supper that you eat.** For in eating, each one goes ahead with his own meal. One goes hungry, another gets drunk. What! Do you not have houses to eat and drink in? Or do you despise the church of God and humiliate those who have nothing? What shall I say to you? Shall I commend you in this? No, I will not. For I received from the Lord what I also delivered to you, that the Lord Jesus on the night when he was betrayed **took bread, and when he had given thanks, he broke it, and said, "This is my body which is for you. Do this in remembrance of me."** In the same way also he took the cup, after supper, saying, **"This cup is the new covenant in my blood. Do this, as often as you drink it, in remembrance of me." For as often as you eat this bread and drink the cup, you proclaim the Lord's death until he comes.** Whoever, therefore, eats the bread or drinks the cup of the Lord in an unworthy manner will be guilty concerning the body and blood of the Lord. Let a person examine himself, then, and so eat of the bread and drink of the cup. For anyone who eats and drinks without discerning the body eats and drinks judgment on himself. That is why many of you are weak and ill, and some have died. But if we judged ourselves truly, we would not be judged. But when we are judged by the Lord, we are disciplined so that we may not be condemned along with the world. So then, my brothers, when you come together to eat, wait for one another--if anyone is hungry, let him eat at home--so that when you come together it will not be for judgment. About the other things I will give directions when I come.
Matthew 26:26-29	Now as they were eating, **Jesus took bread, and after blessing it broke it and gave it to the disciples, and said, "Take, eat; this is my body." And he took a cup, and when he had given thanks he gave it to them, saying, "Drink of it, all of you, for this is my blood of the covenant, which is poured out for many for the forgiveness of sins.** I tell you I will not drink again of this fruit of the vine until that day when I drink it new with you in my Father's kingdom."

Catholicism

Catholicism and Transubstantiation: The Council of Trent summarizes the Catholic faith by declaring: "Because Christ our Redeemer said that it was truly his body that he was offering under the species of bread, it has always been the conviction of the Church of God, and this holy Council now declares again, that by the consecration of the bread and wine there takes place a change of the whole substance of the bread into the substance of the body of Christ our Lord and of the whole substance of the wine into the substance of his blood. This change the holy Catholic Church has fittingly and properly called transubstantiation" (Catechism, 1376).

Mary: The Perpetual Virgin

Biblical Code: MPV

Bible: The Bible describes in multiple places where Jesus or others refer to his brothers and sisters. For instance, in Mathew 13:55-57 it states, "Is not his mother called Mary? And are not his brothers James and Joseph and Simon and Judas? And are not all his sisters with us?" It hard to be a virgin when you have had four additional boys and some girls based on the Scriptures.

Scripture	Content
Matthew 1:25 (18-25)	"but **knew her not until she had given birth to a son**. And he called his name Jesus."
Matthew 12:46-50	"While he was still speaking to the people, behold, **his mother and his brothers** stood outside, asking to speak to him. But he replied to the man who told him, "Who is my mother, and who are my brothers?" And stretching out his hand toward his disciples, he said, "Here are my mother and my brothers! For whoever does the will of my Father in heaven is my brother and sister and mother."
Matthew 13:55-57	"Is not this the carpenter's son? Is not his mother called Mary? **And are not his brothers James and Joseph and Simon and Judas? And are not all his sisters with us**? Where then did this man get all these things?" And they took offense at him. But Jesus said to them, "A prophet is not without honor except in his hometown and in his own household."
Mark 3:31	"And his mother and **his brothers came,** and standing outside they sent to him and called him."
Mark 6:3-4	"Is not this the carpenter, the son of Mary and brother of **James and Joseph and Judas and Simon? And are not his sisters here with us**?" And they took offense at him. 4 And Jesus said to them, "A prophet is not without honor, except in his hometown and among his relatives and in his own household."
Luke 8:19	"Then his mother and **his brothers came to him**, but they could not reach him because of the crowd."
John 2:12	"After this he went down to Capernaum, with his mother and **his brothers and** his disciples, and they stayed there for a few days."
Acts 1:14	"All these with one accord were devoting themselves to prayer, together with the women and Mary the mother of Jesus, and **his brothers.**"
Galatians 1:18-19	"Then after three years I went up to Jerusalem to visit Cephas and remained with him fifteen days. But I saw none of the other apostles except **James the Lord's brother.**"

1 Corinthians 9:4-5	"Do we not have the right to eat and drink? Do we not have the right to take along a believing wife, as do the other apostles and the **brothers of the Lord** and Cephas?"

Catholicism

"Mary remained a virgin in conceiving her Son, a virgin in giving birth to him, a virgin in carrying him, a virgin in nursing him at her breast, always a virgin" (Catechism, 510).

"And so the liturgy of the Church celebrates Mary as Aeiparthenos, the 'Ever-virgin'" (Catechism, 499).

"The Church has always understood these passages as not referring to other children of the Virgin Mary. In fact James and Joseph, 'brothers of Jesus,' are the sons of another Mary, a disciple of Christ..." (Catechism, 500).

Mary was Sinless

Biblical Code: MS

Bible: The Bible states that, "for all have sinned and fall short of the glory of God," (Romans 3:23). No man or woman has ever been sinless except for Jesus.

Scripture	Content
Romans 3:23	"**for all have sinned** and fall short of the glory of God,"
Romans 3:9-19	"What then? Are we Jews any better off? No, not at all. For we have already charged that all, both **Jews and Greeks, are under sin,** as it is written: "**None is righteous,** no, not one; no one understands; no one seeks for God. All have turned aside; together they have become worthless; no one does good, not even one." "Their throat is an open grave; they use their tongues to deceive. The venom of asps is under their lips. Their mouth is full of curses and bitterness. Their feet are swift to shed blood; in their paths are ruin and misery, and the way of peace they have not known. There is no fear of God before their eyes. Now we know that whatever the law says it speaks to those who are under the law, so that every mouth may be stopped, and the whole world may be held accountable to God."
Romans 5:12	"Therefore, just as sin came into the world through one man, **and death through sin, and so death spread to all men because all sinned—"**
Mark 7:21	**"For from within, out of the heart of man, come evil thoughts, sexual immorality, theft, murder, adultery,"**
Galatians 5:17	"For **the desires of the flesh are against the Spirit**, and the desires of the Spirit are against the flesh, for these are opposed to each other, to keep you from doing the things you want to do."
Ecclesiastes 7:20	**"Surely there is not a righteous man on earth who does good and never sins."**

Catholicism

"By the grace of God Mary remained free of every personal sin her whole life long" (Catechism, 493).

"Through the centuries the Church has become ever more aware that Mary, 'full of grace' through God, was redeemed from the moment of her conception" (Catechism, 491).

"Espousing the divine will for salvation whole heartedly, without a single sin to restrain her, she gave herself entirely to the person and to the work of her son..." (Catechism 494).

"Mary is the most excellent fruit of redemption (SC 103): from the first instant of her conception, she was totally preserved from the stain of original sin and she remained pure from all personal sin throughout her life" (Catechism, 508...See also 722).

Mary, "the All-Holy," lived a perfectly sinless life (Catechism 411, 493).

Comparative Doctrine

Old Law Void

Biblical Code: OLV

Bible: The Bible teaches us that, "we have been released from the law [old law of commandments] so that we serve in the new way of the Spirit [Law of the Spirit], and not in the old way of the written code" (Romans 7:6). In addition, we are told that, "...the law was our guardian until Christ came that we might be justified by faith. 25 Now that this faith has come, we are no longer under a guardian" (Galatians 3:24-25).

Scripture	Content
Romans 7:4-6	"So, my brothers and sisters, **you also died to the law** through the body of Christ, that you might belong to another, to him who was raised from the dead, in order that we might bear fruit for God. For when we were in the realm of the flesh, the sinful passions aroused by the law were at work in us, so that we bore fruit for death. But now, by dying to what once bound us, **we have been released from the law so that we serve in the new way of the Spirit, and not in the old way of the written code.**"
Romans 8:1-2	"Therefore, there is now no condemnation for those who are in Christ Jesus, because through Christ Jesus **the law of the Spirit who gives life has set you free from the law of sin and death.**"
2 Corinthians 3:13-18	"We are not like Moses, who would put a veil over his face to prevent the Israelites from seeing the end of what was passing away. But their minds were made dull, **for to this day the same veil remains when the old covenant is read.** It has not been removed, because only in Christ is it taken away. Even to this day when Moses is read, a veil covers their hearts. **But whenever anyone turns to the Lord, the veil is taken away.** Now the Lord is the Spirit, and where the Spirit of the Lord is, there is freedom. And we all, who with unveiled faces contemplate the Lord's glory, are being transformed into his image with ever-increasing glory, which comes from the Lord, who is the Spirit."
Galatians 3:10-14 (1-14)	**For all who rely on the works of the law are under a curse,** as it is written: "Cursed is everyone who does not continue to do everything written in the Book of the Law." Clearly **no one who relies on the law is justified before God,** because "the righteous will live by faith." The law is not based on faith; on the contrary, it says, "The person who does these things will live by them." **Christ redeemed us from the curse of the law** by becoming a curse for us, for it is written: "Cursed is everyone who is hung on a pole." He redeemed us in order that the blessing given to Abraham might come to the Gentiles through Christ Jesus, so that by faith we might receive the promise of the Spirit.
Galatians 3:23-25	"Before the coming of this faith, we were held in custody under the law, locked up until the faith that was to come would be revealed. So **the law was our guardian until Christ came that we might be justified by faith. Now that this faith has come, we are no longer under a guardian.**"

Galatians 4:1-7	"What I am saying is that as long as an heir is underage, he is no different from a slave, although he owns the whole estate. The heir is subject to guardians and trustees until the time set by his father. So also, when we were underage, we were in slavery under the elemental spiritual forces of the world. But when the set time had fully come, **God sent his Son, born of a woman, born under the law, to redeem those under the law, that we might receive adoption to sonship.** Because you are his sons, God sent the Spirit of his Son into our hearts, the Spirit who calls out, "Abba, Father." So you are no longer a slave, but God's child; and since you are his child, God has made you also an heir."
Ephesians 2:14-16	"For he himself is our peace, **who has made the two groups one and has destroyed the barrier, the dividing wall of hostility, by setting aside in his flesh the law with its commands and regulations. His purpose was to create in himself one new humanity out of the two,** thus making peace, and in one body to reconcile both of them to God through the cross, by which he put to death their hostility."
Colossians 2:13-15	"When you were dead in your sins and in the uncircumcision of your flesh, God made you alive with Christ. **He forgave us all our sins, having canceled the charge of our legal indebtedness, which stood against us and condemned us; he has taken it away, nailing it to the cross.** And having disarmed the powers and authorities, he made a public spectacle of them, triumphing over them by the cross."
Hebrews 8:6-13	"But in fact the ministry Jesus has received is as superior to theirs as **the covenant of which he is mediator is superior to the old one, since the new covenant is established on better promises.** For if there had been nothing wrong with that first covenant, no place would have been sought for another. But God found fault with the people and said: "The days are coming, declares the Lord, when I will make a new covenant with the people of Israel and with the people of Judah. It will not be like the covenant I made with their ancestors when I took them by the hand to lead them out of Egypt, because they did not remain faithful to my covenant, and I turned away from them, declares the Lord. **This is the covenant I will establish with the people of Israel after that time, declares the Lord. I will put my laws in their minds and write them on their hearts. I will be their God, and they will be my people.** No longer will they teach their neighbor, or say to one another, 'Know the Lord,' because they will all know me, from the least of them to the greatest. For I will forgive their wickedness and will remember their sins no more." **By calling this covenant "new," he has made the first one obsolete; and what is obsolete and outdated will soon disappear."**
Hebrews 10:9-10	Then he said, "Here I am, I have come to do your will." **He sets aside the first to establish the second.** And by that will, we have been made holy through the sacrifice of the body of Jesus Christ once for all."

Armstrongism

Armstrong taught the adherence to Levitical food regulations and the observance of the 'Holy Days' of the Mosaic Law (Herbert W. Armstrong, Pagan Holidays – Or God's Holy Days – Which, p.26).

Judaism

Does not believe New Testament is God's Will. Only believe in the Torah, which is the first five books of the Old Testament; Genesis, Exodus, Leviticus, Numbers and Deuteronomy.

Seventh-day Adventists

"Lo, here are the people of God mentioned in Revelation 12, having the "testimony of Jesus," which is the "spirit of prophecy" (December, 1844), and keeping the commandments—all ten of them—the Seventh-day Sabbath included. Here the remnant church was born, and these two significant truths identify it (Ellen White's Writings, Believe His Prophets)

Once Saved Always Saved

Biblical Code: OSAS

Bible: Those who believe in Eternal security or OSAS often quote Romans 8:28-30 to prove their point. As was initially stated in this work you can't pick a scripture to support your doctrine. You must look at multiple scriptures. No scripture will conflict with another, and both will be true in some way if you explore it. We suggest that you read the above Scripture along with those shown below. The Bible tells us that God reconciles us to Him through Christ if we continue in the faith (Colossians 1:21-23). He also tells us that some Christians will fall away from the faith (1 Timothy 4:1-2) and lose their reward. That is also very specific. With this in mind multiple Scriptures communicate a warning that tells Christians to be careful of those who would lead us away from the living God. Let's look to see what the Bible says about Once Saved Always Saved.

Scripture	Content
Galatians 5:3-4	"I testify again to every man who accepts circumcision that he is obligated to keep the whole law. You are severed from Christ, you who would be justified by the law; **you have fallen away from grace."** NOTE: You can't fall away from something you don't have!
Hebrews 3:12	"Take care, brothers, lest there be in any of you an evil, unbelieving heart, **leading you to fall away from the living God."**
Romans 11:17-24	"But if some of the branches were broken off, and you, although a wild olive shoot, were grafted in among the others and now share in the nourishing root of the olive tree, do not be arrogant toward the branches. If you are, remember it is not you who support the root, but the root that supports you. Then you will say, "Branches were broken off so that I might be grafted in." That is true. They were broken off because of their unbelief, but you stand fast through faith. So do not become proud, but fear. **For if God did not spare the natural branches, neither will he spare you.** Note then the kindness and the severity of God: severity toward those who have fallen, but God's kindness to you, provided you continue in his kindness. Otherwise you too will be cut off. **And even they, if they do not continue in their unbelief, will be grafted in, for God has the power to graft them in again. For** if you were cut from what is by nature a wild olive tree, and grafted, contrary to nature, into a cultivated olive tree, how much more will these, the natural branches, be grafted back into their own olive tree."
1 Corinthians 9:27	"But I discipline my body and keep it under control, **lest after preaching to others I myself should be disqualified."**
Colossians 1:23	**"if indeed you continue in the faith, stable and steadfast, not shifting from the hope of the gospel that you heard,** which has been proclaimed in all creation under heaven, and of which I, Paul, became a minister."

Colossians 2:18	"**Let no one disqualify you,** insisting on asceticism and worship of angels, going on in detail about visions, puffed up without reason by his sensuous mind,"
1 Timothy 4:1-2	"**Now the Spirit expressly says that in later times some will depart from the faith** by devoting themselves to deceitful spirits and teachings of demons, through the insincerity of liars whose consciences are seared,"
Hebrews 6:4-6	"For it is impossible, in the case of those who have once been enlightened, who have tasted the heavenly gift, and have shared in the Holy Spirit, and have tasted the goodness of the word of God and the powers of the age to come, **and then have fallen away, to restore them again to repentance,** since they are crucifying once again the Son of God to their own harm and holding him up to contempt."
Hebrews 10:26-29	"**For if we go on sinning deliberately after receiving the knowledge of the truth, there no longer remains a sacrifice for sins, but a fearful expectation of judgment, and a fury of fire that will consume the adversaries.** Anyone who has set aside the law of Moses dies without mercy on the evidence of two or three witnesses. How much worse punishment, do you think, will be deserved by the one who has spurned the Son of God, and has profaned the blood of the covenant by which he was sanctified, and has outraged the Spirit of grace?"
James 5:19-20	"My brothers, **if anyone among you wanders from the truth** and someone brings him back, let him know that whoever brings back a sinner from his wandering will save his soul from death and will cover a multitude of sins."
2 John 8-9	"**Watch yourselves, so that you may not lose what we have worked for,** but may win a full reward. Everyone who goes on ahead and does not abide in the teaching of Christ, does not have God. Whoever abides in the teaching has both the Father and the Son."
Revelation 2:4-5	"**But I have this against you, that you have abandoned the love you had at first. Remember therefore from where you have fallen;** repent, and do the works you did at first. If not, I will come to you and remove your lampstand from its place, unless you repent."

See Appendices for an in-depth doctrinal comparison (Pages 362-364).

Arminianism

"ARMINIANISM is a teaching regarding salvation associated with the Dutch theologian Jacob Arminius (1560-1609). The fundamental principle in Arminianism is the rejection of predestination, and a corresponding affirmation of the freedom of the human will. Shortly after his death, the followers of Arminius (later called Arminians) presented a statement to the governing authorities of Holland in which they set forth five articles of doctrine. These were: (1) that the divine decree of predestination is conditional, not absolute; (2) that the Atonement is in intention universal; (3) that man cannot of himself exercise a saving faith, but requires God's help to attain this faith; (4) that though the grace of God is a necessary condition of human effort it does not act irresistibly in man; (5) that believers are able to resist sin but are not beyond the possibility of falling from grace. In essence, the Arminians maintained that God gives indispensable help in salvation, but that ultimately it is the free will of man which decides the issue" (Bible Research, Arminianism, Michael Marlowe, July 2005).

NOTE: A very large portion of all Christendom mostly agree with Arminious when it comes to Eternal Salvation. He does not believe that Eternal Election or Once saved Always Saved is Biblical. The following churches usually do not believe in OSAS; Assembly of God, Lutherans, Methodists, Roman Catholics, Churches of Christ, Disciples of Christ and many others. However, there are some groups within some of these churches that do accept OSAS.

Calvinism

Calvin's **Perseverance of the Saints** is a Christian teaching that asserts that once a person is truly "born of God" or "regenerated" by the indwelling of the Holy Spirit, nothing in heaven or earth "shall be able to separate (him) from the love of God" (Romans 8:39) resulting in a reversal of the converted condition. Perseverance of the Saints, is also referred to as the doctrine of "Once Saved Always Saved; "the impossibility of apostasy;" "the security of the believer;" and "once in grace always in grace."

There are many churches that accept this doctrine. Traditionally, Presbyterian churches that were founded on Calvin's beliefs follow this teaching. Some Baptists and several other churches also accept OSAS or Perseverance of the Saints.

Gnosticism in the Early Church

During the second century A.D. the church was already dealing with a variety of teachings that weren't necessarily from the Apostles or their writings. A Christian church leader named Irenaeus (130-202) wrote a book titled, "Against Heresies" in which he addressed the issue of Once Save Always Saved or **Perseverance of the saints**. In Book I Chapter 6 he wrote the following regarding Gnostic teaching: "But as to themselves, they hold that they shall be entirely and undoubtedly saved, not by means of conduct, but because they are spiritual by nature. For, just as it is impossible that material substance should partake of salvation (since, indeed, they maintain that it is incapable of receiving it), so again it is impossible that spiritual substance (by which they mean themselves) should ever come under the power of corruption, whatever the sort of actions in which they indulged. For even as gold, when submersed in filth, loses not on that account its beauty, but retains its own native qualities, the filth having no power to injure the gold, so they affirm that they cannot in any measure suffer hurt, or lose their spiritual substance, whatever the material actions in which they may be involved. Wherefore also it comes to pass, that the "most perfect" among them addict themselves without fear to all those kinds of forbidden deeds of which the Scriptures assure us that "they who do such things shall not inherit the kingdom of God. And committing many other abominations and impieties, they run us down (who from the fear of God guard against sinning even in thought or word) as utterly contemptible and ignorant persons, while they highly exalt themselves, and claim to be perfect, and the elect seed. For they declare that we simply receive grace for use, wherefore also it will again be taken away from us; but that they themselves have grace as their own special possession, which has descended from above by means of an unspeakable and indescribable conjunction; and on this account more will be given them."

One Christ

Biblical Code: OC

Bible: The Bible teaches us that, "...There is but one Lord, Jesus Christ, through whom all things came and through who we live" (1 Corinthians 8:6b).

Scripture	Content
1 Corinthians 8:6	"yet for us there is but one God, the Father, from whom all things came and for whom we live; and there is but **one Lord, Jesus Christ,** through whom all things came and through whom we live."
Matthew 24:23-24	**"At that time if anyone says to you, 'Look, here is the Messiah!' or, 'There he is!' do not believe it.** For false messiahs and false prophets will appear and perform great signs and wonders to deceive, if possible, even the elect."
Mark 13:6	**"Many will come in my name, claiming, 'I am he,' and will deceive many."**
Ephesians 4:5	**"one Lord,** one faith, one baptism;"

Baha'i

God has sent Divine Messengers known as Manifestations of God—among them Abraham, Krishna, Zoroaster, Moses, Buddha, Jesus Christ, Muhammad, and, in more recent times, the Báb and Bahá'u'lláh—to cultivate humanity's spiritual, intellectual and moral capacities (the official Bahai website). They believe that Jesus was just one of nine manifestations of the divine being and He appeared in her era of time. Today the Ba'u'llah is the source of revelation (Martin, 2003) "The revelation of Jesus was for His own dispensation, that of the Son, and now it is no longer the point of guidance to the world. Baha'is must be severed from all and everything that is past—things both good and bad—everything.....Now all is changed. All the teachings of the past are past (Star of the West Brochure, 1913).

Catholicism

"Let us rejoice then and give thanks that we have become not only Christians, but Christ himself. Marvel and rejoice; we have become Christ" (Catechism, 795).

Unification Church

Sun Myung Moon claims to be Christ, Lord of the Second Advent (Divine Principle, Pg. 500, 510, 520).

"Then they can understand that Rev. Moon is Messiah, the Lord of the Second Advent. . . If only they can understand the fall of man they can understand that Father is the Messiah. . .Father is visible God" (120 Day Training Manual, Pg. 160, 222, 362).

"…to meet the Lord in the air signifies that the saints will receive the Lord in the world of good sovereignty when Christ [Moon] comes again and restores the Kingdom of Heaven on earth by overthrowing the Satanic sovereignty" (Divine Principle Pg. 117).

Jesus was the second Adam. For 2000 years Christians have supposed to prepare for the coming of the second Messiah. That Messiah will be born somewhere in the east. Korea is the only logical place for people there have a strong faith in God. Moon is the second coming of the Messiah (Divine Principle, 519; Yamamoto, 1974).

"I (Moon) am Jesus who came 2000 years ago. My mission still remains to be accomplished. In order to realize God's will, you must be responsible for a great mission" (120 Day Training Manual, p. 324).

One God

Biblical Code: OG

Bible: The Bible teaches us that. "The Lord our God, the Lord in one" (Mark 12:29). In Isaiah 45:22 it is written, "Turn to me and be saved, all you ends of the earth; for I am God, and there is no other." The Bible is clear that God is one; however, it also discusses trinity (see Trinity).

Scripture	Content
Mark 12:29-32	"The most important one," answered Jesus, "is this: 'Hear, O Israel: **The Lord our God, the Lord is one**. Love the Lord your God with all your heart and with all your soul and with all your mind and with all your strength.' The second is this: 'Love your neighbor as yourself.' There is no commandment greater than these." "Well said, teacher," the man replied. "You are right in saying that God is one and there is no other but him."
1 Corinthians 8:4-6	"So then, about eating food sacrificed to idols: We know that "An idol is nothing at all in the world" and that **"There is no God but one."** For even if there are so-called gods, whether in heaven or on earth (as indeed there are many "gods" and many "lords"), yet **for us there is but one God**, the Father, from whom all things came and for whom we live; and there is but one Lord, Jesus Christ, through whom all things came and through whom we live."
Ephesians 4:6	**"one God and Father of all,** who is over all and through all and in all."
1 Timothy 2:5	**"For there is one God** and one mediator between God and mankind, the man Christ Jesus,"
James 2:19	"You believe that **there is one God.** Good! Even the demons believe that—and shudder."
Isaiah 43:10-11	"You are my witnesses," declares the LORD, "and my servant whom I have chosen, so that you may know and believe me and understand that I am he. **Before me no god was formed, nor will there be one after me. I, I am the Lord and besides me there is no savior."**
Isaiah 44:6 (6-8)	"This is what the LORD says— Israel's King and Redeemer, the LORD Almighty: **I am the first and I am the last; apart from me there is no God."**
Isaiah 45:22	"Turn to me and be saved, all you ends of the earth; **for I am God, and there is no other."**

Armstrongism

Armstrong also teaches that men can become Gods. We can rise in the school of advancement, by following Armstrong, and become a God. Those who believe will be given immortal spirit bodies at the resurrection. They will then become God beings and help finish creating many planets in the universe (Just What Do You Mean—Born Again, 1962, Pg. 19).

"But God is not limited. As God repeatedly reveals, his purpose it to reproduce himself into what well may become billions of God persons. It is the false Trinity teaching that limits God, denies God's purpose and has palpably deceived the whole Christian world" (Armstrong, Mystery of the Ages, 1995).

"The ones who accept Jesus will receive the immortal resurrection of a spirit-body. Hence, they become God Beings and finish creating the many planets in the universe" (Armstrong, The Plain Truth, October/November, 1977).

Buddhism

First, there is the more predominant belief of a "Creator God" in major religions. That concept is of course in direct contradiction with not only Buddha Dhamma, but also with modern science. Both Buddha Dhamma and modern science are based on the Principle of Causality: There must be a cause(s) for each and every effect (What Does Buddha Dhamma Say about Creator, Satan, Angels, and Demons? https://puredhamma.net).

Thus there is no "Creator God" or a "Satan". It is each person acting on his/her own free will that is committing good or bad acts. But it is a complex issue, because what we are today is the kind of "cumulative result" of all our actions in the deep past through our previous lives. These can be condensed as our character (or "gati" or "gathi") or sansaric habits (or "āsavas")" (What Does Buddha Dhamma Say about Creator, Satan, Angels, and Demons? https://puredhamma.net).

Catholicism

"For the Son of Man became a man so that we might become God" (Catechism, 460).

"The only-begotten Son of God, wanting to make us sharers in his divinity, assumed our nature, so that he, made man, might make men gods" (Catechism, 460).

Hinduism

"Hindus all believe in one Supreme God who created the universe. He is all-pervasive. He created many Gods, highly advanced spiritual beings, to be His helpers" (www.Hinduismtoday.com Hinduism Magazine).

Idols: "Hindus do not worship a stone or metal "idol" as God. We worship God through the image. We invoke the presence of God from the higher, unseen worlds, into the image so that we can commune with Him and receive His blessings......The stone or metal deity images in Hindu temples and shrines are not mere symbols of the Gods. They are the form through which their love, power and blessings flood forth into this world" (www.Hinduismtoday.com Hinduism Magazine).

Mormonism
*
We too may ascend to the status of Godhood by obedience to all principals and ordinances of the Gospel (The Gospel Through the Ages, pp. 114-117).

God was once a man who lived on another world. There have been many worlds that were created by 'new' gods. There are many gods (Journal of Discourses, Vol. 7, Pg. 333).

"In the Heaven where our spirits were born, there are many Gods, each one of whom has his own wife or wives which were given to him previous to his redemption, while yet in his mortal state (The Seer, by Orson Pratt, pp. 37-38).

"Each of these gods, including Jesus Christ and his Father, being in possession of not merely an organized spirit, but a glorious body of flesh and bones" (Parley P. Pratt, Key to the Science of Theology [1973 Edition] , Pg. 44; See also Doctrine and Covenants, 130:22.

Council of Gods Created the World, (Abraham 4:1-13; Doctrine of Covenants 121:32).

Scientology

"There are gods above all other gods.....There is not argument here against the existence of a supreme Being or an devaluation intended. It is that amongst the gods, there are many false gods elected to power and position.....There are gods above other gods, and gods beyond the gods of the universe" (Scientology, 8-8008,1967 Pg. 73).

Man is basically good and through reincarnation (rebirth) he will ultimately be godlike and will be called "homo novis" (Hubbard, Dianetics, Pg. 26).

Hubbard goes on to say that the next step in the evolution of man is called homo novis.   At this point man becomes a "godlike' being (History of Man, Pg. 5-6, 27-34, 38).

Unification Church

Man will spiritual advance, even after death, until he reaches deity....to even become a god (Speeches, Pg. 14-15).

"Then they can understand that Rev. Moon is Messiah, the Lord of the Second Advent. . . If only they can understand the fall of man they can understand that Father is the Messiah. . .Father is visible God" (120 Day Training Manual, Pg. 160, 222, 362).

Moon stated that, "...Jesus, being one body with God, may be called a second God (image of God), but can by no means be God Himself" (Divine Principle, Pg. 210-211). "Father [Moon] is visible God" 120 Day Training Manual, Pg. 135-136).

"He [God] is living in me [Moon] and I am in the incarnation of Him" (New Hope, P. 361).

Unitarian Universalism

"Our universe, from the smallest particles to the galaxies beyond our galaxy, fills us with profound wonder. Why life exists and for what purpose—humans have struggled to answer that question *for millennia. In a day and age when so much is revealed to us by science, "God" may or may not be part of our worldview": (Official website for Unitarian Universalist Association   uua.org).

"If God is One, then the God of the Jews and the God of the Muslims and the God of the Christians is One. God is One" (Official website for Unitarian Universalist Association   uua.org).

One Heaven

Biblical Code: OH

Bible: In the Bible heaven is portrayed as a place, a city that has been prepared for His children.   It is where Jesus and God reside.   Heaven is referred to as the place where God's throne is located. The Bible speaks of 'a city' multiple times.   Multiple heavens, cities or a variety of places cannot be found (Matthew 7:21).

Scripture	Content
Revelation 7:15-17	**"Therefore, they are before the throne of God, and serve him day and night in his temple; and he who sits on the throne will shelter them with his presence.** They shall hunger no more, neither thirst anymore; the sun shall not strike them, nor any scorching heat. For the Lamb in the midst of the throne will be their shepherd, and he will guide them to springs of living water, and God will wipe away every tear from their eyes."
Acts 4:12	"And there is salvation in no one else, for there is no other name under **heaven [singular]** given among men by which we must be saved."
Luke 15:7	"Just so, I tell you, there will be more joy in **heaven [singular]** over one sinner who repents than over ninety-nine righteous persons who need no repentance."
Matthew 7:21-23	"Not everyone who says to me, 'Lord, Lord,' **will enter the kingdom of heaven**, but the one who does the will of my Father who is in heaven. On that day many will say to me, 'Lord, Lord, did we not prophesy in your name, and cast out demons in your name, and do many mighty works in your name?' And then will I declare to them, 'I never knew you; depart from me, you workers of lawlessness.'
Philippians 3:20-21	"But our citizenship is in **heaven [singular],** and from it we await a Savior, the Lord Jesus Christ, who will transform our lowly body to be like his glorious body, by the power that enables him even to subject all things to himself."
Hebrews 11:10	"For he was looking forward **to the city that has foundations, whose designer and builder is God."**
Hebrews 11:16	"But as it is, they desire a better country, that is, a heavenly one. Therefore God is not ashamed to be called their God, **for he has prepared for them a city."**
Revelation 22:1-5	"Then the angel showed me the river of the water of life, bright as crystal, **flowing from the throne of God and of the Lamb through the middle of the street of the city;** also, on either side of the river, the tree of life with its twelve kinds of fruit, yielding its fruit each month. The leaves of the tree were for the healing of the nations. No longer will there be anything accursed, but the throne of God and of the Lamb will be in it, and his servants will worship him. They will see his face, and his name will be on their foreheads. And night will be no more. They will need no light of lamp or sun, for the Lord God will be their light, and they will reign forever and ever."

Islam

> ### Seven Heavens in the Qur'an
>
> **Here are two of several explanations about the seven heavens. This can be found in Ahlul Bayt Digital Islamic Library Project (Al-Islam.org)**
>
> 1. "Here by seven is meant to be multiplication (to be more). It means that He has created many heavens, i.e. He has created a number of times."
> 2. "Still, according to the views of some great intellectuals, those small stars, galaxies and Milky Way, which are seen, all are part of the first heaven and beyond that six still bigger worlds are there. And by seven heavens the Holy Qur'an means all those seven worlds, which exist in the Universe."

"He it is Who created for you all that is in the earth. Then turned He to the heaven, and fashioned it as seven heavens. And He is Knower of all things" (Surah 2:29, emp. added);

"The seven heavens and the earth and all that is therein praise Him" (Surah 17:44).

In regards to creation the following in found in the Qur'an. "Then He ordained them seven heavens in two Days and inspired in each heaven its mandate; and we decked the nether heaven with lamps, and rendered it inviolable" (Surah 41:12).

"Say: Who is Lord of the seven heavens, and Lord of the Tremendous Throne? They will say: Unto Allah (all that belongeth). Say: Will ye not then keep duty (unto Him)?" (Surah 23:86-87).

"The seven heavens and the earth and all that is therein praise Him" (Surah 17:44).

"See ye not how Allah hath created seven heavens in harmony, and hath made the moon a light therein, and made the sun a lamp? (Surah 71:15-16, see also 23:17; 65:12; 67:3; 78:12).

In regards to creation the following is found in the Qur'an. "Then He ordained them seven heavens in two Days and inspired in each heaven its mandate; and we decked the nether heaven with lamps, and rendered it inviolable" (Surah 41:12).

Jehovah's Witnesses

Jehovah's Witnesses believe there are two peoples of God: (1) the Anointed Class (144,000) will live in heaven and rule with Christ; and (2) the "other sheep" (all other believers) will live forever on a paradise earth. This is an actual heavenly government with a King—Jesus Christ—and 144,000 co-rulers, who are "bought from the earth." (Revelation 5:9, 10; 14:1, 3, 4; Daniel 2:44; 7:13, 14) They will rule over the earth, which will be cleansed of all wickedness and will be inhabited by many millions of God-fearing humans (Proverbs 2:21, 22--See JW.Org Bible Teachings). Earth Becomes a Paradise. Anyone else who is saved – those who prove themselves to be loyal subjects of Jesus – will live in an eternal earthly paradise. Only the 144,000 faithful Jehovah's Witnesses will go to heaven.

Comparative Doctrine

Mormonism

There are three different heavens. The highest of the highest is reserved for good Mormons who become gods and goddesses (Mormon Doctrine, Pg. 348).

Scientology

"Further, we have our hands on an appalling bit of technology where the world is concerned. With rapidity and a Meter it can be shown that Heaven is a false dream and that the old religion was based on very painful lie, cynical betrayal" (L. Ron Hubbard, *HCOB 11 May, 1963*).

Unification Church

According to Moon there are four basic spirit worlds. Evil men go to a place of darkness or what's called hell. Men who attain to only the form stage go to a place of darkness, those who attain to the life-spirit stage (through faith in the Gospel) go to paradise, those who reach the perfection or divine-spirit stage (by serving the Lord in person) go to the Kingdom of Heaven when they die (Divine Principle, pp. 174-175).

One Mediator

Biblical Code: OM

Bible: In the Bible Jesus stated that, "I am the way and the truth and the life. No one comes to the Father except through me" (John 14:6).   We are also clearly told that there is, "...one mediator between God and mankind, the man Christ Jesus" (1 Timothy 2:5-6).   No one else can mediate for us as Christians.

Scripture	Content
1 Timothy 2:5-6	"For there is one God and **one mediator** between God and mankind, the man Christ Jesus, who gave himself as a ransom for all people. This has now been witnessed to at the proper time."
John 14:6	Jesus answered, "I am the way and the truth and the life. **No one comes to the Father except through me.**"
John 16:23	"In that day you will no longer ask me anything. Very truly I tell you, **my Father will give you whatever you ask in my name.**"
Ephesians 3:12	**"In him and through faith in him we may approach God with freedom and confidence."**
Hebrews 7:25	"Therefore he is able to save completely those **who come to God through him, because he always lives to intercede for them.**"

Catholicism

"Therefore the Blessed Virgin is invoked in the Church under the titles of Advocate, Helper, Benefactress, and Mediatrix" (Catechism Pg. 252, #969).

Mary is the Co-Mediator to whom we can entrust all our cares and petitions. (Catechism 968-970, 2677)

"The witnesses who have preceded us into the kingdom, especially those whom the Church recognizes as saints, share in the living tradition of prayer by the example of their lives...They contemplate God, praise him and constantly care for those who they have left on earth. Their intercession is their most exalted service to God's plan. We can and should ask them to intercede for us and for the whole world" (Catechism, 2683).

"Being more closely united to Christ, those who dwell in heaven fix the whole Church more firmly in holiness....they do not cease to intercede with the Father for us, as they proffer the merits which they acquired on earth through the one mediator between God and men, Christ Jesus....So by their fraternal concern is our weakness greatly helped" (Catechism, 956, See 493).

Unification Church

"As Christians, we prayed in the name of the Father, the Son, and the Holy Ghost or Holy Spirit. Now we should pray in the name of the True Parents" (Master Speaks, March and April, 1965, MS-3, p.2).

Original Sin

Biblical Code: OS

Bible: Original Sin was first taught by Augustine around the late 4th Century AD. Which in and of itself suggests that it was not taught by Jesus, the Apostles nor can it be found in the New Testament. Simply stated, the reason Infant baptism is so important to people who believe in Original Sin is that babies are already sinful when they are born and must be baptized to have their sins removed or they could not go to heaven. The Bible suggests otherwise. In Ezekiel the Scriptures communicate that, "You were blameless in your ways from the day you were created till wickedness was found in you" (Ezekiel 28:15). In Revelation, John writes, "...each person was judged according to what they had done" (Revelation 20:13).

Scripture	Content
Matthew 15:18-19	**"But what comes out of the mouth proceeds from the heart, and this defiles a person.** For out of the heart come evil thoughts—murder, adultery, sexual immorality, theft, false testimony, slander."
1 John 3:4	**"Everyone who sins breaks the law;** in fact, sin is lawlessness."
1 John 5:17	**"All wrongdoing is sin,** and there is sin that does not lead to death."
James 4:17	**"If anyone, then, knows the good they ought to do and doesn't do it, it is sin for them."**
2 Corinthians 5:10	"For we must all appear before the judgment seat of Christ, so that each of us may receive what is due us **for the things done while in the body, whether good or bad."**
Revelation 20:12-13	"And I saw the dead, great and small, standing before the throne, and books were opened. Another book was opened, which is the book of life. **The dead were judged according to what they had done as recorded in the books.** The sea gave up the dead that were in it, and death and Hades gave up the dead that were in them, and **each person was judged according to what they had done."**
Ezekiel 18:20 (14-20)	**The soul who sins shall die. The son shall not suffer for the iniquity of the father, nor the father suffer for the iniquity of the son. The righteousness of the righteous shall be upon himself, and the wickedness of the wicked shall be upon himself.**
Ezekiel 28:15	**"You were blameless in your ways from the day you were created till wickedness was found in you."**
Jeremiah 31:30	**"Instead, everyone will die for their own sin;** whoever eats sour grapes—their own teeth will be set on edge."

Catholicism

The Catholics also teach that all men are born sinners as a result of Adam's sin. "...it is a sin "contracted" and not "committed"—a state and not an act" (Catechism, 404).

"Born with a fallen human nature and tainted by original sin, children also have need of the new birth in Baptism to be freed from the power of darkness and brought into the realm of the freedom of the children of God, to which all men are called. The sheer gratuitousness of the grace of salvation is particularly manifest in infant Baptism. The Church and the parents would deny a child the priceless grace of becoming a child of God were they not to confer Baptism shortly after birth" (Catechism 1250).

"Finally the Immaculate Virgin, preserved free from all stain of original sin, when the course of her earthly life was finished, was taken up bodily and soul into heavenly glory, and exalted by the Lord as Queen over all things." (Catechism, 966).

Jehovah's Witnesses

"Adam brought death not only to himself but on all the race descended from him" (New Heavens and a New Earth, Pg. 89).

Other results of Adam's fall included inborn sin, imperfection, and disease (Religion for Mankind, Pg. 63).

Seventh-day Adventists

"Sin...is an inheritance. Men are born sinners. Through disobedience, Adam's nature became changed. He was no longer a holy and righteous being, but a sinful being. And this sinful nature must, of necessity, be transmitted to his children as an inheritance" (Branson, Pg. 43).

Unification Church

"The inherited sin of man has been inherited from the first man and the first woman . . . original sin remains in the flesh and is transmitted continuously from generation to generation" (Divine Principle, Pg. 66, 148).

According to Moon, man's fall was twofold. First, the spiritual fall, then the physical fall. Both falls were the result of illicit sexual intercourse (Divine Principle, Pg. 77).

Eve was tempted and then sinned by having sexual intercourse with Satan. Her sin resulted in the spiritual fall of man (Divine Principle, Pg. 78-79

As a result of Eve's sexual union with Satan she bore Cain (Divine Principle, Pg. 242).

Eve tempted Adam into premature sexual union. His sin resulted in the physical fall of man (Divine Principle, Pg. 26).

"Therefore, all the saints since the resurrection of Jesus through the present day have enjoyed the benefit of the providence of spiritual salvation only. Even in devout men of faith, the original sin remains in the flesh and is transmitted continuously from generation to generation. The more devout a saint becomes in his faith, therefore, the more severe becomes his fight against sin. Thus, Christ (Moon) must come again on the earth to accomplish the purpose of the providence of the physical, as well as the spiritual salvation, by redeeming the original sin which has not been liquidated even through the cross" (Divine Principle, Pg. 148).

Comparative Doctrine

Priests

Biblical Code: PR

Bible: The Bible teaches us that all Christians are Priests. In 1 Peter 2:5 we are told that we are, "a holy priesthood, to offer spiritual sacrifices acceptable to God through Jesus Christ." We are also told that we, Christians, are a "a chosen race, a royal priesthood" (1 Peter 2:9).

Scripture	Content
1 Peter 2:5-9	"You yourselves like living stones are being built up as a spiritual house, **to be a holy priesthood,** to offer spiritual sacrifices acceptable to God through Jesus Christ. For it stands in Scripture: "Behold, I am laying in Zion a stone, a cornerstone chosen and precious, and whoever believes in him will not be put to shame." So the honor is for you who believe, but for those who do not believe, "The stone that the builders rejected has become the cornerstone," and "A stone of stumbling, and a rock of offense." They stumble because they disobey the word, as they were destined to do. But you are a chosen race, a royal priesthood, a holy nation, a people for his own possession, that you may proclaim the excellencies of him who called you out of darkness into his marvelous light."
Revelation 1:6	"and made us a kingdom, **priests to his God and Father**, to him be glory and dominion forever and ever. Amen."
Revelation 5:10	"and you have made them a kingdom and **priests to our God**, and they shall reign on the earth."

Catholicism

"In its document on the ministry of priests, Vatican II says, "The priest receives a special Sacrament by which, through the anointing of the Holy Spirit, he is conformed to Christ the Priest in such a way that he can act, in Persona Christi, that is, in the very Person of Jesus Christ" (In Persona Christi by FATHER RICHARD REGO.

". . . He that despiseth the priest despiseth God; he that hears him hears God. The priest remits sins as God, and that which he calls his body at the alter is adored as God by himself and by the congregation. . . Wherefore they are justly called not only angels, but also God, holding as they do among us the power and authority of the immortal God" (Catholic Doctrine as defined by the Council of Trent, by the Rev. ANampon, S.J.).

Mormonism

Men cannot act legally in the name of the Lord unless they are vested with the priesthood. They must be ordained (Doctrines of Salvation, Vol. 3, Pg. 80).

Men are ordained unto the high priesthood with a holy ordinance (Alma 13:1–9).

Purgatory

Biblical Code: PUR

Bible: The Bible teaches us that when we die there are no more chances to be saved. It is during our life that our eternal destiny is determined. At death we go to the Hadean world which is either paradise for those in Christ (Revelation 2:10; Matthew 1914) or Tartarus or Torment for those who never knew Him (2 Thessalonians 1:9) or who fell away (Galatians 5:4). There is a great Chasm between the two that no one can cross (Luke 16:26). So, at death we will either go to a place of rest, peace and joy (Paradise) or we will go to a place where there is pain (Tartarus). It is where we will await judgment day when all mankind will either be sent to Heaven or Gehenna/Hell for eternity.

Scripture	Content
Luke 16:26	"And besides all this, between us and you a great chasm has been fixed, in order that **those who would pass from here to you may not be able, and none may cross from there to us.**"
Romans 10:9-10	"because, if you confess with your mouth that Jesus is Lord and believe in your heart that God raised him from the dead, you will be saved. **For with the heart one believes and is justified, and with the mouth one confesses and is saved.**"
Hebrews 9:27	"And just as **it is appointed for man to die once, and after that comes judgment,**"
Revelation 20:11-15	"Then I saw a great white throne and him who was seated on it. From his presence earth and sky fled away, and no place was found for them. And I saw the dead, great and small, standing before the throne, and books were opened. Then another book was opened, which is the book of life. **And the dead were judged by what was written in the books, according to what they had done.** And the sea gave up the dead who were in it, Death and Hades gave up the dead who were in them, **and they were judged, each one of them, according to what they had done.** Then Death and Hades were thrown into the lake of fire. This is the second death, the lake of fire. And if anyone's name was not found written in the book of life, he was thrown into the lake of fire."
Revelation 2:10	**"Be faithful unto death, and I will give you the crown of life."**

Catholicism

"All who die in God's grace and friendship, but still imperfectly purified, are indeed assured of their eternal salvation; but after death they undergo purification, so as to achieve the holiness necessary to enter the joy of heaven" (Catechism, 1030).

"The Church gives the name Purgatory to this final purification of the elect..." (Catechism, 1031).

"The Church formulated her doctrine of faith on Purgatory especially at the Councils of Florence and Trent" (Catechism, 1031).

"But at the present time some of his disciples are pilgrims on earth. Others have died and are being purified, while still others are in glory..." (Catechism, 954).

The Catechism of the Catholic Church defines purgatory as a "purification, so as to achieve the holiness necessary to enter the joy of heaven," which is experienced by those "who die in God's grace and friendship, but still imperfectly purified" (Catechism, 1030). It notes that "this final purification of the elect . . . is entirely different from the punishment of the damned" (Catechism, 1031).

Islam

"There will be no one of you who will not enter it [Hell]. This was an inevitable decree of your Lord. Afterwards he may save some of the pious, God-fearing Muslims out of the burning fire" (Surah 19:71).

Mormonism

"...spirit world....is divided into two parts; paradise which is the abode of the righteous, and hell which is the abode of the wicked...when the wicked spirits repent, they leave their prison-hell and join the righteous in paradise" (Mormon Doctrine, Pg. 762).

"It is the duty of men in this life to repent. Every human who hears the gospel message is under obligation to receive it. If he fails, then in the spirit world he will be called upon to receive it..." (Doctrines of Salvation, Vol. 2, Pg.183).

Reincarnation, Rebirth or Reorganization

Biblical Code: RN

Bible: The following scriptures state that once you have died, there is judgment and you don't have an opportunity to live life again. In Hebrews 9:27 we are told, "Just as people are destined to die once, and after that to face judgment..." People are to die once. According to the Bible, there is no reincarnation, there is no dissolved or reorganized spirit that starts over, there is no rebirth, and there are no second chances after you have died.

Scripture	Content
Hebrews 9:27	**"Just as people are destined to die once, and after that to face judgment,"**
Luke 16:19-31	"There was a rich man who was dressed in purple and fine linen and lived in luxury every day. At his gate was laid a beggar named Lazarus, covered with sores and longing to eat what fell from the rich man's table. Even the dogs came and licked his sores. "The time came when the beggar died and the angels carried him to Abraham's side. The rich man also died and was buried. **In Hades, where he was in torment, he looked up and saw Abraham far away, with Lazarus by his side.** So he called to him, 'Father Abraham, have pity on me and send Lazarus to dip the tip of his finger in water and cool my tongue, because I am in agony in this fire.' "But Abraham replied, **'Son, remember that in your lifetime you received your good things, while Lazarus received bad things, but now he is comforted here and you are in agony. And besides all this, between us and you a great chasm has been set in place, so that those who want to go from here to you cannot, nor can anyone cross over from there to us.'** "He answered, 'Then I beg you, father, send Lazarus to my family, for I have five brothers. Let him warn them, so that they will not also come to this place of torment.' "Abraham replied, 'They have Moses and the Prophets; let them listen to them.' "'No, father Abraham,' he said, 'but if someone from the dead goes to them, they will repent.' "He said to him, 'If they do not listen to Moses and the Prophets, they will not be convinced even if someone rises from the dead.'"
John 5:28-29	"Do not be amazed at this, for a time is coming when all who are in their graves will hear his voice and come out—**those who have done what is good will rise to live, and those who have done what is evil will rise to be condemned.**"
2 Corinthians 5:1	"For we know that **if the tent that is our earthly home is destroyed, we have a building from God, a house not made with hands, eternal in the heavens.**"
2 Corinthians 5:10	**"For we must all appear before the judgment seat of Christ, so that each of us may receive what is due us for the things done while in the body, whether good or bad."**

Buddhism

"The universe is subject to a natural causation known as Karma. The merits and demerits of a being in past existences determine his condition in the present one. Each man, therefore, has prepared the causes of the effects which he now experiences" (Fundamental Buddhistic Beliefs).

"With respect to the afterlife, all beings have been embraced within the compassion of Amida's fulfilled Vows. Though they are saved, they do not know it and, therefore, see themselves subject to karmic destiny. But even with such a destiny, the retribution is not eternal and the person eventually is born into the Pure Land. Also for those in whom faith has been awakened, birth in the Pure Land is not entry to a life of eternal bliss apart from worldly suffering. Birth in the Pure Land means taking up the Bodhisattva's task of saving all beings. The Bodhisattva is reborn into the world not as the fulfillment of karma but as his compassionate commitment to the welfare of all beings. It is also imaged as becoming Buddha, whose compassion never ceases to lure and nurture beings on the path to enlightenment. The goal of Pure Land salvation is not only my individual salvation, but the salvation of all beings together and inseparably" (Bloom, Salvation: Christian and Buddhist, Shin Dharma Net).

Hinduism

Hinduism teaches Reincarnation: After many lifetimes of following dharma, the soul is fully matured in love, wisdom and knowledge of God. There is no longer a need for physical birth, for all lessons have been learned, all karmas fulfilled. That soul is then liberated, freed from the cycle of birth, death and rebirth. Evolution then continues in the more refined spiritual worlds....Hindus believe that the soul reincarnates, evolving through many births until all karmas have been resolved, and moksha, liberation from the cycle of rebirth, is attained. Not a single soul will be deprived of this destiny." (www.Hinduismtoday.com   Hinduism Magazine).

By doing good deeds in this life, therefore, one can improve his circumstances in the future, especially in future reincarnations (Bhagavad Gita, p. 9,10).

On Reincarnation: "Yes, we believe the soul is immortal and takes birth time and time again. Through this process, we have experiences, learn lessons and evolve spiritually...[reincarnation] continues its long pilgrimage until it is one with God." (www.Hinduismtoday.com   Hinduism Magazine).

To the Hindu, therefore, punishment consists of continuing to exist on earth. "Eternal life" consists of ceasing to exist in a bodily form and becoming part of the impersonal God. There is no concept of a bodily resurrection, and no ultimate punishment of the wicked. In fact there is no ultimate spirit being who opposes God or urges men to do evil. So, all will eventually progress, after a sufficient number of lives, to liberation, (Bhagavad Gita, p. 19-28; WR142-144; EB-III, 1014; EB-XI, 580; cf. Renou, 40-44).

Hinduism teaches Reincarnation: After many lifetimes of following dharma, the soul is fully matured in love, wisdom and knowledge of God. There is no longer a need for physical birth, for all lessons have been learned, all karmas fulfilled. That soul is then liberated, freed from the cycle of birth, death and rebirth. Evolution then continues in the more refined spiritual worlds....Hindus believe that the soul reincarnates, evolving through many births until all karmas have been resolved, and moksha, liberation from the cycle of rebirth, is attained. Not a single soul will be deprived of this destiny." (www.Hinduismtoday.com   Hinduism Magazine).

"Hinduism explains that the soul reincarnates until all karmas are resolved and God Realization is attained. All souls, without exception, will attain this highest spiritual summit, though it may take many lives. This is a mystical religion ... finally reaching the pinnacle of consciousness where man and God are forever one" (Hinduism Today).

At Death: "At death the soul leaves the physical body. But the soul does not die. It lives on in a subtle body called the astral body. The astral body exists in the nonphysical dimension called the astral plane, which is also the world we are in during our dreams at night when we sleep. Here we continue to have experiences until we are reborn again in another physical body as a baby" (www.Hinduismtoday.com   Hinduism Magazine).

All men will eventually be released from the cycle of birth and death to merge with the One Soul (Brahma).   "Moksha comes when all extraneous karmas have been resolved and God has been fully realized. This means that before Moksha, the soul must have gone through all the experiences of life in the physical world. Once having faced in the spirit of love and understanding all of these various and varies experiences, Moksha comes and marks the way-station where the liberated soul is free from rebirth. When our soul has sufficiently evolved and undergone all necessary karmas in this physical universe and God-Realization has been attained, it will not return to the First World (KARMA AND REINCARNATION: Insights on Two Fundamental Hindu Concepts From the Teachings of Sivaya Subramuniyaswami, Hinduism Today Magazine, July 1987).

Mormonism (Dissolved Spirits: Sons of Perdition Reorganized)

Brigham Young taught that their bodies and spirits would ultimately be dissolved to their original state and that they must then be reorganized to begin life again in another god's universe (Journal of Discourses 1:118). John Widtsoe clarified the teaching further, explaining that, "The ultimate punishment of the Sons of Perdition may be that they, having their spiritual bodies disorganized, must start over again, must begin anew the long journey of existence, repeating the steps that they took in the eternities before the Great Council was held" (Evidence and Reconciliations, pp. 213-214).

Scientology (uses the term rebirth instead of reincarnation)

Not exactly reincarnation, but a similar thought expressed in a different way. "Man is an immortal spiritual being.....His experience extends well beyond a single lifetime" (Does Scientology have a Concept of God? As found on the Official Scientology website).

"Today in Scientology, many people have certainty that they have lived lives prior to their current one. These are referred to as past lives, not as reincarnation. Past lives is not a dogma in Scientology, but generally Scientologists, during their auditing, experience a past life and then know for themselves that they have lived before. To believe one had a physical or other existence prior to the identity of the current body is not a new concept—but it is an exciting one" (Does Scientology Believe in Reincarnation? As found on the Official Scientology website).

Hubbard goes on to say that the next step in the evolution of man is called homo novis.   At this point man becomes a "godlike' being (Hubbard, History of Man, Pg. 5-6, 27-34, 38).

"All these people [Gautama Buddha, Jesus, Mohammad] were saying something that was much more important than 'There is a spiritual side to life.' They were saying, 'There is hope. They can come to you and they can tell you that all is lost and that you are dead, you are trapped, and that there's no hope for you. They can come to you and say this, but this is not true. There is hope. You do go on living. This life is not all there is. There is some future life in which you can do better, succeed more worthily than you have.' That is all these men said...." (The Hope of Man, a lecture given on June 3, 1955, Mr. Hubbard).

Man continues to be reborn until he reaches something akin to deity. "Man is an immortal spiritual being.....His experience extends well beyond a single lifetime" (Does Scientology have a Concept of God? As found on the Official Scientology website).

"The manifestation that our Hereafter is our 'next life' entirely alters the general concept of spiritual destiny. There is no argument whatever with the tenets of any faith, since it is not precisely stated uniformly by all religions that one immediately goes to a Heaven or Hell. It is certain that an individual experiences the effect of the civilization, which he has had part in creating, in his next lifetime. In other words, the individual comes back. He has a responsibility for what goes on today since he will experience it tomorrow."

Unity

"Eventually all souls reincarnate on the earth as babes and in due time take up their problems where they left off at death" (Teach Us to Pray, Pg. 13).

"...Jesus demands of the Pharisees, 'What think ye of Christ? Whose son is he?' They answered, not as one might ordinarily expect, 'The son of Joseph,' but 'The son of David.' In other words, He was the reincarnation of David" (Have We Lived Before, 1936).

Relationship with Unbelievers

Biblical Code: RU

Bible: The Scriptures show us that we need to be wise, gracious, and avoid corrupting talk when relating with non-Christians. In addition, we should always be "prepared to make a defense to anyone who asks you for a reason for the hope that is in you; yet do it with gentleness and respect" (1 Peter 3:15b).

Scripture	Content
Colossians 4:5–6	"Walk in wisdom toward outsiders, making the best use of the time. **Let your speech always be gracious, seasoned with salt, so that you may know how you ought to answer each person.**"
1 Corinthians 9:22	"To the weak I became weak, that I might win the weak. **I have become all things to all people,** that by all means I might save some."
1 Peter 3:13-15	"Now who is there to harm you if you are zealous for what is good? But even if you should suffer for righteousness' sake, you will be blessed. Have no fear of them, nor be troubled, but in your hearts honor Christ the Lord as holy, **always being prepared to make a defense to anyone who asks you for a reason for the hope that is in you; yet do it with gentleness and respect,**"
2 Corinthians 6:14	**"Do not be unequally yoked with unbelievers. For what partnership has righteousness with lawlessness? Or what fellowship has light with darkness?"**

Islam

"O you who believe! Take not My enemies and your enemies as friends showing affection toward them, while they have disbelieved in what has come to you of the truth….and have driven out the Messenger and yourselves because you believe in Allah your Lord!" (Surah 60:1).

"Fight and slay the idolaters wherever you find them, and seize them, and besiege them and lie in wait for them" (Surah 9:5).

"The punishment of those who wage war against God and His Apostle, and strive with might and main for mischief through the land is execution, or crucifixion, or the cutting off of hands and feet from opposite sides, or exile from the land" (Surah 5:33).

"From those, too, who call themselves Christians, We did take a Covenant, but they forgot a good part of the Message that was sent them; so We estranged them, with enmity and hatred between the one and the other, to the Day of Judgment. And soon will Allah show them what it is they have done" (Sural 5:14).

"O ye who believe! Take not the Jews and the Christians for your friends and protectors; they are but friends and protectors to each other. And he amongst you that turns to them (for friendship) is with them. Verily, Allah guideth not a people unjust" (Surah 5:51).

Revelation-Current Day Prophecy

Biblical Code: (RV)

Bible: Both Jesus and the Apostles were concerned that radical individuals would seek to pervert the Gospel and teach something other than what Christ taught. "But false prophets also arose among the people, just as there will be false teachers among you, who will secretly bring in destructive heresies, even denying the Master who bought them, bringing upon themselves swift destruction" (2 Peter 2:1). In addition, the Apostle Paul wrote, "But though we, or an angel from heaven, preach any other gospel unto you than that which we have preached unto you let him be accursed" (Galatians 1:8). Based on Scriptures, any new 'revelation' would be counter to what Jesus and the writers of the Bible taught.

Scripture	Content
Galatians 1:7-9	**"not that there is another one, but there are some who trouble you and want to distort the gospel of Christ.** But even if we or an angel from heaven should preach to you a gospel contrary to the one we preached to you, let him be accursed. As we have said before, so now I say again: If anyone is preaching to you a gospel contrary to the one you received, let him be accursed."
2 Timothy 3:16-17	**"All Scripture is breathed out by God and profitable for teaching, for reproof, for correction, and for training in righteousness, that the man of God may be competent, equipped for every good work."**
Hebrews 1:1-2	"Long ago, at many times and in many ways, God spoke to our fathers by the prophets, **but in these last days he has spoken to us by his Son, whom he appointed the heir of all things, through whom also he created the world."**
Hebrews 13:20-21	"Now may the God of peace who brought again from the dead our Lord Jesus, the great shepherd of the sheep, by the blood of the eternal covenant, **equip you with everything good that you may do his will, working in us that which is pleasing in his sight, through Jesus Christ, to whom be glory forever and ever. Amen."**
2 Peter 1:3	**"His divine power has granted to us all things that pertain to life and godliness,** through the knowledge of him who called us to his own glory and excellence,"
Jude 3-4	"Beloved, although I was very eager to write to you about our common salvation, **I found it necessary to write appealing to you to contend for the faith that was once for all delivered to the saints.** For certain individuals whose condemnation was written about long ago have secretly slipped in among you. They are ungodly people, who pervert the grace of our God into a license for immorality and deny Jesus Christ our only Sovereign and Lord."

2 Peter 2:1	"But false prophets also arose among the people, just as there will be false teachers among you, who will secretly bring in destructive heresies, even denying the Master who bought them, bringing upon themselves swift destruction."
1 John 4:1	"Dear friends, do not believe every spirit, but test the spirits to see whether they are from God, because many false prophets have gone out into the world."
Matthew 5:18	"For truly, I say to you, until heaven and earth pass away, not an iota, not a dot, will pass from the Law until all is accomplished."

Armstrongism

Armstrong claimed that he was, "His [Jesus] one apostle for this twentieth century" (Armstrong, The Plain Truth, July 1977, 1; and February 1978, 43).

State that they teach the Bible, but their beliefs are based on Herbert W. Armstrong's interpretations. Armstrong's interpretation of Bible content is found in his book titled, 'Mystery of the Ages'.

"The paramount mysteries confronting all humanity. The revelation of these mysteries was lost, even to the Church of God, although the revelation of them has been preserved in the writings of the Bible. Why, then, has the world not clearly understood? Because the Bible was a coded book, not intended to be understood until our day in this latter half of the twentieth century (Mystery of the Ages, 1995).

NOTE: See Armstrong False Prophecy. There are multiple prophecies that were found to be false!

Baha'i

God has sent Divine Messengers known as Manifestations of God—among them Abraham, Krishna, Zoroaster, Moses, Buddha, Jesus Christ, Muhammad, and, in more recent times, the Báb and Bahá'u'lláh—to cultivate humanity's spiritual, intellectual and moral capacities (the official Bahai website).
"The revelation of Jesus was for His own dispensation that of the Son, and now is no longer the point of guidance to the world. Baha'is must be severed from all and everything that is past--- things both good and bad---everything. Now all is changed. All the teaching of the past are past" (Baha'i apologist and teacher Udo Schaefer as quoted in The Kingdom of the Cults by Walter Martin).

"...the revelation of Baha'u'llah supersedes such claims (Baha'i apologist and teacher Udo Schaefer as quoted in The Kingdom of the Cults by Walter Martin).

"The writings of Baha'u'llah, since they are the last manifestation, are to be considered the final authority in matters of religion so far as the Baha'i faith is concerned" (Baha'i apologist and teacher Udo Schaefer as quoted in The Kingdom of the Cults by Walter Martin).

"It's robe is the Revelation vouchsafed unto it by God. Whenever this robe hath fulfilled its purpose, the Almighty will assuredly renew it. For every age requireth a fresh measure of the light of God. Every Divine Revelation hath been sent down in a manner that befitted the circumstances of the age in which it hath appeared" (Gleanings from the Writings of Bahá'u'lláh, XXXIV).

Many, unable to examine the claim of the Tah'a'u'llah objectively because the are not sufficiently unbiased and detached from their old-fashioned traditional doctrines, nevertheless pass judgment on the Cause of God (55:2). (The Light that Shineth in the Darkness, Udo Schaefer).

Catholicism

"The Roman Pontiff... enjoys this infallibility in virtue of his office, when, as supreme pastor and teacher of all the faithful - who confirms his brethren in the faith - he proclaims by a definitive act a doctrine pertaining to faith or morals... This infallibility extends as far as the deposit of divine Revelation itself" (Catechism, 891).

The Catholic Church teaches that when the bishops officially teach doctrine relating to faith and morals, then God super naturally prevents them from making any errors. This is called "infallibility". It applies to official councils, such as the Second Vatican Council. It also applies to other teachings, as long as the bishops and the Pope are in agreement about them. (Catechism 890, 891, 939, 2033, 2034, 2049)

The Pope is said to be infallible whenever he makes an official decree on matters of faith and morals. According to Catholic doctrine, it is impossible for the Pope to teach false doctrine. Catholics are expected to obey the Pope without question even when he is not making an "infallible" statement about doctrine. They are expected to submit their wills and minds to the Pope without question (Catechism 892, 2037, 2050).

Christian Science

"In the year 1866, I discovered the Christ Science or divine laws of Life, Truth, and Love, and named my discovery Christian Science. God had been graciously preparing me during many years for the reception of this final revelation of the absolute divine Principle of scientific mental healing (Science and Health, Pg.107).

Islam

At the age of 40, Muhammad is said to have been visited by the angel Gabriel. It was here that he received the beginnings of revelation that would become the Qur'an. This process of revelation, which was sometimes mediated through Gabriel and other times came directly to his heart, lasted approximately 23 years, and ended shortly before his death (Muslim Information Service of Australia. "Beginning of Revelation". Missionislam.com. Retrieved 2015-07-24).

The Qur'an teaches abrogation. This is a legal term that suggests the "destruction or annulling of a former law by an act of the legislative power, by constitutional authority, or by usage' (Black, 1983). Surah 2:100 ff says, "And for whatever verse we abrogate or cast into oblivion, we bring one better or like it." In Surah 13:39 is says, "Every term has a Book. God blots out, and he establishes whatsoever he will;' and with him is the Mother of all Books."

The Qur'on is the most recent revelation from God (Allah) to man. In Qur'an, Allah says: "And we have sent down to thee the Book explaining all things, a guide, a mercy and glad tidings to Muslims" (Qur'an, 16:89)

Allah says in Qur'an: "We have without doubt, sent down the message; and We will assuredly guard it (from corruption)" (Qur'an, 15:9).

This is part of the tidings of the unseen which we reveal unto thee (O Messenger) by inspiration". (Qur'an, 3:44)

"Those who reject the Book and the (revelations) with which we sent Our messengers; but soon shall they know – When the yokes (shall be) round their necks, and the chains; they shall be dragged along – in boiling fetid fluid, then in the Fire shall the be burned" (Surah 40:70-72).

Jehovah's Witnesses

Charles Taze Russell stated, "Be it known that no other system of theology even claims, or has ever attempted to harmonize in itself every statement of the Bible, yet nothing short of this can we claim" (Charles Taze Russell Studies in the Scripture, 1:348)

In the Watchtower it is stated, "It [the Watchtower] is God's sole collective channel for the flow of Biblical truth to men on earth (The Watchtower, July 16, 1960).

F.W. Franz, president of the Watchtower, relaying how their interpretations come from God, stated, "They are passed to the Holy Spirit who invisibly communicates with Jehovah's Witness – and the Publicity Department" (Scottish Daily Express, November 24, 1954).

Jehovah's Witnesses leaders claim that both the holy spirit and angels communicate information to them (Watchtower, March 1, 1972, p. 155 & August 1, 1987, p. 19).

Governing Body: "the governing body of the Jehovah's Witnesses has unquestioned power. Members reveal new truths, such as revisions to previous claims about the end of the world, and have organizational power, such as choosing elders in local congregations" (How Does Jehovah Direct His Organization?" Watchtower Online Library).

Mormonism

The Angel Moroni appeared to Joseph Smith on September 21, 1823 and told him of a book that deposited, written upon gold plates, giving an account of the former inhabitants of this continent,. This book contained the fullness of the Gospel that was delivered to the inhabitants by Jesus Christ himself. Once translated, this became the Book of Mormon (Pearl of Great Price, Joseph Smith History).

Mormons believe that God speaks to them today through revelation. "We believe in the gift of tongues, prophecy, revelation, visions, healing, interpretation of tongues, etc." (Articles of Faith, 7).

The Mormon church believes that the Book of Mormon is True Restored Gospel (2 Nephi 29:1-4).

The Mormon Church believes that the Bible has changed, that errors in translation have been made through the years. As a result, they only believe in it "as far as it is correctly translated" (Articles of Faith, 8).

The Mormon church believes that the Book of Mormon is True Restored Gospel. "Many Gentiles will reject the Book of Mormon—They will say, We need no more Bible—The Lord speaks to many nations—He will judge the world out of the books which will be written. About 559–545 B.C. 1 But behold, there shall be many—at that day when I shall proceed to do a marvelous work among them, that I may remember my covenants which I have made unto the children of men, that I may set my hand again the second time to recover my people, which are of the house of Israel; 2 And also, that I may remember the promises which I have made unto thee, Nephi, and also unto thy father, that I would remember your seed; and that the words of your seed should proceed forth out of my mouth unto your seed; and my words shall hiss forth unto the ends of the earth, for a standard unto my people, which are of the house of Israel; 3 And because my words shall hiss forth—many of the Gentiles shall say: A Bible! A Bible! We have got a Bible, and there cannot be any more Bible. 4 But thus saith the Lord God: O fools, they shall have a Bible; and it shall proceed forth from the Jews, mine ancient covenant people. And what thank they the Jews for the Bible which they receive from them? Yea, what do the Gentiles mean? Do they remember the travails, and the labors, and the pains of the Jews, and their diligence unto me, in bringing forth salvation unto the Gentiles?" (2 Nephi 29:1-4).

Mormons also believe that Jesus spoke additional words for other books that would be written. "9 And I do this that I may prove unto many that I am the same yesterday, today, and forever; and that I speak forth my words according to mine own pleasure. And because that I have spoken one word ye need not suppose that I cannot speak another; for my work is not yet finished; neither shall it be until the end of man, neither from that time henceforth and forever. 10 Wherefore, because that ye have a Bible ye need not suppose that it contains all my words; neither need ye suppose that I have not caused more to be written. 11 For I command all men, both in the east and in the west, and in the north, and in the south, and in the islands of the sea, that they shall write the words which I speak unto them; for out of the books which shall be written I will judge the world, every man according to their works, according to that which is written. 12 For behold, I shall speak unto the Jews and they shall write it; and I shall also speak unto the Nephites and they shall write it; and I shall also speak unto the other tribes of the house of Israel, which I have led away, and they shall write it; and I shall also speak unto all nations of the earth and they shall write it. 13 And it shall come to pass that the Jews shall have the words of the Nephites, and the Nephites shall have the words of the Jews; and the Nephites and the Jews shall have the words of the lost tribes of Israel; and the lost tribes of Israel shall have the words of the Nephites and the Jews" (2 Nephi 29:9-13).

Current Day Revelation proclaimed! The book of Mormon is Christs new Gospel to the world. (HJS 1:15-20, 30-32; 2 Nephi 28:30-31; 2 Nephi 29:1-14).

Seventh-day Adventists

"Lo, here are the people of God mentioned in Revelation 12, having the "testimony of Jesus," which is the "spirit of prophecy" (December, 1844), and keeping the commandments—all ten of them—the Seventh-day Sabbath included. Here the remnant church was born, and these two significant truths identify it" (Ellen White's Writings, Believe His Prophets).

The 18th of the **28 Fundamentals** states the Adventists viewpoint on the Gift of Prophecy: "One of the gifts of the Holy Spirit is prophecy. This gift is an identifying mark of the remnant church and was manifested in the ministry of Ellen. G. White. As the Lord's messenger, her writings are a continuing and authoritative source of truth which provide for the church comfort, guidance, instruction, and correction.

SDA church had a dynamic concept of what they called present truth, opposed to creedal rigidity, and had an openness to new theological understandings that built upon the landmark doctrines, or Pillars of Adventism that had made them a people (Knight, 2000). A Search for Identity. Review and Herald Pub.) The 18 of the 28 Fundamentals states the Adventists viewpoint on the Gift of Prophecy: "One of the gifts of the Holy Spirit is prophecy. This gift is an identifying mark of the remnant church and was manifested in the ministry of Ellen. G. White . As the Lord's messenger, her writings are a continuing and authoritative source of truth which provide for the church comfort, guidance, instruction, and correction. They also make clear that the Bible is the standard by which all teaching and experience must be tested. (Joel 2:28, 29; Acts 2:14-21; Heb. 1:1-3; Rev. 12:17; 19:10.).

Ellen G White stated, "I have had no claims to make, only that I am instructed that I am the Lord's messenger.... Early in my work I was asked several times, Are you a prophet? I have ever responded, "I am the Lord's messenger." I know that many have called me a prophet, but I have made no claim to this title. My Savior declared me to be His messenger. "Your work," He instructed me, "is to bear My word. Strange things will arise; and in your youth I set you apart to bear the message to the erring ones, to carry the word before unbelievers, and with pen and voice to reprove from the Word actions that are not right. Exhort from the Word. I will make My Word open to you.... My spirit and My power shall be with you" (1 October 1904, while preaching in the Battle Creak Tabernacle, reported by D.E. Rebox in the book titled, Believe His Prophets).

Unification Church

"There are many who receive revelations indicating that the Holy Spirit is a female spirit. . . this is the age in which man can communicate directly with God…there are many people today who can communicate with the spirit world. God gives him (man) the revelation that he is lord" (Divine Principle, pp. 215, 177-178).

 "You may again want to ask me, 'With what authority do you weigh these things?' I spoke with Jesus Christ in the spirit world. And I spoke with John the Baptist. This is my (Sun Myung Moon) authority. If you cannot at this time determine that my words are the truth, you will surely discover that they are in the course of time. These hidden truths presented to you as a new revelation. You have heard me speak the Bible. If you believe the Bible, you must believe what I am saying" (Christianity in Crisis, p. 98).

"Until our mission with the Christian church is over, we must quote the Bible and use it to explain the Divine Principle. After we receive the inheritance of the Christian church we will be free to teach without the Bible" (Master Speaks, March and April, 1965, MS-7, p. 1).

"The Divine Principle. . . is truth in its fullest meaning, but not the Bible word for word. The Divine Principle clearly shows how the Bible is symbolic and how it is parabolic. . . the Bible is based upon the truth. The Divine Principle gives the true meaning of the secret behind the verse" (Master Speaks, March and April, 1965, MS-7, p. 1).

"I (Moon) am Jesus who came 2000 years ago. My mission still remains to be accomplished. In order to realize God's will, you must be responsible for a great mission" (120 Day Training Manual, p. 324).

Comparative Doctrine

Sabbath or Sunday

Biblical Code: SOS

Bible: The Bible teaches us that Christians worshiped God on the first day of the week. They came together to break bread on the first day of the week (Acts 20:7). They were also told to set aside some money on the first day of the week (1 Corinthians 16:2). In addition, they were warned that they were not to "submit again to a yoke of slavery" or the commands of the Old Law, that included circumcision (Galatians 5:1), festival or a new moon or the Sabbath (Colossians 2:16).

Scripture	Content
Ephesians 2:14-15	For he himself is our peace, who has made us both one and has broken down in his flesh the dividing wall of hostility **by abolishing the law of commandments expressed in ordinances, that he might create in himself one new man in place of the two, so making peace,** Comment: The law of Moses and the rest of the Old Law was nailed to cross including the commandment to observed the Sabbath.
Romans 7:4-6	Likewise, my brothers, **you also have died to the law through the body of Christ, so that you may belong to another,** to him who has been raised from the dead, in order that we may bear fruit for God. For while we were living in the flesh, our sinful passions, aroused by the law, were at work in our members to bear fruit for death. **But now we are released from the law, having died to that which held us captive, so that we serve in the new way of the Spirit and not in the old way of the written code.** Comment: We have been released from the Old Testament Law and we now are under the Law of the Spirit.
Galatians 5:1-6	"For freedom Christ has set us free; stand firm therefore, and **do not submit again to a yoke of slavery.** Look: I, Paul, say to you that if you accept circumcision, Christ will be of no advantage to you. **I testify again to every man who accepts circumcision that he is obligated to keep the whole law.** You are severed from Christ, you who would be justified by the law; you have fallen away from grace. For through the Spirit, by faith, we ourselves eagerly wait for the hope of righteousness. For in Christ Jesus neither circumcision nor uncircumcision counts for anything, but only faith working through love. Comment: Paul compared the observance of the Sabbath to the observance of the rite of circumcision. It is no longer necessary.
Acts 20:7	"On the first day of the week, when we were gathered together to break bread, Paul talked with them, intending to depart on the next day, and he prolonged his speech until midnight."
1 Corinthians 16:2	**"On the first day of every week,** each of you is to put something aside and store it up, as he may prosper, so that there will be no collecting when I come."

Colossians 2:16-17	"**Therefore let no one pass judgment on you in questions of food and drink, or with regard to a festival or a new moon or a Sabbath.** These are a shadow of the things to come, but the substance belongs to Christ."

Armstrongism

"Sunday observance – this is the Mark of the Beast…If in your forehead and your hand, you shall be tormented by Gods plagues without mercy, yes, you!" (Herbert Armstrong, The Mark of the Beast, Pasadena: Ambassador College Press, 1957, Pg. 10, 11).

The Worldwide Church of God conducted its worship Services during that period, accordingly, on Saturdays. Armstrong further explained that Christ is "Lord of the Sabbath" (Matthew 12:8) for it is He who 'made' it for mankind, thus it is a "blessing... to be ENJOYED, to spiritually REFRESH, in blessed fellowship and communion with CHRIST!" (Armstrong, Herbert. "Which Day Is The Christian Sabbath?", Chapter 8)

Armstrong taught a form of Sabbatarianism, explaining that; by creating the Sabbath (on the seventh day of creation, through resting – not working) God "HALLOWED the Seventh-day of every week (Ex. 20:11)" and therefore made "future TIME holy!" Resting on the Sabbath day is thus commanded for all mankind and should be kept holy from Friday sunset to sunset on Saturday (Armstrong, Herbert W. Which Day Is The Christian Sabbath?, Chapter 2).

Judaism

"The Sabbath (in Hebrew, Shabbat , pronounced shah-BAHT–or in some communities, Shabbos, "SHAH-bis") may be Judaism's most distinctive and characteristic practice….A weekly 25-hour observance, from just before sundown each Friday through the completion of nightfall on Saturday…. At the major worship service on Saturday morning, a portion of the Torah is read aloud as part of a year-long cycle, supplemented by a passage from one of the prophetic books (called a haftarah)" (myjewishlearning.com Shabbat 101).

"Why is the Jewish Sabbath observed on Saturday? Genesis, Chapter 1 provides the basis for the Jewish week and the understanding of its days – God creates on days 1 to 6 and rests on day 7; hence Shabbat is day 7 (ReformJudaism.org).

Seventh-day Adventists

"Lo, here are the people of God mentioned in Revelation 12, having the "testimony of Jesus," which is the "spirit of prophecy" (December, 1844), and keeping the commandments—all ten of them—the Seventh-day Sabbath included. Here the remnant church was born, and these two significant truths identify it" (Ellen White's Writings, Believe His Prophets).

"It was on the first Sabbath in April, 1847, that she had her first vision regarding the Sabbath. By putting together Testimonies for the Church 1:75 ff., and a letter to Joseph Bates written April 7, 1847, now appearing in Early Writings, 32-35, we get the whole story of what she saw and heard. She seemed to be transferred from earth to heaven, and in vision she was taken through the heavenly sanctuary, where she saw the most holy place and the ark containing the law. She was amazed to see the fourth commandment shining above all the others in glory, with a sort of halo of light all around it. She was told of the change of the Sabbath, of the significance of its acceptance and observance, especially in the troublous times ahead, when it will become a sign or a mark for the people who have chosen to obey God rather than man" (Ellen White's Writings, Believe His Prophets).

". . . in the last days the Sabbath test will be made plain. When this time comes anyone who does not keep the Sabbath will receive the mark of the beast and will be kept from heaven" (The Great Controversy, p. 449).

Assemble together on the Sabbath (Saturday). The fourth commandment of God's unchangeable law requires the observance of this Seventh-day Sabbath as the day of rest, worship, and ministry in harmony with the teaching and practice of Jesus, the Lord of the Sabbath (General Conference of Seventh-day Adventists, 2015).

Saints

Biblical Code: STS

Bible: The Bible teaches us that all Christians are saints. You don't have to be dead to be a saint. You don't have to have done anything special. You just have to accept Jesus as the Christ and become one of God's children. In Philippians 1:1 "Paul and Timothy, servants of Christ Jesus, to all the saints in Christ Jesus who are at Philippi, with the overseers and deacons:" The message is to all the 'Saints' or Christians who are at Philippi.

Scripture	Content
Philippians 1:1-2	"Paul and Timothy, servants of Christ Jesus, to **all the saints** in Christ Jesus who are at Philippi, with the overseers and deacons: Grace to you and peace from God our Father and the Lord Jesus Christ."
Acts 9:13	But Ananias answered, "Lord, I have heard from many about this man, how much evil he has done to your **saints at Jerusalem.**
Acts 9:32	Now as Peter went here and there among them all, he came down also to the **saints who lived at Lydda.**
Ephesians 4:12	"to **equip the saints** for the work of ministry, for building up the body of Christ,"
Psalm 34:9	"Oh, fear the Lord, **you his saints**, for those who fear him have no lack!"

Catholicism

The intercession of the saints. "Being more closely united to Christ, those who dwell in heaven fix the whole Church more firmly in holiness.... they do not cease to intercede with the Father for us, as they proffer the merits which they acquired on earth through the one mediator between God and men, Christ Jesus.... So by their fraternal concern is our weakness greatly helped" (Catechism, 956, See 493).

"The witnesses who have preceded us into the kingdom, especially those whom the Church recognizes as saints, share in the living tradition of prayer by the example of their lives, the transmission of their writings, and their prayer today. They contemplate God, praise him and constantly care for those whom they have left on earth. When they entered into the joy of their Master, they were "put in charge of many things" (Catechism 2683). Their intercession is their most exalted service to God's plan. We can and should ask them to intercede for us and for the whole world.

Comparative Doctrine

Salvation Before Death

Biblical Code: SBD

Bible: The Bible teaches us that to obtain salvation, you must choose salvation while you are alive. Once you die, there is judgment, and you no longer have an opportunity to be saved. In Hebrews 9:27-28 the author states, "27 And just as it is appointed for man to die once, and after that comes judgment, 28 so Christ, having been offered once to bear the sins of many, will appear a second time, not to deal with sin but to save those who are eagerly waiting for him." Christ will come for those who were saved.

Scripture	Content
Luke 16:26	**"And besides all this, between us and you a great chasm has been fixed, in order that those who would pass from here to you may not be able, and none may cross from there to us."**
Romans 10:9-10	"because, **if you confess with your mouth that Jesus is Lord and believe in your heart that God raised him from the dead, you will be saved.** For with the heart one believes and is justified, and with the mouth one confesses and is saved."
Hebrews 9:27	"And just as it is **appointed for man to die once, and after that comes judgment,**"
Revelation 20:11-15	"Then I saw a great white throne and him who was seated on it. From his presence earth and sky fled away, and no place was found for them. And I saw the dead, great and small, standing before the throne, and books were opened. Then another book was opened, which is the book of life. **And the dead were judged by what was written in the books, according to what they had done.** And the sea gave up the dead who were in it, Death and Hades gave up the dead who were in them, **and they were judged, each one of them, according to what they had done.** Then Death and Hades were thrown into the lake of fire. This is the second death, the lake of fire. And if anyone's name was not found written in the book of life, he was thrown into the lake of fire."

Armstrongism

"The Armstrongites do not seem concerned about the salvation of lost sinners now. They think people will have a better chance 'at the great white throne of judgment' of Revelation 20:11-15." All will have a chance to be saved after death (Anderson, 1973 p. 124).

Baha'i

"The Bahá'í teachings state that there is no such physical place as heaven or hell, and emphasize the eternal journey of the soul towards perfection. They explain that references to "heaven" and "hell" in the Holy Scriptures of other religions are to be understood symbolically, describing states of nearness to and distance from God in this world and in the realms beyond. 'Abdu'l-Bahá has said that when human beings "become illuminated with the radiance of the sun of reality, and ennobled with all the virtues, they esteem this the greatest reward, and they know it to be the true paradise" (bahai'.org The Human Soul-Heaven and Hell).

"From the moment of conception, man's soul begins to progress. However, life on the physical plane is only the first stage of a spiritual journey which does not require us to return to this world again. The progress we have achieved at the moment of death will continue in the "invisible realms which the human intellect can never hope to fathom nor the mind of man conceive. Thus, to progress, the soul is not required to take a circular path moving again and again through the material world as reincarnationists suggest, but a linear one, moving through this physical world once and then continuing eternally in the worlds of spirit" (On Reincarnation and Related Subjects 25 April 1995, on behalf of Universal House of Justice).

Buddhism

"The bhikshu, full of delight, who is calm in the doctrine of Buddha will reach the quiet place (Nirvana), cessation of natural desires, and happiness" (Dhammapada V. 381).

"According to Pure Land Buddhism, anyone who faithfully calls on the Buddha of the Pure Land, Amitabha, regardless of actions in life or previous karma, can be reborn in the Pure Land. While the Pure Land has many heavenly attributes, and those who arrive there need not fear further rebirths into samsara, it is not technically a final destination. Under Amitabha's tutelage, one can continue to practice and study toward the eventual goal of nirvana, or the dissolution of self [Nirvana]" (Religion Library Zen, Afterlife and Salvation).

Catholicism

"Communion with the dead. In full consciousness of this communication of the whole Mystical Body of Jesus Christ, the Church in its pilgrim members, from the earliest days of the Christian religion, has honored with great respect the memory of the dead; and because it is a holy and wholesome thought to pray for the dead that they may be loosed from their sins she offers her suffrages for them. Our prayer for them is capable not only of helping them, but also of making their intercession for us effective" (Catechism, 958).

"The Church also commends almsgiving, indulgences, and works of penance undertaken on behalf of the dead:" (Catechism, 1032).

"All who die in God's grace and friendship, but still imperfectly purified, are indeed assured of their eternal salvation; but after death they undergo purification, so as to achieve the holiness necessary to enter the joy of heaven" (Catechism, 1030).
"The Church gives the name Purgatory to this final purification of the elect..." (Catechism, 1031).

"The Church formulated her doctrine of faith on Purgatory especially at the Councils of Florence and Trent" (Catechism, 1031).
"But at the present time some of his disciples are pilgrims on earth. Others have died and are being purified, while still others are in glory..." (Catechism, 954).

Comparative Doctrine

Christian Science

"Man's probation after death is the necessity of his immortality, for good dies not and evil is self-destructive, therefore evil must be mortal and self-destroyed. If man should not progress after death, but should remain in error, he would be inevitably self-annihilated" (Miscellaneous Writings, Pg. 2).

Christian Science teaches that some kind of spiritual progress is made after 'death' and continues until the error of believing in matter is totally discarded. "Man is not annihilated nor does he lose his identify, but passing through the belief called death. After the momentary belief of dying passes from mortal mind, this mind is still in a conscious state of existence..." (Miscellaneous Writings, Pg. 47).

"The period required for this dream of material life, embracing its so-called pleasures and pains, to vanish from consciousness. "Knoweth no man.....neither the Son, but the Father." This period will be of longer or shorter duration according to the tenacity of error" (Science and Health, Pg. 77).

Hinduism

All men will eventually be released from the cycle of birth and death to merge with the One Soul (Brahma). "Moksha comes when all extraneous karmas have been resolved and God has been fully realized. This means that before Moksha, the soul must have gone through all the experiences of life in the physical world. Once having faced in the spirit of love and understanding all of these various and varies experiences, Moksha comes and marks the way-station where the liberated soul is free from rebirth. When our soul has sufficiently evolved and undergone all necessary karmas in this physical universe and God-Realization has been attained, it will not return to the First World (KARMA AND REINCARNATION: Insights on Two Fundamental Hindu Concepts From the Teachings of Sivaya Subramuniyaswami, Hinduism Today Magazine, July 1987).

Islam

"There will be no one of you who will not enter it (Hell). This was an inevitable decree of your Lord. Afterwards he may save some of the pious, God-fearing Muslims out of the burning fire" (Surah 19:71).

Mormonism

Eternal damnation is a state that does not allow man to progress to godhood. "Eternal punishment is, thus, the kind of punishment imposed by God who is Eternal, and those subject to it may suffer there for either a short or a long period. After their buffetings and trials cause them to repent, they are freed from this type of eternal damnation" (Mormon Doctrine, Pg. 236, 1966).

Hell is temporary (Mormon Doctrine, Pg. 349-351; Doctrine of Salvation 2:133-134). Joseph Smith stated, "Is it the duty of men in this life to repent. Every man who hears the gospel message is under obligation to receive it. If he fails, then in the spirit world he will be called upon to receive it..." (Doctrines of Salvation, Vol. 2, Pg. 183). Joseph Smith and others will teach those in spirit prison. Most people will then accept the 'Mormon Gospel' and will go to paradise and ultimately to a heavenly realm.

"...spirit world....is divided into two parts; paradise which is the abode of the righteous, and hell which is the abode of the wicked...when the wicked spirits repent, they leave their prison-hell and join the righteous in paradise" (Mormon Doctrine, Pg. 762).

"It is the duty of men in this life to repent. Every human who hears the gospel message is under obligation to receive it. If he fails, then in the spirit world he will be called upon to receive it…" (Doctrines of Salvation, Vol. 2, Pg.183).

Scientology

Salvation is being free of the endless cycle of birth and rebirth (Reincarnation or Rebirth). "Scientology further holds Man to be basically good, and that his spiritual salvation depends upon himself, his fellows and his attainment of brotherhood with the universe" Does Scientology have a Concept of God? As found on the Scientology website).

Unification Church

All mankind get to progress; even after death. Four stages of progression from Hell to Heaven (Divine Principle, Pg. 172-174).

> **Hell:** Reserved for evil men. Evil men who have died must torment sinful people on earth, eventually leading them to the formation stage of development.

> **Place of Darkness--Formation Stage:** Reserved for good men who followed laws and commandments. Must influence those living to believe in Jesus and the Lord of the Second Advent [Moon].

> **Paradise—Growth Stage:** Reserved for those who believed in Jesus while on earth. Must influence saints that they must serve and believe in Moon.

> **Kingdom of Heaven—Perfection Stage:** Reserved for those who believe in and serve Moon. No further progression is needed, they are one with God!

Man will spiritually advance, even after death, until he reaches deity….to even become a god (Speeches, Pg. 14-15). Can progress after death (Divine Principle, Pg. 181-182).

Salvation - Most Men Lost

Biblical Code: MML

Bible: In Matthew 7:13-14 the gospel writer communicates that the way is easy that leads to destruction. When you look at how many religious groups define eternity, it becomes evident that they believe that most, if not all men will eventually be saved. However, Matthew shares that the way to heaven and eternal life with God is difficult and few will find it.

Scripture	Content
Matthew 7:13-14	**"Enter by the narrow gate. For the gate is wide and the way is easy that leads to destruction, and those who enter by it are many. For the gate is narrow and the way is hard that leads to life, and those who find it are few."**
Luke 13:23-24	"And someone said to him, Lord, will those who are saved be few?" And he said to them, **"Strive to enter through the narrow door. For many, I tell you, will seek to enter and will not be able."**

Christian Science

Christian Science teaches that some kind of spiritual progress is made after 'death' and continues until the error of believing in matter is totally discarded. "Man is not annihilated nor des he lose his identify, but passing through the belief called death. After the momentary belief of dying passes from mortal mind, this mind is still in a conscious state of existence..." (Miscellaneous Writings, Pg. 47). "The period required for this dream of material life, embracing its so-called pleasures and pains, to vanish from consciousness. "Knoweth no man.....neither the Son, but the Father." This period will be of longer or shorter duration according to the tenacity of error" (Science and Health, Pg. 77).

Hinduism

All men will eventually be released from the cycle of birth and death to merge with the One Soul (Brahma). "Moksha comes when all extraneous karmas have been resolved and God has been fully realized. This means that before Moksha, the soul must have gone through all the experiences of life in the physical world. Once having faced in the spirit of love and understanding all of these various and varies experiences, Moksha comes and marks the way-station where the liberated soul is free from rebirth. When our soul has sufficiently evolved and undergone all necessary karmas in this physical universe and God-Realization has been attained, it will not return to the First World (KARMA AND REINCARNATION: Insights on Two Fundamental Hindu Concepts From the Teachings of Sivaya Subramuniyaswami, Hinduism Today Magazine, July 1987).

"Hindus believe that the soul reincarnates, evolving through many births until all karmas have been resolved, and moksha, liberation from the cycle of rebirth, is attained. Not a single soul will be deprived of this destiny." (www.Hinduismtoday.com   Hinduism Magazine).

Jehovah's Witnesses

Teach that most men will be saved. 144,000 will go to heaven and reign with God as joint heirs and co-rulers. All others, the sheep, who believe will live on an earthly paradise (New Heaven and a New Earth, Pg. 360).

Mormonism

Most people will go to one of the three heavens god had prepared. Only Satan, his fallen angels and the 'Sons of Perdition' will be thrown into the lake of fire (Doctrine and Covenants, 76:44). However, Brigham Young stated that their bodies and spirits would ultimately be dissolved to their original state and that they must then be reorganized to begin life again [reincarnation of sorts] in another god's universe (Journal of Discourses 1:118)

Scientology

Man continues to be reborn until he reaches something akin to deity. "Man is an immortal spiritual being.....His experience extends well beyond a single lifetime" (Does Scientology have a Concept of God? As found on the Official Scientology website). Hubbard goes on to say that the next step in the evolution of man is called homo novis. At this point man becomes a "godlike' being (History of Man, Pg. 5-6, 27-34, 38).

Unification Church

Everyone will eventually be perfected and as a result be saved (Divine Principle, Pg. 187, 190). There are three stages of progression; the Formative Stage, the Growth Stage and the Perfection Stage (Divine Principle, Pg. 174-175). Can progress after death (Divine Principle, Pg. 181-182).

Unity

"Eventually all souls reincarnate on the earth as babes and in due time take up their problems where they left off at death" (Teach Us to Pray, Pg. 13).

Salvation Through Christ

Biblical Code: STC

Bible: The Bible teaches us that Jesus is the Christ, the son of God and Savior of all who would believe. He is the one and only way to obtain salvation. In Acts 4:10-12 Luke writes, "10 let it be known to all of you and to all the people of Israel that by the name of Jesus Christ of Nazareth, whom you crucified, whom God raised from the dead—by him this man is standing before you well. 11 This Jesus is the stone that was rejected by you, the builders, which has become the cornerstone. 12 And there is salvation in no one else, for there is no other name under heaven given among men by which we must be saved." The following Scriptures also clearly reveal this.

Scripture	Content
Acts 4:10-12	"Let it be known to all of you and to all the people of Israel that by the name of Jesus Christ of Nazareth, whom you crucified, whom God raised from the dead—by him this man is standing before you well. This Jesus is the stone that was rejected by you, the builders, which has become the cornerstone. **And there is salvation in no one else, for there is no other name under heaven given among men by which we must be saved.**"
John 14:6	Jesus said to him, **"I am the way, and the truth, and the life. No one comes to the Father except through me."**
Ephesians 1:7	**"In him we have redemption through his blood, the forgiveness of our trespasses,** according to the riches of his grace,"
John 10:7-9	So Jesus again said to them, **"Truly, truly, I say to you, I am the door of the sheep.** All who came before me are thieves and robbers, but the sheep did not listen to them. I am the door. **If anyone enters by me, he will be saved and will go in and out and find pasture."**
Hebrews 9:11-14	**"But when Christ appeared as a high priest of the good things that have come,** then through the greater and more perfect tent (not made with hands, that is, not of this creation) he entered once for all into the holy places, not by means of the blood of goats and calves but **by means of his own blood, thus securing an eternal redemption.** For if the blood of goats and bulls, and the sprinkling of defiled persons with the ashes of a heifer, sanctify for the purification of the flesh, **how much more will the blood of Christ, who through the eternal Spirit offered himself without blemish to God, purify our conscience from dead works to serve the living God."**
Hebrews 10:10	"And by that will **we have been sanctified through the offering of the body of Jesus Christ once for all."**
1 John 2:2	**"He is the propitiation for our sins, and not for ours only but also for the sins of the whole world."**

Matthew 1:21	"She will bear a son, and you shall call his name Jesus, **for he will save his people from their sins.**"
John 4:42	They said to the woman, "It is no longer because of what you said that we believe, for we have heard for ourselves, and we know that **this is indeed the Savior of the world.**"
Acts 5:31	**"God exalted him at his right hand as Leader and Savior, to give repentance to Israel and forgiveness of sins.**"
Acts 13:23	"Of this man's offspring **God has brought to Israel a Savior**, Jesus, as he promised."
2 Timothy 1:10	"And which now has been manifested through the appearing of our **Savior Christ Jesus, who abolished death and brought life and immortality to light through the gospel,**"
1 John 4:14	"And we have seen and testify that **the Father has sent his Son to be the Savior of the world.**"

Bahai

"We accept the fact that no one is perfect, but by the practice of principles laid down by Bahu'u'llah and by making every effort through prayer and personal sacrifice to live in accord with the character of the divine being revealed in him, we can arrive at eventual salvation as you like to term it" (Baha'i apologist and teacher Udo Schaefer as quoted in The Kingdom of the Cults by Walter Martin).

"A Christian may find spiritual peace in believing in a substitutionary atonement. In Bahaism this is unnecessary. That age is past. The new age of spiritual maturity has dawned through Bahá'u'lláh, and we are to listen to his words" (Baha'i apologist and teacher Udo Schaefer as quoted in The Kingdom of the Cults by Walter Martin).

Buddhism

"The bhikshu, full of delight, who is calm in the doctrine of Buddha will reach the quiet place (Nirvana), cessation of natural desires, and happiness" (Dhammapada V. 381).
"Salvation is liberation from such bondage through the transformation of our consciousness and our awakening to our true nature, our Buddha nature. It is the awareness that we are more than we appear; that we all possess the potential to express compassion rather than turning to violence. Ego is not abolished, but its condition is made clear" (Bloom, Salvation: Christian and Buddhist, Shin Dharma Net).

Catholicism

"Even though incorporated into the Church, one who does not however persevere in charity is not saved" (Catechism, 837).

"The Second Vatican Council's Decree on Ecumenism explains: 'For it is through Christ's Catholic Church alone, which is the universal help toward salvation, that the fullness of the means of salvation can be obtained'" (Catechism, 816).

"Taken up to heaven she (Mary) did not lay aside this saving office but by her manifold intercession continues to bring us the gifts of eternal salvation..." Catechism, 969).

"Being obedient she (Mary) became the cause of salvation for herself and for the whole human race" (Catechism, 494).

"She (Mary) is inseparably linked with the saving work of her Son" (Catechism, 1172).

Christian Science

"To get rid of sin through Science, is to divest sin of any supposed mind or reality, and never to admit that sin can have intelligence or power, pain or pleasure. You conquer error by denying its verity" (Science and Health, Pg. 399). In other words YOU must believe that there is no such thing as sin and that where there is no sin there is 'salvation'. Other than a Jesus has nothing to do with your 'salvation'.

Hinduism

"All performance of dharma is meant for ultimate liberation (moksha). It should not be performed for material gain. Furthermore, one who is engaged in the ultimate occupational service (dharma) should not use material gain (artha) simply for sense gratification (karma)" (Bhagavat Purana 1.2.9). To explain, dharma or righteousness. Artha is economic development. Karma is sensual enjoyment. Moksha is the liberation or the ultimate goal man. Salvation for a Hindu is called Moksha. Moksha is achieved through union with God. Moksha occurs when an enlightened human being is freed from the cycle of life-and-death (the endless cycle of death and reincarnation) and comes into a state of completeness. He then becomes one with God.

Islam

On the one hand, the Qur'an teaches that salvation is based on purification by good deeds (Qur'an 7:6–9).

However, Allah predetermines every person's destiny. The problem is that one's righteous acts may or may not affect Allah's decision (Qur'an 57:22).

The Qur'an also teaches that everyone, both the righteous and the unrighteous, will be led into hell by Allah. At this point the righteous will enter heaven (Qur'an 19:67–72).

The above suggests that no Muslim can know what his eternal destiny will be. Muhammad was unsure of his salvation (Qur'an 31:34; 46:9).

Jehovah's Witnesses

To receive everlasting life in the earthly paradise we must identify that organization and serve God as part of it (Watchtower, February 15, 1983, p. 12).

Mormonism

". . . no man of woman in this dispensation will ever enter into the celestial kingdom of God without the consent of Joseph Smith . . . every man and woman must have the certificate of Joseph Smith, junior, as a passport to their entrance into the mansion where God and Christ are--

. . . I cannot go there without his consent. . . He reigns there as supreme a being in his sphere, capacity, and calling, as God does in heaven" (Journal of Discourses, Vol. 7, p. 289).

Scientology

"Scientology further holds Man to be basically good, and that his spiritual salvation depends upon himself, his fellows and his attainment of brotherhood with the universe" (Does Scientology have a Concept of God? As found on the Official Scientology website).

Salvation is being free of the endless cycle of birth and rebirth (Reincarnation or Rebirth).

Unification Church

"With the fullness of time, God has sent one person to this earth to resolve the fundamental problems of human life and the universe. His name is Sun Myung Moon. For several decades he wandered through the spirit world so vast as to be beyond imagining. He trod a bloody path of suffering in search of the truth, passing through tribulations that God alone remembers. Since he understood that no one can find the ultimate truth to save humanity without first passing through the bitterest of trials, he fought alone against millions of devils, both in the spiritual and physical worlds, and triumphed over them all. Through intimate spiritual communion with God and by meeting with Jesus and many saints in Paradise, he brought to light all the secrets of Heaven" (Divine Principle (translated 1966).

Moon's shed blood drawn during his persecution provides for the forgiveness of man's sins. Without Moon there is no forgiveness of sin (Unification Church 120 Day Training Manual, pp. 135-136).

"Therefore, all the saints since the resurrection of Jesus through the present day have enjoyed the benefit of the providence of spiritual salvation only. Even in devout men of faith, the original sin remains in the flesh and is transmitted continuously from generation to generation. The more devout a saint becomes in his faith, therefore, the more severe becomes his fight against sin. Thus, Christ (Moon) must come again on the earth to accomplish the purpose of the providence of the physical, as well as the spiritual salvation, by redeeming the original sin which has not been liquidated even through the cross" (Divine Principle, p. 148).

"Through father [Moon] and Mother [his wife] we can be born anew, sinlessly" (120 Day Training Manual, Pg. 41-42).

Unitarian Universalism

"The lack of formal creed has been a cause for criticism among some who argue that Unitarian Universalism is thus without religious content. "We know there is no "one right answer" when it comes to belief, and we don't let that stop us from taking action for a better world. We build a community that welcomes us in our wholeness, cherishes our doubts, and invites our ongoing search for truth" (Official website for Unitarian Universalist Association   uua.org).

Unity

"The forgiveness of sin is an erasure of mortal thoughts from consciousness. The joy which comes to the converted Christian is the inflow of Divine Love after the mind has been cleansed by denial of sin" (Christian Healing, Pg. 55).

Being 'born-again' or 'born from above' is not a miraculous change that takes place in man; it is the establishment of that which has always existed as the perfect man idea of divine Mind" (Christian Healing, Pg. 24).

"We have thought that we were to be saved by Jesus' making personal petitions and sacrifices for us, but now we see that we are to be saved by using the creative principles that he developed in himself and that He is ever ready to cooperate with us in developing in ourselves by observing the law as He observed it. 'I in them, and thou in me, that they may be perfected into one" (Jesus Christ Heals, Pg. 162).

Comparative Doctrine

Satan–Devil

Biblical Code: SAT

Bible: Satan is the prince of evil spirits and primary adversary of God. Satan rebelled against God and was cast out of heaven along with other "fallen" angels before Adam and Eve were created (Ezekiel 20:14–18 and Isaiah 14:12–17). In the New Testament, Jesus stated that he saw Satan fall like lightning from heaven (Luke 10:18). He, along with his fallen angels, will be sent to hell for eternity.

Scripture	Content
Matthew 4:8-9	Again, **the devil took him to a very high mountain and showed him all the kingdoms of the world and their glory**. And he said to him, "All these I will give you, if you will fall down and worship me."
2 Corinthians 11:14	"And no wonder, for even **Satan disguises himself as an angel of light.**"
1 John 3:8	"Whoever makes a practice of sinning is of the devil, **for the devil has been sinning from the beginning.** The reason the Son of God appeared was to destroy the works of the devil."
1 Peter 5:8-9	"Be sober-minded; be watchful. **Your adversary the devil prowls around like a roaring lion, seeking someone to devour.** Resist him, firm in your faith, knowing that the same kinds of suffering are being experienced by your brotherhood throughout the world."
Revelation 12:7-9	"Now war arose in heaven, Michael and his angels fighting against the dragon. And the dragon and his angels fought back, but he was defeated, and there was no longer any place **for them in heaven. And the great dragon was thrown down, that ancient serpent, who is called the devil and Satan, the deceiver of the whole world**--he was thrown down to the earth, and his angels were thrown down with him."
Revelation 20:1-2	"Then I saw an angel coming down from heaven, holding in his hand the key to the bottomless pit and a great chain. **And he seized the dragon, that ancient serpent, who is the devil and Satan, and bound him for a thousand years,**"
Genesis 3:1-5	**Now the serpent was more crafty than any other beast of the field that the LORD God had made. He said to the woman, "Did God actually say, 'You shall not eat of any tree in the garden'?"** And the woman said to the serpent, "We may eat of the fruit of the trees in the garden, but God said, 'You shall not eat of the fruit of the tree that is in the midst of the garden, neither shall you touch it, lest you die.'" **But the serpent said to the woman, "You will not surely die. For God knows that when you eat of it your eyes will be opened, and you will be like God, knowing good and evil."**

Isaiah 14:12-17	**"How you are fallen from heaven, O Day Star, son of Dawn! How you are cut down to the ground, you who laid the nations low! You said in your heart, 'I will ascend to heaven; above the stars of God I will set my throne on high; I will sit on the mount of assembly in the far reaches of the north; I will ascend above the heights of the clouds; I will make myself like the Most High.'** But you are brought down to Sheol, to the far reaches of the pit. Those who see you will stare at you and ponder over you: 'Is this the man who made the earth tremble, who shook kingdoms, who made the world like a desert and overthrew its cities, who did not let his prisoners go home?'

Baha'i

There is no entity that is Satan. "The reality underlying this question is that the evil spirit, Satan or whatever is interpreted as evil, refers to the lower nature in man. This baser nature is symbolized in various ways. In man there are two expressions, one is the expression of nature, the other the expression of the spiritual realm…. God has never created an evil spirit; all such ideas and nomenclature are symbols expressing the mere human or earthly nature of man. It is an essential condition of the soil of earth that thorns, weeds and fruitless trees may grow from it. Relatively speaking, this is evil; it is simply the lower state and baser product of nature" (Abdu'l-Baha, Promulgation of Universal Peace, Pg. 294–295).

"The reality underlying this question is that the evil spirit, Satan or whatever is interpreted as evil, refers to the lower nature in man. This baser nature is symbolized in various ways. In man there are two expressions, one is the expression of nature, the other the expression of the spiritual realm…. God has never created an evil spirit; all such ideas and nomenclature are symbols expressing the mere human or earthly nature of man. It is an essential condition of the soil of earth that thorns, weeds and fruitless trees may grow from it. Relatively speaking, this is evil; it is simply the lower state and baser product of nature" (Abdu'l-Baha, Promulgation of Universal Peace, Pg. 294–295).

"The meaning of the serpent is attachment to the human world" (Abdu'l-Baha, Some Answered Questions, Pg. 123).

Buddhism

"Thus there is no "Creator God" or a "Satan". It is each person acting on his/her own free will that is committing good or bad acts. But it is a complex issue, because what we are today is the kind of "cumulative result" of all our actions in the deep past through our previous lives. These can be condensed as our character (or "gati" or "gathi") or sansaric habits (or "āsavas")" (What Does Buddha Dhamma Say about Creator, Satan, Angels, and Demons? https://puredhamma.net).

Christian Science

The Devil is "evil"; "a lie"; "error" (Science and Health, 584).

There is no devil, (Science and Health 469).

314

Hinduism

"Not a single soul will be deprived of this destiny.....There is no eternal hell, no damnation in Hinduism, and no intrinsic evil--no satanic force that opposes the will of God" (Hinduism Today, 9/2011).

To the Hindu, therefore, punishment consists of continuing to exist on earth. "Eternal life" consists of ceasing to exist in a bodily form and becoming part of the impersonal God. There is no concept of a bodily resurrection, and no ultimate punishment of the wicked. In fact there is no ultimate spirit being who opposes God or urges men to do evil. So, all will eventually progress, after a sufficient number of lives, to liberation, (Bhagavad Gita, p. 19-28; WR142-144; EB-III, 1014; EB-XI, 580; cf. Renou, 40-44).

Scientology

Satan or the Devil is not mentioned in Scientology works!

Second Coming

Biblical Code: SC

Bible: The Bible teaches us that only God knows when Christ will return. However, it is a fact that he will return. In Matthew 24:36 we are told, "But concerning that day and hour no one knows, not even the angels of heaven, nor the Son, but the Father only. It won't be a secret when He comes. It will be obvious to all when Jesus returns.

Scripture	Content
Matthew 24:36	**"But concerning that day and hour no one knows, not even the angels of heaven, nor the Son, but the Father only."**
Matthew 16:27	**"For the Son of Man is going to come with his angels in the glory of his Father,** and then he will repay each person according to what he has done."
Matthew 24:29-30	"Immediately after the tribulation of those days the sun will be darkened, and the moon will not give its light, and the stars will fall from heaven, and the powers of the heavens will be shaken. Then will appear in heaven the sign of the Son of Man, and then all the tribes of the earth will mourn, and **they will see the Son of Man coming on the clouds of heaven with power and great glory.**
Matthew 24:44	"Therefore you also must be ready, for **the Son of Man is coming at an hour you do not expect."**
Mark 13:32	**"But concerning that day or that hour, no one knows,** not even the angels in heaven, nor the Son, but only the Father.
John 5:28-29	"Do not marvel at this, for **an hour is coming when all who are in the tombs will hear his voice and come out,** those who have done good to the resurrection of life, and those who have done evil to the resurrection of judgment."
1 Thessalonians 4:13-18	"But we do not want you to be uninformed, brothers, about those who are asleep, that you may not grieve as others do who have no hope. For since we believe that Jesus died and rose again, even so, through Jesus, God will bring with him those who have fallen asleep. For this we declare to you by a word from the Lord, that we who are alive, who are left until the coming of the Lord, will not precede those who have fallen asleep. **For the Lord himself will descend from heaven with a cry of command, with the voice of an archangel, and with the sound of the trumpet of God. And the dead in Christ will rise first. Then we who are alive, who are left, will be caught up together with them in the clouds to meet the Lord in the air, and so we will always be with the Lord."**
1 Thessalonians 5:2	"For you yourselves are fully aware that **the day of the Lord will come like a thief in the night."**

2 Thessalonians 1:7-8	"And to grant relief to you who are afflicted as well as to us, **when the Lord Jesus is revealed from heaven with his mighty angels in flaming fire, inflicting vengeance on those who do not know God and on those who do not obey the gospel of our Lord Jesus.**"
2 Peter 3:10-13	"**But the day of the Lord will come like a thief, and then the heavens will pass away with a roar,** and the heavenly bodies will be burned up and dissolved, and the earth and the works that are done on it will be exposed. Since all these things are thus to be dissolved, what sort of people ought you to be in lives of holiness and godliness, waiting for and hastening the coming of the day of God, because of which the heavens will be set on fire and dissolved, and the heavenly bodies will melt as they burn! But according to his promise we are waiting for new heavens and a new earth in which righteousness dwells."
Revelation 1:7	"**Behold, he is coming with the clouds, and every eye will see him**, even those who pierced him, and all tribes of the earth will wail on account of him. Even so. Amen."

Armstronism

Armstrong preached that Jesus Christ will return to earth to "rescue" humanity from the brink of self-annihilation, resulting in the establishment of "God's government" upon earth, during a 'Millennium' period, under the rulership of Christ and first-resurrected saints. After His return, those surviving the "great tribulation" will be given the chance to voluntarily accept "God's way of life." (Herbert Armstrong, Mystery of the Ages, p. 344-345).

Christ is in heaven "until" the "times of restitution" (Acts 3:19–21) when God's government, world peace and utopian conditions shall be restored to this earth (Armstrong, Herbert. "Mystery of the Ages". Chapter 7 "Mystery of the Kingdom of God").

Baha'i

The Baha'is claim that Baha'u'llah is the fulfillment of the Biblical prophecies of the return of Christ (Selections from the Writings of Abdu'l-Baha, 110-12). "Know that the return of Christ for a second time doth not mean what the people believe, but, rather, signifieth the One promised to come after Him. He shall come with the Kingdom of God and His power which hath surrounded the world. This power (or reign) is in the world of hearts and spirits and not in that of matter (or bodies). For the material world is not comparable to a single wing of a fly, or rather less in the sight of thy Lord, wert thou of those who know! Verily Christ came with His Kingdom from the beginning which hath no beginning and will come with His Kingdom to the eternity of eternities, inasmuch as in this sense Christ is an expression of the divine reality, the simple essence and heavenly entity which hath no beginning or ending. It hath appearance, arising and manifestation and setting in each of the cycles." (Abdu'l-Baha, Tablets of Abdu'l-Baha v1, Pg. 137).

Comparative Doctrine

Christian Science

Christ will not literally come back. Mrs. Eddy writes, "The second appearing of Jesus is, unquestionably, the spiritual advent of the advancing idea of God, as in Christian Science" (Retrospection and Introspection, Pg. 70).

"It is authentically said that one expositor of Daniel's dates fixed the year 1866 or 1867 for the return of Christ – the return of the spiritual idea to the material earth or antipode of heaven. It is a marked coincidence that those dates were the first two year of my discovery of Christian Science" (The First Church of Christ, Scientist, and Miscellany, Pg. 181).

Jehovah's Witnesses

Jehovah's Witnesses believe that the second coming of Jesus was an invisible, spiritual event that occurred in the year 1914. On October 1 of the year 1914, it is contended, the "appointed times of the nations" ended, and God's heavenly kingdom, with Christ enthroned as King, began (Paradise Lost, PG. 178, 203).

Second Coming has already happened: On October 1, 1914 the "appointed times of the nations" ended, and God's heavenly kingdom began with Christ enthroned as King (Paradise Lost, Pg. 173-174).

Mormonism

Signs of Christ's Return: Signs that Must be Fulfilled show below!

"14 But, behold, I say unto you that before this great day shall come the sun shall be darkened, and the moon shall be turned into blood, and the stars shall fall from heaven, and there shall be greater signs in heaven above and in the earth beneath; 15 And there shall be weeping and wailing among the hosts of men; 16 And there shall be a great hailstorm sent forth to destroy the crops of the earth" (Doctrine and Covenants, 29:14-16).

"24 And this I have told you concerning Jerusalem; and when that day shall come, shall a remnant be scattered among all nations; 25 But they shall be gathered again; but they shall remain until the times of the Gentiles be fulfilled. 26 And in that day shall be heard of wars and rumors of wars, and the whole earth shall be in commotion, and men's hearts shall fail them, and they shall say that Christ delayeth his coming until the end of the earth" (Doctrine and Covenants, 45:24).

"6 To lift up your voice as with the sound of a trump, both long and loud, and cry repentance unto a crooked and perverse generation, preparing the way of the Lord for his second coming. 7 For behold, verily, verily, I say unto you, the time is soon at hand that I shall come in a cloud with power and great glory. 8 And it shall be a great day at the time of my coming, for all nations shall tremble. 9 But before that great day shall come, the sun shall be darkened, and the moon be turned into blood; and the stars shall refuse their shining, and some shall fall, and great destructions await the wicked" (Doctrine and Covenants, 34:6-9).

"40 And they shall see signs and wonders, for they shall be shown forth in the heavens above, and in the earth beneath. 41 And they shall behold blood, and afire, and vapors of smoke. 42 And before the day of the Lord shall come, the sun shall be darkened, and the moon be turned into blood, and the stars fall from heaven. 43 And the remnant shall be gathered unto this place; 44 And then they shall look for me, and, behold, I will come; and they shall see me in the clouds of heaven, clothed with power and great glory; with all the holy angels; and he that watches not for me shall be cut off" (Doctrine and Covenants, 45:40-44).

During the Millennium, Jesus will "reign personally upon the earth" (Articles of Faith 1:10). Joseph Smith explained that Jesus will "reign over the Saints and come down and instruct" (Teachings of Presidents of the Church: Joseph Smith, 2007, P. 258.

Seventh-day Adventists

Jesus failed to come as they had expected. "Let us now project ourselves in imagination back to the year 1844. Many, with William Miller in the lead, were fervently preaching that the coming of Christ and the end of the world would be on October 22, 1844. Excitement ran high. Thousands upon thousands were seriously preparing to meet Christ as He would come in the clouds of heaven. Hundreds of thousands stood by a bit restless and uncertain, but hoping to make the right decision by the fateful day, afraid that He might come, and at the same time hoping that He would not come..... I could almost feel myself among that group on October 22, looking at the sky, watching for the appearance of Christ, as a small cloud, which would come closer and closer. But the sun went down that fateful evening and He did not come. I could actually sense the disappointment of that early Advent group. My heart went out to them in their bitter disappointment" (Ellen White's Writings, Believe His Prophets)

Second Coming. When He returns, the righteous dead will be resurrected, and together with the righteous living will be glorified and taken to heaven, but the unrighteous will die (General Conference of Seventh-day Adventists, 2015). The "remnant church" is understood to act as a catalyst for the formation of this group. The eschatological remnant will consist of some (but not all) constituents of the present "remnant church", together with a cohort of believers from other (that is, non-Adventist) churches. Only members of the eschatological remnant will be saved through the end-times (Official website of the Seventh-day Adventist Church).

Only the Righteous Resurrected. The resurrected righteous and the living righteous will be glorified and caught up to meet their Lord (General Conference of Seventh-day Adventists, 2015).

Unification Church

"Then they can understand that Reverent Moon is Messiah, the Lord of the Second Advent....If only they can understand the fall of man they can understand that Father is the Messiah....Father is visible God" (120 Day Training Manal, Pg. 160, 222, 352).

"...to meet the Lord in the air signifies that the saints will receive the Lord in the world of good sovereignty when Christ [Moon] come again and restores the Kingdom of Heaven on earth by overthrowing the Satanic sovereignty" (Divine Principle Pg. 117).

"Consequently, he most important matter of all is the viewpoint from which one interprets the Bible.....since it is absolutely incomprehensible to the intellect of modern men that the Lord would come on the clouds, it is necessary for us to consider the Bible in detail a second time..." (Divine Principle, Pg. 500).

Jesus was the second Adam. For 2000 years Christians are have supposed to prepare for the coming of the second Messiah. That Messiah will be born somewhere in the east. Korea is the only logical place for people there have a strong faith in God. Moon is the second coming of the Messiah (Divine Principle, 519; Yamamoto, 1974).

"I (Moon) am Jesus who came 2000 years ago. My mission still remains to be accomplished. In order to realize God's will, you must be responsible for a great mission" (120 Day Training Manual, p. 324).

Sin

Biblical Code: SIN

Bible: The Bible says that "For all have sinned, and come short of the glory of God" (Romans 3:23).   In Revelation 15:4 we are told, "Who shall not fear thee, O Lord, and glorify thy name? For thou only art holy". In Romans 3:10 it says, "There is none righteous, no, not one".

Scripture	Content
Romans 3:23	**"For all have sinned and fall short of the glory of God,"**
Romans 3:10	**"As it is written: None is righteous, no, not one;"**
Romans 5:12	"Therefore, just as sin came into the world through one man, and death through sin, **and so death spread to all men because all sinned—"**
Romans 7:16-23	"Now if I do what I do not want, I agree with the law, that it is good. So now it is no longer I who do it, but sin that dwells within me. For I know that nothing good dwells in me, that is, in my flesh. For I have the desire to do what is right, but not the ability to carry it out. **For I do not do the good I want, but the evil I do not want is what I keep on doing.** Now if I do what I do not want, it is no longer I who do it, but sin that dwells within me. So I find it to be a law that when I want to do right, evil lies close at hand. For I delight in the law of God, in my inner being, but **I see in my members another law waging war against the law of my mind and making me captive to the law of sin that dwells in my members."**
1 John 1:8-10	**"If we say we have no sin, we deceive ourselves, and the truth is not in us.** If we confess our sins, he is faithful and just to forgive us our sins and to cleanse us from all unrighteousness. If we say we have not sinned, we make him a liar, and his word is not in us."
Revelation 15:4	"Who will not fear, O Lord, and glorify your name? **For you alone are holy.** All nations will come and worship you, for your righteous acts have been revealed."

Catholicism

Mary, "the All-Holy," lived a perfectly sinless life (Catechism 411, 493).

"By the grace of God Mary remained free of Every personal sin her whole life long" (Catechism, 493).

"Espousing the divine will for salvation wholeheartedly, without a single sin to restrain her, she gave herself entirely to the person and to the work of her son..." (Catechism 494).

"Mary is the most excellent fruit of redemption (SC 103): from the first instant of her conception, she was totally preserved from the stain of original sin and she remained pure from all personal sin throughout her life" (Catechism, 508…See also 722).

Christian Science

There is no sin, it is not real. It is an illusion, (Science and Health, Pg. 71, 480).

Jesus "…came to destroy the belief of sin" (Science and Health, Pg. 473).

"Therefore, the only reality of sin, sickness, or death is the awful fact that unrealities seem real to human, erring belief, until God strips off their disguise" (Science and Health, Pg. 472).

"Nothing unspiritual can be real, harmonious, or eternal. Sin, sickness and mortality are the suppositional antipodes of Spirit and must be contradictions of reality" (Science and Health, Pg. 335).

Unity

"Sin is man's failure to express the attributes of Being—life, love, intelligence, wisdom, and the other God qualities" (The Revealing Word, Pg. 180).

Comparative Doctrine

Tithing or Giving

Biblical Code: TI

Bible: The following scriptures state that giving is essential for the Christian. You should give as you prosper (1 Corinthians 16:2), do so in a cheerful way (2 Corinthians 9:7) and set aside your giving for the first day of the week (1 Corinthians 16:2). In addition, it is stated that your giving should be done in secret to avoid being tempted to be praised by others (Matthew 6:1-4). We are also told to, 1) not neglect to do good, and 2) to share what you have with others (Hebrews 13:16). The New Testament does not use the word Tithing.

Scripture	Content
1 Corinthian16:2	**"On the first day of every week, each of you is to put something aside and store it up, as he may prosper,** so that there will be no collecting when I come."
Matthew 6:1-4	"Beware of practicing your righteousness before other people in order to be seen by them, for then you will have no reward from your Father who is in heaven. **"Thus, when you give to the needy, sound no trumpet before you,** as the hypocrites do in the synagogues and in the streets, that they may be praised by others. Truly, I say to you, they have received their reward. **But when you give to the needy, do not let your left hand know what your right hand is doing, so that your giving may be in secret. And your Father who sees in secret will reward you."**
Luke 6:38	**"Give, and it will be given to you.** Good measure, pressed down, shaken together, running over, will be put into your lap. For with the measure you use it will be measured back to you."
Acts 2:44-45	"And all who believed were together and had all things in common. **And they were selling their possessions and belongings and distributing the proceeds to all, as any had need."**
2 Corinthians 9:7	**"Each one must give as he has decided in his heart, not reluctantly or under compulsion, for God loves a cheerful giver."**
1 Timothy 6:17-19	"As for the rich in this present age, charge them not to be haughty, nor to set their hopes on the uncertainty of riches, but on God, who richly provides us with everything to enjoy. They are to do good, to be rich in good works, **to be generous and ready to share, thus storing up treasure for themselves as a good foundation for the future, so that they may take hold of that which is truly life."**
Hebrews 13:16	"Do not neglect to do good and to **share what you have,** for such sacrifices are pleasing to God."

Islam

"Save yourself from hellfire even by giving half a date-fruit in charity" (Surah 2:498; bkhari 2.24.498).

"Those who believe, and do deeds of righteousness, and establish regular prayers and give zakat, will have their reward; on them shall be no fear nor shall they grieve" (Surah 2:277). Note: Muslims are expected to give 2.5 percent (zakat) of their overall estate each year to the poor.

"The Prophet said, "Do not with-hold your money by counting it (that is, hording it), for if you did so, Allah would also withhold His blessings from you'" (Surah 2:514; Bukhari 2.24.513).

Judaism

"Some Rabbinic sources make reference to a tithe of money as well as of produce, although it is not too clear whether this was seen as a voluntary contribution rather than an obligation. Nevertheless, many observant Jews today do donate a tenth of their annual income to charity. This is known as maaser kesafim, 'the money tithe' or 'wealth tax." See Numbers 18:21-32 and Deuteronomy 14:22-7 and 26:12 (taken from myjewishlearning website).

Mormonism

"Behold, now it is called today until the becoming of the Son of Man, and verily it is a day of sacrifice, and a day for the tithing of my people; for he that is tithed shall not be burned at his coming" (Doctrine and Covenants 64:23).

"Will a man rob God? Yet ye have robbed me. But ye say, Wherein have we robbed thee? In tithes and offerings. 9 Ye are cursed with a curse: for ye have robbed me, even this whole nation. 10 Bring ye all the tithes into the storehouse, that there may be meat in mine house, and prove me now herewith, saith the Lord of hosts, if I will not open you the windows of heaven, and pour you out a blessing, that there shall not be room enough to receive it" (Malachi 3: 8-10).

Comparative Doctrine

Trinity or Godhead

Biblical Code: TR

Bible: The Bible teaches us that God, Jesus and the Holy Spirit are one. In John 10:30 we are told that God and Jesus are one. In 2 Corinthians 3:17 we are told that God and the Holy Spirit are one. So, if God and Jesus are one and God and the Holy Spirit are one that would suggest that the three are one.

Scripture	Content
John 1:1	**JESUS AND GOD ARE ONE.** "In the beginning was **the Word, and the Word was with God, and the Word was God.**"
John 10:30, 38b	**JESUS AND GOD ARE ONE.** "**I and the Father are one.**" "The Father is in me and I am in the Father."
Matthew 28:19	**FATHER, SON AND THE HOLY SPIRIT CONNECED.** "Go therefore and make disciples of all nations, baptizing them in the name of the **Father and of the Son and of the Holy Spirit,**"
2 Corinthian 3:17	**GOD AND THE SPIRIT ARE ONE.** "Now the **Lord is the Spirit,** and where the Spirit of the Lord is, there is freedom."
Genesis 1:26	**JESUS AND GOD ARE ONE.** "Then God said, "**Let us make man in our image, after our likeness.** And let them have dominion over the fish of the sea and over the birds of the heavens and over the livestock and over all the earth and over every creeping thing that creeps on the earth."

Words in Bold and CAPITOLIZED are Comments!

We are going to vary from our initial statement that we would not give opinions. The concept of Trinity is so difficult for some that we thought we would give some examples of what others have said regarding how you could better understand the concept of Trinity in the Godhead.

1. Some earlier Christians explained that the Father is like the mind that conceives the thoughts, the Word (Christ) is the expression of that thought, and the Spirit is the voice that carried the thought along. The three are separate in person, but in essence one.
2. The Trinity is NOT a triplex: (1+1+1=3). Norman Geisler and Abdul Saleeb observe, "His one essence has multiple "personalities." Thus, there is no more of a mathematical problem in conceiving the Trinity than there is in understanding 1 to the third power (1^3).
3. Another description is that the Trinity is water. Water can be frozen, but still water. It can be steam, but it is still water. Obviously, it can be liquid water. So, water can have three different forms, but in essence is still water.
4. In Hebrews 1:3 it says, "The Son is the radiance of God's glory." Just as the one sun emits light, heat, and radioactive waves, and by encountering any of those you experience the sun itself, so in encountering Jesus you experience the very essence of God.

Armstrongism

"The false Trinity teaching does limit God to three persons. But God is not limited. As God repeatedly reveals, his purpose it to reproduce himself into what well may become billions of God persons. It is the false Trinity teaching that limits God, denies God's purpose and has palpably deceived the whole Christian world" (Armstrong, Mystery of the Ages, 1995).

Bahai

Believes that God is one person as does Judaism and Islam. Cannot accept the idea that God is both three and one (Martin's Interview with Udo Schaefer, a well known Baha'i apologist and teacher).

Christian Science

"The theory of three persons in one God (that is, a personal Trinity or Tri-unity) suggests polytheism, rather than the one ever-present I AM" (Science and Health, Pg. 256).

The Trinity is Life, Truth, and Love, (Science and Health, Pg. 331:26).

"Life, Truth, and Love constitute the triune Person called God, -- that is, the triply divine Principle, Love. They represent a trinity in unity, three in one, -- the same in essence, though multiform in office: God the Father-Mother, Christ the spiritual ideal of sonship; divine Science or the Holy comforter" (Science and Health, Pg. 331-332).

"Jesus is not God..." (Science and Health, Pg. 361).

Islam

Allah explicitly condemns the Christian doctrine of the Trinity (Surah 5:116). Qur'an is very clear in denouncing Trinity (4:171; 5:73).

Jehovah's Witnesses

"God through His Word, appeals to our reason. This Trinity doctrine is a negation of both the scriptures and reason" (Should You Believe in the Trinity, 1989).

He is not part of a Trinity (See JW.Org Bible Teachings).

The Holy spirit is defined as "the invisible active force of Almighty God which moves His servants to do His will" (Let God Be True). Both the personality of the Holy Spirit and his deity are rejected.

The apostle Paul wrote that after Jesus was resurrected, God "exalted him [Jesus] to a superior position." Obviously, Paul did not believe that Jesus was Almighty God. Otherwise, how could God exalt Jesus to a superior position? —Philippians 2:9 (See JW.Org Bible Teachings). Thus Jesus cannot be God!

"The trinity doctrine was not conceived by Jesus or the early Christians" (Let God Be True 1952).

The Son "did not follow the course of the Devil and plot and scheme to make himself like or equal to the Most Hight God and to rob God or usurp God's place" (Let God Be True, Pg.34-35). They believe that Jesus was a god, but not God.

"The obvious conclusion is, therefore, that Satan is the originator of the Trinity doctrine" (Let God Be True, Pg. 101).

Comparative Doctrine

Judaism

Jehovah God or Yahwa is the only God. There are no others. "The New Testament also include numerous verses testifying to Jesus as equal to God and as divine — a belief hard to reconcile with Judaism's insistence on God's oneness" (taken from myjewishlearning website).

Unification Church

Rhodes summarized Moon's believe regarding the Trinity by writing, "According to Moon, it was God's original intention in creating Adam and Eve to form a Trinity by uniting them into one body with himself (that is God, the "True Father" [Adam], and the "true Mother" [Eve]). This plan was foiled because Adam and Even did not perfect themselves and fell into sin. Because of the fall, a Satanic trinity was formed with Satan, Adam, and Eve (false parents). Later, once Jesus perfected himself spiritually, God formed a spiritual Trinity with Jesus and the Holy Spirit (who is a female spirit; hence Jesus and the Holy Spirit supposedly took the roles of "second Adam' and "second Eve"). But because Jesus died on the cross before getting married, God could not form a physical trinity with Jesus and the woman he might have married. Moon claims that the members of the physical Trinity will be God, the Lord of the Second, and the Lord of the Second Advent's wife. Moon teaches that when this physical Trinity is formed, the kingdom of heaven will be established on earth" (Divine Principle, 519; Yamamoto, 1974; Rhodes, 2001).

"Christ must come again in the flesh in order that he may become the True Parent both spiritually and physically, by forming substantial Trinity centered on God. He will the, by giving them rebirth both spiritually and physically, have all fallen men form (by couples) substantial trinities centered on God, after having liquidated the original sin" (Divine Principle, pg. 218, 1977).

"It is plain that Jesus is not God himself" (Divine Principle, Pg. 211).

Unity

"The Father is Principle, the Son is that Principle revealed in the creative plan, the Holy Spirit is the executive power of both Father and Son carrying out the plan" (Metaphysical Bible Dictionary, 1931).

"The doctrine of the trinity is often a stumbling block, because we find it difficult to understand how three persons can be one. Three persons cannot be one...God is the name of the all-encompassing Mind, Christ is the name of the all-loving Mind. Holy Spirit is the all-active manifestations. These three are one fundamental Mind in its three creative aspect" (The Revealed Word, 1959).

Unconditional Election

Biblical Code: UE

Bible: Calvin teaches Unconditional Election. He states that man is unable to initiate a response to God. He cannot choose to come to God for Salvation. This doctrine also communicates that God picked specific people who would become saved before the foundation of the world and everyone else was destined for the Lake of Fire. If you look at all Scriptures that address this issue, it is evident that this doctrine is not Biblical. What does the Bible teach about the Elect? God elected that all men be saved. The Bible is extremely clear on this point (John 3:16-17; 1 Timothy 2:3-4; 2 Peter 3:9). Who are the Elect and who can be saved according to the Bible? Let's see what the Scriptures say.

Scripture	Content
John 3:16-17	"For God so loved the world, that he gave his only Son, that **whoever believes in him should not perish but have eternal life.** For God did not send his Son into the world to condemn the world, but in order that the world might be saved through him.
1 Timothy 2:3-4	This is good, and it is pleasing in the sight of God our Savior, **who desires all people to be saved** and to come to the knowledge of the truth.
2 Peter 3:9	The Lord is not slow to fulfill his promise as some count slowness, but is patient toward you, **not wishing that any should perish**, but that all should reach repentance.
2 Peter 3:9	The Lord is not slow to fulfill his promise as some count slowness, but is patient toward you, **not wishing that any should perish**, but that all should reach repentance.
1 John 2:2	He is the propitiation for our sins, and not for ours only but also **for the sins of the whole world.**
1 John 4:14	And we have seen and testify that the Father has sent his Son to be the **Savior of the world.**
Acts 2:21	And it shall come to pass that **everyone who calls upon the name of the Lord shall be saved.'**
Romans 10:12-13	For there is no distinction between Jew and Greek; for the same Lord is Lord of all, bestowing his riches on all who call on him. For **"everyone who calls on the name of the Lord will be saved."**
Acts 17:30	The times of ignorance God overlooked, but now **he commands all people everywhere to repent,**
Free Will in the Bible	
John 15:10	**If you keep my commandments, you will abide in my love,** just as I have kept my Father's commandments and abide in his love.

James 1:12	Blessed is the man who remains steadfast under trial, **for when he has stood the test he will receive the crown of life**, which God has promised to those who love him.
Revelation 20:13 (11-15)	And the sea gave up the dead who were in it, Death and Hades gave up the dead who were in them, and **they were judged, each one of them, according to what they had done.**
1Tim 2:4 – 6	who **desires all people to be saved** and to come to the knowledge of the truth. For there is one God, and there is one mediator between God and men, the man Christ Jesus, who gave himself as a ransom for all, which is the testimony given at the proper time.

See appendices where Arminian vs Calvinistic beliefs are reviewed.

Arminian Election

Cottrell clearly defines Election based on Arminian beliefs. "Election, says Cottrell, is "the idea that God predestines to salvation those individuals who meet the gracious conditions which he has set forth" ("Conditional Election"). When a person by free will meets these conditions (faith and repentance), we must not think of him as performing meritorious works of righteousness, because the conditions are sovereignly and graciously imposed by God. Since man did not deserve to have these conditions made available to him whereby he might be saved, the election which results from his meeting those conditions remains wholly of grace. "Thus," Cottrell concludes, "having set forth these conditions for being in Christ, God foreknows from the beginning who will and who will not meet them. Those whom he foresees as meeting them are predestined to salvation" (61). The crucial point in this Arminian concept of election is this: If and when a person fulfills the condition of faith and repentance, it is he or she alone who does so. It is not God but the individual himself who is the ultimate cause of the decision" (The Arminian Concept of Election, Sam Storms.org).

Calvinism' Unconditional Election

Election is the unchangeable purpose of God, whereby, before the foundation of the world, he hath out of mere grace, according to the sovereign good pleasure of his own will, chosen, from the whole human race, which had fallen through their own fault, from their primitive state of rectitude, into sin and destruction, a certain number of persons to redemption in Christ, whom he from eternity appointed the Mediator and Head of the elect, and the foundation of Salvation (Canons of Dort, I:7).

Unconditional Election is the doctrine which states that God chose those whom he was pleased to bring to a knowledge of himself, not based upon any merit shown by the object of his grace and not based upon his looking forward to discover who would "accept" the offer of the gospel. God has elected, based solely upon the counsel of his own will, some for glory and others for damnation (Romans 9:15,21). He has done this act before the foundations of the world (Ephesians 1:4-8)" (http://www.reformed.org/calvinism).

Virgin Birth

Biblical Code: VB

Bible: The Bible teaches us that Jesus was conceived and born by his mother Mary through the power of the Holy Spirit and without the help of a human father. Mary was a virgin before and after Jesus was conceived.   However, Jesus did have brothers, as shown in the Bible, documenting that she did have other children (Matthew 12:46-50, 13:55-56; Mark 3:31, 6:3; Luke 8:19; John 2:12, 7:3; Acts 1:14; 1 Cor. 9:5; Galatians 1:19; Matthew 13:55; Mark 6:3).

Scripture	Content
Matthew 1:18	"Now the birth of Jesus Christ took place in this way. When his mother Mary had been betrothed to Joseph, before they came together **she was found to be with child from the Holy Spirit**."
Matthew 1: 23-25	"Behold, **the virgin shall conceive and bear a son**, and they shall call his name Immanuel" (which means, God with us). When Joseph woke from sleep, he did as the angel of the Lord commanded him: he took his wife, but knew her not until she had given birth to a son. And he called his name Jesus."
Luke 1:26-35	"In the sixth month the angel Gabriel was sent from God to a city of Galilee named Nazareth." He was to explain to Mary even thought **she was a virgin she was to bear a child**. And the angel answered her, "The Holy Spirit will come upon you, and the power of the Most High will overshadow you; therefore the child to be born will be called holy--the Son of God."

Catholicism

"Mary remained a virgin in conceiving her Son, a virgin in giving birth to him, a virgin in carrying him, a virgin in nursing him at her breast, always a virgin" (Catechism,510).

"And so the liturgy of the Church celebrates Mary as Aeiparthenos, the 'Ever-virgin'" (Catechism, 499).

"The Church has always understood these passages [Matthew 13:55; Mark 6:3; Galatians 1:19] as not referring to other children of the Virgin Mary. In fact James and Joseph, 'brothers of Jesus,' are the sons of another Mary, a disciple of Christ..." (Catechism, 500).

"Jesus is Mary's only son, but her spiritual motherhood extends to all men whom indeed he came to save: "The Son whom she brought forth is he whom God placed as the first-born among many brethren, that is, the faithful in whose generation and formation she co-operates with a mother's love" (Catechism, 501).

Christian Science

Jesus, the Galilean prophet, was born of the virgin Mary's spiritual thought of life and its manifestation. "Mary's conception of him was spiritual, for only purity could reflect Truth and Love, which were plainly incarnate in the good and pure Christ Jesus" (Science and Health, Pg. 332).

Jehovah's Witnesses

"Jehovah then placed the life force' of Michael [Archangel] in the womb of the virgin Mary so Jesus cold be born a human being (Watchtower Book, The Kingdom at Hand).

Unification Church

Jesus was the son of Zechariah, not born of a virgin. "Jesus was born of a father and a mother, just as anyone is, but in his case the Spirit of God was working also" (Master Speaks, Pg. 9).

Mormonism

God the Father came to earth in his physical form and had sexual intercourse with Mary to produce Jesus. (Journal of Discourses, V. 8, pp. 115, 211).

Scriptural Study for Common Core Beliefs

Section Five

The rest of this work is meant to help you understand various beliefs and whether or not they are scripturally sound or not. This section addresses Core Beliefs that can be found in most churches who claim to Believe in the Bible and follow Jesus Christ. These core beliefs are important Biblical facts about Christianity that we all should know well. We should also be able to show others what the Bible says about these core beliefs. You will have the option marking and chaining each of these common core beliefs as shown in this Section and in Section Eight.

- Marking Common Core Beliefs
- Common Core Beliefs

  - Bible Inspiration (BI)
  - Consciousness, Life After Death (CAD)
  - Elder Qualifications (EQ)
  - Death (DE)
  - Forgiveness of Sins (FOS)
  - God Created the World (GCW)
  - God is Spirit (GS)
  - God and Creation Separate (GCS)
  - God and Man Separate (GMS)
  - God Never Changes (GNC)
  - Heaven is a Place (HAP)
  - Hell is Eternal (EH)
  - Holy Spirit (HS)
  - Jesus' Birth (JB)
  - Jesus' Blood/Sacrifice Sufficient (JBS)
  - Jesus is the Christ-Deity (JIC)
  - Jesus is Eternal (JE)
  - Jesus' Mission (JM)
  - Jesus' Physical Death (JPD)

  - Jesus' Physical Resurrection (JPR)
  - Jesus was Sinless (JS)
  - Judgment Day (JMT)
  - Kingdom Established (KE)
  - Old Law Void (OLV)
  - One Christ (OC)
  - One God (OG)
  - One Heaven (OH)
  - One Mediator (OM)
  - Priests (PR)
  - Relationship with Unbelievers (RU)
  - Sabbath or Sunday (SOS)
  - Saints (STS)
  - Salvation Before Death (SBD)
  - Salvation-Most Men Lost (MML)
  - Salvation is Through Christ (STC)
  - Satan-Devil (SAT)
  - Sin (SIN)
  - Tithing or Giving (TI)
  - Trinity (TR)
  - Virgin Birth (VB)

Comparative Doctrine

Marking Common Core Beliefs

Keep in mind that even though these are common core beliefs among Christians, there are a multitude of people who have different beliefs and either, 1) don't know what the Bible teaches, or 2) come from another religious system that has their own creed or beliefs. Many of the core beliefs are distorted by cults and other religions who have their own agenda. Again, we need to let the Bible speak for itself. We don't want or need to listen to the words or works of any man, no matter who he is, or what he claims to be.

NOTE: Don't use large bold letters when you code your Bible. Some Scriptures address a variety of different doctrines or false teachings that some churches or cults believe in. Leave yourself room for other coding when possible.

Instructions for Marking

- Find a Blank Page in your Bible where you can tape or paste your Core Beliefs chain reference guide.
- Mark a Vertical red line next to each verse in each chain.
- Next to the line write the Initial of the topic and the designated code for the belief or denomination indicated (see example below ('JPD').
- At the end of the verse(s) write the initials of the doctrine that is being addressed, then record the next Scripture in the chain (see example below).

EXAMPLE: JESUS' PHYSICAL DEATH---LUKE 23:46

'JPD' CS IS UC	"Jesus called out with a loud voice, 'Father, into your hands I commit my spirit.' When he had said this, he breathed his last." 'JPD' Luke 23: 52-53

> This is the next Scripture in a chain. Place this Scripture underneath or to the side in your Bible.

'JPD'	=	Code for Jesus' Physical Death
CS	=	Stands for Christian Science
IS	=	Stands for Islam
UC	=	Stands for Unification Church

The beliefs that are listed under the code teach doctrine regarding this issue that is contrary to Bible Scripture.

Comparative Doctrine

Common Core Beliefs

Use the following chart to chain your scriptures for each area identified. Once you put in scriptures that are listed in the Scripture column you can add others that you believe would be appropriate. Once finished listing all Scriptures in a chain, you can put the first Scripture underneath the last Scripture. It will then be a loop. No matter where you start it will address the issue with multiple scriptures that are easy to find.

Teaching	Doct. Code	Scriptures	Churches/Beliefs that Disagree	Church Code
Bible Inspiration	'BI'	2 Peter 1:3 John 14:26 John 16:12-15 1 Corinthians 2:13 2 Timothy 3:16-17 Hebrews 1:1-2 2 Peter 1:20-21	Armstrongism Baha'i Catholicism Christian Science Islam Jehovah's Witnesses Judaism Mormonism Scientology Seventh-day Adventists Unification Church Unity	ARM BHI CA CS IS JW JU MO SCI SDA UC UN
Consciousness and Life After Death	'CAD'	Matthew 17:1-3 Luke 16:25 (19-30) Revelation 5:9 Revelation 6:9-11 Revelation 7:9-10 Revelation 14:11-13 Revelation 20:10 Revelation 20:11-14	Armstrong Jehovah's Witnesses Seventh-day Adventists Unitarian Universalist	ARM JW SDA UU
Death	'DE'	Hebrews 9:27 1 Corinthians 15:52-57 Ecclesiastes 12:7	Armstrong Christian Science Hinduism Scientology Unification Church Unity Unitarian Universalist	ARM CS HIN SCI UC UN UU
Elder Qualifications	'EQ'	Acts 20:28-31 1 Timothy 3:1-7 Titus 1:5-9	Catholicism Mormonism	CA MO
Forgiveness of Sins	'FOS'	Mark 2:10 Acts 2:38 Acts 10:43 Acts 13:38 Ephesians 1:7 Colossians 1:13-14 1 John 1:8-10	Catholicism Mormonism Scientology Unification Church	CA MO SCI UC

God Created the World	'GCW'	Genesis 1:1(1-31) Nehemiah 9:6 Colossians 1:15-17 Hebrews 11:3 Genesis 2:2-3 (1-25)	Armstrong Buddhism Christian Science Hinduism Islam Mormonism Scientology Unification Church Unitarian Universalist	ARM BUD CS HIN IS MO SCI UC UU
God is Spirit	'GS"	John 4:24 Matthew 16:17 1 Corinthians 15:50 2 Corinthians 3:17 Genesis 1:2	Christian Science Mormonism Scientology	CS MO SCI
God and Creation Separate	'GCS'	Genesis 2:2-3 Hebrews 11:3	Christian Science Hinduism Unification Church	CS HIN UC
God and Man Separate	'GMS'	Genesis 1:26-27 Numbers 23:19 Hosea 11:9 Hebrews 1:2	Christian Science Scientology Unification Church	CS SCI UC
God Never Changes	'GNC'	Malachi 3:6 Isaiah 40:28 Isaiah 44:6-8 Isaiah 57:15-27 Habakkuk 1:12 Romans 1:20 1 Timothy 6:15-16 Revelation 1:8 Revelation 10:5-6	Buddhism Hinduism Mormonism	BUD HIN MO
Heaven is a Place	'HAP'	John 14:1-3 2 Corinthians 5:1 Philippians 3:20 Colossians 1:5 1 Thessalonians 4:17 Hebrews 11:16 Revelations 21:1-7 Psalm 11:4	Baha'i Buddhism Christian Science Islam Hinduism Jehovah's Witnesses Mormonism Unification Church Unitarian Universalist Unity	BHI BUD CS IS HIN JW MO UC UU UN
Hell is Eternal	'EH'	Matthew 25:45-46 (41-46) Matthew 13:49-50 (47-50) Luke 16:22-23 (19-31) Revelation 14:9-11 Revelation 20:10 Revelation 21:8 Matthew 5:22 Matthew 10:28 Matthew 25:46	Armstrongism Baha'i Hinduism Christian Science Jehovah's Witnesses Mormonism Scientology Seventh-day Adventists Unification Church	ARM BHI HN CS JW MO SCI SDA UC

		2 Thessalonians 1:8-9 Jude 7 Revelations 20:11-15		
Holy Spirit	'HS'	Matthew 28:19 John 14:26 John 15:26 John 16:13-14 (7-15) Acts 13:4 Acts 8:29 Romans 8:26-27 (20-28) 1 Corinthians 12:11	Armstrongism Baha'i Christian Science Jehovah's Witnesses Unification Church Unity	ARM BHI CS JW UC UN
Jesus' Birth	'JB'	Matthew 1:18-25 Matthew 2:1-12 Luke 2:4-7 Luke 2:12-15 Isaiah 7:13-14 (10-15) Isaiah 9:6 Micah 5:2	Christian Science Islam Jehovah's Witnesses	CS IS JW
Jesus' Blood/ Sacrifice Sufficient	'JBS'	Hebrews 9:14-15 (9-28) Romans 5:6-9 Matthew 26:27-28 Hebrews 10:10-14 1 John 1:7 Revelation 1:5 Ephesians 2:13-18	Baha'i Christian Science Islam Judaism Unification Church Unitarian Universalist	BHI CS IS JU UC UU
Jesus is the Christ -Deity	'JIC'	Matthew 16:16 Mark 14:61-62 John 1:1 John 1:14 Romans 8:3 Colossians 2:9 Hebrews 1:1-4 (1-14) 1 John 2:22 Revelation 1:17-18	Baha'i Christian Science Islam Jehovah's Witnesses Judaism Scientology Unification Church Unitarian Universalist Unity	BHI CS IS JW JU SCI UC UU UN
Jesus is Eternal	'JE'	John 1:1 Colossians 1`:17 Hebrews 7:3 Hebrews1:8-12	Christian Science Islam Jehovah's Witnesses Mormonism Scientology	CS IS JW MO SCI
Jesus' Mission	'JM'	Matthew 20:28 Luke 4:43 Luke 19:10 John 12:27-33 1 John 4:14	Unification Church Unitarian Universalist	UC UU

Jesus' Physical Death	'JPD'	Matthew 27:58-60 Mark 8:31 Mark 15:39 (33-39) Luke 23:46 Luke 23:52-53 John 10:11-18 John 19:33 (31-42) Rev. 1:18 Mark 15:45-47	Christian Science Islam Jehovah's Witnesses Unification Church	CS IS JW UC
Jesus' Physical Resurrection	'JPR'	Luke 24:13-29 Luke 24:30-32 Luke 24:38-43 John 2:19-21 John 20:17 John 21:12-14	Armstrongism Baha'i Christian Science Islam Jehovah's Witnesses Judaism Unification Church	ARM BHI CS IS JW JU UC
Jesus was Sinless	'JS'	2 Corinthians 5:21 Hebrews 4:15 1 Peter 1:18-19 1 Peter 2:22 1 John 3:5	Christian Science Unification Church	CS UC
Judgment Day	'JMT'	Matthew 12:36 Matthew 25:31-46 John 12:48 Acts 17:31 Romans 2:16 2 Corinthians 5:10 2 Thessalonians 1:5-10 2 Timothy 4:8 Hebrews 9:27 2 Peter 2:4 2 Peter 2:9 Revelation 20:15	Baha'i Christian Science Jehovah's Witnesses Mormonism Scientology Unification Church	BHI CS JW MO UC SCI
Kingdom Established	'KE'	Colossians 1:12-13 Acts 8:12 Matthew 16:18-19 Matthew 16:28 Mark 9:1 Luke 17:21 Revelation 1:6, 9 Revelation 5:10	Armstrongism Jehovah's Witnesses Mormonism Seventh-day Adventists Unification Church Unitarian Universalist	ARM JW MO SDA UC UU
Old Law Void	'OLV'	Romans 7:4-6 Romans 8:1-2 2 Corinthians 3:13-18 Galatians 3:10-14 Galatians 3:23-25 Galatians 4:1-7 Ephesians 2:14-16 Colossians 2:13-15 Hebrews 8:6-13 Hebrews 10:9-10	Armstrongism Judaism Seventh-day Adventists	ARM JU SDA

One Christ	'OC'	1 Corinthians 8:6 Matthew 24:23-24 Mark 13:6 Ephesians 4:5	Baha'i Catholicism Unification Church	BHI CA UC
One God	'OG'	Mark 12:29-32 1 Corinthians 8:4-6 Ephesians 4:6 1 Timothy 2:5 James 2:19 Isaiah 43:10-11 Isaiah 44:6 (6-8) Isaiah 45:22	Armstrongism Buddhism Catholicism Hinduism Mormonism Scientology Unification Church Unitarian Universalists	ARM BUD CA HIN MO SCI UC UU
One Heaven	'OH'	Revelation 7:15-17 Acts 4:12 Luke 15:7 Matthew 7:21-23 Philippians 3:20-21 Hebrews 11:10 Hebrews 11:16 Revelation 22:1-5	Islam Jehovah's Witnesses Mormonism Scientology Unification Church	IS JW MO SCI UC
One Mediator	'OM'	1 Timothy 2:5-6 John 14:6 John 16:23 Ephesians 3:12 Hebrews 7:25	Catholicism Unification Church	CA UC
Priests	'PR'	1 Peter 2:5-9 Revelation 1:6 Revelation 5:10	Catholicism Mormonism	CA MO
Relationship with Unbelievers	'RU'	Colossians 4:5–6 1 Corinthians 9:22 1 Peter 3:13-15 2 Corinthians 6:14	Islam	IS
Sabbath or Sunday	'SOS'	Ephesians 2:14-15 Romans 7:4-5 Galatians 5:1-6 Acts 20:7 1 Corinthians 16:2 Colossians 2:16-17	Armstrongism Judaism Seventh-day Adventists	ARM JU SDA
Saints	'STS'	Philippians 1:1-2 Acts 9:13 Acts 9:32 Ephesians 4:12 Psalm 34:9	Catholicism	CA

Salvation Before Death	'SBD'	Luke 16:26 Romans 10:9-10 Hebrews 9:27 Revelation 20:11-15 Revelation 22:11-12	Armstrongism Baha'i Buddhism Catholicism Christian Science Hinduism Islam Mormonism Scientology Unification Church	ARM BHI BUD CA CS HIN IS MO SCI UC
Salvation – Most Men Lost	'MML'	Matthew 7:13-14 Luke 13:23-24	Christian Science Hinduism Jehovah's Witnesses Mormonism Scientology Unification Church Unity	CS HIN JW MO SCI UC UN
Salvation is Through Christ	'STC'	Acts 4:10-12 John 14:6 Ephesians 1:7 John 10:7-9 Hebrews 9:11-14 Hebrews 10:10 1 John 2:2 Matthew 1:21 John 4:42 Acts 5:31 Acts 13:23 2 Timothy 1:10 1 John 4:14	Bahai Buddhism Catholicism Christian Science Hinduism Islam Jehovah's Witnesses Mormonism Scientology Unification Church Unitarian Universalists Unity	BHI BUD CA CS HIN IS JW MO SCI UC UU UN
Satan-Devil	'SAT'	Matthew 4:8-9 2 Corinthians 11:14 1 John 3:8 1 Peter 5:8-9 Revelation 12:7-9 Revelation 20:1-2 Genesis 3:1-5 Isaiah 14:12-17	Baha'i Buddhism Christian Science Hinduism Scientology	BHI BUD CS HIN SCI
Sin	'SIN'	Romans 3:23 Romans 3:10 Romans 5:12 Romans 7:16-23 1 John 1:8-10 Revelation 15:4	Catholicism Christian Science Unity	CA CS UN
Tithing or Giving	'TI'	1 Corinthian16:2 Matthew 6:1-4 Luke 6:38 Acts 2:44-45 2 Corinthians 9:7 1 Timothy 6:17-19 Hebrews 13:16	Islam Judaism Mormonism	IS JU MO

Trinity	'TR'	John 1:1 John 10:30 Matthew 28:19 2 Corinthian 3:17 Genesis 1:26	Armstrongism Baha'i Christian Science Islam Jehovah's Witnesses Judaism Unification Church Unity	ARM BHI CS IS JW JU UC UN
Virgin Birth	'VB'	Matthew 1:18 Matthew 1:23-25 Luke 1:26-35	Catholicism Christian Science Jehovah's Witnesses Mormonism Unification Church	CA CS JW MO UC

Scriptural Study of Common Doctrinal Differences

Section Six

The section addresses Common Doctrinal Differences that have occurred in a variety of churches who follow New Testament teachings. You will have the option marking and chaining each of these common doctrinal differences as shown in this Section and in Section Eight.

- Marking Common Doctrinal Differences
- Common Doctrinal Differences

  - ➢ Baptism (BAP)
  - ➢ Infant Baptism (IB)
  - ➢ Judged by Grace through Faith (JGF)
  - ➢ Lord's Supper (LS)
  - ➢ Once Saved Always Saved (OSAS)
  - ➢ Original Sin (OS)
  - ➢ Second Coming (SC)
  - ➢ Unconditional Election (UC)

NOTE: It is important to remember that if the Bible says something in multiple passages, all of them must be true. As a result, you must compile all of the scriptures regarding that particular belief to come up with a true Biblical answer. Ignoring one Scripture or focusing a particular Scripture when there are other Scriptures that should be considered will produce an invalid or inaccurate description of that belief or doctrine.

Marking Common Doctrinal Differences

Varying Biblical interpretations of Scripture have occurred almost from the inception of the church. Today, there are many churches who have different beliefs that appear to be Biblical, but are in disagreement with other churches interpretations. This section allows you to look at the Scriptures to see what the Bible says about these particular doctrinal issues.

NOTE: Don't use large bold letters when you code your Bible. Some Scriptures address a variety of different doctrines or false teachings that some churches or cults believe in. Leave yourself room for other coding when possible.

Instructions for Marking

- Find a Blank Page in your Bible where you can tape or paste your Common Doctrinal Differences chain reference guide.
- Mark a Vertical red line next to each verse in each chain.
- Next to the line write the Initial of the topic and the designated code for the belief or denomination indicated (see example below 'IB').
- At the end of the verse(s) write the initials of the doctrine that is being addressed, then record the next Scripture in the chain (see example below).

EXAMPLE: INFANT BAPTISM---MARK 16:15-16

'IB' CA CAL	(Must be capable of believing!) He said to them, "Go into all the world and preach the gospel to all creation. Whoever believes and is baptized will be saved, but whoever does not believe will be condemned."

'IB' Acts 2:38

> This is the next Scripture in a chain. Place this Scripture underneath or to the side.

'IB'	=	Code for Infant Baptism
CA	=	Stands for Catholicism
CAL	=	Calvinism

Each of these forms of religion teach doctrine contrary to Bible Scripture.

Comparative Doctrine

Common Doctrinal Differences

Use the following chart to chain your scriptures for each area identified. Once you put in scriptures that are listed in the Scripture column you can add others that you believe would be appropriate. Once finished listing all Scriptures in a chain, you can put the first Scripture underneath the last Scripture. It will then be a loop. No matter where you start it will address the issue with multiple scriptures that are easy to find.

Teaching	Doct. Code	Scriptures	Churches/Beliefs that Disagree	Church Code
Baptism	'BAP'	Acts 2:38 Matthew 28:18-20 Mark 16:15-16 John 3:5 1 Peter 3:21 Acts 22:16 Romans 6:3 1 Corinthians 12:13 Galatians 3:26-27 Titus 3:5 (Note: See Conversion Examples in Appendix)	Catholicism Christian Science Mormonism	CA CS MO
Infant Baptism	'IB'	Mark 16:15-16 Acts 2:38 Romans 10:9-10 Galatians 3:26-27	Calvinism Catholicism	CAL CA
Judged by Grace through Faith	'JGF'	Ephesians 2:8-10 Romans 1:16 Galatians 2:16-21 Titus 3:4-8 John 6:29 (26-29) James 2:24 (18-26) Colossians 2:11-12 Romans 10:9-10 Acts 2:38	Armstrongism Baha'i Buddhism Catholicism Hinduism Islam Jehovah's Witnesses Judaism Mormonism Unity	ARM BHI BUD CA HIN IS JW JU MO UN
Lords Supper	'LS'	1 Corinthians 10:16 Acts 20:7 1 Corinthians 11:20-34 Matthew 26:26-29	Catholicism	CA

Once Saved Always Saved	'OSAS'	Galatians 5:3-4 Hebrews 3:12 Romans 11:17-24 1 Corinthians 9:27 Colossians 1:23 Colossians 2:18 1 Timothy 4:1-2 Hebrews 6:4-6 Hebrews 10:26-29 James 5:19-20 2 John 8-9 Revelation 2:4-5	Calvinism* Gnosticism	CAL GNO
Original Sin	'OS'	Matthew 15:19 1 John 3:4 1 John 5:17 James 4:17 2 Corinthians 5:10 Revelation 20:12-13 Ezekiel 18:20 Ezekiel 28:15 Jeremiah 31:30	Calvinism Catholicism Jehovah's Witnesses Seventh-day Adventists Unification Church	CAL CA JW SDA UC
Second Coming	'SC'	Matthew 24:36 Matthew 16:27 Matthew 24:29-30 Matthew 24:44 Mark 13:32 John 5:28-29 1 Thessalonians 4:13-18 1 Thessalonians 5:2 2 Thessalonians 1:7-8 2 Peter 3:10-13 Revelation 1:7	Armstrong Baha'i Christian Science Jehovah's Witnesses Mormonism Seventh-day Adventists Unification Church	ARM BHI CS JW MO SDA UC
Unconditional Election	'UE'	John 3:16-17 1 Timothy 2:3-4 2 Peter 3:9 2 Peter 3:9 1 John 2:2 1 John 4:14 Acts 2:21 Romans 10:12-13 Acts 17:30 John 15:10 James 1:12 Revelation 20:13 (11-15) 1 Tim 2:4–6	Calvinism*	CAL

*   See Calvinism in the appendices for information about churches that believe these doctrines.

Scriptural Study for Doctrines Not Supported in the Bible

Section Seven

Section seven addresses False Teaching that occur in Churches, cults and other religious beliefs. You will have the option marking and chaining each of these false teaching as shown in this Section and in Section Eight.

- Marking False Doctrine or Doctrines Not Supported in the Bible
- False Doctrine or Doctrines Not Supported in the Bible

  ➢ Baptism for the Dead (BD)
  ➢ Born of God (BOG)
  ➢ Foods Prohibited (FP)
  ➢ God Causes Some to go Astray (GCA)
  ➢ Heavenly Deception (HD)
  ➢ Infallibility (IN)
  ➢ Mary the Perpetual Virgin (MPV)
  ➢ Mary was Sinless   (MS)
  ➢ Purgatory (PUR)
  ➢ Reincarnation, Rebirth or Reorganized (RN)
  ➢ Revelation (RV)

Marking False Doctrine or Doctrines Not Supported by the Bible

Not everyone who says to me, 'Lord, Lord,' will enter the kingdom of heaven, but only he who does the will of my Father who is in heaven. Many will say to me on that day, 'Lord, Lord, did we not prophesy in your name, and in your name drive out demons and perform many miracles?' Then I will tell them plainly, 'I never knew you. Away from me, you evildoers!' Matthew 7:21-23.

There are some who teach that they have new revelation or a better understanding of what the Bible really means. As a result, there are new doctrinal beliefs that are promoted as being from God. Usually, these new doctrinal beliefs are in contrast to what the Bible teaches. The teachings listed in this section are in that category. They are obvious contradictions to Scripture.

Instructions for Marking

- Find a Blank Page in your Bible where you can tape or paste your False Doctrine or Doctrines Not Supported by the Bible chain reference guide.
- Mark a Vertical red line next to each verse in each chain.
- Next to the line write the Initial of the topic and the designated code for the belief or denomination indicated (see example below 'RN').
- At the end of the verse(s) write the initials of the doctrine that is being addressed, then record the next Scripture in the chain (see example below).

EXAMPLE: REINCARNATION – Hebrews 9:27

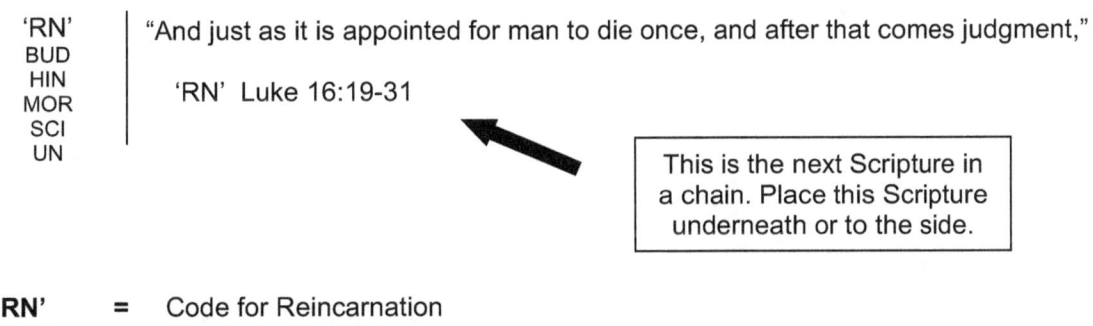

| 'RN' BUD HIN MOR SCI UN | "And just as it is appointed for man to die once, and after that comes judgment," 'RN' Luke 16:19-31 | This is the next Scripture in a chain. Place this Scripture underneath or to the side. |

'RN'	=	Code for Reincarnation
BUD	=	Stands for Buddhism
HIN	=	Stands for Hinduism
MOR	=	Stands for Mormonism
SCI	=	Stands for Scientology
UN	=	Stands for Unity Church

Each of these forms of religion teach doctrine contrary to Bible Scripture.

False Doctrine or
Doctrines Not Supported in the Bible

Teaching	Doct. Code	Scriptures	Churches/Beliefs that Disagree	Church Code
Baptism for the Dead	'BD'	Acts 2:38 Hebrews 9:27 Revelation 20:11-15 2 Corinthians 6:1-2 Mark 16:16 Romans 10:8-17	Catholicism Mormonism	CA MO
Born of God	'BOG'	John 3:3-5 1 Jn. 2:29 1 Jn. 3:9 1 Jn. 4:7 1 Jn. 5:1	Armstrong	A
Foods Prohibited	'FP'	Acts 15:28-29 Acts 10:10-15 Matthew 15:11 Romans 14:20 (1-23) 1 Timothy 4:3-4 (1-5) Colossians 2:16 (16-23)	Catholicism Hinduism Islam Judaism Mormonism Seventh-day Adventists	CA HIN IS JU MO SDA
God Causes Some to Go Astray	'GCA'	Luke 6:35-36 Romans 5:8	Islam	IS
Heavenly Deception	'HD'	John 8:44 Colossians 3:9 1 Timothy 1:10 Revelation 21:8 Revelation 22:15	Islam Unification Church	IS UC
Infallibility	'INF'	Galatians 1:7-9 Hebrews 1:1-2 Hebrews 13:20-21 2 Peter 1:3	Catholicism	CA
Mary the Perpetual Virgin	'MPV'	Matthew 1:25 (18-25) Matthew 12:46-50 Matthew 13:55-57 Mark 3:31 Mark 6:3-4 Luke 8:19 John 2:12 Acts 1:14 Galatians 1:18-19 1 Corinthians 9:4-5	Catholicism	CA

Mary was Sinless	'MS'	Romans 3:23 Romans 3:9-19 Romans 5:12 Mark 7:21 Galatians 5:17 Ecclesiastes 7:20	Catholicism	CA
Purgatory	'PUR'	Hebrews 10:17-18 Luke 16:26 Romans 10:9-10 Hebrews 9:27 Revelation 20:11-15 Revelation 2:10	Catholicism Islam Mormonism	CA IS MO
Reincarnation, Rebirth, or Reorganization	'RN'	Hebrews 9:27 Luke 16:19-31 John 5:28-29 2 Corinthians 5:1 2 Corinthians 5:10	Buddhism Hinduism Mormonism Scientology Unity	BUD HIN MO SCI UN
Revelation	'RV'	Galatians 1:7-9 Luke 16:27-31 Romans 15:19 2 Timothy 3:16-17 Hebrews 1:1-2 Hebrews 13:20-21 2 Peter 1:3 Jude 3-4 2 Peter 2:1 1 John 4:1 Matthew 5:18	Bahai Buddhism Catholicism Christian Science Hinduism Islam Mormonism Unification Church	BHI BUD CA CS HIN IS MO UC

Chain Reference Guides for Biblical Doctrine

Section Eight

There are four possible Chain Reference guides in this section that you can choose to use.

- Common Core Doctrinal Beliefs
- Common Doctrinal Differences in Christ Centered Churches
- False Doctrine or Doctrine not Supported in the Bible
- Common Quick References
- Personal Quick References

Common Core Doctrinal Beliefs

The following are some of the more 'Common Core Doctrinal Beliefs' that Christ believing Churches often share. There is room on this chain reference guide for additional beliefs if you want to add them. If you want to use this as a resource in your Bible, simply copy this page and tape or paste it into a page in your Bible. Premade sticky backed reference guide for 'Common Core Doctrinal Beliefs' is available from this author.

Comparative Doctrine
Common Core Doctrinal Beliefs Quick Reference
That Most Christ-Centered Beliefs Adhere To

Common Core Beliefs	Doct. Code	Location
Bible Inspiration	'BI'	2 Peter 1:3
Consciousness after Death	'CAD'	Matthew 17:1-3
Death	'DE'	Hebrews 9:27
Elder Qualifications	'EQ'	Acts 20:28-31
Forgiveness of Sins	'FOS'	Mark 2:10
God Created the World	'GCW'	Genesis 1:1 (1-31)
God is Spirit	'GS'	John 4:24
God and Creation Separate	'GCS'	Genesis 2:2-3
God and Man Separate	'GMS'	Genesis 1:26-27
God Never Changes	'GNC'	Malachi 3:6
Heaven is a Place	'HAP'	John 14:1-3
Hell is Eternal	'EH'	Matthew 25:41-46
Holy Spirit	'HS'	Matthew 28:19
Jesus' Birth	'JB'	Matthew 1:18-25
Jesus' Blood/Sacrifice Sufficient	'JBS'	Heb. 9:14-15
Jesus is the Christ - Deity	'JIC'	Matthew 16:16
Jesus is Eternal	'JE'	John 1:1
Jesus' Mission	'JM'	Matthew 20:28
Jesus' Physical Death	'JPD'	Matthew 27:58-60
Jesus' Physical Resurrection	'JPR'	Luke 24:13-29
Jesus was Sinless	'JS'	2 Corinthians 5:21
Judgment Day	'JMT'	Matthew 12:36
Kingdom Established	'KE'	Colossians 12:13
Old Law Void	'OLV'	Roman. 7:4-6
One Christ	'OC'	1 Corinthians 8:6
One God	'OG'	Mark 12:29-32
One Heaven	'OH'	Revelation 7:15-17
One Mediator	'OM'	1 Timothy 2:5-6
Priests	'PR'	1 Peter 2:5-9
Relationship with Unbelievers	'RU'	Colossians 4:5-6
Sabbath or Sunday	'SOS'	Ephesians 2:14-15
Saints	'STS'	Philippians 1:1-2
Salvation before Death	'SBD'	Luke 16:26
Salvation – Most Men Lost	'MML'	Matt. 7:13-14
Salvation is through Christ	'STC'	Acts 4:10-12
Satan-Devil	'SAT'	Matthew 4:8-9
Sin	'SIN'	Romans 3:23
Tithing or Giving	'TI'	1 Corinthians 16:2
Trinity	'TR'	John 1:1
Virgin Birth	'VB'	Matt. 1:18

F. Russell Crites, Jr. and Derek Russell Crites

Common Doctrinal Differences
in Christ-Centered Churches

The following are some of the more common doctrinal differences that Christ believing Churches often experience. There is room on this chain reference guide for additional differences if you want to add them. If you want to use this as a resource in your Bible, simply copy this page and tape or paste it into a page in your Bible. Premade sticky backed reference guide for 'Common Doctrinal Differences' is available from this author.

Comparative Doctrine
Common Doctrinal Differences Quick Reference in Christ Centered Churches

Common Doctrinal Differences	Doct. Code	Location
Baptism	'BAP'	Acts 2:38
Infant Baptism	'IB'	Mark 16:15-16
Judged by Grace through Faith	'JGF'	Ephesians 2:8-10
Lord's Supper	'LS'	1 Corinthians 10:16
Once Saved Always Saved	'OSAS'	Galatians 5:3-4
Original Sin	'OS'	Matthew 15:19
Second Coming	'SC'	Matthew 24:36
Unconditional Election	'UE'	John 3:16-17

False Doctrine or
Doctrine not Supported in the Bible

The following are some false doctrines that are not supported by the Bible. There is room on this chain reference guide for additional False Doctrines if you want to add them. If you want to use this as a resource in your Bible, simply copy this page and tape or paste it into a page in your Bible. Premade sticky backed reference guide for 'Doctrine not Supported by the Bible' is available from this author.

Comparative Doctrine
False Doctrine Quick Reference
or Doctrine not Supported by the Bible

Doctrine Not Supported	Doct. Code	Location
Baptism for the Dead	'BD'	Acts 2:38
Born of God	'BOG'	John 3:3-5
Foods Prohibited	'FP'	Acts 15:28-29
God Causes Some to go Astray	'GCA'	Luke 6:35-36
Heavenly Deception	'HD'	John 8:44
Infallibility	'INF'	Galatians 1:7-9
Mary: Perpetual Virgin	'MPV'	Matthew 1:25
Mary was Sinless	'MS'	Romans 3:23
Purgatory	'PUR'	Hebrews 10:17-18
Reincarnation	'RN'	Hebrews 9:27
Revelation-Current Day	'RV'	Galatians 1:7-9

Common Quick References

The 'Personal Quick Reference' guide is meant to be used for specific teachings that are important to you that have not been addressed in the other reference guides. Most people have interests in specific topics in the Bible. Simply identify the name of the topic, give it a specific code (make sure the code is not used elsewhere in this work) and write down the first Scripture you want to go to if you want to review that topic. Chain multiple scriptures to the first one if desired. Follow the chaining model used for the other Chain Reference Guides in this section. If you want to use this as a resource in your Bible, simply copy this page and tape or paste it into a page in your Bible. Premade sticky backed reference guide for 'Personal Quick References' is available from this author. You can decide your first Scripture and those that you chain to it. Some examples of topics that some people choose to have a quick reference for:

- Conversion Examples 'C'
- False Teaching 'FT'
- Faith 'FA'
- Marriage 'MAR'
- Miracles 'M'
- One Anothering 'OA'
- Parables 'PAR'
- Prayer 'PR'
- Prophecies Fulfilled-Jesus 'PF'

- Spiritual Gifts 'SG'
- Spiritual Growth 'SG'
- Stages of Spiritual Growth 'SSG'
- Grace 'GR'
- Justification 'JUS'
- Sanctification 'SAN'
- Baptism 'BAP'
- Sins Against the Holy Spirit 'SAS'

Comparative Doctrine
Common Quick Reference

Topic	Code	Location
Conversion Examples	'C'	Acts 2:37-41
False Teaching	'FT'	Matthew 7:15-23
Faith	'FA'	Hebrews 11:1
Marriage	'MAR'	Genesis 2:24
Miracles	'M'	Matthew 8:5-13
One Anothering	'OA'	Mark 9:50
Parables	'PAR'	Matthew 5:14-16
Prayer	'PR'	Mark 11:24
Prophecies - Jesus	'PF'	Micah 5:2
Spiritual Gifts - Motivational	'SGT'	Romans 12:4–8
Spiritual Growth	'SG'	Hebrews 5:11-14
Stages of Spiritual Growth	'SSG'	1 Corinthians 3:1-4
Grace	'GR'	Ephesians 2:8-9
Justification	'JUS'	Colossians 2:10
Sanctification	'SAN'	Philippians 3:12
Baptism	'BAP'	Acts 2:38
Sins Against the Holy Spirit	'SAS'	Matthew 12:31-32

Comparative Doctrine
Personal Quick References

Topic	Code	Location

Appendices

- Book Series on Christianity
- Identifying False Doctrine Checklist
- Prophet Test
- Arminianism or Calvinism
- Key Beliefs in Arminianism and Calvinism
- Conversion Examples
- The 1837 Debate on Roman Catholicism Between Alexander Campbell and Bishop John Purcell (Initial statement by Campbell)

From Salvation to Discipleship
Book Series on Christianity

There are four books in this series. These fiver works take you on a journey towards a deeper understanding of Christianity and your place in the Christian world. The following books are presented in order in which they probably should be read and studied.

Grace and Salvation: This work is actually the first work in the series. It was intended to primarily be read by those who are searching and want to know more about Grace and Salvation. It can also be very helpful for any Christian who wants to have a deeper grasp on what Grace really means and how someone can become a Christian. Learn about all the aspects of grace, and what the Bible says about salvation.

Journey Into Discipleship: This work will take you on a journey that helps you understand how to become a fully mature godly Christian. It describes the ups and downs that Christians face and how they can get the help they need to overcome. Some of the topics are; building faith, how to combat your carnal or fleshly nature, stages of spiritual growth, how to grow spiritually, learning how to allow the Holy Spirit to aid you, understanding and preparation for Spiritual warfare, balanced Discipleship and much more.

Comparative Doctrine: This work will help you learn how to identify Scriptures that address over fifty doctrinal issues. It also shows how several religions have ignored the Bible or have attempted to alter what it says. To help people, or yourself, you must understand what the Bible teaches. This work will help you see specifically what the Bible says about important doctrines. God wants you to internalize His word. Studying it and developing a better understanding of what the Bible teaches will help you grow spiritually and is necessary in helping you identify Biblical doctrine. It also helps you when you are faced with sharing your Biblical beliefs with someone who wants to know more about the Bible and the Life of Jesus.

Spiritual Gifts and Ministry: This work helps you identify the spiritual gift that God specifically gave you so that you can function in the body where He wants you to function. Using your gift is a natural way to serve your brothers and sisters and to reach out to those who need to learn about God. It is also how God wants you to participate in ministry and service in the local body. Outreach of any kind is much more natural when you use your God given gift.

Discipleship Family Manual: The Discipleship Family is a method by which you or your church can implement an easy way to help others learn about God while at the same time practically learning how to become better disciples. The following statement is taken from the preface to the Discipleship Family manual. This work provides you with a model that you can use or adapt for your own purposes. Small groups can meet five key elements for personal growth and Discipleship. They are:

- Prayer
- Study of God's Word: Discussions sharing God's will and teaching for development and edification.
- Outreach, evangelism, seeking the lost: This includes church members who are not active or need help in some way.
- Fellowship: Serving and building each other up as well as enjoying Christian relationships. Growing together.
- The sharing of meals. Eating is both a bonding experience and a way to get others to participate in your group.

Each of these methods can promote spiritual and relational growth. They also provide an avenue to reach out to the unchurched or to Christians who are unsure, wandering or hurting in some way. This group method also helps elders become more directly involved with those in the church that are struggling or need help in some way. Their task to shepherd a large congregation can be overwhelming at times. The Discipleship Family provides them with a way to be able to touch and care for every person in their congregation.

There are some other supportive books written by this author or others that are listed in the appendices that can also be helpful for specific situations.

Comparative Doctrine
Identifying False Doctrine Checklist

Doctrine To be Checked:	Yes	No
Did this doctrine come from any other work, personal beliefs or any other means other than the Bible?		
Was this doctrine identified as a result of any new revelation other than what is shared with us in the Bible and New Testament teachings?		
Does this doctrine delete, minimize, change or disregard Bible or specifically the New Testament teachings?		
Does this doctrine minimize or deny the deity or work of Jesus Christ?		
Does this specific doctrinal point use a selected Scripture or Scriptures as proof, instead of considering how other Scriptures may be in disagreement?		

Note: If you answer "Yes" to any of the above questions, the doctrine you are considering is most likely a false doctrine. If you answer "Yes" to several of these questions it becomes more obvious that the doctrine you are checking is false. Keep in mind that the truth about any doctrine can be found in the Bible and no other book.

The Prophet Test

Prophecies in _____

Prophecy	Fulfillment	Prophecy True False	

Comparative Doctrine

Arminianism or Calvinism

Arminianism

"Arminianism is a teaching regarding salvation associated with the Dutch theologian Jacob Arminius (1560-1609). The fundamental principle in Arminianism is the rejection of predestination, and a corresponding affirmation of the freedom of the human will. Shortly after his death, the followers of Arminius (later called Arminians) presented a statement to the governing authorities of Holland in which they set forth five articles of doctrine. These were: (1) that the divine decree of predestination is conditional, not absolute; (2) that the Atonement is in intention universal; (3) that man cannot of himself exercise a saving faith, but requires God's help to attain this faith; (4) that though the grace of God is a necessary condition of human effort it does not act irresistibly in man; (5) that believers are able to resist sin but are not beyond the possibility of falling from grace. In essence, the Arminians maintained that God gives indispensable help in salvation, but that ultimately it is the free will of man which decides the issue" (Bible Research, Arminianism, Michael Marlowe, July 2005).

Calvinism

"Therefore original sin is seen to be an hereditary depravity and corruption of our nature diffused into all parts of the soul . . . wherefore those who have defined original sin as the lack of the original righteousness with which we should have been endowed, no doubt include, by implication, the whole fact of the matter, but they have not fully expressed the positive energy of this sin. For our nature is not merely bereft of good, but is so productive of every kind of evil that it cannot be inactive. Those who have called it concupiscence [a strong, especially sexual desire, lust] have used a word by no means wide of the mark, if it were added (and this is what many do not concede) that whatever is in man from intellect to will, from the soul to the flesh, is all defiled and crammed with concupiscence; or, to sum it up briefly, that the whole man is in himself nothing but concupiscence. . . ." (Institutes of the Christian Religion, Calvin Op. ii. 3I sq. edition of 1559, Book II. chap. i).

Christian Churches in Today's World

According to Ron Rhodes who wrote a book titled, The Complete Guide to Christian Denominations, there are eighteen basic 'Christian' churches.   Most of these churches do not have new books or works that include revelations communicating God's 'new' plan for man. Within those eighteen core churches there have been many splits over different doctrinal issues. As a result, to totally understand the beliefs of each of those hundreds of churches would be a monumental task.   With that in mind, the list below identifies a select group of churches that conform partially to either Arminianism or Calvinism.   This covers most mainline churches that you read or hear about.   The core eighteen types of churches are:

Adventist Churches	Friends (Quaker) Churches
Baptist Churches	Holiness Churches
Brethren Churches	Lutheran churches
Catholic Churches	Mennonite Churches
Christian Churches	Methodist Churches
Congregational Churches	Orthodox Churches
Episcopal and Anglican Churches	Pentecostal Churches
Fundamentalists, Bible and Conservative	Presbyterian Churches
Evangelical Churches	Reformed Churches

If you want to learn more about the basic doctrine of the churches listed above, you may want to take a look at Ron Rhodes book.

Key Beliefs in Arminianism and Calvinism

Arminianism	Calvinism
Jacob Arminius (1560-1609) "The scriptures know no election by which God precisely and absolutely has determined to save anyone without having first considered him as a believer."	John Calvin (1509-1564) The TULIP memory tool was solidified at the Synod of Dort (1618-1619).
Sinner Can do Good and Respond to God Man is sinful, but has the freedom of the human will and can choose God if they follow his plan.	**Total Depravity** **Because of Original Sin** People cannot independently choose God because sinfulness pervades all areas of life and human existence. They cannot save themselves. God must intervene to save people.
God Elects Man on the Basis of Foreseen Faith. Predestination is conditional, not absolute.	**Unconditional Election** **Predestination** God chooses who will be saved. He Elects Man According to His Good Pleasure, because man is unable to initiate a response to God....they are totally depraved. The saved people are called the Elect.
Christ Died for All Mankind. Jesus' Atonement is meant for all men. It is universal. He wants all people, who choose, to come to him by faith.	**Limited Atonement** Jesus Christ died only for the sins of the Elect.
Man Can Resist God's Grace. The grace of God is a necessary condition of human effort, but it does not act irresistibly in man.	**Irresistible Grace** Unconditional. God brings his Elect to salvation through an internal call, which they are powerless to resist. The call comes from God and cannot be resisted by his Elect.
The Believer Can Lose Salvation. Believers are able to resist sin, but are also capable of falling from grace.	**Perseverance of the Saints** Those Elected by God cannot Lose Salvation. They are eternally secure. God Knew who they were, selected them, and because he chose them for salvation they cannot lose it.

Arminianism	Calvinism
Jacob Arminius (1560-1609) "The scriptures know no election by which God precisely and absolutely has determined to save anyone without having first considered him as a believer."	John Calvin (1509-1564) The TULIP memory tool was solidified at the Synod of Dort (1618-1619),
Sinner Can do Good and Respond to God Assembly of God Catholic Church Church of Christ Disciples of Christ	**Total Depravity** Methodist Church Presbyterian Church
God Elects Man on the Basis of Foreseen Faith. Episcopal Assembly of God Baptist* Catholic Church Church of Christ Disciples of Christ	**Unconditional Election** 'Predestination' Baptist Church* Lutheran Church Methodist Church Presbyterian Church
Christ Died for All Mankind. Methodist Lutheran Roman Catholic Church of Christ Disciples of Christ	**Limited Atonement** Presbyterian Church
Man Can Resist God's Grace. Assembly of God Church Baptism Church Lutheran Church Catholic Church Church of Christ Disciples of Christ	**Irresistible Grace** Episcopal Church Presbyterian Church
The Believer Can Lose Salvation. Assembly of God Church Methodist* Lutheran Church Catholic Church Church of Christ Disciples of Christ	**Perseverance of the Saints** OSAS or Eternal Security Episcopal Church Baptist* Methodist Church* Presbyterian Church
Information above was taken from multiple sources within each church; websites, books, Creeds, Doctrinal stances. Many churches have split over doctrine more than once. As a result, doctrinal stances may be different from church to church. Some are simply not clear on what they teach. * Some teach this, some don't.	

Conversion Examples

Instructions

1. Find a place in your Bible or use the Personal Quick References insert to write down the initial Scripture for the Conver sions found in Acts.
2. Draw a red line next to the Scripture.
3. Put a 'C' next to each Scripture that shows Conversion examples in the book of Acts.
4. Start with Acts 2:37-41 and then chain them until you have all the Conversion examples listed in your Bible.

CONVERSIONS: In the book of Acts several examples of Conversions are described.   Each Scripture shows how the individual(s) responded to the Gospel.

'C' | "37 Now when they heard this they were cut to the heart, and said to Peter and the rest of the apostles, "Brothers, what shall we do?" 38 And Peter said to them, "Repent and be baptized every one of you in the name of Jesus Christ for the forgiveness of your sins, and you will receive the gift of the Holy Spirit. 39 For the promise is for you and for your children and for all who are far off, everyone whom the Lord our God calls to himself." 40 And with many other words he bore witness and continued to exhort them, saying, "Save yourselves from this crooked generation." 41 So those who received his word were baptized, and there were added that day about three thousand souls."

C Acts 8:12

> This is the next Scripture in a chain. Place this Scripture underneath or to the side.

Conversion Examples
These scriptures show you how others have responded to the Gospel.

Scripture	Who	Hear	Faith/Belief	Repentance	Confession	Baptism
Acts 2:37-41	Jews	vs 37		vs 38		vs 38
Acts 8:12	Samaritans		vs 12			vs 12
Acts 8:13	Simon		vs 13			vs 13
Acts 8:26-40	Ethiopian Eunuch	vs 35	vs 37		vs 37	vs 38
Acts 10:34-48	Cornelius	vs 34-44	vs 43			vs 47-48
Acts 16:14-15	Lydia	vs 14				vs 15
Acts 16:25-34	Jailor	vs 30-32				vs 33
Acts 18:8	Corinthians	vs 8	vs 8			vs 8
Acts 19:1-7	Ephesians	vs 5				vs 5
Acts 22:1-16	Paul (Saul)	vs 15				vs 16

STS: The Scriptures shown above may be underlined in Yellow since they address Salvation.

The 1837 Debate on Roman Catholicism Between Alexander Campbell and Bishop John Purcell

This is a short section of the 1837 debate where Alexander Campbell shared his concerns about the Catholic church.

Points at Issue

In order to meet, as far as possible, the arrangements entered into for conducting the contemplated debate for seven days, Mr. Campbell, according to agreement, sent to bishop Purcell, on Thursday morning, Jan. 12, the following statement of the POINTS AT ISSUE.

1, The Roman Catholic Institution, sometimes called the "Holy, Apostolic, Catholic. Church," is not now, nor was she ever, catholic, apostolic, or holy; but is a sect in the fair import of that word, older than any other sect now existing, not the "Mother and Mistress of all Churches," but an apostasy from the only true, holy, apostolic, and catholic church of Christ.

2. Her notion of apostolic succession is without any foundation in the Bible, in reason, or in fact;, an imposition of the most injurious consequences, built upon unscriptural and anti-scriptural traditions, resting wholly upon the opinions of interested and fallible men.

3. She is not uniform in her faith, or united in her members: but mutable and fallible, as any other sect of philosophy or religion—Jewish, Turkish, or Christian—a confederation of sects with a politico-ecclesiastic head.

4. She is the "Babylon" of John, the "Man of Sin" of Paul, and the Empire of the "Youngest Horn" of Daniel's Sea Monster.

5. Her notion of purgatory, indulgences, auricular confession, remission of sins, transubstantiation, supererogation, &c.. essential elements of her system, are immoral in their tendency, and injurious to the well-being of society, religious and political.

6. Notwithstanding her pretensions to have given us the Bible, and faith in it, we are perfectly independent of her for our knowledge of that book, and its evidences of a divine original.

7. The Roman Catholic religion, if infallible and unsusceptible of reformation, as alleged, is essentially anti-American, being opposed to the genius of all free institutions, and positively subversive of them, opposing the general reading of the scriptures, and the diffusion of useful knowledge among the whole community, so essential to liberty and the permanency of good government.

A. CAMPBELL.

Points of Interest in Campbell's Debate

"PROP. I. The Roman Catholic Institution, sometimes called the 'Holy, Apostolic. Catholic. Church.' is not now, nor was she ever, catholic, apostolic, or holy; but is a sect in the fair import of that word, older than any other sect now existing, not the 'Mother and Mistress of all Churches,' but an apostasy from the only true. holy, apostolic, and catholic church of Christ." As this is the place and time for logic rather than rhetoric, I will proceed to define the meaning of the important terms contained in this proposition. The subject is the Roman Catholic Institution. This institution, notwithstanding its large pretensions, I affirm, can be proved clearly to be a sect, in the true and proper import of the term. Though she call herself the mother and mistress of all churches, she is, strictly speaking, a sect, and no more than a sect. We now propose to adduce proof to sustain this part of the proposition. In the first place, the very term Roman Catholic indicates that she if a sect, and not the ancient, universal and apostolic church, the mother and mistress of all churches. If she be the only universal or Catholic church, why prefix the epithet Roman? A Roman Catholic church is a contradiction. The word Catholic means universal—the word Roman means something local and particular. What sense or meaning is there in a particular universal church? It is awkward on another account. If she pretends to be considered the only true and universal church of Christ among all nations and in all times, why call herself Roman? To say the Roman Catholic church of America, is just as absurd as to say the Philadelphia church of Cincinnati, — the London church of Pittsburgh,—the church of France of the United States. The very terms that she chooses indicates that she cannot be the universal church. It will not help the difficulty to call her the Church of Rome. These words indicate a sect and only a sect, as much as the words Roman Catholic. They signify strictly, only the particular congregations meeting in that place. The Roman Catholic historians endeavor to reconcile this discrepancy of terms by saying that, though those particular congregations are meant, in their larger sense the terms are used to designate all those congregations, scattered throughout the world, who are in communion with the church of Rome.

Thus testifies Du Pin— "It is true, that at the present time, the name of the church of Rome, is given to the Catholic church, and that these two terms pass for synonymous. "But in antiquity no more was intended by the name of the church of Rome, than the church of the city of Rome, and the popes (bishops) in their subscriptions or superscriptions, look simply to the quality of bishops of Rome. The Greek schismatics seem to he the first who save the name of the church of Rome to all the churches of the west, whence the Latins made use of this to distinguish the churches which communicated with the church of Rome, from the Greeks who were separated from her communion. From this came the custom to give the name of the church of Rome to the Catholic church. But the other churches did not from this lose their name or their authority."

I shall hereafter give the day and date of this separation, when she received this sectarian designation and "became a sect, in the proper acceptation of that term. It may, perhaps, appear that it was not only unscriptural, but dishonorable; as opprobrious as ever were the terms Lutheran or Protestant. But suppose we call her "Catholic" alone; and her advocates now endeavor to impress the idea that she is no longer to he called "Roman Catholic," but Catholic, this term equally proves her a sect; for in the New Testament and primitive antiquity there is no such designation. It is simply the church of Christ. It is one thing for us to choose a name for ourselves, and another to have one chosen for us by our enemies. Societies, like persons, are passive in receiving their names. It is with churches as it is with individuals; they may not wear the name they prefer. She wishes now to he called no longer Roman Catholic, but Catholic. She repudiates the appellation of Roman; and claims to be the only Catholic church that ever was, and is, and ever more shall he. But we cannot allow her to assume it; and we dare not, in truth, bestow it, for she is not catholic. But, as there is no church known in the New Testament by that name, could we so designate her, still she would be a sect. But let me ask, what is the church of Rome of the nineteenth century, or rather, what is the present Roman Catholic institution? Permit me here to say, most emphatically, that I have not the slightest disposition to use terms of opprobrium in speaking of this church; or of the worthy gentleman who is opposed to me in this debate. I do not wish or intend to use the slightest expression which could be construed into an unfriendly tone of satire, irony or invective towards the respectable gentleman, or towards his church. I shall speak freely of her pretensions as to the only true church, &c., but I shall observe a scrupulous respect in all my language towards the present representatives of the Catholic church in the nineteenth century.

Are we then to understand her as the immutable, universal, ancient, primitive, apostolic church of Christ? Are we to understand this by the Roman Catholic church of the nineteenth century, with her popes, her cardinals, her patriarchs, primates, metropolitans, archbishops, archdeacons, monks, friars, nuns, &c. &c. teaching and preaching the use and worship of images, relics, penances, invocation of departed men and women, veneration for some being whom they call "the mother of God," teaching and preaching the doctrine of priestly absolution, auricular confession, purgatory, transubstantiation, extreme unction, &c. &c.

Is this the ancient, universal, holy apostolic church? Not one of these dogmas can be found in the bible. They originated hundreds of years since, as I am prepared to show, from the evidence of Roman Catholic authors themselves. How then can we call it the ancient apostolic church? Not one of these offices nor dogmas is mentioned in the New Testament. Hear Du Pin on this point. In exposing the imposition, practised, by an effort, so late as the ninth century, to foist into the history of the church certain pretended decrees or writings of those called the first popes, Du Pin, an authentic Roman Catholic historian, proves these decrees and writings to be spurious, because in them there are numerous allusions to offices and customs not yet existing in the times referred to.

"The following" proves them spurious. 1st. The second epistle of St. Clement directed to St. James, speaks of the Ostiarii or doorkeepers, archdeacons and other ecclesiastical officers, that were not then introduced into the church." 2nd. "This letter mentions sub-deacons, an order not then established in the church." p. 584. 3d. "In the first Epistle attributed to St. Sixtus, he is called an 'archbishop.' a word not used in this time." 4th. "The second, attributed to the same pope, mentions consecrated vessels, and appeals to Rome, the grandeur of the church. It is there pretended that all bishops wait for the pope's decision, and are instructed by his letters; modes of speaking never used by the first bishops of Rome." 5th. "The epistle attributed to Telesphorus calls him an archbishop, a name unknown in the first ages." 6th. "There is a decree in it. to enjoin three masses on our Savior's nativity, a custom not so ancient." 7th. "We find several passages in the letter attributed to Anicetus, which does not agree with the time of that pope; as. for instance, what is there laid down concerning the ordinations of bishops, sacerdotal tonsure, archbishops and primates, which were not instituted till long after: besides many things of the same nature." p. 585. How, then, can we suppose that this church of the nineteenth century, with so many appendages, is the apostolic church—the only original, primitive, universal institution of Christ? But she glories in the name of mother and mistress of all churches throughout the world. This astonishes me still more; for with the bible in his hand and history before him, who can stand up and say, that this church ever was the mother and mistress of all churches! The most ancient catholic church was the Hebrew. She was the mother, though not the mistress of all churches; for the Christian church has no 'reigning queen on earth, to lord it over her—as Paul says, on another occasion —"Jerusalem is the mother of us all."

If the gentleman admit Luke to be a faithful historian, he must not, only place the Hebrew church first, but the Samaritan, Phoenician, Syrian and Hellenist churches as older than the church in Rome. I say if we speak of churches, as respects antiquity, the Hebrew, Samaritan, Syrian and Phoenician churches must be regarded as prior to her. The Acts of the Apostles close with Paul's first appearance in Rome. But that the Roman Catholic institution may stand before you in bold relief as a sectarian establishment, I will give you a definition of her pretensions, from an authentic source, one of her own standards. The Douay catechism, in answer to the question—" What are the essential parts of the church?" teaches "A pope, or supreme head, bishops, pastors and laity." p. 20. These, then, are the four constituent and essential elements of the Roman Catholic church. The first is the pope, or head. It will be confessed by all, that, of these, the most essential is the head. But should we take away any one of these, she loses her identity, and ceases to be what she assumes. My first effort then shall be to prove that, for hundreds of years after Christ, she was without such a head; the most indispensable of these elements; and consequently, this being essential to her existence, she was not from the beginning. Because no body can exist before its head. Now, if we can find a time when there was no pope, or supreme head, we find a time when there was no Roman Catholic party. By referring to the scriptures, and to the early ecclesiastical records, we can easily settle this point. Let us begin with the New Testament, which all agree, is the only authenticated standard of faith and manners—the only inspired record of the Christian doctrine. This is a cardinal point, and I am thankful that in this we all agree. What is not found there, wants the evident sanction of inspiration, and can never command the respect and homage of those who seek for divine authority in faith and morality. I affirm then, that not one of the offices, I have enumerated, as belonging to the Roman Catholic church, was known in the days of the apostles, or is found in the New Testament. On the contrary, the very notion of a vicar of Christ, of a prince of the apostles, or of a universal head, and government in the Christian church is repugnant to the genius and spirit of the religion. We shall read a few passages of Scripture, from the Roman version, to prove that the very idea of an earthly head is unscriptural and anti-scriptural. The version from which I am about to quote was printed in New York, and is certified to correspond exactly, with the Rhemish original, by a number of gentlemen, of the first standing in society. If it differs from any other and more authentic copy, I will not rely upon it. I am willing to take whatever bible the gentleman may propose.

I read from the twentieth of Matthew. "Jesus said to his disciples, You know that the princes of the Gentiles overrule them, and those that are the greater exercise power against them. It shall not be so among you, but whosoever will be the greater among you, let him be your minister!" Does this convey the idea of a prince among the apostles, a vicar of Christ, a lord over the people of God? Does it not rather say there shall not be any lordship amongst you! This command is express, that there shall not be a pope, a supreme lord of the Christian church. Again, Matt. 23. 8, "Be not you called Rabbi, for one is your Master and all ye are brethren: and call none father (i. e. pope,) for one is your father, he that is in heaven. Neither be you called masters, for one is your master, Christ. He that is the greater of you shall be your servitor!" If the very question about a pope had been before the Messiah at this time, he could not have spoken more clearly. This expression indicates the most perfect equality of rank among the apostles and disciples of Christ, and positively forbids, in a religious sense, the assumption of the title of father or pope. The commandment which says "thou shalt not steal," is not more clearly laid down than the command "call no man father." Now will the gentleman deny that "pope" (in Greek "pappas," in Latin, "papa") means "father?" and that the case clearly comes within the command. Jesus Christ says, "call no man pope;" yet they ordain a bishop and call him pope; and this pope claims the title of "universal father "—supreme head and governor of the church of Christ. He is sometimes called Lord God the pope.

This testimony of Christ will outweigh volumes. Put all the folios and authorities, which the gentleman may bring, on one side, and this text of Jesus Christ on the other, and the former, in comparison, will be found light as the chaff which is blown away by a breath. Can anyone, then, who fears God and believes in the Messiah, call the pope, or any human being "father," in the sense here intended. The Lord anticipated the future in all his precepts, and spoke with an eye to it as well as to the men of his own time. He had the pride and assumptions, of the Rabbis of Jerusalem, in his eye, who coveted renown, who loved such greetings in the market place, and received such compellations in the synagogues. Describing these men to his disciples, he cautions them against their example, and teaches them to regard each other as brethren. I hope the gentleman will pay particular attention to this point in his reply to these remarks.

The third testimony on which we rely will be found in Ephesians iv. 11. This passage sums up all the officers or gifts which Jesus gave the church after his ascension into heaven. "And" says Paul "he gave some apostles, and some prophets, and some evangelists, and some pastors, and doctors" or teachers. In this enumeration, which contains the whole, there is no pope. The highest or first rank is given to apostles. In every other enumeration found in the epistles, there is the same clear reference to the apostles as the first class. 1 Cor. xii. 28. But let Peter himself speak as to his rank. We see that in his own 1st Epistle, ch. 1, he calls himself an apostle, not the apostle of Jesus, not the prince of apostles, not the supreme head of the church. Peter had no idea of such headship and lordship. Again in addressing the "seniors" or elders, chap. v. 1, he says, "I myself am a fellow senior." They were all co-elders, co-bishops, co-apostles, as respected each other; and as respected all other officers the apostles were first. The thought of a supreme head amongst them is not found in the New Testament; only as reprobated by our savior.

I will not, at present, advance any more scriptural authority upon the point, but shall proceed to examine what foundation this element of the Roman church, has in ancient history. But I would here say distinctly, once for all, that I will not open a single document to prove any doctrine, tenet, or principle of Protestantism, other than this holy record of the prophets, and apostles, the holy men of God, who spake as they were moved by the Holy Spirit. On these I rely, and I affirm that these contain no authority for the assumption of the doctrine of a universal father, pope, or head of the church. There was no such person mentioned—no such idea cherished until hundreds of, years after the death of the apostles. I will read the following general remarks by this learned historian. The title page is as follows:—

A New History of Ecclesiastical Writers, containing an account of the authors of the several books of the Old and New Testaments; of the lives and writings of the primitive Fathers: an abridgment and catalogue of their works; their various editions, and censures, determining the genuine and spurious. Together with a judgment upon style and doctrine. Also a compendious history of the Councils; with Chronological Tables of the whole, written in French by Lewis Ellies Du Pin, doctor of the Sorbonne, and Regius Professor at Paris. 3 vols. Folio. The Third Edition corrected, Dublin, printed by and for George Grierson, at the Two Bibles in Essex Street, MDCCXXIV.

I am happy to find, appended to the preface, the seals and signatures of men high in the church, which I cannot now stop to read. From this work I will proceed to read some passages in proof of. the proposition I have advanced, that there is not a vestige of evidence in favor of the cardinal idea, of the Roman Catholic religion, that there was a pope in the first ages of the church. At the close, of the third century the highest advance yet made towards any supremacy in the church on the ground of metropolitan standing, is thus described by Du Pin. "The bishops of great cities had their prerogatives in ordinations, and in councils; and as in civil affairs men generally had recourse to the civil metropolis, so likewise in ecclesiastical matters, they consulted with the bishop of the metropolitan city. The churches of the three principal cities of the world were looked upon as chief, and their bishops attributed great prerogatives to themselves. The church of Rome, founded by St. Peter and St. Paul, was considered as first, and its bishops as first amongst all the bishops of the world; yet they did not believe him to be infallible: and though they frequently consulted him, and his advice was of great consequence, yet they did not receive it blindfold and implicitly, every bishop imagining himself to have a right to judge in ecclesiastical matters." p. 590.

Observe the bishops of the principal cities attributed to themselves great prerogatives. And Rome, the chief city, began to assume the chief prerogatives. But the general character of the clergy as detailed by this writer was not yet favorable to such assumption—for, says he, "The clergy were not distinguished from others by any peculiar habits, but by the sanctity of their life and manners, they were removed from all kind of avarice, and carefully avoided every thing that seemed to carry the appearance of scandalous, filthy lucre. They administered the sacrament gratis, and believed it to be an abominable crime to give or receive any thing for a spiritual blessing. Tithes were not then appropriated to them, but the people maintained them voluntarily at their own expense."

"The clergy were prohibited to meddle with any civil and secular affairs. They were ordained against their will and did not remove from one church to another out of a principle of interest or ambition. They were extremely chaste and regular. It was lawful for priests to keep the wives they married before they were ordained." Nothing indeed like an ecclesiastical establishment was yet in existence: for says Du Pin, speaking of these times, "After all, it must be confessed, that the discipline of the church has been so extremely different and so often altered, that it is almost impossible to say any thing positively concerning it." p. 590.

So stood the matter at the close of the third century. But we have still more definite and positive testimony, in the great councils of the 4th and 5th centuries. Let us then examine the early councils. The famous council of Nice which sat in 325, is the first general council that ever assembled; for although they call the consultations of the apostles—Acts 15., a council, yet in the enumeration of general councils, of which they establish eighteen, that of Nice is called the first. At this council there were present 318 bishops. It was called by the Roman emperor in order to settle certain discords in what was then called the church. By the sixth canon of this first council it appears, according to Du Pin, that the idea of a pope, or supreme head, had not begun to he entertained. The sixth canon of the council of Nice is as follows. "The 6th canon is famous for the several questions it has occasioned. The most natural sense that can be given to it, is this: 'We ordain that the ancient custom shall be observed, which gives power to the bishop of Alexandria, over all the provinces of Egypt, Libya, and Pantapolis, because the bishop of Rome has the like jurisdiction over all the suburbicary regions (for this addition must be supplied out of Rufinus;) we would likewise have the rights and privileges of the church of Antioch and the other churches preserved: but these rights ought not to prejudice those of the metropolitans. II any one is ordained without the consent of the metropolitan, the council declares, that he is no bishop: but if any one is canonically chosen by the suffrage of almost all the bishops of the province. and if there are but one or two of a contrary opinion, the suffrage of the far greater number ought to carry it for the ordination or those particular persons. This canon being thus explained has no difficulty in it. It does not oppose the primacy of the church of Rome, but neither does it establish it.'

"In this sense it is, that it compares the church of Rome to the church of Alexandria, by considering them all as patriarchal churches. It continues also to the church of Antioch and all the other great churches, whatsoever rights they could have; but lest their authority should be prejudicial to the ordinary metropolitans, who were subject to their jurisdiction, the council confirms what had been ordained in the fourth canon concerning the authority of metropolitans in the ordination of bishops. This explication is easy and natural, and we have given many proofs of it in our Latin dissertation concerning the ancient discipline of the church."

"This canon," says Du Pin, who be it remembered was always anxious to find some authority for the pope's supremacy, "DOES NOT ESTABLISH THE SUPREMACY OF THE CHURCH OF ROME." Willing as he was to have this primacy traced to the beginning of Christianity, he is constrained to admit, that even the council of Nice does not establish it. Nay more—it is in truth against it; for it gives the Bishop of Alexandria like jurisdiction with the church of Rome; and also preserves to the church of Antioch its metropolitan dominion. It would be too tedious to go into an exposition of the causes, why so much power was accumulated in the hands of four or five bishops. It originated in the divisions of the empire. In Roman jurisdiction, there were four great political dioceses, (for diocese was then a political term) and to these the church conformed. Hence the patriarchal sees of Rome, Constantinople, Antioch, and Alexandria. In process of time, Jerusalem was added, and these all became radiating centres of ecclesiastical power and patronage. The bishop of each diocese assumed a sort of primacy, in his own district; and as various interferences and rivalries in jurisdiction occurred, the council of Nice so far decided that the same power should be given to them all—that all primates should be co-ordinate. Hence Du Pin could not find in that council authority for the supreme primacy of Rome. In the canons of the second and third general councils there is no reference to these matters whatever. I shall therefore proceed to the great council of Chalcedon, of preeminent authority, the greatest of the first four general councils. From all. the canons of the council relating to government, it is evident that they had not yet excogitated the idea of a supreme head. Says Du Pin, "The 28th canon grants to the church of the city of Constantinople, which is called New Rome, the same privileges with old Rome, because this city is the second city in the world. It also adjudges to it, besides this, jurisdiction over the dioceses of Pontus, Asia, and Thrace, and over the churches which are out of the hounds of the emperor, and a right to ordain metropolitans in the provinces of These dioceses." p. 678.

Thus this council, composed of 340 bishops, and assembling in the year of our Lord 451, gave the same power to the patriarch of Constantinople as to the patriarch of Rome, and makes the supremacy of the one equal to the supremacy of the other. I have examined the proceedings of all the councils of the first six centuries, of which I find about 170, promulgating in all about 1400 canons. I have read and examined the twenty creeds of the fourth century with all their emendations down to the close of the sixth; and I affirm, without the fear of contradiction, that there is not in all these a single vestige of the existence of a pope or universal head of the church down to the time of Gregory the great, or John the Faster of Constantinople. I shall now proceed to show from the same learned historian when this idea began to be divulged. And be it emphatically observed that the title of pope in its peculiar and exclusive sense was first assumed by the patriarch of Constantinople, and approved by the patriarch of Rome. Du Pin says in his life of Gregory, chap. 1, "He did often rigorously oppose the title of universal patriarch, which the patriarchs of Constantinople assumed to themselves."

Indeed he calls the title, "proud, blasphemous, anti-Christian, diabolical," and says, the bishops of Rome refused to take this title upon them "lest they should seem to encroach upon the rights of other bishops." But the following document or remonstrance against the title shews what a novelty the idea of an universal head, father, or pope was even at Rome, A. D. 588: — "St. Gregory does not only oppose this title in the patriarch of Constantinople, but maintains also, that it cannot agree to any other bishop. and that the bishop of Rome neither ought, nor can assume it. John the younger, patriarch of Constantinople, had taken upon him this title in a council held in 586, in the time of pope Pelagius, which obliged this pope to annul the Acts of this council. St. Gregory wrote of it also to this patriarch; out this made no impression on him, and John would not abandon this fine title. B. 4. Ep. 36. St. Gregory addressed himself to the emperor Mauritius, and exhorted him earnestly to employ his authority for redressing this abuse, and force him who assumed this title to quit it. He remonstrates to him in his letter, that although Jesus Christ had committed to St. Peter the care of all his churches, yet he was not called universal apostle. That the title of universal bishop is against the rules of the gospel, and the appointment of the canons: that there cannot he an universal bishop but the authority of all the other will be destroyed or diminished; that if the bishop of Constantinople were universal bishop, and it should happen that he should fall into heresy, it might be said that the universal church was fallen into destruction. That the council of Chalcedon had offered this title to Leo. but neither he nor his successors would accept it, lest by giving something peculiar to one bishop only, they should take away the rights which belong to all the bishops. That it belongs to the emperor to reduce by his authority him who despises the canons, and does injury to the universal church by assuming this singular name." B. 4. Ep. 32.

But at this time the patriarchs of Constantinople and Rome were contending for the supremacy, and while it appeared to Gregory that his rival of the east was likely to possess the title, he saw in it, everything anti-Christian and profane. When a new dynasty, however, ascended the throne and offered the title to a Roman bishop, it lost all its blasphemy and impiety, and we find the successor of Gregory can wear the title of universal patriarch when tendered him by Phocas, without the least scrupulosity. It is then a fact worthy of much consideration in this discussion, that John bishop of Constantinople first assumed the title of universal head of the whole Christian church, and that the bishop of Rome did in that case oppose it as anti-scriptural and anti-Christian. Concerning the reputation of Saint Gregory I need not be profuse. Of the Gregories he is deservedly called the Great. Renowned in history as one who stamped his own image on the Roman world for a period of five hundred years, yet he could not brook the idea of a pope, especially when about to be bestowed on his rival at Constantinople. St. Gregory, be it remembered, says Du Pin, did not only oppose the title in the case of John the Faster, as proud, heretical, blasphemous, &c., but could not agree to its being assumed by any other bishop; he affirmed that the bishops of Rome ought not, dare not, cannot assume this pompous and arrogant title. Thus stood matters as respects a supreme head up to within 14 years of the close of the 6th century.— [Time expired.]

This debate can be found in book form and in PDF form on the internet.   For more of information about what was discussed review, "A DEBATE on the ROMAN CATHOLIC RELIGION Between ALEXANDER CAMPBELL, Bethany, Va. AND THE Right Reverend JOHN B. PURCELL, Bishop of Cincinnati Held in the Sycamore Street Meetinghouse, Cincinnati, from the 13th to the 21st of January, 1837. Taken down by reporters, and revised by the parties.

References and Recommended Readings

Armstrong or Worldwide Church of God (Grace Communion International)

Armstrong, H. Mystery of the Ages. Philadelphia Church of God: 1995.

Armstrong, H. "End Vietnam War Now!" The Plain Truth, February, 1967.

Armstrong, The Plain Truth, July 1977, 1; and February 1978, 43

Armstrong, Just What Do You Mean—Born Again. Pasadena: Radio Church of God, 1962,19.

Armstrong, H. World Tomorrow Telecast; What is the Holy Spirit? From Herbert W Armstrong website.

Armstrong, H. The Mark of the Beast. Pasadena: Ambassador College Press, 1957.

Armstrong, H. The Incredible Human Potential. Everest House; 1978.

Armstrong, H. Which Day Is The Christian Sabbath? Booklet from Herbert W Armstrong website

Armstrong, H. Do You have an Immoral Soul--Booklet, Pasadena, CA: Ambassador College Press, 1973.

Armstrong, H. Ambassador College Correspondence Course, Lesson 6.

Armstrong, H (1955). What is the True Gospel (PDF) (1972 ed.). Pasadena, California: Ambassador College

Flurry, G. "Personal," The Philadephia Trumpet, February 1997, 1). Armstrong, H. W. The Plain Truth, January, 1979.

The Real Truth: A magazine Restoring Plain Understanding

The Pillar Magazine: The Pillar is a unique bimonthly publication sent to members of The Restored Church of God (RCG).

World Tomorrow Telecast. What is the Holy Spirit? October 2, 1978.

The official website rcg.org

Free online Library: Books and Booklets, e.g., The True Jesus Christ, Saturday or Sunday, the Ten Commandments, The Trinity, How Gods Kingdom will Come, Life After Death, Understanding Tongues and more.

Baha'i

Star of the West Brochure, 1913

Baha'u'llah and Shoghi Effendi Gleanings from the Writings of Bahá'u'lláh, 2005.

Schaefer, Udo The Light that Shineth in the Darkness. George Ronald, 1980.

The official Bahai website

Buddhism

Bodhi, B. (translator) The Noble Eightfold Path: Way to the End of Suffering. Pariyatti Publishing; 3rd edition, 2006.

Bodhi, B. (Translator) In the Buddha's Words: An Anthology of Discourses from the Pali Canon (The Teachings of the Buddha). Wisdom Publications,   2005.

Gautama, Siddhartha (Buddha) Dhammapada (Wisehouse Classics - The Complete & Authoritative Edition), 2017   (Translator: Muller, F.)

Olcott, H. S. The Buddhist Caechism.   Publication Division Ministry of Cultural Affairs, 135, Dharmapala Mawatha, Colombo 7 SRI LANKA, 1903. (Approved and recommended for use in Buddhist Schools by H. SUMANGALA, Pradhana Nayaka Sthavira, High Priest of Sripada and the Western Province and Principal of the Vidyodaya Pirrftna.)

Catholicism

Catechism of the Catholic Church Second Edition Twenty-sixth Printing, 2016. (A Catechism is a summary of the principles of Christian religion in the form of questions and answers, used for the instruction of Christians. Pope John Paul II was instrumental in the creation of this work on December 8, 1992, is a collection of Catholic doctrine that is used as a reference text for teaching and particularly for preparing local catechisms.)

The Catholic Church, Code of Canon Law: Latin-English Edition. Canon Law Society of America; Third Printing edition, 1983. (Canon law is a set of ordinances and regulations made by ecclesiastical authority, for the government of a Christian organization or church and its members)

Rev. A. Nampon, S.J., Catholic Doctrine: As Defined by the Council of Trent: Expounded in a Series of Conferences Delivered in Geneva. Philadelphia, PN: Peter F. Cunningham and Son, Catholic Booksellers, 1809.

Christian Science

Eddy, M. B. Miscellaneous Writing. Boston: Trustees, 1924.

Eddy, M. B. Retrospection and Introspection. Boston: Trustees, 1920.

Eddy, M. B. Science and Health with Key to the Scriptures, Boston: Trustees, 1934.

Eddy, M. B. The Peoples Ideal About God.   Boston, MA: 1936.

Comparative Doctrine

Hinduism

Hinduism: An Overview, Hinduism Today, 9/2011; hinduismtoday.com

Nine Beliefs of Hinduism, Hinduism Today, 9/2011; hinduismtoday.com
Nikhiilananda, Swami The Upanishads - A One-Volume Abridgment. Advaita Ashrama; Second, first printing edition, 2008.

Prabhupada, Bhaktivedanta Bhagavad Gita as it is. Los Angeles, CA: The Bhaktivedanta Book Trust, 1972.

Wilson, H. (Translator) The Visnu Purana: Sanskrit Text and English Translation. Parimal Publications, 2011

Islam

Imam Bukhari, Bengali: Sahih Al-Bukhari - Vol. 3. Houston, TX: Dar-Us-Salam Publications, 2012 edition.

Muslim Information Service of Australia. "Beginning of Revelation". Missionislam.com.

The Holy Qur'an Translated by Abdullah Yusuf Ali, The Islamic Propagation Centre.

Tafsir ibn Kathir Tafsir al-Surah al-'Azim (5 v. sader) Publisher: DAR SADER (2009).
Yaseen M., Human Nature in Islam. A.S. Noordeen, 1998.

Jehovah's Witnesses

JW.Org Bible Teachings

Let God Be True. Watchtower Bible and Tract Society: 1953.

New World Translation of the Holy Scriptures. Watchtower Bible and Tract Society, 2013.

Scottish Daily Express, November 24, 1954

Religion for Mankind. Watchtower Bible and Tract Society, 1953.

Reasoning from the Scriptures, Watch Tower Bible and Tract Society of Pennsylvania, 1989

Russell, C. Studies in the Scriptures (7 Volumes). Bible Students Congregation of New Brunswick, 1996)

Russell, C. Thy Kingdom Come, Studies in the Scriptures, series 3. 1st Edition 1891. Divine Plan, 1990

The Kingdom is at Hand, Watchtower Bible and Tract Society, Original Edition 1944.

Rutherford, J. The Harp of God: Proof Conclusive That Millions Now Living Will Never Die. (Originally delivered by Rutherford in a speech given in 1918. This brochure was published two years later in 1920), 2016

Watchtower Reprints, Vol. I, March, 1880, Pg. 82.

Watchtower, This Means Everlasting Life, Watchtower Bible and Tract Society Inc.; First Edition, 1950.

Watchtower, <u>Make Sure of All Things</u>. Watchtower Bible and Tract Society of New, 1965.

Judaism

The Torah

Ramban, Mishneh Torah Set 18 volumes Hebrew and English - Updated version Hardcover, 1998.

myjewishlearning.com

Palano, H. <u>The Talmud.</u> Daly City, CA: Book Tree, 2003. First translated into English by Palano in 2003. It is a collection of early Biblical discussions, with the comments of teachers going back generations. It discusses law, civil and penal, human and divine. It records the thoughts of those men and it also discusses oral traditions.

Note: The Berakhot is the first tractate of Seder Zeraim of the Mishnah and of the Talmud. The tractate discusses the rules of prayers, particularly the Shema and the Amidah, and blessings for various circumstances.

Mormonism

<u>A Comprehensive History of the Church of Jesus Christ of Latter-day Saints, Century 1, Vol. 1</u> by the Church Brigham Young University Press, Provo Utah, 1965 and 1976.

<u>Achieving Celestial Marriage</u>, Student Manual, Church Educational System, The Corporation of the President of the Church of Jesus Christ of Latter-day saints, Salt Lake City, 1976 and 1992.

<u>Book of Commandments</u> (now Doctrine & Covenants), Published in 1833. (See Joseph Smith Begins His Work Vol. 2 (Can be obtained from Utah Lighthouse Ministry).

<u>Book Mormon 1920 Edition</u> Salt Lake City: Corporation of the Church of Jesus Christ of Latter-day Saints, 1920.

<u>Book Mormon</u> 1981 Edition Salt Lake City: Corporation of the Church of Jesus Christ of Latter-day Saints, 1981.

<u>Deseret Weekly News 1888 – 1898</u> The Deseret News was the first newspaper published in the Utah Territory, just three years after Mormon pioneers settled the Great Salt Lake valley. In 1865, the weekly became a semi-weekly, appearing on Tuesdays and Saturdays.

<u>Doctrine and Covenants 1835 Original Edition,</u> Herald Heritage Publishing House/Facsimile Reprint, Independence, Missouri, 1971.

<u>Doctrine and Covenants of the Church of Jesus Christ of Latter-day Saints, 1883 Edition,</u> Deseret News Company, Salt Lake City.

<u>Ensign Magazine</u>   An official periodical of The Church of Jesus Christ of Latter-day Saints.

Guide to the Scriptures. The Guide to the Scriptures defines selected doctrines, principles, people, and places found in the Holy Bible, the Book of Mormon, the Doctrine and Covenants, and the Pearl of Great Price.

Joseph Smith Begins His Work Vol. 1 Book of Mormon, 1830 Original Edition (can be obtained from Utah Lighthouse Ministry)

Comparative Doctrine

Joseph Smith Begins His Work Vol. 2 The Book of Commandments, 1833; The Doctrine and Covenants, 1835; The Lectures on Faith; and the Fourteen Articles of Faith (can be obtained from Utah Lighthouse Ministry)

Journal of Discourses (The Journal of Discourses (often abbreviated J.D.) is a 26-volume collection of public sermons by early leaders of The Church of Jesus Christ of Latter-day Saints). McConkie, Bruce R. (Quorum of the Twelve's Apostles) Mormon Doctrine 2nd Edition. Bookcraft, Salt Lake City, 1966.

Millennial Star Periodical The Latter-day Saints' Millennial Star was the longest continuously published periodical of The Church of Jesus Christ of Latter-day Saints, being printed in England from 1840 until 1970.

Missionary Handbook, 2006.

"Ordinance and Blessing Policies", Handbook 1: Stake Presidents and Bishops (Salt Lake City, Utah: LDS Church, 2010).

Smith, Joseph   Man: His Origins and Destiny.   Salt Lake City: Deseret Book Co., 1954.

Smith, Joseph Teachings of the Prophet Joseph Smith. Salt Lake City: Deseret Book Co., 1976.

Smith, Joseph   Doctrines of Salvation, Vol. 1. Bookcraft: Salt Lake City, 1954.

Smith, Joseph   Doctrines of Salvation, Vol. 2. Bookcraft: Salt Lake City, 1955.

Smith, Joseph   Doctrines of Salvation, Vol. 3. Bookcraft: Salt Lake City, 1956

Smith, Joseph   Pearl of Great Price. Salt Lake City: Corporation of the Church of Jesus Christ of Latter-day Saints, 1951, revised 1981.

Times and Seasons (Mormon Document): Times and Seasons, was published in 135 issues of sixteen pages each between November 1839 and February 1846. It was published monthly from November 1839 to October 1840. After 1940 it became a biweekly work. This continued until February 15, 1846. During the seven months in 1842 that the Prophet Joseph Smith was the editor, he published several important documents of Mormon history in its pages including the translation and facsimiles of the book of Abraham, the Wentworth Letter, and the early segments of the History of the Church.

Widtsoe, J. Evidences and Reconciliations, Salt Lake City, Utah: Bookcraft, 1943.

Scientology

Hubbard, L.   Dianetics: The Modern Science Of Mental Health. Los Angeles, CA: Bridge Publications Inc., 2007 edition.

Hubbard, L. The Factors: Admiration & the Renaissance of Beingness. Golden Era Publications, 2007 edition.

Hubbard, L. Self Analysis. Los Angeles, CA: Bridge Publications Inc., 2007 edition.

Hubbard, L. Scientology: The Fundamentals of Thought. Los Angeles, CA: Bridge Publications Inc., 2007 edition.

The Hope of Man, a lecture given on June 3, 1955, Mr. Hubbard
Official Scientology Website

Scientology Clear Procedure, Issue One – 1969, Pg. 21

Position on Reincarnation & Past Lives: Official Church of Scientology". scientology.org. January 2001.

Seventh-day Adventists

Branson, W. In Defense of the Faith. Washington, D.C.: Review and Herald, 1933.

Seventh-day Adventist Church Manual. Inter-American Division Publishing Association, 2016.

Seventh-day Adventist Questions on Doctrine: An Explanation of Certain Major Aspects of Seventh-day Adventist Belief. Review and Herald Publishing Association Washington, D.C.

White, E. G. Steps to Christ, World Christian Library, 2009 Edition.

White, E.G. The Desire of Ages. Oakland, CA: Pacific Press Publishing Association; Deluxe ed. Edition, 2002

White, E. G. The Great Controversy. Oakland, CA: Pacific Press Publishing Association; Revised ed. Edition, 2002.

White, E. G. Believe His Prophets Writings (see Ellenwhite.org).

Ellen G White Estate Writings @ellenwhite.org

Unification Church

Divine Principle. Washington, D.C.: Holy Spirit Association for the Unification of World Christianity, 1973.

Jones, W. A Prophet Speaks Today: The Words of Sun Myung Moon. New York, N.Y.: HSA-UWC Publications, 1975.

Kim, Y. O. An Introduction to Theology. Holy Spirit Association for the Unification of World Christianity, 1983.

Kim, Y. O. The Divine Principles. San Francisco, CA: HSAUWC, 1969 & 1963.

Kim, Y. O. Speeches on Unification Teaching. Barrytown, N.Y.: Unification Theological Seminary, 1986.

Kim, Y. O. Unification Theology. New York, N.Y.: HSAUWC, 1987.

Kim, Y. O. Unification Theology and Christian Thought. New York, N.Y.: Golden Gate Publishing Company, 1975.

Kim, Y. O. Master Speaks, March and April, 1965, MS-3, Pg. 2.

Moon, S. M. New Hope: Twelve Talks. (The talks in this book have been compiled from among the many speeches given by Sun Myung Moon in 1971, 1972, and 1973).

Moon, S. M. The New Future of Christianity. Washington, DC: The Unification Church, 1974.

Moon, S. M. Christianity in Crisis. New Hope, Washington, DC: The Holy Spirit Association of the Unification of World Christianity, 1974.

Moon, S. M. God's Warning to the World. New York, N.Y.: HSAUWC, 1985.

Sudo, K. Unification Church 120 Day Training Manual. Barry town, New York: Holy Spirit Association for the Unification of World Christianity, n.d.

The Divine Principle Study Guide. Belvedere Tarrytown, N.Y.: HSW-UWC, 1973.

The Way of the World (Unification Church Magazine)

Time Magazine (September 30, 1974)

Who, K. Y. The Principle of Creation. Belvedere Tarrytown, N.Y.: Holy Spirit Association for the Unification of World Christianity, 1973.

Yamamoto, Unification Church, 31-32, Divine Principle 2nd ed., trans. Won Pok Choi Washing, DC: The Holy Spirit Association for the Unification of World Christianity, 1974.

Unity

Cady, H. Lessons in Truth. Lee's Summit, MO.: Unity School of Christianity, 1944.

Fillmore, C. Jesus Christ Heals. Lee's Summit: Unity School of Christianity, 1947.

Filmore, C. Metaphysical Bible Dictionary. Lee's Summit, MO.: Unity School of Christianity; Fifth Edition, 1982.

Fillmore, C. Christian Healing; The Science of Being.   Wentworth Press, 2016.

Fillmore, C. The Revealed Word. Lee's Summit, MO.: Unity School of Christianity, 1959.

Fillmore, C. Teach Us to Pray. Lee's Summit, MO.: Unity Books Unity School of Christianity, 1997

Scott, S. The True Character of God. Lee's Summit, MO: Unity School of Christianity, n.d.

Taylor, E. What Unity Teaches. Lee's Summit, MO.: Unity School of Christianity, 1952.

Unity. October 1896, vol. 7, 400.

Wilson, E. Have We Lived Before? Kansas City: Unity, 1936.

Universal Unitarianism

Trudeau, R. Universalism 101: An Introduction for Leaders of Unitarian Universalist Congregations. Charleston, SC: Book Surge Publishing, 2009

Buehrens, J.; Church, F. A Chosen Faith: An Introduction to Unitarian Universalism. Boston, MA: Beacon Press: 1998.

Early Church History

Allen, C. Discovering Our Roots: The Ancestry of Churches of Christ. Abilene, TX: Abilene Christian University Press, 1988.

Cottrell, Jack   Baptism: Zwingli or The Bible?   Mason, OH: The Christian Restoration Association, 2022.

Curtis, A. The 100 Most Important events in Christian History. Grand Rapids, MI: Revel, 1998.

Ferguson, E. The Early Church & Today: Vol. 1. Abilene, TX: Abilene Christian University Press, 2012.

Josephus: The Complete Works Translated by William Whiston, A.M., Nashville, TN: Thomas Nelson Publishers,1998.

Kurian, G. A Quick Look at Christian History. Eugene, OR: Harvest House, 2015.

Latourette, S. Christianity Through the Ages. New York, NY: Harper & Row, 1965.

Lietzmann, H. A History of the Early Church, Vols 1, 2. New York, NY: Charles Scribner's Sons, 1937.

Reformation Movement

Jacobs, C. M., Luther, Martin MARTIN LUTHER Premium Collection: Theological Works, Sermons & Hymns: The Ninety-five Theses, The Bondage of the Will, A Treatise on Christian Liberty, ... Prayers, Hymns, Letters and many more (Kindle Edition)

Picken, Stuart D.B. Historical Dictionary of Calvinism (Historical Dictionaries of Religions, Philosophies, and Movements Series)

Restoration Movement

Cobb, B, Campbell, A. et al. Alexander Campbell: A Collection: Volume 1 (Restoration Movement), 2013.

Campbell, A., Stone, B., Campbell, T., Errett, I, Garrison, J. Historical Documents Advocating Christian Union. The Restoration Movement Library, 2017.

Hines, M. History of the American Restoration Movement. Jun 26, 2014

Restoration Movement - Abilene Christian University

General Books and Resources

Anderson, S. E. Armstrongism's 300 Errors Exposed. Grand Rapid: Baker Book House, 1973.

Ankerberg, J et.al., The Facts on Jehovah's Witnesses. Harvest House Publishers: Eugene, Or. 1984.

"Barley and Wheat in the Book Mormon". Featured Papers. Maxwell Institute. Archived from the original on 23 February 2007.

Bjornstad, J. The Moon is Not the Son. Minneapolis: Bethany Fellowship, 1976.

Boa, K. Cults, World Religions, and You. Wheaton, Illinois: Victor Books, 1977.

Boettner, L. Roman Catholicism. Philadelphia: The Presbyterian and Reformed Publishing Company, 1962.

Campbell, A. A DEBATE on the ROMAN CATHOLIC RELIGION Between ALEXANDER CAMPBELL, Bethany, Va. AND THE Right Reverend JOHN B. PURCELL, Bishop of Cincinnati

Held in the Sycamore Street Meetinghouse, Cincinnati, from the 13th to the 21st of January, 1837. Taken down by reporters, and revised by the parties.

Coe, Michael "Mormons and Archeology: An Outside View," Dialogue: A Journal of Mormon Thought, Vol. 8, No. 2 (Summer 1973)

Crites, R., Crites, D. Sharpening the Sword on Mormonism: Mormon Documents, The Bible and the Truth-Revised. Dallas, TX: CPC, 2018.

Crites, F. R. Sharpening the Sword on the Unification Church. Abilene, TX: 1981.

Crites, F.R. & Hill, R. Journey Into Discipleship-Revised. Dallas, TX: CPC, 2022.

Curtis, K. The 100 Most Important Events in Christian History.   Grand Rapids, MI: Revell, 1998.

Geerhardus V. The Pauline Eschatology. Grand Rapids: William B. Eerdmans Publishing Co., 1972.

Greear, J. Breaking the Islam Code: Understanding the Soul Questions of Every Muslim. Eugene, Or.: Harvest House, 2010.

Hoekema, A. The Four Major Cults. Grand Rapids: Eerdmans Publishing Company, 1976.

Holden, J. (Author), Geisler, Norman The Popular Handbook of Archaeology and the Bible: Discoveries That Confirm the Reliability of Scripture.   Harvest House Publishers, 2013.

Hunter, M. R. The Gospel Through the Ages, Salt Lake City: Steven and Wallis, 1945.

Isbouts, Jean-Pierre Archaeology of the Bible: The Greatest Discoveries From Genesis to the Roman Era. National Geographic,   2007.

Kurian, G. A Quick Look at Christian History: A Chronological Timeline Through the Centuries. Eugene,OR: Harvest House, 2015.

Lewis, C. S. The Great Divorce, NY, New York: Harper One, 1946 (Revised April 21, 2015).

Lightfoot, Neil How we Got the Bible. Grand Rapids, MI: Baker books, 2003.

Marlowe, M. Bible Research, Arminianism, July 2005.

Martin, W. The Kingdom of the Cults: The Definitive Work on the Subject.   Bethany House: Bloomington, MN, 2019.

McDowell, J. & McDowell, S Evidence That Demands a Verdict: Life-Changing Truth for a Skeptical World. Nashville, TN.: Thomas Nelson, October 3, 2017.

Miller, D.   The Qur'an Unveiled: Islam and New Testament Christianity in   Conflict. Montgomery, AL: Apologetics Press, 2008.

Miller, D. What the Bible says about the Mormon Church. Montgomery, AL: Apologetics Press, 2019.

Parley P. Pratt, Key to the Science of Theology [1973 Edition]

Patheos Library of World Faiths & Religions (online)

Pinedo, M. What the Bible Says About the Catholic Church. Montgomery, AL: Apologetics Press, 2008.

Ridenour, F. So What's the Difference? A look at 20 Worldviews, Faiths and Religions and How They Compare to Christianity. Ventura, CA: Regal Books, 2001.

Rhodes, R. The Challenge of the Cults and New Religions. Grand Rapids, MI: Zondervan, 2001.

Rhodes, R. The Complete Guide to Christian Denominations: Updated & Expanded. Eugene, OR: Harvest House, 2015.

Sanders, P Evangelism Handbook of New Testament Christianity: Searcy, Arkansas: Kachelman Publications, 2017

Shank, R. Elect in the Son. Minneapolis, MN: Bethany House Publishers, 1989.

Shank, R. Life in the Son. Springfield, MO: Westcott Publishers, 1961.

Singer, Ben. "A Brief History of the Horse in America; Horse Phylogeny and Evolution". Canadian Geographic Magazine. Archived from the original on 2014-08-19.

Sparks, J. The Mind Benders. New York: Thomas Nelson, 1977.

Strobel, L The Case for Christ: A Journalist's Personal Investigation of the Evidence for Jesus. Grand Rapids, MI: 1998.

St. Irenaeus of Lyons: Against the Heresies Book 1, Translated by Dominic J. Unger on January 1, 1991.

Tanner, J & Tanner, S. Flaws in the Pearl of Great Price: A Study of Changes and Plagiarism in Joseph Smith's Pearl of Great Price. Utah Lighthouse Ministry, 1991.

Tanner, J. & Tanner, S. Mormonism: Shadow or Reality? Utah Lighthouse Ministry; Fifth Edition 1987; Reformatted 2008.

Tanner, J & Tanner, S. The Case Against Mormonism, Vol. 1. Utah Lighthouse Ministry, 1967.

Tanner, J. & Tanner, S. The Changing World of Mormonism: A Behind-the-Scenes Look at Changes in Mormon Doctrine and Practice. Moody Press; 1st edition June 1979.

Tanner, J.; Tanner, S. 3,913 Changes in the Book of Mormon. A photo Reprint of the Original 1830 Edition of the Book of Mormon with the changes Marked. Utah Lighthouse Ministry.

Tanner, S. 41 Unique Teachings of the LDS Church. Utah Lighthouse Ministry; 2012.

Thompson, B. In Defense of the Bible's Inspiration, Apologetics Press, 1998.

Thompson, D. Witness to Mormons in Love: The Mormon Scrapbook, Revised Edition. CreateSpace, 2014.

Tucker, R. Another Gospel: Cults, Alternative Religions, and the new Age Movement. Zondervan: Grand Rapids, MI., 1998.

Valachos, C. <u>Brigham Young's False Teaching: Adam is God.</u> (Reprint of an article appearing in the Journal of Pastoral practice, Vol. III, number 2, pages 93-119, 1979. Reprinted with permission of the author.) 1979.

Other Biblical Works by These Authors

Grace and Salvation: This work is the first work of this series on Christianity. It was intended to primarily be read by those who are searching and want to know more about Grace and salvation. It can also be very helpful for any Christian who wants to have a deeper grasp regarding what Grace really means. The different aspects of Grace including Adoption, Justification, Righteousness, Sanctification, Glorification and what they do to and for you as you respond to God's Grace is discussed. It also discusses the history of salvation and provides an in-depth study of what the Bible says about how you go about becoming a Christian. This is available on Amazon, from your local bookstore or through this author.

Journey Into Discipleship-Revised: This is the second work of this series on Christianity. It covers many aspects of the God-Man Relationship. It is a wonderful reference guide for teaching new converts or those who simply want to know more about God and His plan for us. This work will take you on a journey that helps you understand how to become a fully mature, godly Christian. It describes the ups and downs that Christians face and how they can get the help they need to overcome. Some of the topics are: knowing God, saving faith, the Holy Spirit, new life and sin, sins against the Holy Spirit, brokenness and the foundation of spiritual maturity, understanding and preparation for spiritual warfare, assurance of salvation, prayer, knowing God's Word, outreach, fellowship, balanced discipleship and much more. It has been significantly updated with new helpful information. This is now available through Amazon, your local bookstore or through this author.

Journey Into Discipleship Workbook-Revised: This workbook is a shortened work that covers many of the core issues identified in the Journey into Discipleship manual. This is currently being revised. Coming soon on Amazon, your local bookstore or through this author.

Comparative Doctrine: This is the third work of this series on Christianity. This work will help you learn how to identify Scriptures that address over fifty doctrinal issues. It also shows how several religions have ignored Biblical doctrine or have attempted to alter it in some way. This work will help you understand what the Bible teaches about each doctrinal issue addressed. As you study and internalized what you learn, you will grow spiritually. It will also be very helpful when you are faced with sharing your Biblical beliefs with someone who wants to know more about the Bible and what it teaches. This is available on Amazon, your local bookstore or through this author.

Spiritual Gifts and Ministry - Leader and Participant Workbooks: This is the fourth work of this series on Christianity. This work helps you identify the spiritual gift that God specifically gave you so that you can function in the body where He wants you to function. Using your gift is a natural way to serve your brothers and sisters and to reach out to those who need to learn about God. It is also how God wants you to participate in ministry and service in the local body. Outreach of any kind is much more natural when you use your God given gift. This is available on Amazon, your local bookstore or through this author.

Discipleship Family Leader's Manual: This is the fifth work of this series on Christianity. This manual helps individuals or churches develop a consistent method for having optional groups for Sunday evenings or weekdays. It has procedures, forms, suggestions for structure of meetings and more. The Discipleship Family is a method by which you or your church can implement an easy way to help others learn about God while at the same time practically learning how to become better disciples. This work provides you with a model that you can use or adapt for your own purposes. Small groups can meet five key elements for personal growth and Discipleship. They are: 1) prayer, 2) study of God's Word, 3) outreach, evangelism or seeking the lost (this includes church members who are not active or need help in some way, 4) fellowship (serving and building each other up as well as enjoying Christian relationships), and 5) the sharing of meals (eating is both a bonding experience and a way to get others to participate in your group). This is available on Amazon, your local bookstore or through this author.

Prayer Journal: Keep track of prayers, who they are for, when God answers them. This is available on Amazon, your local bookstore or through this author.

Sharpening the Sword on Mormonism - Mormon Documents, the Bible and the Truth: This manual is an advanced Sharpening the Sword work that describes the works of Mormonism, how they contradict themselves, how they have changed (additions and deletions in the text), and how their teachings conflict with the Bible. An overall method for working with those believe in Mormonism is included. This is available on Amazon, your local bookstore or through this author.
Sharpening the Sword on the Unification Church: This is an advanced Sharpening the Sword work that describes the beliefs of the Unification church and how they conflict with the Bible. This is currently being revised. Will be available soon on Amazon or through this author.

Foundations in Spiritual Growth: This workbook helps the reader define what is healthy using Jesus as a model. In Luke 2:42 we are told that Jesus grew in wisdom, stature and in favor with God and Man. We too must be healthy and grow in those four areas that are redefined as Mental, Social, Physical and Spiritual. To be healthy in all four areas you must identify weaknesses in yourself in each area and seek to replace those weaknesses with healthy, spiritual ways of thinking and socializing. You must also seek to take care of the temple that is your body and treat it as something precious. Last, you must internalize the foundational spiritual beliefs that help you become more and more like Jesus. You must get rid of the worldly or unhealthy aspects of self and put on a Christlike nature in all four areas. This workbook helps you accomplish this in a practical and very helpful way. This workbook is currently being revised. The revision will be available on Amazon, your local bookstore or through this author soon.

Guilt and Grace Workbook: This workbook explains the different aspects of Grace including Justification, Righteousness, Sanctification, what they do to and for you and what your response to Grace should be. It also discusses different kinds of Guilt that can paralyze you and keep you from enjoying the fulness of God's Grace in your life. This is currently being revised. Will be available soon on Amazon or through this author.

Marriage Go Round Basic Workbook: This workbook addresses nine steps to improving your relationship and rekindling love in your life. Several aspects of how you can improve your relationship are included. As in all relationships, it is important to have a life that is founded on spiritual beliefs. That is just one of many aspects of a healthy relationship that are addressed in this workbook. The *Marriage Go Round Couple Therapy Resources* Manual provides a more thorough look at thirty-two areas that improve the quality of any relationship. Both of these works are available on Amazon, your local bookstore or through this author.

For more information about the Biblical works please go to www.cpcchristianministry.com.

For other Professional Works by this author please go to Amazon.com/author/russcrites